TRUE LIES

TRUE LIES

Margaret
Johnson-Hodge

KENSINGTON PUBLISHING CORP.
http://www.kensingtonbooks.com

DAFINA BOOKS are published by

Kensington Publishing Corp.
850 Third Avenue
New York, NY 10022

All Kensington titles, imprints and distributed lines are available at special quantity discounts for bulk purchases for sales promotion, premiums, fund-raising, educational or institutional use.

Special book excerpts or customized printings can also be created to fit specific needs. For details, write or phone the office of the Kensington Special Sales Manager: Kensington Publishing Corp., 850 Third Avenue, New York, NY 10022, Attn. Special Sales Department. Phone: 1-800-221-2647.

Dafina Books and the Dafina logo Reg. U.S. Pat & TM Off.

ISBN 0-7582-0004-8

First Hardcover Printing: October 2002
First Trade Paperback Printing: September 2003
10 9 8 7 6 5 4 3 2 1

Printed in the United States of America

"Because you love one human being, you see everyone else differently . . . you are both stronger and more vulnerable, free and bound."

—James Baldwin

Chapter 1

The odds were against them.

A house party was the last place statistics said you could meet someone eligible and interested, but Dajah and David did just that.

Neither of them had been what the other had been looking for, but something sparked across the crowded living room anyway. They danced together that evening, taking their drinks to the balcony that overlooked Guy R. Brewer Boulevard and talked. They talked about things and life, each discovering a worth in the other, bits and pieces that stuck.

For Dajah it was the concave shape of David's cheeks and the squareness of his jaw. For David it was Dajah's hands moving through the air when expressive, the soft liveliness that came into her eyes when she wanted to make a point.

When the May night turned cool, it became David's jacket going around Dajah's shoulders, carrying the scent of him, the fit of him and more importantly the warmth.

In the weeks that followed Dajah became all to David and David all to Dajah. He showed up when he was supposed to and treated her well. They went places and did things. In every sense of the word, they were a couple headed toward Nirvana.

Dajah fell in love, and David, a pace behind, fell in love too. For the next year they were in the same place, at the same time, feeling the same things and doing okay. But familiarity began to breed contempt and the relationship grew less than. Less than their purpose. Less than their need to stay together.

Dajah's eyes began to wander, and she tried hard to fight it. But the harder she tried, the less she loved. The less she loved, the less she began to care. David, following in the same footsteps, began looking elsewhere too.

They were wise enough to know that there was no real future. Tactful enough to let go. Remaining friends, they called each other from time to time, became a significant other when social proclivities required it.

When David's company had its annual picnic, it was Dajah at his side. When Dajah's cousin got married, it was the two of them dancing the Electric Slide and wishing the happy couple good luck. When Dajah came down with a very bad case of the flu, it was David who brought her soup and ginger ale. They never forgot a birthday, checked in with each other on a regular basis and just considered themselves cool like that.

Maybe if she hadn't gone to see the Alvin Ailey Dance Company all by herself and the E train hadn't gone out of service at Sutphin Boulevard, two stops short of hers—169th Street—she might not have left the crowded platform and headed for the exit. Maybe if Frieda had been able to join her, they would have stopped for pizza, shared a cab.

Maybe if David didn't live less than a block away, she would have waited for the Q88, got off at 169th Street, then boarded a second bus that would have taken her half a block from home. But he did and she found herself heading up the old crooked stairs to his second-floor apartment over the extermination store.

She was coming unannounced on a Saturday night, but they were friends and Dajah was certain he wouldn't mind. Second floor landing conquered, she'd just raised her hand to knock when the door swung open. Head down, mind elsewhere, for a hot second David didn't see her. When he did, surprise claimed him.

"Day?" Black baggy pants, a loose shirt, the cologne Pi drifting from the slope of his cheeks, there was no doubt of his intentions.

He was going out. "What's doing?" he asked, pulling the door closed, locking it.

"I was coming in from Ailey's concert. The train went out of service at Sutphin so I thought I'd drop by."

He took a quick reading, sensing things in her eyes. "I'm on my way out."

"I'm seeing."

"Running late."

Running late. Running away—same difference. Either way you sliced it, he was off to somewhere else, someone else. "Go ahead," she uttered. "I'll catch you later."

David did just that, bounding down the stairs and swinging back the lobby door before her foot reached the first floor. He disappeared around some corner before she made it to the sidewalk, and Dajah knew that whoever *she* was, she was a very lucky woman indeed.

During the day Leonardo's Coffee House on Sutphin Boulevard was a pit stop for lawyers, judges and everyday people who had business at the courthouse down the street. Nighttime drew a different type of clientele: women who plied their trade in the cover of darkness and the homeless who had scrounged up enough change for a cold soft drink against the humid summer night.

There were the bleary-eyed workers who had put in that extra shift, cleaning women with swollen ankles and stiff, ashy hands. The eatery held its share of club-hoppers gathered in huddles, the excitement of the night ahead, surrounding them like acoustic confetti.

All people just trying to get from Point A to Point B, Dajah found herself one of them as she sat at the counter. Taking up her burger, she took a bite and chewed, thinking about David, where he was off to and with whom.

She was mapping out scenarios in her head when the bell over the door jingled, drawing her attention. *City,* was her first thought, taking in the white shirt, the collection of patches on the arm. *Law enforcement,* her second as the holstered gun glided into her line of vision.

She saw the body, tight and fit beneath the long-sleeved white shirt, the way the belt gathered around the slim waist. Dajah caught the fine rise of behind inside the dark blue slacks, the snug fit of the belt, as he moved by.

Not a cop, she was thinking, as he settled on the stool next to her. A knee bumped her leg. Her head turned, anticipating apology. It came with eyes that, despite a weariness, shone with such intensity that they looked backlit.

"Sorry," he mumbled, looking away. "Hey, Joe, let me get a root beer and a burger, rare." The voice did not go with the body, one that suggested power and depth. The tone that left him was soft and tender, gentle as a Maxwell ballad.

His knee hit her leg a second time, but he was lost to some other place. Dajah shifted on the stool, took up her cup of ice and soda and sipped through the straw, producing a gurgling sound. Empty. She looked down at her plate—no food there either.

It was time to go.

A glance at her watch said it was past midnight. Eyes toward the window told her she was eight miles from home. For the first time since she'd left the subway, fear claimed her as the knee made contact a third time.

"You want me to move over?"

"What?"

"I said do you want me to move over?" She pointed to the space between them, his knee flush against her thigh. "Your knee keeps on touching me."

"Sorry. Rough shift." He drew it away.

"Shift?"

But he didn't seem to hear, his eyes drifting off. Dajah looked into her empty glass, felt the awaiting darkness. A tingle of anxiety tap-danced along her spine, settling as she eased off the stool, adjusted her pocketbook and tugged at the hem of her suddenly too-tight, too-short blouse.

Then she was out of things to adjust and her next concern became the too revealing blouse, the anticipatory darkness and her fear. She forced her mouth open. "Not NYPD, right?" The City of New York had a slew of law enforcers, everything from the Fire Department down to the Department of Sanitation. And though the arm patch would tell her, it was on the other side.

"No."

"What then?"

"Corrections."

She nodded, looked out toward the glass windows. He followed her gaze, felt something in her. Asked where she was headed.

"Home."

"Where's home?"

She laughed, a fragile sound that revealed her fears. "About eight miles from here."

"Driving?"

She shook her head no.

"Busing it?"

"Kinda."

His expression changed from concern to disappointment. "Kinda late in the night for you not to be knowing how you're getting home."

"The train went out of service, so I ended up here."

"Where you headed?"

"A hundred and sixty-ninth."

"You're walking?"

"Bus probably."

"Blue bus?"

"Yeah."

"Want company?"

"Aren't you on duty?"

"Doing a double. Have to take the bus back to Riker's."

"Island?"

"Yeah. Where I work."

Riker's Island, a major penitentiary for the best and worst of New York felons. Criminals big and small were sent there. Dajah had never been there, but she had friends with family members who had.

"So, you want that escort?"

He was a stranger, but he was of the law. Better to have him with her as she waited than not. "That would be great."

He leaned toward the counter. "Joe. Hold that order." He eased off the stool and pointed to the door. "Let's go."

They hit the sidewalk, heading toward the closed HSBC Bank, the lawless scattering in the approach of the law.

Dajah laughed, a sound only half bent on being shared. "You have them scrambling."

"They need to."

"I'm Dajah," she offered as they passed the subway entrance.

"Rick."

"As in James?"

A smile came, the first since they'd met. "Yeah. See my Jherri Curl and guitar?" He studied her. "What you doing out here anyway?"

"I came from a concert in the city. The train went out of service at Sutphin. I didn't feel like standing down there waiting for another one." She lied a little. "So I came up to get a bite to eat."

"All by your lonesome?"

"I'm a big girl."

"That much I can see. Still, kind of uncool to be taking mass transit by yourself this time of night. Where's your car?"

Who said she had one? But Dajah took that thought back. Most woman her age living in the borough of Queens did. "I left it home. I'm one of those fools who still enjoys the subway."

"So you went all the way to Manhattan by mass transit and you have a ride at home?"

"Yeah."

"Takes all kinds."

"There's nothing wrong with the subway."

"Tell that to the victims."

They reached the bus stop. Not another soul there. "You're the first C.O. I've ever seen running around in uniform without some prisoner hitched to their wrist."

"Supposed to have been a straight run, but I got hungry. I'm doing a double. On 'til eight."

"In the morning?'

"Something like that."

"Night shift?"

"Just for today. Normally I work the four to midnight . . . overtime."

A bus turned the corner. It was the right color, but the wrong number. Rick looked at his watch. "Should be here soon."

They waited, red lights going to green, fast cars zipping by tossing out loud flashes of too much bass and the lyrics lost to them. They stood, silent and separate, eyes from each other. Affected.

"I thought you were somebody else at first."

She was glad to hear him break the silence; she had feared it would go on forever. "Who?"

He shrugged. "Not important."

"We look that much alike?"

"Same shape face, same height, same shape. Hair's different, eyes not quite the same, but yeah, you look like her."

"Her got a name?'

"Not important."

She felt him draw back and instantly regretted her words.

Four minutes passed, the bus nowhere in sight. Rick looked at his watch again. "I'm going to have to get back." Dajah sensed that. She knew that he could not stand there with her forever. She appreciated the time he had spent with her so far.

He unclipped a portable canister of Mace from his belt and handed it to her. "Anybody ask, you found it."

"Don't you need it?"

Rick shrugged. "I can get another one."

"I can give it back . . . tomorrow or something."

His brow rose. "Or something?"

"Yeah. I mean, I probably won't even use it and what's the sense of buying another one."

There was something in her eyes, something that said it was about more than the Mace, or could be. Time bent the laws of physics, one second becoming ten as Rick took his time in responding "There's something you have to know."

"What?"

"Besides not wanting to see anything happen to a fine sister like you, and liking very much what I'm seeing, my life, where I'm at, is complicated."

"Like how?"

Rick looked off, shifting the fit of his hat back off his forehead. He looked back at her, needing her to fully understand. "My situation . . . got a daughter, four. Her name's Kanisha and I love her. She's my heart. Nobody comes before she does. Me and Kanisha's mother? Complicated."

"Together or apart?"

"Both."

She nodded, heart fluttering.

"So if you still want me to come over and get the can of Mace to-morrow, I'd be more than willing to. If you don't, I understand."

Dajah looked at the canister held so many times the lettering had worn off. Looked back at Rick, a superhero for her night of misfortune. Searched her bag for scrap paper. Asked to borrow his pen.

"You sure?"

"I'm not offering twice."

Rick slipped the pen out of his shirt pocket, eyes drawn to the butternut-brown face, the shoulder-length braids. He appreciated the mouth painted in shades of sienna and gold, the cheekbones that suggested Native American heritage.

Pretty and bubbly, that's how she looked, like the letters and numbers she wrote on the scrap paper. "I get off at eight in the A.M. I can be there around quarter to nine—too early?"

"I'll be up."

"Tomorrow then."

Dajah nodded.

"Be safe," he offered, prayer-soft, turning and heading up the street. Dajah watched until he disappeared around the corner of the bank. Clutching her Mace like a precious gem, she kept her watch on the corner, relief filling her as her bus lumbered out of the darkness.

Understatements.

As a rule Rick didn't like to use them when it came to explaining his life and the situation in which he was now living, but there was no way he was going to tell the whole truth to a woman he had only known for ten minutes.

Complicated did not fully encompass the true business of how bad his relationship with his daughter's mother was. It was a full-blown mess.

Thirteen years ago, Rick Trimmons, at age eighteen had found the courage to ask one Bridget Campbell out after secretly being in love with her since ninth grade. Bridget Campbell, having just been dropped by her first love, said yes.

For Rick it was love; for Bridget it was convenience. Rick had a summer job, a fast car and a heart eager to please. A lap dog, he stayed devoted to Bridget even when Bridget had no interest in staying devoted to him. Four years later, when her true love returned, Bridget Campbell dropped a then twenty-two-year-old Rick like a bad habit, without so much as a blink of her eye.

Three years later Rick was still wound licking when he spotted a foxy, brash seventeen-year-old, Gina Alexander, in the park one day. One look was all it took before she came up to him, asking his name. Ten minutes of conversation, all it took for Gina to invite herself over to Rick's apartment. Twenty-three minutes later Rick decided she was just what the doctor ordered.

Despite warnings from both friends and family, he didn't leave the young thing alone. Rick went with her and into and all about her full force, she a perfect balm to his wounded ego, making him feel manly, important—all that.

Gina gave as good as she got, and being with Rick opened up a whole new world for her. For the first time in her life she felt important. Through Rick her life gained purpose.

Formerly a high school dropout, Gina went back to school and completed the tenth grade. She decided she wanted to do what her friend Shabreica had done twice—have a baby.

Riding the wave of Gina's ocean of love and devotion, Rick thought it was a good idea. He loved Gina and Gina loved him. He had been with Corrections for four years by then, pulling in a decent salary, and in his heart and mind it was doable.

He wanted to get married first but Gina said they could do that later. Soon after, little Kanisha was on her way and Gina left her mother's house and moved in with Rick. They set up the second bedroom as a nursery.

Gina basked in pre-motherhood, the envy of her friends. Rick was good-looking, hard-working and faithful, and as far as her friends were concerned Gina had gone for the gold.

But the idea of something and the reality were two separate things. Once Kanisha was born, Gina found she could no longer run the streets with her friends and had to give up necessities like partying and sleeping.

Rick found himself working more hours to keep the roof over their head, formula in Kanisha's belly and clothes on Gina's back. All too late Gina realized she really wasn't ready to be a mother. Like a caged animal, she longed for freedom. She began dropping her daughter off at her mother's house and allowed the streets to reclaim her.

When Rick complained, Gina told him to fuck himself and moved back home with her mother. When her mother got on her nerves, she told her mother she didn't have to listen to her and moved back in with Rick. When Rick pissed her off again, she went back home to Momma, thus beginning a vicious cycle.

Maybe if Rick hadn't loved his daughter so much, desired a picture-perfect life with the imperfect Gina, he would have walked away a long time ago. But he did love his daughter and still wanted Gina. He was trying to hold on.

But even the most determined grow weary. Rick was no different. These days his main concern was his daughter, who deserved the stability that he had had coming up. Always a thinker, Rick came up with a plan.

He began taking the steps toward it two years ago. As he eased the prison bus over the bridge to Riker's Island, he wasn't sure of its validity, but in that moment, it was all he had. A little something was always better than a whole lot of nothing.

Chapter 2

The canister of Mace lay on Dajah's night table, in the space between her lamp and her alarm clock. She had stared at it for a good five minutes before she forced herself to roll over, get comfortable and try to get to sleep.

It was trouble; everything in her gut was saying so. *Just trying to make lemonade without the benefit of sugar or water.* Rick was involved, and that was not a game Dajah played.

Dajah didn't share—a affirmation she'd had since the age of thirteen when her father told her she didn't have to. Thirteen, when her first real maybe-I-can-go-with-you crush on a boy arrived and he asked her out and four days later she spotted him with a lanky arm around somebody else.

Tender in age, new to the full scope of emotions attraction could warrant, everything in her had boiled up and in a heartbeat she was bum-rushing him, her voice loud, screechy and so hurt-filled that her throat ached as she told him that she hated him. She barely knew herself as she went on to say that he was no good and she never wanted to see him again, the whole of it—surprising, betraying—bringing on an uncontrollable anger that jumped her for the first time ever, leaving her trembling, teary-eyed and bewildered.

In the aftermath Dajah had stood on 147th Street near Foch Boulevard uncertain of what she'd experienced, even why, only that it hurt deeply and she had lost control. That somehow in a blink of an eye some boy had turned her from a mannerly, well-behaved quiet child into a crazy female who should have known better.

She had turned on her heels, head down, trying to vanish, and made her way home. Tears drying with every step she took, confusion filled her with every breath as she labored on. Dajah went into her house, saw her mother and could not speak.

"You okay?" Delia Moore had asked.

"I need to talk to Daddy," was all Dajah could manage.

"Somebody hurt you?"

Dajah couldn't answer that either. All she could ask was, "Where's Daddy?" She loved her mother and her mother no doubt loved her, but in that moment she had needed her father more. He was a man and one day that stupid, knuckle headed fool who had made her crazy would be one too. Her father could fill in the blanks, explain it. Make sense of it all.

"Something happen to you?" her mother asked concerned. "You tell me, tell me right now what happened to you," she demanded, her voice full of a rising fear.

It had been that fear that drew Hank Moore, coming into the living room, seeing a wife full of anguish and a child just as grieved. "Baby?" he uttered, his arms opening automatically and Dajah going into them, her wet face against his chest.

"She won't tell me, Hank. Says she needs to talk to you."

Hank Moore had looked to his wife, nodded his head twice and gently eased his only child from his waist. "Let's go in the kitchen. We can talk in there."

Hank Moore had sat and listened to Dajah's tale, eyes kind and heart knowing. When Dajah was finished, he took away her anguish by explaining the cause of it. "Your first broken heart Cookie, that's all. Kind of early in the game for you, but there's no time like the present to learn. Now he obviously thought you was going to share him, but I'm glad to see you had other plans. If a boy want you, then he should just want you. If he wants somebody else too, then you don't want him, got it?"

Dajah did. It became gospel.

It wasn't always easy to adhere to that rule and moments came when she wasn't willing to do the foot work, but not even the dazzling-eyed, muscle-bound, *five inches taller than me* Rick could make her.

So he could come and get his canister. She wouldn't even let him inside. She would make him stand in the hallway when she handed it over. Send him on his way.

This was what Dajah had decided by the time her doorbell rang the next morning. This was what rode her brain, her breath and her heart as she swung open the downstairs door, testy and decisive. But when she caught sight of him, it all slipped away, vanishing like a magician's trick.

Injured.

It was the only word that came to her as she took in the man she had known for less than twenty-four hours, seeing the dirt-smeared shirt, a nasty nick on his cheek. Those eyes, haunted and glazed.

"You okay?"

Rick nodded, brought his hands to his face. He worked the flesh with his fingers, as if to rub away old skin. Looked up at her, a brief explanation leaving him. "A fight."

"A fight?"

"Yeah, in Cell Block Nine. We almost lost one."

Nine words so heavy with danger Dajah had to swallow hard just to digest them. Nine words so powerful she forgot she wasn't supposed to care.

"You almost lost one?" she managed, closing the front door behind him.

"Yeah, a C.O. The prisoners nearly got him." His whole body shuddered, fresh with the memory. He looked beyond her, up the stairs, in need of comfort, any kind he could get. She followed his gaze, debating with herself. Nodded her head. Told him, "Come on up."

They took the stairs, Dajah in the lead, Rick behind her. She opened the door and he moved through it, taking refuge on her thick, lush sofa. She had no plans to sit next to him, no plans to invade his tempered private space. But in a heartbeat she was there beside him. Close.

"One time I needed my Mace." His voice fell off, heavy, leaden.

She eyed the canister still in her hand. "You gave it—"

"Yeah, to you."

"Rick, I am so sorry."

"Not your fault. That's how life goes, right?"

She wanted to tell him no, but everything about him said he was already a full-fledged convert. She waited for more words to come, but he was tucked away somewhere so she sat there, eyes on her large Charles Bibb reprint, feeling him.

The lithograph reminded her of who she was, and all that she wanted to become. The woman, drawn large, looming, loving, had become a visual mantra. *I am fierce, I am strong, yet tender. I am the love that has set the world in motion, the love that can never be denied.*

This was what the picture reaffirmed in her as Rick huddled in his silence. She wasn't certain how much longer he would stay that way but opened herself to the intensity of his presence.

The air shifted, broke up, scattered. Rick came back, tilted his neck, unloosening a kink. "I'm all right." He looked around him, the horror, once real, fading as his reason for coming arrived. "My Mace?"

She handed it over. Watched as he hooked it onto his belt. His eyes suggested secrets as they found hers, as he uttered, "Guess that's that."

She felt it then, the tender soul harbored beneath the sullied uniform. Felt as if she had just climbed into his heart and was drawn to all that she'd found. He was a good guy, a bona-fide do-right man. She found herself wishing they had met sooner.

She wanted him to stay, but she couldn't ask because share wasn't a part of her game plan. Still an option left her, words she'd never spoken or considered leaving her soul. "If you're ever free . . ."

Rick nodded and headed back down the stairs.

If I'm ever free?

Had he ever been? Wasn't there always some chaining, some claiming, something holding him back, keeping him tethered? Even as a child he had been in servitude to his parents. High school and Bridget had only added more shackles. Free? Rick could not even begin to comprehend what it would feel like.

He could feel Dajah, though, feel her as he walked down the stone pathway and opened the gate. He could smell her, a mixture of hair oil and perspiration as he got into his car.

It was more than her looking like the first woman to ever own her heart, more than her street savvy, the apartment kept neat and straight. It went beyond the desire he sensed from her, the unspoken reluctance at seeing him go.

She was his equal.

About the same age, no doubt the same level of education, he could tell it in the way she said things, the expressions that elongated her face. Rick could tell by the empathy that poured from her like sunshine on a rainy day.

Intuitiveness. Rick had never realized the importance of it, had never respected the merit of it until five minutes ago. He hadn't understood that Gina lacked it until Dajah showed him it existed and it took a certain type of person to possess it.

Had he ever felt that with Gina?

Rick tried to remember. Tried to find one moment in their lives when Gina knew him without him saying a word. In the beginning she had. The day they'd met in the park, she had possessed the same canny insight, but that had been too long ago to count.

Lately any concern or consideration she gave was affixed to some personal need, like fifty dollars to get her hair done or going to another party without him.

Gina had become a planet unto herself, rotating in a personal orbit, oblivious to everything else. But Dajah was different. She came off like the moon and the stars, a visible comfort but just too far, in that moment, to reach.

Dajah rolled the chair back from the computer hutch, clicked off the monitor and got up. She didn't need to look at the clock to know that she had been online for three hours, that only an empty belly had pulled her away.

She knew she was spending way too much time online, her vast membership in various chat sites not helping any. There was the Single Black Females Network, Livin' Large In Da En Y Cee, Rita's Reading Corner and Diva's Divarama, all sites she belonged to, shared thoughts with. Her moniker was Greenhouse. She had a thing for plants.

Logging on was a nice diversion in her life. She needed something to take her mind off Rick. But the more she tried, the less she succeeded, parts of him flowing through her without effort.

Nice height, nice build. Protective. Honest. *And taken.* Apprehended in the worst way, he had all the complications of a marriage from which he could never be divorced. His daughter made it so.

Children were forever. They were a bond made of blood. It could not be washed away, willed away or even emotionally removed. Rick was forever claimed.

In truth Dajah wanted what her parents had, old love like a legacy to be passed on even if their commitment had yet to reach her. It had taken thirteen years for her to admit it. Thirteen years of hit and miss to acknowledge it. She had never seriously considered settling down, but recently her life had hit a fork in the road. Suddenly she wanted it.

Stretching she headed to the kitchen to find something to eat. She thought to give her friend Frieda a call, then changed her mind. Tied up with a love life and an overburdened work schedule, Dajah knew Frieda didn't have time for her own self, much less her best friend.

Close for years, the friendship began the day Dajah had started on a new job.

"Frieda," was how she introduced herself, extending her hand Dajah's way that long-ago day.

Dajah had looked up from her desk, the newness still with her and took the hand extended. "I'm—"

"Dajah. Dajah Moore. Yeah, I know." Frieda had looked her over carefully, making some private determinations. "You busy for lunch?"

First day on the job, Dajah hadn't thought about it. "No, I don't think so."

"Great. There's this place on Main Street. Service is fast, food is good. We can go there."

"We?"

"You plan on being here a while?"

"Yeah."

"Well, then, the first thing you need to know is how things go around here. We can do lunch and you can get the divvy, or you can just go along blindly. Your choice."

Dajah took option A.

Frieda took her car, Dajah feeling like a hostage as Frieda drove fast, dipping in and out of traffic as they made their way toward Flushing. She talked as fast as she drove, and by the time they pulled up to the diner, Frieda had pointed out all the people Dajah needed to be careful of. Who could be trusted and who couldn't.

"County Hospital ain't no joke," Frieda had warned. "Especially their Accounting Department. The pay's good, the benefits are excellent and somebody always got a niece or a cousin looking for a spot so you have to look out for yourself because, believe me, nobody else will."

"You did."

"Because you a sister like me."

That had been eight years ago. Dajah eventually left County Hospital to work at General Management in Long Island, but they had remained best friends. Still, nothing stayed the same and getting together regularly became a thing of the past.

When Frieda met Barry, the tide began to turn. When her staff got laid off and Frieda was forced to pick up the slack, the turn was complete. The last time Dajah and Frieda had spent any time together had been about two weeks ago. Finding her friend exhausted beyond belief, Dajah had hardly recognized Frieda when she'd opened her door.

Dajah didn't stay long, just long enough to tell Frieda to get some rest and they would hook up later. But that later was overdue, and in moments like this Dajah could have used the company.

The next night Rick pulled his Navigator into the metered space, unable to believe his luck. Normally he had to park as far as two blocks away, but there was a spot right in front of his building.

After midnight, in a few hours, he would have to start feeding the meter quarters, but that was the price he had been willing to pay to live here. He used to have a love affair with the apartment building he called home, but the residents had gone from good to not so good, and the same young men he had seen locked up in Riker's often crossed his path as he came and went.

Years ago the brick apartment complex on 89th Avenue had been near exclusive, well kept and highly maintained. A credit check, a background check and an interview were needed before they even considered your application.

Rick would never forget his own interview as a nattily dressed young white man asked him questions, all the while taking in the red carpet, the heavy drapes and the furniture that looked tooled in Italy that filled his parents' living room.

The questions had been analytical, with no clear right or wrong. It had taken a few minutes before Rick understood it was a method of registering the type of person he was. Being young, black and male had been a first strike against him, and though the neighborhood he had grown up in had still been well kept and stable, rough elements had started to infiltrate the main corners and boulevards, which became an automatic second strike.

So Rick had been extra careful with his answers, keeping direct eye contact, sitting up straight and speaking with all the good English both his parents and his teachers in elementary school had taught him. He understood the interview was not so much about his potential as a tenant but about eliminating him as a candidate, and with the two strikes in place before he even shook the man's hand, Rick knew had to tread on careful ground.

He had wanted the two-bedroom apartment with the high ceilings, the smooth, eggshell walls. He wanted the convenience of walking to the E or F Train if the need hit and being close to the shopping mecca of Jamaica Avenue.

He liked stepping into the marbled lobby, riding the brass-plated elevator to the fourteenth floor and being able to look out of his apartment window, getting a panoramic view of Jamaica, Queens, proper.

Mostly he wanted to step out from under his parents' shadow and live his life on his own, showing the two people who raised him that they had done well.

Two weeks later, when his notification of acceptance letter arrived, he started packing up his things. Rick took his parents and his brother and sister with him on moving day, wanting to impress them with his capabilities.

There had been tears in his mother's eyes, a reserved wonder in his father's, and for the first couple of months his younger brother stopped by on the way home from high school on a near-daily basis.

His sister came by with friends, hoping one of them would be able to cure the broken heart he toted after Bridget. And while he was polite, even dated a few, none had the ability to jumpstart his heart.

A nice stream of unity had run through Rick's family, parents and siblings proud of him. But that changed when he met Gina.

Gina's presence in Rick's life altered how his parents viewed him. The closeness he had shared with his younger brother slid away. His sister stopped coming by with friends and then stopped coming by at all.

When Kanisha was born, it took a whole week before his family came to inspect the new addition. Blood being thicker than water, it became love at first sight.

Rick's relationship with his parents had suffered, but he was wise enough to know that nothing stayed the same, except for the feeling he was getting now as he fitted the key into his apartment door. Day to day, hour to hour, he never knew if Gina was going to be there or if she had decided it was time to go.

"Gina?"

He clicked on the hallway light, dispelling the darkness. He tried to sense subtle changes as he made his way through. He poked his head into the kitchen and saw dishes in the sink. Dirty dishes meant Gina had been there to eat. And if she took time to cook, perhaps she was still around.

Rick moved to the living room, saw his daughter's collection of Power Puff dolls on the floor. Going to the first bedroom, he stuck his head in. There before him, looking like a true gift from God, lay Kanisha, fast asleep and more beautiful than any angel ever conceived.

Rick closed the door, headed to his bedroom and found Gina, clothes on, fast asleep across the bed. Quietly he took off his clothes, shaking her, telling her to get in. She sat up, eyes dazed, blinking a few times.

"Time is it?'"

"Quarter to one."

She scratched at a lay of weave against the back of her head with a long acrylic nail, smacked her lips and squinted. "Damn." Standing, she dragged herself to the mirror, unhappy with the sight. Straggling off to the bathroom, she closed the door hard.

Gina came back, still more sleepy than awake, but her hair was fixed, her clothes rearranged and Cool Water filled the space about her. "You got a twenty?"

In truth he had it and a lot more, but he did not want her going out tonight. He was looking forward to having her beside him. "One o'clock in the morning, Gina."

"And? Look, I'm already late. You got a twenty?"

He took in the black Gap khakis hugging her hips, revealing the still firm flesh of her waist, the inny of her navel. He took in the white T-shirt two sizes too small hugging her round, high breasts that had no benefit of a bra. Took in the eyes, witchy and riddled with sleep. Wanted her.

"I got to go, Rick. Come on now, damn."

Despite it all, he understood. She was young, and just because he was too tired to go somewhere didn't mean she was. If he didn't give her the money, she'd go anyway. "Look in my wallet."

Gina turned, giving him a nice view of rump. She went through his wallet like a thief, snatched up her keys and left.

There was no sense asking where she was going; she never told. Just that she'd be back later, a time span that encompassed the world.

Chapter 3

Pink Lotion.

It was a gooey, slick concoction with an odor that couldn't decide if it wanted to be sweet or oily, but it tamed the wildness of Rick's daughter's hair and made the two ponytails doable.

"Ouch!"

"If you hold still, it won't hurt." It was a lie, but it was all Rick had as he eyed the clock, seeing he had five minutes to head out the front door. He was going to piss his mother off, again.

Hours after Gina had raided his wallet, snatched up her keys and headed out the front door, she still hadn't returned and the New York City Department of Corrections didn't care. Rick was expected in his assigned cellblock in a little under an hour, which meant once again he had to take his daughter to his mother's.

The first time he had dropped Kanisha off because Gina hadn't come home and he had to go to work, the dismay evident in his mother's voice over the phone vanished at the sight of her grand-baby.

By the eighth time, not even the kiss Kanisha gave could banish her ire. Rick knew he wasn't about to score any brownie points with an-other drop-off, but he had no choice.

"Hold still now," he said, too harsh for even his own ears. He worked the brush gathering loose strands and placed a rubberband around the hair, fluffing out the end. With a sigh, he began the other.

He glanced at the clock, seeing what he already knew. He had exactly two minutes to get out the door.

Kanisha's clothes still had to be ironed but there was no time, which meant his child would be showing up at his mother's in rough-dried shorts. It was another demerit and at some point Rick knew he would stop counting, but for now it mattered. Mattered a whole lot.

"Ain't you suppose to be somewhere?"

Gina looked up from the close inspection she was giving her nails and gazed at her friend Tarika. After hanging out at the after-hours club on Francis Lewis, she had crashed at Tarika's house. Awaking past noon, they had gone to White Castles for a quick, hot, cheap meal, made a pit stop at the grocery for two forties and had retreated to the park to drink it.

Time had gone by as it often did, slow and in no hurry to get to the next point until Tarika asked her about being somewhere.

"Oh, shit, what time is it?"

Tarika looked at her Concord watch. Outside of her gold earrings, it was the only precious possession she owned. "Three-twenty-seven."

The words lifted Gina off the park bench, her Coach bag hitting the ground in her haste. She picked it up, studied the horizon for a hot minute and looked around. The chronic she had smoked, the forty she had drunk, were still with her. Even in her fuzzy-minded state she knew where her daughter was. Knew too that Rick's mother would be able to smell her indulgences a mile away.

She wouldn't go over there now. Would wait until later, when her high was gone and the summer breeze had taken the smell of burnt weed from her clothes.

Gina sat back down.

"You ain't going?"

"Too fucking late now." Leaning back, she sucked out the last inch of malt liquor, watching the world go by.

Loretta Trimmons eyed her granddaughter as she wiped down the kitchen counter. Joy and pain was what she felt. Joy because Kanisha was the only grandchild she had, pain because the momma was a no-good run-around little juvenile who had trapped her son in the worst way.

"You know where your mother's gone to?" It was the fourth time Loretta had asked, but she kept hoping that sooner or later Kanisha would come up with an answer. It had been after three when Rick dropped her; now it was getting close to dark. Kanisha's bedtime was coming up soon, and once Loretta put the child down for the night she hated having to wake her later.

"Unh-uh."

"Don't say 'unh-uh,' Kanisha. Say no, Granny, I don't."

Brown eyes found her. "No, Granny, I don't."

"Well if she's not here in fifteen minutes, then we're going to get you into the tub and then it's bedtime."

"Not sleepy, Granny." And Kanisha wasn't. She didn't go to bed until late, and it was far from late. There was still some light out.

"Now you know when you stay with me you go to bed on time. I'll leave the TV on, but you have to be in the bed—that is, if your momma don't get here soon." Loretta rubbed a dishtowel over the plastic bowl and handed it to Kanisha. "Put that away for me."

It wasn't that Loretta couldn't do it herself; it was that her grand-child needed training in keeping house. Certain that Gina wasn't showing her, Loretta took it upon herself every chance she got. Just because the momma was nothing didn't mean she was going to stand by and let her grand-baby be the same nothing.

"Grab that dustpan from the corner." Kanisha may not have been old enough to wield a broom, but she could hold the dustpan steady for the day's worth of kitchen floor droppings.

Floor swept, dishes washed, counters wiped and condiments put away, the older woman and the little girl headed up the stairs to the bathroom. The tub was filled and Kanisha was undressing to get in when the doorbell rang. "I'll get it," Loretta called out to her husband Al.

Loretta didn't like Al answering the door when Gina came. He was too nice to her when he did. Gina wasn't welcome, and Loretta wanted her to know it every chance she got. Most times her husband forgot to be unkind and even when he did, it was a half attempt.

She moved down the steps, took a deep breath and opened the

door. The woman who had entered her son's life like a hurricane, leaving nothing but destruction in its wake, stood there.

"I was just about to bathe her."

"She can get one at home," Gina decided stepping past her.

No hello. No thank-you. Not even I'm sorry you had to be inconvenienced. Not a drop of common courtesy had Gina ever expressed, and Loretta knew it was far too late for Gina to start now; still, she itched to knock Gina in the back of her head. Correct her with one good smack. Teach her respect.

But Gina wasn't her child. Loretta wasn't certain just whose child Gina was because she had never met the mother. But a child learns at home, and it was obvious Gina's mother didn't teach her a thing.

Footsteps on the stairs drew her eyes; the sight of Gina coming down, her daughter in tow, broke Loretta's heart anew. Before her was the bitter and the sweet, the bad and the good. The hopelessness and the hope.

"I fed her." Loretta said, giving Gina an expectant look. "So she shouldn't be hungry for the rest of the night."

Gina urged her daughter toward Loretta. "Go tell Granny good night."

Kanisha went, placing her tiny arms about her Grandmother's hips. "Good night, Granny."

Loretta bent down and kissed her forehead. "Good night, Baby. You be good, hear?"

"I will." Then they were out the door and Loretta was closing it, wishing her heart the same capability.

When her eldest son had shown up that fateful day, the too young, too brass little girl at his side, Loretta knew whatever became of them would be no good. Six years later her opinion had not changed. Why her son even picked up with a girl like Gina had become an enigma over the years—not hers to determine, know or resolve. Still, she wished life had turned out different.

Rick had been a good boy. He had a habit of loving a little too hard and a little too deep for his own good, but he had been a B student, never got into the troubles some of Loretta's friends' children had gotten into, and had actually gone to college.

He only stayed for three years, but it was enough that he had tried it. When he announced he was taking the test to be a prison guard, it hurt her heart because she and her husband had envisioned so much more for their son, but it was an honest living despite the dangers.

Loretta was certain working with the riffraff of society must have rubbed off, that he must have found something alluring about no-good people. Why else would he ever get involved with a wild thing like Gina?

Her husband insisted that he had a tender heart, felt a need to help those who could not help themselves, and that was fine and good but you did not extend yourself in a way that became detrimental and that's all Gina Alexander was, detrimental and uncaring and just wrong.

Loretta Trimmons made her way back up the steps. She stuck her hand into the tub of bubbles, warm water lapping her elbows as she found the plug and pulled.

As always Kanisha struggled to keep up with the fast stride her mother used. She knew enough at four that to falter meant an arm being grabbed, angry hot words in her face, or worse. So Kanisha kept up, her little Fubu sneakers hitting the ground steadily enough to keep her from falling, but her legs hurt from the effort.

"What you eat at Granny's?"

"Fish."

"No vegetables?"

Kanisha had to think about it. She had a tendency to remember what she liked and forget what she didn't. "Ledduce."

"Salad then."

"Um-hum."

The boulevard was crowded and thick; dozens of people moved down the sidewalk stained with old gum, grease and litter. Up ahead the sign of the bus stop seemed like an oasis in the desert to Kanisha. It had been a long four-block walk, and she was tired and hot.

"Don't tell me we missed the bus," Gina said, making Kanisha wonder how she knew that. "Damn it." Her mother's footsteps slowed, drifted to a near halt as she stopped at the store, pushed against the glass door with the cowbell fixed over it.

Kanisha turned a blind eye to the row of chocolate candy bars pushed against the thick plexiglass and the stack of potato chips in all kinds of flavors. She knew enough to follow her mother as she moved down the tight aisle, heading for the refrigerated cases in back.

The cold air was like a breath of sweetness as her mother opened the glass door, reached in and grabbed a Heineken. Kanisha found herself missing the sensation as the door swung abruptly shut. She wet her lips, thirsty.

They were nearly to the register when her mother stopped and turned, finding Kanisha's eyes for the first time since they had left Rick's mother's house. "You want something?"

Kanisha nodded furiously.

"Soda?"

There before Kanisha was the look she didn't get to see too often but could not get enough of when it arrived. It was the pretty pecan face, the normally tight eyes made wide and special by plucked brows and motherly concern. It was a look that made Kanisha want to jump in it and never come out, drown even, if it meant she could have it forever.

"Un-huh."

"Hurry up and get it."

It hadn't been a particularly bad shift, but on Riker's Island there were few good ones. Rick eased his white shirt off his back, unlooped the hook on his belt, and stood for a moment in his underwear. He closed his eyes, sighed, then went about the business of putting his civilian clothes on.

He was thinking about Dajah, knowing the futility of that probing. She would have nothing to do with him until he was through with Gina. As Rick slipped his gun from around his leg, forced his work shirt into his duffle bag and hung his work pants on the hanger, he was only mildly surprised to find himself thinking about doing just that.

For years he had tried to make the best of his situation with Gina, times when his patience was sorely tested. Like today. Gina knew he had to leave for work by three-fifteen and where the fuck was she?

Missing in action, her main coda these days.

She was unreliable as the mother of his child. Just as unreliable as the love in his life. He slammed the locker shut, left the noisy locker room and headed for the front door.

Minutes later, as Rick got into his SUV and headed home, he wondered like always what he would find.

* * *

Innocence and passion.

That was what greeted him as he came into his bedroom, Gina sleeping, covers tossed off against the summer heat. There before him were the round orbs of her behind, the straps of the thong giving it no discretion and a face that in sleep revealed the twenty-three years that she was, soft as butter, pretty as spring, nestled and closed to the outside world.

He stood there, studying her, things moving through his heart, his loins, wanting her like the first time. Leaving the room quietly, he went to the other bedroom and found his daughter Kanisha just as lost to slumber. Flat on her back, sheet to her chin, the total sum of his heart was before him.

Without thought he reached down and kissed her forehead, reached for a small, warm hand, held it in his own in awe of its tininess. He gave it a squeeze. Left the room.

He yawned and began undoing his shirt. Made his way back to his bedroom and got into bed. The heat of Gina found him without effort, his longing arms pulling her close.

She came awake to his hand on her belly. Came awake to his breath, pungent and warm against her neck. Smiling in half-sleep, she moved close until they nestled, moved onto her back, taking him along for the journey.

Even through the condom Rick could tell she was wet and slippery as he eased into her, her eyes finding his as he did. "You love me, Rick?"

It had been so long since she'd asked that, so long since he even sensed she wanted to know, that it took him by surprise. "What do you mean?"

He felt her body tense, a closing off of herself even as he glided into her again. "What I said. You love me?"

He looked at the woman-child who had entered his life those many years ago, recalled the healing balm she had been to his wounded heart. Tried to find an answer. Couldn't quite catch one. Just lowered his lips to her collarbone and kissed it gently, feeling her relax, feeling her welcoming him deep inside of her. Knew that for the moment, it was enough.

* * *

The next morning he found Kanisha in pajamas on the living room floor, a bowl of Froot Loops before her, Cartoon Network blasting. The side of his bed had been empty, Gina nowhere in sight.

"Where's Mommy?"

Kanisha shrugged, bringing a tablespoon of cereal and milk to her mouth.

"She didn't say where she was going?"

"Didn't see her."

Which meant Gina had just got up and gone out without telling anybody anything. He headed to the kitchen, spying the sink full of dishes, crumbs on the table and floor. Opening the refrigerator in need of a glass of orange juice, Rick discovered there was none.

Just leftover Chinese food in greasy sauce-stained containers and other odds and ends that said Gina hadn't cooked dinner in a while.

Rick tried to remember the last time Gina had done any cooking, any cleaning. Couldn't. Resigned, he started on the kitchen and found himself straightening up the living room, both bedrooms and the bathroom. Two hours later he took a shower, gave Kanisha a bath and pressed out their clothes.

Half an hour after that they were in his car on their way to Waldbaum's to do food shopping. By the time they got back and put the food away, it was time for Rick to get ready for work, Gina nowhere to be found.

Doreen had always been suspicious of her daughter's boyfriend. She was suspicious of any grown man wanting to get with someone who was too young and too immature to be an equal. While the passing years had shown that Rick was in for the long haul, Doreen Alexander's reservations had not ceased.

Doreen had little interest in raising her own daughter and so she really wasn't interested in raising any grandchildren. But it was clear from the tone in Rick's voice that he was in a bind, and so she relented, telling him she would watch Kanisha but not to make it a habit.

"Them days of being stuck with Kanisha are over. You two got into this mess. You best find a way to get out."

There had been nothing new to the words, but for some reason they stuck to Rick like glue. They stayed with him as he headed for work, were right there beside him as he put in his eight-hour shift and were still keeping him company when he got home and found the apartment empty. Quarter to one in the morning, and there was no indication Gina had been back since she'd left the previous morning.

Rick found himself searching out better times, a sweeter life. Soul on automatic, he found himself reaching out to brighter days, but life was what it was—a horizon full of gray.

Getting some share time with her friend hadn't been easy, but Dajah was determined to do just that. She didn't need Frieda to tell her that even though it was just Monday she was exhausted. It was all in Frieda's voice.

"You sound beat," Dajah told her.

Beat ain't the word, Frieda thought to herself.

When her department manager had come to her some three months before and announced that they were going to have cutbacks, Frieda just knew her position as an accountant with County Hospital was out the window.

Frieda was certain that her eight years of struggle to attain the position were about to be snatched from under her, that she was about to be transferred to some other place.

When she heard her manager say that her two assistants were being laid off but Frieda wasn't, she'd been so relieved that she actually giggled. She managed to catch most of it before it left her mouth, but enough of it had spilled out to cause her manager to raise a brow.

"I'm sorry," Frieda said. "I'm not laughing at anyone's misery." She was just relieved that it wasn't hers.

She'd have a bigger workload, her boss went on to say, but the situation would only be for a little while. "June is our fiscal year, and we're requesting new help in that budget. You can hang on till then."

It had been March when they had that talk. It was now the middle of June. At the time she thought she could handle the workload, but the reality was showing her different.

The whole hour lunch she used to take became six minutes at her desk. Her work day that used to begin at 9:05 A.M. now started at 7:45. Quitting time no longer had an exact number, just when she became too brain-dead to calculate another stat. Frieda understood how premature her relief had been.

Still, she couldn't remember the last time she had spent some time with Dajah. "Come on by tomorrow."

"You sure?"

"Of course I am. We haven't seen each other in a while. Time for catch-up." But even as Frieda said this, she could not stop her yawns. Her body tingled to hang up the phone and crawl into bed, tired beyond belief.

The next day Dajah made it her business to get there by seven. A red-eyed, beat-down-looking Frieda answered the door.

"Damn, Frieda." Dajah hadn't meant for those words to leave her, but the sight of her friend looking closer to forty than thirty took her by surprise.

"You coming in or you're going to stand there and stare at me."

"You look terrible."

"Well, thanks a lot." Frieda turned away, but Dajah was still making her a case study.

"This isn't good, Frieda."

"Don't start," she insisted, plopping onto her love seat.

"But you don't."

"I know that, Day, okay? I know I look tore up from the floor up. I know I'm working too hard for not enough money. I know I can't go on like this, all right?"

"Okay . . . so still no word?"

Frieda cut her eyes Dajah's way. "What do you think?"

Dajah was smart enough to switch channels. "I met this guy." The hostility that had infused Frieda faded away, a new light coming into her eyes.

"Yeah?"

"Yeah."

"When?"

"Last week."

"Where?"

"At that diner up the street from David's."

Eyebrows went up. "David's?"

"Long story. But yeah. Went to that concert, train went out of service at Sutphin. Figured I drop by David's, 'cept he was on his way out.

So I stop at the diner and this guy comes in, takes a seat next to me . . . kinda all that."

"Kinda?" was Frieda's question.

"Yeah. Nice body, okay face, just a shade short of cute."

"So what happened?"

"Well, he kept on bumping his knee against my leg, and I finally asked him if he wanted me to move over and he apologized. Then it was time to go and I didn't realize how late it was and how I had to take two buses home. Guess he must have seen my face or something. He offered to walk me to the bus stop."

"He was on foot?"

"He was on duty."

"Duty?"

Dajah knew like breathing how her friend felt about any man who took a job in law enforcement—he had to be a little loco. "Corrections."

"Prison guard?"

"Yeah."

"So he walks you, then what?"

"He gave me his Mace."

"Gave?"

"Yeah. For protection. Came the next day to pick it up."

"And?"

This was the hard part, the unoptimistic, 'why are you even bothering to consider him' part. "He has a daughter and hasn't quite broken up with the mother."

Frieda's brow rose again, not believing the words leaving her friend's mouth. "You can't be serious."

"I'm not getting with him. Just met him, that's all."

Frieda could read Dajah especially when Dajah wasn't up to the task. Frieda didn't let her slide, never gave her an easy out. Always made her face what was before her. Now was no different. "You playing yourself now?"

"I'm not 'playing' myself. I won't see him until he stops seeing her." Still, it did not quite fit the confines of her soul. It became a square peg trying to fit into a round hole.

The last bit of weariness left Frieda as the drama of her friend's life took hold. "And just how are you suppose to know when that is? Men do it all the time."

"He didn't have to tell me at all."

"So that makes him honest?"

"No, but it doesn't make him a liar."

Frieda could not stop herself from shaking her head, could not stop herself from putting a roadblock square in front of her friend's wrong path. Because this was not the Dajah she had known and loved.

This was not the woman who had never been desperate or foolish about men. The one who put self-worth above all else. This was some impostor wearing Dajah's jeans and black sandals. Frieda had to show her for the impostor she was.

"Why would you even want to risk that? Risk a world of trouble for someone you've seen for just a few minutes? Why would you want to put yourself in that position?"

Dajah had no verbal answer, only what she felt. She could only remember how everything in her wanted to just hold him, forever. Came up with the best answer she could find. "Sometimes you have to take a risk."

"For a man that's already taken?"

The phone rang, and Dajah was glad when Frieda got up to get it. Because she had no answer for her friend. She hardly had one for herself.

Chapter 4

Wednesdays and Thursdays were Rick's days off. Time away from work meant time being a family, and when Thursday morning rolled around, he had the day mapped out.

Everyone would get up and dressed, hop in his Navigator and make a stop at McDonald's for breakfast. They would get on the Van Wyck Expressway and head toward Staten Island and arrive at Sesame Place in Pennsylvania in no time.

Kanisha would spend the day riding and climbing and being a happy child while Rick and Gina would play the doting parents. They would indulge themselves in the overpriced lunch menus, buy souvenirs and a few hours later head back to Jamaica, Queens.

This was what was on his mind when he opened his eyes, ready to reach over and shake Gina awake. But the space besides him was empty.

Rick sat up, strained to hear the sound of cartoons blaring, his daughter's sweet melodious voice. But silence was all he heard, as thick and full as morning pressing against his window.

He rolled out of bed and went down the hall. Opening his daughter's bedroom, he saw her fast asleep. He went to her and shook her gently. Waited for her mirror eyes to find his, for cognizance to fill the sleepy spaces.

"Hey."

"Hi, Daddy."

"You know where your mommy is?"

Kanisha shook her head no.

"I was thinking about going to Sesame Place today. Sound like a plan?"

The only thing good about Mustapha was the bankroll. Not those pitch-black eyes that had found her a few weeks ago. Not the Sean John supersized baggy jeans that had been hanging off his hips, showing the waistband of his matching Sean John underwear.

Not the Timberlands unlaced or the diamond stud in his left ear. Not the real Rolex watch on his long, muscular vein-filled arm or those lips that looked made for kissing.

Just his money, Gina realized, extracting herself from the weight of him as she rolled off the king-size bed and sat on the edge. She cast a glance at his sleeping face, mindful of the pitiful sex he had given, knowing the only thing Mustapha really knew about was making bank.

He had the merchandise but was clueless about how to use it. Didn't spend any time touching her, trying to get her wet or anything. Thirty seconds of pounding, six of grunting and then he was pulling out and rolling over, condom still on when the snores began.

Gina didn't give her goodies away to just anyone, and she was mad at herself. Mad at him too because for all that he didn't do she should have kept it to herself this time around.

Ain't no Rick, she thought, looking around for her underwear, refusing to pay close attention to the milk crate turned nightstand next to his bed or the other shambled pieces of make-do furniture that filled the room.

As much money as Mustapha made on the corners, Gina expected him to live better than this. But when he had taken her down into the basement of his mother's house and clicked on the light, she realized where his money didn't go.

The sheets had been dirty and the pillowcases smelled foul, but she hadn't been there looking for clean linen, just to get her freak on.

She hadn't, and the thought turned her gut more as she got up, turned on a light and searched out the rest of her clothes.

She could smell the basement on her, could smell Mustapha on her. Wanted a shower but would wait until she got home.

Clothes on, she moved close to Mustapha's face. "Moo. Moo, wake up. I got to go." He came to, eyes opening, a few lashes sticky with mucus. A lascivious smile filled his face as one hand reached for her, but Gina stepped back from his grasp. "Ain't got time for all that. I got to go."

She had seen him padlock the trapdoor leading down into the basement at the back of the house and knew that the one leading to his mother's kitchen was heavy duty, made of steel and needed two keys to open it. She understood that if he didn't want to let her leave, he could keep her there, and the expression on his face said he wasn't ready for her to depart just yet.

"Where you in a rush to?"

Gina was glad he was still looking at her with that hungry look and not the one he normally wore when he was running his corner crew. They called him the Exterminator; he was a dangerous man, which at one time had been part of his charm. It no longer was.

"I got to get home to my child. My momma has someplace to go soon, and if I'm not there she's gonna be pissed."

"Where your momma live?"

She wasn't going to tell him. Wasn't going to expose her life to him anymore than she already had. Gina just wanted to get away from him and never come back. "You ain't got to take me there and shit."

He stood, tall, defiant, a totem pole of sculptured blackness. Muscles everywhere she looked, as if he had been carved with a sharp knife. "Why?"

"'Cause my momma don't play that, that's why. We roll up in your ride and she's gonna know what you do. I'll never be able to get her to baby-sit."

Uncertainty danced in his eyes. It took a few seconds before he realized a smile, a smile that used to turn her on. Now it chilled.

"Awright. Let me get some pants on. I'll let you out."

She accepted the hug he gave her, the roll of hundreds he deposited into her hand. Smiling like she meant it, she told him, yeah, they could hook up again and stepped out in the hot morning air.

* * *

"Rick?"

The apartment gave back no answer. "Rick, you here?" The silence told her he wasn't. She went into the kitchen and checked the small chalk board on the refrigerator. He often left messages for her, but the slate had been wiped clean.

Gina peeped her head into her daughter's room and saw the bed was made up nice and neat. She understood that Rick and Kanisha had gone out, but had no idea just where.

She went to her bedroom and searched her underwear drawer. Could not believe her bad luck when she couldn't find a single pair of clean panties.

She felt dirty, slimed, and just wanted a hot shower. Gina wanted to scrub away Mustapha, the basement smell clinging to her. She wanted to put on clean clothes, but she didn't have any underwear. She had standards and dirty panties didn't fit them.

She took a five-dollar bill from her pocketbook. Grabbing her keys, she left and headed for Cheap John's. Like a contrail, the funk rode the beckoning heat. If she could smell herself, she was certain others could.

She entered Cheap John's and moved toward to the back, went to the bin and began to search out a pair of size-four panties. She found nines and tens and even a couple of twos, but there didn't seem to be any loose fours, what she needed.

There were a bunch of them hanging on the rack, but they were a four-pack and were a dollar-fifty more than she had brought with her. Gina grabbed one, kept her hands low and ripped it open.

She took out one, dropped the rest and kicked it under the table. She brought her hand slowly to the bin of loose ones and began moving her hands through the pile. She went on searching, her bounty tight in one fist. Straightening herself up, size four in hand, she headed for the register.

The salesgirl, all of seventeen, searched the panties, and could not find a scanner tag. She looked around the store, ready to call out for a manager, but Gina cut her off.

"They're a dollar. Got them from the bin."

The salesgirl looked at her, looked at the panties, felt the quality and knew better. She looked back at Gina, and Gina returned the look with fire; held it as the girl looked away, shrugged and rang up a dollar sale. She stuffed the underwear into the bag and took Gina's five. She gave her the change, and Gina headed out of the store.

Gina bought a slice of pizza, a donut and a coke. Making her way back home, she ate, and then hopped into the shower.

She didn't leave until its hot, stinging rays turned cold, stayed under the chilly spray until it had her shivering. She got out, dried herself off and put on her new underwear. Putting her old ones into a plastic bag, she made her way to the hall and pitched them down the incinerator.

The hole in Rick's heart that morning had not lessened a bit as he carried Kanisha into the apartment building, she half asleep and fastened to his chest. Sitting in Sesame Place, watching the *mothers* and fathers enjoying the park with their children, had only widened it.

Even Kanisha, who normally loved Sesame Place and always begged for one more ride, seemed ready to go after an hour. Her normally chatty voice was missing on the ride there, and she chose slumber over singing him songs on the ride back.

Shifting her in his arms, Rick stepped off the elevator and headed for his door. He heard the ear-busting music pouring from behind it and knew Gina was back from wherever she had been.

"Where y'all went?" she asked from the confines of the sofa, a Source magazine in her hand.

But Rick refused to answer. He headed for the stereo and turned down the sound, then took his sleepy-eyed daughter to her bedroom.

"You deaf?" she asked, getting up and following. "Where y'all been? I came home and nobody here."

Rick eased Kanisha onto the bed, moved her toward the wall, turned and walked out of the room.

"Nigga, I'm talking to you."

He hated the N-word. Hated the variants that had manifested through time. Nigger, nigga', nigga's, they were all horrible expressions unworthy of leaving anybody's mouth for any reason. Up in the prison it was all he heard.

He turned, surprising himself, surprising Gina even more. His expression made her shrink, his body taut, ready to spring. "Who the fuck you calling a nigga?"

Gina had never seen such fire in his eyes, never felt such insolence in his body. It scared her, and a nervous laugh left her, throat tight, eyes skittish. "I didn't mean it like that."

Rick glared at her, hating her as he had never hated her before. He felt his fist ball, ready for battle. He was on the edge, and Rick knew he could hurt her real bad, knew that his hands and fist and feet were just awaiting the call.

He caught himself and turned away. Marching off to his bedroom, he slammed the door and locked it. Rick sat on the bed and held his head, while the sound of Gina asking about doing the laundry filled the hot, tense air.

Shut up, he was thinking. *Just shut the fuck up. Don't ask me about shit, just go the fuck away.* His brain felt ready to explode. Blood pounded inside it like a tom-tom. He squeezed his eyes shut, forcing down his rage.

Rick wasn't certain when she stopped asking, when she left the door, when the silence came. Only that he fell back against the bed and gave in to a weariness he did not even know he possessed, fast asleep in no time.

"He's trippin'," Gina said, half an hour later, as she sat holding herself.

"What you mean?" Tarika asked, seeing her friend as she had never seen her friend before—bugged-out scared.

"Nigga was going to hurt me, Tarika. Was five seconds off my ass." "Rick?"

Gina cast her with a wild-eyed look. "Who the fuck you think?" "He was going to hit you?"

"Ain't that what I said? He didn't, but he wanted to. I ain't never seen him look like that before."

"What happened?"

"When I got home, no one was there. So like four hours later, he comes through the door with Kanisha sleeping in his arms. All I said was where you been? Wouldn't answer. So I follows him to Kanisha's room and ask him again. But he's acting like I'm air or some shit. So I say, Rick, I'm talking to you and he just turns on me with this crazy fucking look in his eyes. Next thing I know he's stomping off to the bedroom and he slamming the door. Locked it and shit." Gina took a breath, looked off. "I hauled ass out of there."

It was not the Rick Tarika knew. Not the Rick who had been with her best friend for all those years, but Tarika understood why. The Rick Gina had seen this day was long overdue.

Tarika had a man, and his name was Sha-Keem. Sha-Keem had a job, but it was selling five-and ten-dollar vials of crack on the corner, and though he made a couple hundred a day, since he had come back from prison, he was no longer sharing his bounty with her.

In fact he was no longer sharing much with her, least of all his time. If he dropped by once a week it was a miracle. She knew about Angie, knew that Sha-Keem had taken a real liking to her, but they had gone through so much together and she was certain their love could survive.

Hadn't Tarika been the one who sat through his bail hearing? Hadn't she been the one who took the bus to Riker's every day to visit him when he was in jail and had been there on the day he got out? But it didn't seem to be enough. Sha-Keem was more gone from her life than in it, and here Gina was, with a man any girl would want, and she just refused to do right. Rick broke rank? It was about time. Still, Tarika knew better than to voice that. "So what you gonna do?" she asked sympathetically.

Gina looked around Tarika's room. It was dark, dank, full of old clothes, broken appliances and discarded furniture. Tarika's uncle's basement wasn't fit for anything, but he had been the only family member who had been willing to take Tarika in.

Her bed was a discarded mattress on the floor that spiders liked to crawl in at night. To earn her keep, Tarika had to keep upstairs clean and spotless, cook dinner every night and do her uncle's laundry. In return he gave her forty dollars a month and the basement.

If life had been different for her, at twenty-three Tarika would have had her high school diploma and a job that could afford her at least a studio apartment.

But life hadn't treated her different. And when her mother kicked her out at the age of twelve and she bounced from relative to relative, she had never tried to be any more than what she was—a high school dropout with no goals. "Where you gonna go?" she asked Gina.

Tarika's basement was a lifetime from the two-bedroom apartment on 89th Avenue, but at the moment Gina couldn't go back there. Ditto her momma's house. "Was thinking I could stay with you for a while."

Tarika's eyes grew wide. "Here, Gina? You know my uncle won't have it."

Gina fished into her back pocket and pulled out the three hundred dollars Mustapha had given her. Peeled off two. "I'll pay him two hundred if he let me stay here for a week. Rick'll cool down by then and I can go back home."

Tarika looked at the money, glanced toward the aged, exposed support beams over her head. "Let me go ask." She took two hundred from Gina's hand and headed up the stairs.

Three minutes later, Tarika was back. She didn't have to say it. It was all over her face, but she told it anyway. "My uncle said no."

No.

The word was still rocking inside Gina's head as she left Tarika's house, so angry her blood boiled and so hurt it was all she could do not to cry. Though she had never really had a conversation with the man, she knew his type. Money always talked.

Money made Tarika's uncle's world go round. Money was his beginning and his end. But he had refused hers. Had refused her cash as if it was tainted, wasn't good enough. As if Gina was such bad news that there wasn't enough of it in the world to let her stay in his shabby basement.

That hurt. Nothing else had in a long time, but that really wounded.

Back on the street, Gina considered her options. Mustapha would take her in for a while, but she feared he would never let her go. She could go knock on her mother's door but wasn't up to the battle.

That left option number three. Flagging a gypsy cab, she headed back to Rick's.

Rick wasn't sure how long he was out, only that the sound of his daughter's voice brought him back to the world.

"Daddy."

She was sitting on the bed when he came to. He sat up, tried to remember how he had fallen asleep in the first place and found himself back to the moment he was about to hurt Gina. His heart sank at the memory and he closed his eyes to the shame. It took a few seconds to get his emotions together before he could face his child.

"How you open the door?" He remembered he had locked it.

Kanisha picked up the butter knife by her side, its shiny surface glinting in the soft light. "I seen Momma do it."

"She home?"

Kanisha knew he would ask. It was what everyone seemed to want to know. Everywhere she went someone was asking her about her momma. She didn't know why they thought she could answer. Rarely was she able to tell them. This time was no different.

"Nope."

Rick sat up. Looked at the clock. Saw it was after seven and tried to calculate how much time had slipped past. His stomach growled, and he realized he was hungry. He got up, made a pit stop in the bathroom and then headed for the kitchen.

There were food items but nothing he wanted to eat. He tried to determine what his stomach was calling for, but couldn't get a clear fix on it. Rick asked his daughter what she wanted, already knowing the answer. He told her to go put on her shoes.

Like a deer caught in the headlights, that was how Gina looked as she came face-to-face with Rick in the apartment lobby. He had never seen her look so terror-stricken, and for a hot minute considered using it against her, but Kanisha was there and the ugliness had to end.

His eyes drifted from her. "We're on our way to McDonald's."

It took a minute for Gina's mouth to work. She wasn't sure what she should say, wasn't certain if it was the old Rick or the new one before her. "On my way up."

"You coming, Mommy?" Kanisha asked, sensing that she needed to be a part of the trip.

Gina looked at Rick for an answer. He nodded his head. "Yeah, she's coming." The three of them made their way toward Jamaica Avenue, closed stores drifting by in a parade of heavy-duty locks and shutters of steel.

Chapter 5

Sweet summer.

Dajah could feel it, even though her eyes were closed. She could sense it even as she lay in bed, trying to get herself up from its confines. She had a shower to take, clothes to get into, a commute to work to make, but she did not want to abandon the comfort of her bed, the mind puzzle she was playing called what does Rick look like?

She could see his eyes, but not the face that they dwelled in. Dajah could see the tight fit of his work pants, but not the torso and chest above. She knew he had hair but couldn't remember if it was cut scalp-close or had an inch of growth. "Enough," she uttered to no one, tossing back the sheet.

Planting her feet on the area rug, she went to the window, separated the mini-blinds and looked out into the sun-splashed day. Heat radiated through the glass, rolled over the asphalt street in seductive shimmers, and she knew that the day was going to be a scorcher.

The beach.

The idea came, stayed, as she heard the faint tweet of morning birds mingle with the rush of faraway traffic.

An Aries by birth and nature, nothing in her or about her matched the longing her soul had for the ocean, but in recent years she had found herself more times than she could count on the boardwalk of Jones Beach, watching the sun vanish into the void between heaven and earth.

Dajah would stand there, elbows pressed against the boardwalk railing until the darkness was near complete and the lights of the boardwalk twinkled on. Sunset comforted her, its presence made her feel a part of the universe. At a time in her life when she needed to feel a part of something, she knew that the beach was where she'd be after work.

General Management was a one-floor office tucked into the glass and steel mini-tower on Old Country Road in Seaford, Long Island. A financial firm for various small to midsize businesses, on a good day it was a twenty-two minute commute. With the flow of heavy traffic headed in the opposite direction, toward Manhattan, bad traffic days were rare.

Dajah had found the job when working for County Hospital became too stifling for her taste. In need of a less tense working environment, with a BA in accounting and a love for numbers, she had no trouble taking the position of junior accountant with the firm.

The work challenged her, the benefits were good and she'd gotten along well with her co-workers without being entangled in their lives. Dajah couldn't complain if she wanted to. Her job was a good thing.

She pulled in to her designated parking space, left her car and made her way up the wide marbled steps. Through the heavy glass doors she went, the lobby softly lit with recessed lighting, the whisper of nylons and the tap of leather soles echoing across the dark green-tiled lobby floor.

She stopped at the concession stand, got a black coffee and a plain croissant. Then she was off to the elevator banks, where she spotted Elias, the building maintenance worker who had been retirement age when Dajah first started.

Where once she had wondered why he was still pushing a broom, now she looked forward to seeing him in the mornings. There was something comforting in the brown wrinkled-raisin face. Something comforting in the onyx eyes that suggested old forgotten pleasures.

"Good morning, Miss Moore."

"Morning, Mr. Elias. How are you?"

"Just fine."

The elevator door slid open. Dajah stepped in. "Well, you have a good day."

"I'm sure gonna try, Miss Moore." That was the bulk of their conversation. But like the coffee in her hand, the little bit was a pick-me-up at the start of her day.

The elevator door closed on his smiling face, and Dajah found her own reflected in the shiny panels. She could not see much detail to her face, but her legs looked sturdy and her battleship-gray dress was hitting the right spot—three and a half inches above her knees.

Slightly bowed, her legs did not touch, and beneath the sheen of her stockings the scar that ran across one kneecap could not be seen. But Dajah knew it was there. A battle scar from childhood, it was a permanent marker from a long-ago dare.

"*Try it,*" her friend Jennifer had urged those many decades ago. "*Go 'head, try it.*"

Age eight, Dajah had stood at the top of the too-steep hill, legs fast to the ground, bike steady between them, and gazed down the long expanse of empty roadway. She had stood there debating with herself, wondering about the quickness of the descent and the abilities of her back-pedal brakes.

She had witnessed Jennifer take the flying ride three times, the wind lifting heavy braids off her back in flight. She had heard the squeal of delight in Jennifer's voice as the thrill took hold, forcing her mouth open in delicious freedom. Dajah had wanted to try it too, but the sensible part of her mind wasn't convinced.

"You chicken?" Jennifer had asked, more question than statement. "You are. You a chicken." A final decision.

"Am not," was all Dajah could throw back, even though she was.

"Yeah, you are. Dajah's a chicken. Dajah nothing but a big old chicken." As if to prove her point, Jennifer mounted her bike and took off down the hill, braids flying, voice squealing.

In the next second Dajah was taking off too, breath gone, heart in her throat. She had nearly reached to the bottom when she let go of her fears and started to enjoy it. She was nearly to the bottom when she realized she should have applied her brakes a few seconds before.

Dajah was shooting toward the oncoming traffic of the cross street when she did, feet slamming back against the pedals, sending her and the bike onto its side, her knee making impact with the jagged edge of a broken bottle.

The sound of screeching brakes was all she remembered before the world went dark. Needles and stitches and being on punishment for a month was what she recalled afterward. She never attempted to ride that hill again.

Cautious, wise, that's who Dajah had been.

The elevator arrived at her floor with the gentlest of bumps. Massive, the office was a sea of gray-burlap cubicles, each seemingly as unspecific as the next. But inside a true struggle for individuality was waged, with everything from first-grade artwork down to mini cappuccino makers filling the space.

Sean Ellis achieved it with the New York Rangers memorabilia, banners, coffee mugs and old tickets tacked to the natty walls in every available space. Helene Mortimer's cubicle was a homage to her three grandchildren, elementary school portraits and hand-drawn pictures in fancy frames topping her lateral files.

Webster O'Donnell chose the alumni route, his two college degrees, graduation photos and tassel from Old Westbury on prominent display.

For Dajah, it was plants.

Her Wandering Jew had fastened its lush green leaves along the divider wall and was making its way over into the cubicle next to it. Half a dozen cactus with little heads of fuchsia and orange stood like soldiers along her utility nook. A big floppy frond explored the recess of one corner, and a spider plant hung in a basket from the other.

An oasis of green in a sea of gray, the sight always lifted her spirits. For no matter what was and wasn't going on in her life, this was her one true thing, comforting and near effortless.

It was the whine of the vacuum that woke him. It was the smell of coffee and cooked sausage that made him leave his bed.

Rick stood in his living room, seeing a sight he had not seen in weeks. Everything sparkled and shined and he hadn't lifted a finger.

His stomach led him to the kitchen, where Gina was attacking burnt-food stains on the stove. Sensing him more than she saw him, she turned, uncertainty on her face. "I made you breakfast. Pancakes and sausage. It's ready any time you want."

She had pushed too hard and too far the other day, that much she knew even though she was unable to pinpoint exactly how and when. Whatever it was it had turned Rick into someone she didn't know and she just wanted to make it right again.

"You hungry?" she went on to say. She couldn't control her need to be "out there", could not stop her desire to see other men, but she loved Rick; he was her rock. She wanted to keep it that way. "Are you?" she asked again.

Rick took in the stack of pancakes, the nubby links of sausage. Felt hunger nudge his belly. "Let me shower first," he said, and left the kitchen.

The clean apartment was fine and the breakfast awaiting his mouth was better. But there was more to life, and Rick found he wanted it. Just because Gina wasn't capable of giving it to him didn't mean it wasn't still due.

Jones Beach.

Seashell-littered ochre sand. Seagulls circling the breeze. Afternoon bathers offered up their skin to the sun, and foam-capped waves rushed the shore in whispers.

Dajah stood on the boardwalk, inhaling the hot briny air, the heat of the sun burning into the top of her head, the exposed flesh of her arms. There was no need to do what she'd normally do—go deep inside herself to determine what needed to be addressed.

That knowledge had been with her for a few weeks. Right there beside her from the moment she had uttered those words—*if you're ever free*—filling her with both hope and despair.

She'd felt immediacy with Rick. Like Legos clicking into place, she'd felt as if she'd known him forever, or from some long-ago place.

A part of her said there was no sense in hoping. That to want Rick meant destruction of a family unit, no matter how unstable it was. And even if he left his baby's mother, he would always be tethered to her.

But another part of her said that it had worked for other people, that a man with a child by someone did not limit a new relationship with someone else. Dajah believed there were no accidents in life.

Everything happened for a reason and stopping by the diner that night held validity, for both herself and Rick. Something was to come of it. She just wasn't certain what or when.

Call her.

And say what?

The truth, something told him.

The thought, like a flower blooming, had been with Rick since morning. But while it yo-yoed back and forward in his mind, putting the idea into action was a scary proposition. He hadn't left Gina. But he wanted to.

Since he'd met Dajah, the idea of a new life had taken root, finding fertile ground in the woman whose mere presence told him how much he was missing out on, what he was due and all that he wasn't getting.

The unhappiness between him and Gina wasn't new. It had been there for a while. Rick saw possibility in Dajah. Knew he had to keep the lines of communication open.

Waiting until he was on his work break, he dug out the piece of paper with the bubbly script. Staring at the digits as if they could reveal the future, Rick began to dial.

You leave her yet?

That was what should have come out of Dajah's mouth when she picked up the phone and heard Rick on the other end. What she managed was, "Hey, you're calling."

"Yeah, I am. How've you been?"

"I've been okay. Any more fights?"

"What do you mean?"

"At work. You're keeping safe, right?"

"Safe enough." Rick paused. "It's not done yet."

"What's not done?"

"Me and my baby's mother."

His words were so unexpected she couldn't respond. He wasn't supposed to be making this call until it was over. Phoning her when it wasn't, wasn't a part of the deal.

"Just wanted you to know," Rick went on to say, her silence saying much. "It's not that I'm not, I'm still leaving her, and soon, but just not yet."

"Then I got to go."

"I understand," but Rick's words were lost to the abrupt click of the phone.

"Put on that Prince CD . . . that song 'Can't Make You Love Me.'"

Tarika got up off her bed and went to the stack of CDs on the floor. That Gina was asking to hear it, that she didn't want to hear Ja Rule or Nelly, was speaking volumes into the effervescent silence that had trailed her since the moment Gina had arrived.

She hadn't said much, just plunked down on the old chair as though the world was resting on her shoulders. That she had barely looked at Tarika, uttered few words, told her that she was hurting in a way she'd never hurt before.

Tarika wanted to ask if she was okay, ask what was wrong, but she knew a part of it. She knew Gina's life had been shaken and stirred, the contents settling into something unfamiliar. It was a place Tarika had been a few times in her life, and she was ready to offer some comfort, but she knew Gina wasn't quite ready to hear it.

It took a while to find the CD, but only a few seconds to slip the disc in, program the number, push play and allow Prince's voice to ache its way across the dimness. Gina leaned back and closed her eyes, mouth moving in painful lip-synch.

It took four replays before Gina had her fill. Four trips to the CD player before she opened her eyes, a shiny wetness clinging to the corners and a pain real enough to touch on her face. "I'm losing him, Tarika."

"Rick?"

"Who the fuck you think?"

Tarika looked away, searched for words, a soothing comfort. Found none.

"Just been fucking strange since that day. Acting like I'm not even there . . . got up yesterday morning, cleaning and cooking like a muthafucker and he ain't so much as said thank you . . . won't give me none either."

Which was a true sign that things had changed, for even Tarika knew that when that basic need ceased to be a consideration, a large part of him was already gone.

"What am I gonna do?"

Tarika had a truckload of answers but knew her friend wasn't capable of doing any of them. So she did what good friends did. She told a lie. "He ain't leaving you, girl. You the mother of his child. Rick love you mad crazy, you know that. All that stuff he done did for you, shoot."

Gina looked at her friend a long time, trying to find the truth in those words. She clung to the hope even though it felt hollow in her heart. "Yeah, guess you right. Shit, we done been together all these years, where the fuck he going?"

Rick looked down at his bank statement, eyes dancing over the five-figure number, The Plan like honey in his mouth. He was almost there. By September, he'd be ready to go.

But it was only June.

Only June and freedom was singing in his ear. Only June and he wanted out. Only June and he was craving happiness like a dope fiend. Only June and he was craving Dajah.

He lay in bed at night and remembered how it felt to be close to her, the soft heat, the fullness of her presence. Rick found himself remembering how scared she'd looked that night they met in the diner and the ease that came into her when he offered to take the walk with her.

Life had become a memory lane of slow sweeps across the not-so-faraway past until Gina happened into the room. Rick began to feel as if he couldn't breathe, could not draw another good breath until he was away from her. Feeling like an inmate for the first time in his life, Rick wanted to be free.

He had to give his daughter The Talk first. Had to try and explain why they could no longer live together, why her and her mother had to go. It wasn't that Rick didn't want Kanisha with him; it was that Gina would never allow it. Though Kanisha got on Gina's nerves on a regular basis, Gina wouldn't even think about living away from her child.

Rick would try and break it down to Kanisha in a way that wouldn't hurt so much, that would allow her to understand that she was his heart, would always be.

Gina gave him the opportunity.

Wednesday morning she was up, showered and dressed. Said she was going to Tarika's and she would be back later. With few words being spoken between them in the last week, she didn't wait for a response and Rick didn't give her one. He wanted her gone.

As soon as the front door closed, he told Kanisha to go take a shower and brush her teeth. That he was taking her out for the day.

Half an hour later, father and daughter were on their way to McDonald's for breakfast, then it was off to Toys "R" Us for a shopping spree. A hundred dollars worth of toys later, they went to the park, where Kanisha zipped around the playground as if she owned it.

When the Mr. Softee ice cream truck rolled up, they sat on the bench and ate vanilla cones with chocolate sprinkles. Kanisha was still working on hers when The Talk began.

"You think me and Mommy are happy?"

Kanisha's eyes lit upon his, wide, curious, followed by a touch of sadness. "Yeah."

"Tell the truth, Kanisha. What do me and Mommy do most of the time?"

"Well, most da time you at work and she be with her friend. And den sometimes we all go to McDonald's."

"And?" She looked away, torn. Rick lifted her face toward him. "You can tell me. I won't tell her."

Liquid filled the spaces of her eyes. "She always mad, Daddy. Always mad. She curses a lot and she yells."

"At me, right?" Rick asked as carefully as he could.

"Yeah . . . me too."

"So if Mommy's always mad and cursing at us, you think it's because we're happy?"

The little lips pouted. "Nope."

Rick swallowed. "No, we're not." A tear rolled down her cheek. Rick wiped it. Gathered her onto his lap, latched his arms around her tightly, drew her head to his chest. Rick sat there for a moment allowing the full impact to find a settling place.

Her tiny body shuddered against him. He balled up the ice cream napkin and patted the corner of her eyes. When Rick spoke again, his voice was tight, choked with pain. "I want to be happy, Kanisha. I want you to be happy. And we can't be happy the way things are now. I love you more than anyone or anything. You my heart, and I want you to always remember that."

She pulled away from him, wet eyes finding his, a terror inside pitched. "You leaving, Daddy? You leaving, me?"

"Oh, no, Baby, I could never leave you. Just your mother."

"We leaving Mommy?" Her voice a near whisper.

"We're not. I am."

"Can I come with you?"

"In a little while. But for right now, I have to send you and mommy back to your grandmother's house. But it's only going to be for a little while, and I'll come and see you every day, I promise. And we'll still go places and do things and it'll be like now, but we'll be living in different places."

Little arms wrapped around him like a python, squeezing. "I don't want you to leave, Daddy. I don't want you to."

"I know, Kanisha. I know. But it'll only be for a little while, I swear, just for a little while." But in that moment he was feeling it the way Kanisha was expressing it. A little while was a void as deep and as wide as the universe.

"You can't tell Mommy none of this. Not what we talked about, not that I'm sending her away and not that we'll be together later, okay, Baby?"

Her head nodded against his chest, father and daughter holding fast, emotionally stockpiling against the future, no direct destination in sight.

A mini-mountain of boxes and plastic bags pushed against the south wall was the first thing Gina noticed when she let herself in. Then she noticed Kanisha sitting red-eyed on the sofa.

"Where your daddy?"

"In da room."

Gina made her way, found Rick emptying out one of her dresser drawers. Words jumped her tongue, but caution made her speak them carefully. "What you doing, Rick?"

"Packing up your stuff."

"Why? We moving?"

"No, Gina, 'we' ain't moving. You and Kanisha are."

She chuckled because she was scared, not because it was funny. "Moving where? Why?"

"Because it's time for you to go and for me to live my life."

"You kicking me out?"

"Something like that." He closed the empty drawer and grabbed the one beneath it. He pulled it open and immediately began grabbing tops and jeans.

"You playing, right?"

"Does it look like I'm playing?"

"You can't do this."

"Says who?"

She had no answer, only self-preservation. "Me, that's who. I ain't leaving." She charged across the room, snatching her clothes from his hand. She managed two items before he shoved her hard. The fall was quick, the pain that echoed through her behind quicker.

Before she could catch her breath, he was standing over her, a tower of fierce determination. "Now we can do this two ways, Gina. Let me pack up your shit and get you to your momma's or knock your ass out and then take you to your momma's. Which one you prefer?"

It wasn't even a choice.

After she had gotten her hurt behind off the floor, Gina attempted the soft approach, her laugh careful, her eyes wanting, her arms reaching out to hold him. When that didn't work, she went back to the rage, a caboose of vile words leaving her until he gave her that cold look that shut her mouth.

When they were in his Navigator, filled to the brim with things, and they were making their way down 169th Street, she tried again with tears. Tears so real and gut-deep Rick could not tune the sorrow out.

"Please, Rick. Please don't do this. All those years we had? How you gonna throw all that away?"

Kanisha joined the chorus. "We don't want to go, Daddy. Don't make us go."

In a heartbeat the Navigator was pulled to the side of the road, gear in park, hazard lights on, one finger so close to Gina's face, it took her breath and made her blink. "Shut up. Just shut the fuck up, hear?

Don't say another thing to me, you got it?" Rick turned, anger on him like lava, found his daughter's eyes as his whole body trembled.

"What I tell you earlier? Didn't I explain it, didn't I? So you just shut up too." Then he twisted back around, put his car in drive, flicked off his hazards and moved back into the flow of traffic. Not another word was spoken the rest of the way.

Poker face.

That was what Rick presented as he unloaded his SUV, taking the contents into Gina's mother's house, ignoring Gina's mother, who said they couldn't stay there, and the silent but pressing plea he felt from both Gina and Kanisha that they didn't want to be there.

Rick held it all together as he hugged his daughter good-bye. Held it as she ran after him and he screamed to Gina to come get her. He held it as he got into his SUV and started the engine and drove away. Held it as he made his way back home.

Rick held it as he waited for the elevator to come and the too-long ride up. Held it until he was letting himself into the apartment that felt haunted with a thousand moments. But when he closed the door and locked it, there was nothing left to hold on to.

Nothing to keep him steady, poker-faced, upright as he slid to the floor and wept like he had never wept before.

Doreen Alexander had stopped beating her only child at the age of twelve, when her only child grabbed a broom and started swinging back. Until that moment Doreen Alexander had ruled her household with a vicious mouth and more than enough backhands. But that day she had stood cornered in her own kitchen while her pubescent twelve-year-old held the broom over her head looking for the slightest excuse to bring it crashing down, she ceased.

She still mouthed but she no longer hit. As her daughter and her daughter's daughter put away clothes in the second bedroom, Doreen Alexander found herself missing the old days. "How he think he can just drop y'all off like this? What man abandons his woman and his child? Always knew he was no damn good. And who he think he is that I can be taking care of what he suppose to take care of?"

Gina ignored her mother. Her heart was too wounded to argue, and she knew that whatever words her mother tossed her could not touch the pain she already felt.

"Don't think you gonna be here long, Gina 'cause I ain't having it and don't think you gonna be mooching offa me either. I ain't taking care of you or your child. You big enough to lay down and have her, then you big enough to raise her."

Gina threw clothes into the dresser drawer. Shook her possessions out on the bed, the whole thing surreal. She wanted some tree and a nice ice-cold forty to go with it but she had to get some order to the tiny bedroom. Had to get some part of her life straight first.

She'd put Kanisha to bed and go over to Tarika's house and chill. Tell her stupid-ass friend how fucking wrong she'd been.

"Tomorrow you best be out looking for a J-O-B, not that you'd even know what that is . . . stupid heifer you are. Had a good-ass man and what you do? Get your ass kicked out. Always said you ain't had a bit of sense in your head."

As far as Gina was concerned her mother was the real stupid one, standing up there talking trash and not meaning a drop of it. If her mother really wasn't going to let her stay, Gina, her child and their possessions would be out on the street by now.

"Always knew you wasn't going to be nothing. Now look atcha. You really ain't shit." Familiar parting words. Gina continued to put things away, sensing more than seeing her mother leave.

"She don't want us here, Momma," the first words Kanisha had spoken since Rick pulled off.

"Don't matter what she want, Kanisha. We here."

"I'm calling."

"Rick?"

"Yeah. I'm calling like I promised."

"You two are finished?"

"Yep. Over and done."

"You're sure?"

"Wouldn't be making this phone call if I wasn't." But he sounded so sad.

"You doing okay?"

No, he wasn't. Rick was tired, weary, hurt. He felt as if he had been beaten with an ugly stick; every part of him just ached. "Could be better."

"That bad?"

"Yeah, Dajah, that bad."

"For the right reasons, right?'

"What?"

"I just need to know what you did was for the right reasons."

In that moment it was a hard question to answer. He had sent Gina away and had to send his daughter away as well. Suddenly the trade-off didn't seem fair. He'd wanted out, but it had been a rough journey. "The right reasons, yeah . . . Can I see you?"

Dajah swallowed, his pain felt like a cocoon of sticky nettles. "When?"

"Like now? Can I come over?"

He had turned his whole world upside down for her. How could she tell him no?

He had barely stepped out of his car before her front door was swinging open, Dajah not quite recognizing the worn-down, red-eyed, sorrow-filled man who hit the alarm on his Navigator and moved toward her as if every bone inside of him had been broken.

A second before, she had not remembered the whole of Rick, only bits and pieces of his being that made an incomplete picture. But as she stepped out of her doorway and waited, the sight of him became as familiar as her own name.

Her arms lifted to him, letting him know that she would draw him near, hold him close, give all the comfort he was in need of. He embraced her, held her hard, tight, and she remained there with him on her front stoop, their bonding on full display.

Tears trickled onto her neck. The muscles of his forearms sent a crushing squeeze against her ribs. But in that moment she was willing to be broken in half if he needed her. And there was no doubt he did.

"I didn't know it would hurt so much," Rick was saying minutes later as he sat in her apartment.

"Breaking up is never easy."

"No, not Gina. Kanisha. The way she cried, didn't want to let me go." His head shook. "Just tore me up." His eyes found hers, those backlit wonders no longer full of light. "Didn't want her to hurt behind it."

"She'll be okay."

"Will she? Riker's full of kids who went through stuff like that and never got over it."

"But those kids didn't have you for a father. No doubt you love your little girl. You're going to be there for her."

"I guess you right." He massaged his temple. "Got some aspirin or something? My head's killing me."

"Advil?"

"That'll work."

Dajah went to the kitchen and came back with one tablet and a glass of water. She stood by as he popped the pill into his mouth, swallowed, winced and handed back the glass. She took the glass to the kitchen and came back, her mind running full speed ahead with what would happen next, full speed ahead with what Rick's baby's mother would and wouldn't do. "You change the locks?"

"On?"

"Your apartment."

He had not thought of that. The idea that Gina could still come and go made his head hurt worse. "Damn . . .didn't think about it." He considered Dajah with pained eyes. "I just wanted to get here, with you."

"I never been in a situation like this," she confessed, "but I have to believe you left her for a good reason and not just because of me."

"Not, it wasn't about you, not the whole thing anyway. It's about wanting more happiness than grief. Wanting more for myself, my daughter. You just gave me the courage."

"You need to know that I don't do half ass. I don't play the you-see-me-and-her-too."

"I don't do that."

"Never?"

"No, never."

"Just me and you?"

"Yeah, just me and you."

Dajah eased into the new shoes life had given her and asked if he wanted some wine.

"No, I'm cool. Besides, took that Advil. Shouldn't mix the two."

"Drug free?"

"Any other way to be?"

She leaned beyond him, peeked around his back. "Anymore like you? Because I swear you need to be cloned."

"Just who I am, Dajah. I work hard, I don't lie, don't do drugs."

"Never?"

"Well, when I was a teenager, I messed around a—"

"No, I mean lie."

"Little white ones to my daughter, yeah, but everything else, I'm straight up."

Dajah considered the man before her, head shaking. "She's crazy."

Rick didn't ask who.

Saying good night was not easy. Leaving off without taking the next step, a hard thing to do. But Dajah wanted time "to get to know you first." Prudent and old-fashioned, by the time Rick was heading home, the idea pleased him.

Life *had* been zooming by him for a while. It was time to slow things up, give each moment its due. No more speed chases through life. For now Rick just wanted to cruise.

Euphoria moving inside of him, Rick pulled up to his apartment building, a soft, fuzzy warmth filling his heart. But all that had happened hijacked his soul the moment he opened his apartment door, the rooms dark, silent, stifling with summer heat.

He could feel his daughter's absence. Understood that the pain was part of the process of the healing. Rick didn't try and fight it off; he opened up to it. Picked up the phone. Made a call.

Rick did not expect his daughter to answer. He had been certain that he would have a verbal battle with Gina or her mother just to hear Kanisha's voice. But it was hers that reached him, tiny and afraid.

"Kanisha?"

"Daddy." She said it as if she had been holding on to it forever, a surprising relief within each syllable. "You coming?"

"Coming where?" But he knew.

"Here, to get me like you promised."

"I will, but I can't yet."

"I don't like it here. Want to come home, Daddy."

"Who dat?" Rick heard in the background. Then there was a grappling with the phone, Gina's voice filling his ear. "Hello?"

"It's me, Rick."

"What you want?"

"Just wanted to check on Kanisha."

"She fine." Gina hung up.

Rick hit redial, the phone ringing until the voice mail came on.

Chapter 6

The next day Rick went out early, heading toward Gina's mother's house before he set off for work. Her mother's old battered Lincoln wasn't in the driveway, but Rick was certain Gina was home.

He rang the doorbell. Stood on the top stoop waiting for an answer. It didn't come. The windows were open, and he could hear both the sound of the television and the radio drifting from inside. He rang the bell again, giving it a few extra taps for good measure. Waited.

Rick peered up the street, in hopes that Gina had run to the store and would be making her way back. But the only sight he saw were children playing jump rope. He found himself envying the uncomplicated scene.

Moving to the top step, Rick pressed his face to the screen and peered inside. He saw the back of a sofa, an area rug, walls in need of painting, but not much else. "Gina," he called, the high summer sun beaming on his head, the breeze about him hot. "Gina, it's me—Rick."

No answer. He switched gears. "Kanisha," he shouted, his forehead pressed to the dusty screen. "Kanisha, you there? It's me, Daddy."

A car door slammed behind him. Rick turned and saw an older man leaving his car, his eyes on Rick, suspicious, unkind. Rick looked away, holding his breath until the man went inside his house.

Rick ran his hand across his brow, sweat and dirt coming off in warm drops. He wiped it on the back of his dark slacks, pressed the bell again, then again, its hollow ring ricocheting back to him.

He stared at the old wood door, understanding much with aching clarity.

He had devised The Plan, had given his daughter The Talk, but had not foreseen Gina's ingenuity. She couldn't force Rick to take her back, but she had the power to keep Kanisha away.

The hand over Kanisha's mouth was removed as the sound of a car driving off reached her. She labored for breath, her back sticky from being pressed into her mother's leg.

"Nigga crazy," Gina muttered, eyes wide, seeing nothing.

"Daddy?" Kanisha asked.

Her mother didn't answer. Somehow Kanisha didn't expect her to.

Rick drove, soul on fire. He picked up his cell phone, pressed the number sign, entered 02, and listened to the phone ring, five in all before the voice mail came on. "I ain't here right now, so leave a message," Gina's mother's voice demanded. Rick disconnected and tossed the phone into the passenger seat. But found himself reaching for it again.

He hit the number sign, entered 04, his heart a land mine as Dajah came on the line.

"Dajah Moore speaking."

"Hey, Dajah, it's Rick."

"Hi."

"Hi back. Listen, the day just started for me, and it's already jacked. You up to some company?"

"When?"

"Tonight. When I get off from work?"

"Like past midnight tonight?"

"Yeah."

Past midnight was bedtime. Past midnight, heavy with implications. Implications that Dajah was trying to make her way toward slowly.

"Can I?"

It took a while for her answer "Sure," to come; a while for her to accept rules were about to be broken.

"Thanks."

"For?"

"Understanding." Rick disconnected the call.

Candles. Music. Wine. She wanted to make it special.

But the candles, the music, the wine were neither noticed nor appreciated as Rick reached for her the moment she opened her door to him at ten to one in the morning. Her effort to offer up a "hey" became lost to arms that moved around her so quick, squeezed her so hard, her ribs ached.

His mouth was on her so fast, she had no time to take a next breath. Like a python, he encompassed her, back-walking her to the bedroom, his lips glued to hers, his arms too tight about her.

She tripped, nearly fell, but Rick did not seem to notice as his feet trampled hers urging her to the queen-size mattress. Her butt hit it hard and he was pushing her back when she broke away, stood, looking at him like he was crazy.

"What is wrong with you?"

"I just want you."

"Yeah, and I want you too, but a hello would be nice."

Rick stared at her, confused, caught up. He tasted desperation in the back of his throat, realization making a fast sweep. "Damn . . . I'm sorry."

"Well, you should be."

"I'm sorry, Dajah," he offered again.

"Well, good. Now." She took a breath. "We're going to do this the right way, or not at all." She pointed toward the living room. "I have wine, I have candles. Music. Let's go and settle into that before we settle into this."

She poured two tulip glasses of wine, handed him one. Sat back. Took a long sip. Looked off, Maxwell voice mocking the moment, the feel of Rick's too-tight arms still with her.

"Hey," he said softly.

It took a moment for her to look at him, anger and hurt inside her eyes. "I'm listening."

"I'm not normally like this."

"I hope not."

He twirled the delicate glass between his palms; old scars like slashes of magic markers across the knuckles. "Just never thought it would be like this."

"Like what?"

"So messed up . . . she won't let me see my kid."

There it was, the reason behind all of it. His call earlier, his need to see her. The assault when she opened her door. It didn't make her feel any better, but at least she knew. "How can she do that?"

"Simple."

"It's only been a day. Give her some time," the subject unwanted. Dajah didn't want that part of Rick's life in theirs now. But as he finished off the wine, reached for the bottle, she knew it would be.

"Not enough time in the world," he decided, filling the glass to the brim. "I went by there right before I called. She wouldn't even answer the door."

"Why?"

"Why what?'

"Why did you go by there?"

"To see my kid, why else?"

"Just asking." But Dajah was doing more than that. She was thinking, deciding, debating, considering. The more her brain worked, the more she felt invaded. It was too early in the game for issues with his child's mother to be infiltrating their life. "Maybe this isn't a good idea. Maybe you should go until you get that stuff settled."

"It's already settled."

"Doesn't feel like it."

"Don't you know how much I want to be with you?"

"I thought I did."

"I've given up my world to be here, with you, and you trying to insinuate that I'm not serious?"

No, that wasn't what she was insinuating, but it was messy and imposing and not how she wanted it. "Day two and there's already drama."

"You think I want this either?"

She saw it then, the hurt in his eyes. The confusion. The pain. She took a breath, released the doubt. "You're right, just tripping."

Rick felt the shift in her, took up one of her hands. Brought it to his lips. Kissed each fingertip. Her hand and body tingled. Her eye closed as one digit was engulfed in the warmth of his mouth.

His hand moved around her waist, drawing her close, against him, then on top. Her lips replaced her fingers as Maxwell crooned about a woman's work. Dajah released her soul, the body beneath her, an unknown mystery requesting that it be solved.

His hands found the slope of her back, palms smoothing already smooth flesh. He slipped them into the fit of her loose house shorts, tugged them past her hips, down her calves, his own feet finishing the task.

The bottom half of her naked, his belt buckle pinched her belly, making her pull away. "The buckle," she uttered, thighs spread, inner secrets on soft display.

He eased from beneath her, took off his pants, his shirt, boxers, clothes forming a pool of white and blue on the floor. Then he was naked before her, want apparent as she asked about condoms.

Rick reached into his discarded pants pocket, a roll of three appearing. Beckoning, he extended his hand her way. A hand Dajah took, glad, grateful and on fire, a fire that never got quenched as they made their way to her bedroom, condom on, him inside of her, coming too rough and too fast for her to even be a part of the final destination.

He rolled off, sweaty, winded, silence rushing, crushing hopes, extinguishing desire. Dread filled the air. Two for two, she was thinking as she lay there, unfulfilled.

"Too good," he muttered.

"What?"

"You . . . too hot, too wet. Couldn't help it."

Despite herself, she smiled. Despite other things strumming through her, she took the compliment. "I am who I am and I can't change how I feel."

"Don't want you to." Rick sat up. "Let me use your bathroom." He disappeared up the hall, came back. Reached for a second condom, making love to her a second time as if the first attempt had never happened. Making it delicious and slow, as if he had all night. As if there were no other place he wanted to be in that moment but between her soft, sticky thighs.

* * *

They slept.

Close, cuddled. Dajah and Rick slept inseparable, lost to a long overdue slumber. Then her alarm was going off and she hit the button quickly, getting out of bed. Behind her gentle snores came and she took a moment to study his face. Sweet, angelic, she could not wake him, not yet.

Showered and dressed Dajah perked Jamaica Blend, making two cups. She slipped into her bedroom, nudged the bed with a knee. Waited for those eyes to find her. "Morning," she offered, putting a mug on the nightstand.

Aroma made him sit up, reach for it. Rick inhaled the fragrance, took a fast hot sip. "Good."

"Jamaica Blend . . . listen, I'm heading out in about ten."

"I'll be ready." Nine minutes later they were heading out her front door.

Frieda held the phone to her ear, eyes on Barry, knowing that their evening was about to be interrupted. She listened to the giddiness in Dajah's voice, respected their friendship and said, "Sure, I'll be here."

She hung up. "Dajah's coming by."

"Tonight?"

"Yeah. She's on her way." Barry looked off. "She is my friend," Frieda said, understanding everything Barry wasn't going to utter.

"You hear me say anything?"

"It's not like she's going to spend the night."

"I'm not complaining."

But he was, quietly and intensely. It had been days since Frieda hadn't been too tired to spend some time with him and now that he was here, the last thing he wanted was to have to share his time with her friend.

They spent weekends together, but the few times they managed to go somewhere, Frieda would start yawning before half the evening was through. He'd look up from his drink, or glance over at her from his movie seat and there'd she'd be, glassy-eyed, blinking; just zombied-out.

So Barry pulled back a little, giving her space, time to rest. But obviously there wasn't enough of it in the world because Frieda was still looking like the walking dead.

It hurt him.

It hurt Barry that Frieda was putting in all that time without so much as a protest. It hurt him that she felt her job was more important than their relationship and, from the looks of things, her own well-being.

His insistence that she put her foot down was met with deaf ears. They had had too many verbal arguments about it to count. *"Get another job,"* he had insisted to her.

"You think I'm going to throw away all those years I put in with City and start all over? Forty thousand dollars a year, Barry. You hearing me? I'm not walking away from that to start all over again."

And be dead too soon to enjoy it, he had thought. He loved Frieda, and the last place he wanted to be was without her. But every time he saw her tired, haggard face, every time he glimpsed her hair that seem thinner and duller with every passing week, every time she got undressed and he saw a little less flesh on her bones, his heart ached.

"She won't be here long."

"Whatever." Barry headed off to her bedroom. But the moment he got there, he turned around, came back. "Just trippin'."

"No, I understand. How my life's going now isn't easy. And I know I'm as hardheaded as they come. But I have to handle it the way I have to handle it. It may not seem like the best way, or the wisest, but I'm doing what I can do."

"I'm just worried about you, Free."

"Kind of worried about myself. But I know it won't be for too long, and then we'll be back."

"Back to where?"

Her eyes grew soft. "To where we used to be."

"Well, that's a good thing, because I swear I miss you. Miss the you you used to be."

"Is it that bad?"

She had never asked before, and times came when Barry wanted to march her off to a mirror for her to take a good hard look. But in that moment he felt he could tell it. "Yeah, it's that bad." He pinched her butt. "Half of it has disappeared. Got circles under your eyes." He fingered her hair. "Your hair . . ." His voice trailed.

She felt his hurt, felt it as if she was feeling her own. She went out, then came back with a shoebox. She opened the lid; inside were puffs of what used to be on her head. "I comb my hair, and it just comes out in clumps." There was awe in her voice.

Barry looked at the collection, fascinated and repelled. "When were you going to tell me?"

"Never." She closed the lid.

"How long do you plan on keeping it?"

She shrugged.

He ran his fingers through the edges of her hair. What used to hang on her shoulders like a curtain of velvet had vanished into a thinness you could glimpse the wall through. "That's not good, Frieda."

She shrugged away from his touch, her emotions a yo-yo. "I know that. I just haven't had time to go to Michael's. I'm in need of a serious trim."

And a perm, some conditioner, Barry thought. "Take a day."

"A day what?"

"To at least get your hair done. Just take a personal day. Tell your boss to go fuck himself and take a day. Go get your hair done. A manicure. That spa you used to go to."

Frieda tried to imagine going to work tomorrow and telling her boss she was taking a personal day. Tried to imagine waking up during a weekday not to the sound of the ringing alarm, but sometime past noon.

She saw the extra work she would return to and couldn't hold the vision. "Sounds good." But her smile was too careful.

"No, it sounds like a plan."

"It's not that simple, Barry."

"Not if you believe it isn't. You're hurting yourself, Frieda, and hurting us in the process. This was only supposed to be for a little while. But it hasn't been. Just forever, is how it feels. Like our life, your health, is on serious lockdown. You're turning thirty-one in two weeks. But I'm looking at you and—" He stopped himself.

"And what?"

His head shook, refusing to go there. "Nothing."

"No, say it."

"Why should I? So we can just get mad at each other?"

"No, I want you to say it because you've been wanting to say it for a while. So go ahead and tell me how tore up I look. How it embarrasses you sometimes how haggard I've become. How you can't remember the last time I had my nails done."

He looked at her, a million things swimming in the air between them. "No need now, right? Just be wasting my breath."

"You think I like this?"

"No, Frieda, I don't think you like this, I'm starting to think you just love the shit out of it. Makes you some kind of freaking martyr or something, holding up a fort all by your lonesome even if it kills you."

"That's not fair or true."

"Proof is in the pudding."

"I got to eat."

"What about your mutual funds? Your nice little nest egg you've saved up? You don't have to stay there. You can find another gig. Less money, maybe, but that money you've got socked away will see you through whatever bad times you can perceive."

"That's for my retirement."

"What good is a retirement fund if you aren't going to be around to enjoy it." The anger in his eyes had vanished, slipping back into familiar territory she had seen too often to count lately.

"I'm not dying, Barry."

He took the box out her hand. Opened the lid. "And this says you're living?"

The doorbell rang. They exchanged a final look. Barry went off to the bedroom, Frieda to answer the door.

"Hey, girl," she said, a too-big smile on her face.

Dajah reached for the shoe box. "You bought shoes?"

Frieda pulled it back, shook her head. "No. Just stuff . . . be back." She went to the bathroom, opened the cabinet beneath the sink and put the box inside. She took a glance at her shabby hair in the bathroom mirror. Went and joined her friend.

"So, what's up?"

"Rick."

One brow raised. "Rick?"

"Oh, yeah."

"Mr. Baby Momma Drama?"

"Not anymore. She's gone."

"Really?"

"Absolutely. He has officially kicked her to the curb and my heart is just like *whew!*"

"I bet."

"You look in my face, my smiling, happy face and tell me it's not a good thing."

"It's always good in the beginning, Dajah. You know that."

"You're such a damn naysayer, you know that?"

"No, I'm a realist."

"Like there's a difference? I finally meet a man I can get with and all you can do is sit back and think about why it won't work." Dajah shook her head. "Can't you be happy with me? I remember the days when I wouldn't even have to ask."

"And I remember the days when hooking up with some man who had a child wasn't even a part of your thinking."

"Life changes, Frieda. Life, people, perceptions."

"No, people give up, that's what really happens. They get tired of the struggle and just say what the hell, that's what happens. And you know I'm glad you're sitting over there thinking that your world has just become complete, but I don't believe it has, Dajah."

Straight, no chaser, that was how Frieda always came. She didn't pull punches, didn't bite her tongue, none of that. Dajah shouldn't have been surprised or stung, but she was. "Fine, you are entitled to your thoughts."

"You think I don't want you to be happy? I do. I know it's been a year since you and David. I know that, but you don't get anywhere short-changing yourself."

"Well, look who's calling the kettle black. You working your ass into the ground over some stupid City job that would give two fucks if you died tomorrow, and you talking about not short-changing yourself?"

"I'm not short-changing myself."

"Oh, yeah, right. You just holding on, relief is coming . . . you know you may think the world is all black and white, Frieda, and maybe in your world it is, but I'm not living in your world. I'm living in mine, and right now Rick is working for me. I came way over here just to share that with you because you're my friend—or at least was."

"Don't even go there."

"Go where? When the last time we did anything together? Can you tell me, please, because I sure would like to know?"

"What is it with you people? You think I freaking like how my life is going?"

"Well, damn it, do something about it."

"I am. Every single day I go to work, I'm doing something about it."

"Something or nothing."

Frieda fixed her with a cool eye. "Tell you what. You don't tell me how to run my life, and I won't tell you how to run yours."

"Fine." Dajah stood up. "Guess I'll catch you later."

Frieda didn't sleep good that night.

She tossed and turned, head full of thoughts, her soul crowded with the hurt of others—Barry and Dajah. When her alarm went off at six, she had to force herself from the bed. By seven-fifteen, she was at her desk.

Two hours later Frieda had barely registered that someone had opened her office door when a stack of printouts rustled through the air like a captive bird. "What is this?"

She looked up, and saw her boss Herman, the stack of paper in his hand. She knew exactly what it was. She had stayed late last night working on it. "It's the figures from last quarter."

"Wrong."

Herman's cheeks were puffing; a bead of sweat dotted the top of his lip. But all Frieda really calculated in that moment were the brown eyes fixed like lasers, ready to obliterate.

"What do you mean, wrong?" Frieda asked, reaching for the pages, but they were airborne before she could secure them, landing on her desk, disturbing her cup of coffee. In fascination she watched it become an oil slick of Mountain-Grown and half-and-half. It took another second of staring before instinct sent her up from her chair.

She tried to remember if there were paper towels in her desk, the absorbency of plain copy paper. Tried to determine what would do more damage—a smack in the face or cursing him out.

She was still trying to decide her next move when her boss's voice came at her again. "Fifteen minutes. I need those correct figures in fifteen. Not seventeen, not sixteen and a half, but fifteen." And then he was gone, the door slamming behind him so hard, it rattled in its frame.

She glanced down at the edge of one sheet, saw the wrong date, the wrong year in the corner. She had stayed late working on the new numbers, but somehow had printed from the wrong database.

Frieda wasn't a weeper, could not remember the last time she'd shed a tear, but in that moment she became one.

She just hung her head and let the tears fall, allowing the pain to assault her from all angles. She did not try to pick apart the horrors she was feeling, or which one hurt worse. She just hung her head and cried.

She took four minutes of those precious fifteen, grieving as silently as she could. Then she wiped her eyes, cleaned up spilled coffee and blew her nose one last time. Understanding that exhaustion had made her careless, Frieda blinked and blinked again, then got down to work.

Like the air she breathed, she knew Herman would call her into his office later that day. Frieda found herself looking forward to it. Barry and Dajah were right; enough was enough. She was steely and hard-edged as she took a chair, her eyes making no attempt to hide her hostility. She glared at her boss, daring him to say one bad thing about her. Was surprised when he didn't.

"I want to apologize, Frieda. I lost my head this morning, and I wanted to say I'm sorry."

She sat there, stunned, feeling cheated in the worst way. He wasn't supposed to begin like that. He was supposed to confront her, so that she could in turn confront him. "Apologize?"

"Yes. Yelling like that, knocking your coffee over. You know how much pressure we've been under . . ."

"Yes, we have," Frieda volleyed, sitting back in her seat. "I haven't had a lunch break in months. I come in at seven and don't leave until six. I need staff, Herman. I can't go on much longer. I'm weary. Just beat down."

She was using black vernacular. As a black man, her boss understood words like "weary", an emotion so ingrained at times it seemed genetic. She was looking to him to help her, be the boss he had once been. But Herman was in the same boat she was, and he had no more means than she.

"I'm there with you. Right there, but I just had a talk with the head of Human Resources. Still no word."

"So I'm just supposed to work myself down to the bone? I'm not even getting overtime."

"We're working on that as we speak. Trying to get that changed."

Spilled coffee and salty tears. Her head shook. "I can't go on like this, Herman. I just can't."

"I'd hate to lose you, Frieda. You've been one of my best."

His words drew her eyes, made her search out his. Bluff or absolute, she wasn't sure, only that the ball was in her court.

"You'd do that? Let me walk out of here?"

It had never been spoken, only hinted at. But in that moment Frieda needed him to deny it or affirm it. Needed him to say it one way or the other, out loud.

"If you think the job is too much for you, I won't make you stay."

"Let me get this straight, Herman. You'd let me walk after all the time I've put in, being one of your 'best'?"

Herman sighed. Looked at her plainly, honestly and openly. "This is a city hospital tending to the poor and downtrodden. What do they care about us? Nothing. You working eleven hours a day and getting paid for eight, tough luck. They don't care about me, you and anybody else here. So yeah, I can stroll into Mancini's office and demand they get me more staff, and the only thing it will do is get me transferred."

Frieda sat back, her head swinging to and fro. She felt the need to cry again, but resolved against it. "Do they even have it in the budget?"

Herman shook his head no.

Her voice was tight, cracked. "So all this time I've been waiting?"

Herman did not answer.

"The glory days" was what Frieda's father called those times of yore when a City of New York job was a bounty of goodness and the pros outweighed the cons.

Frieda knew about the glory days and found herself sitting in the midst of all they had yielded. It was the well-kept two-story home with the nice backyard and the just-enough-to-mow front. It was in the remodeled kitchen, the big overstuffed furniture in the living room and the trips her parents made each year to Cancun.

Yes, the glory days had put Frieda through college, had gotten her

her first car at eighteen and had paid in full the braces she had needed at twelve. Back then there were no deductibles, prescriptions were filled for free and there was no such thing as being understaffed. Back then the city seemed to be just giving money away.

But that came to an abrupt end with the Reaganomics of the eighties. The glory days were gone, something her father was telling her as they sat in the living room talking.

"Then quit," he told her after hearing her tale.

"You know I can't."

"So why are we even having this conversation? You know, in everybody's life there comes a time where you have to do or die. Now I know the last thing you want to do is leave, but if it means living long enough to see your grandchildren, I can't see why you would stay."

"Where am I going, Daddy?"

"There're jobs out there, especially for someone with your experience. Have you even looked?"

In truth she had been buying the New York Times every Sunday but had been too tired to go through the classifieds. "Yeah, I've been looking."

"How many applications you put in?" Her father looked at her with knowing eyes. Frieda looked away. "You don't really know if you can work somewhere else unless you try. So you make up your mind. Stay where you're at and go to an early grave or start looking somewhere else."

"Even if I got an interview, when would I have time to go, with the hours I work?"

"Is it important to you?"

"I guess."

"Then you'll make the time."

Chapter 7

Frieda didn't like how things had ended when Dajah came to visit. She couldn't let the rift between them remain. So she phoned, not to outright apologize, but in need of a way back in. Calling about her upcoming celebration gave her that.

"Just calling to remind you about my birthday party."

"When is it?"

"When it always is—third week in June, next Saturday."

"Your folk's place?"

"The same."

"What time?"

"Two 'til whenever."

Silence. Both women thinking, feeling, wanting to get beyond their tiff, each a little too strong-willed to try.

"You need me to bring anything?" Dajah asked, sky-blue quick.

"Just you and Rick," Frieda answered, giving an opening without saying the sorry word.

"You sure you want me to bring him?"

"If he's going to be in your life, I might as well get a good look."

"Daddy Wilkes working the grill?" Daddy Wilkes, Frieda's father. A man so congenial and good-natured, calling him by a parental moniker was as easy as breathing.

"Wouldn't be a party unless he did . . . you are coming early, right?"

Dajah laughed, the first bit of joy she'd felt since she had picked up the phone. "Like I have a choice."

"Just words, Dajah—you know that, right?"

"Words that hurt, words that pissed us off, but yeah, I know."

"So I'll see you next weekend around noon?"

"I'll be there."

Gina lay in bed, eyes staring at the ceiling, the sound of her mother in the kitchen drifting through the closed door. She looked at the clock, saw it was nearing eight-thirty, time seeming to pass in too-slow motion.

Gina was waiting for the sound of running water, the impact of a cup hitting the ceramic sink. She was waiting for the tap-tap of heels on the hard linoleum floor, followed by the *bam* of the closing front door.

She was in need of the rev of the old Lincoln engine and the *shish* of its tires as it left the driveway. Gina was in need of her mother off and gone to work so she could get up, find something to eat, decide the rest of her day.

She could not stand her mother's mouth first thing in the morning, could hardly stand it at all.

Day nine of being back home felt like forever. She had been spending a lot of time at Tarika's house, but she missed sorely the comfort of the two-bedroom up on 89th Avenue.

Gina missed being able to walk around any way she wanted to. Missed her thirty-six-inch color television and the eight-hundred-dollar stereo system that she used to play as loud as she liked. She missed the queen-size bed with the good mattress, being able to go into the kitchen any time she wanted.

She missed never worrying about money. Last count she had six dollars. Her mother made it clear that she was not going to give her a single red cent.

She ran her fingers through her hair. Felt the weave track half an inch from her scalp. She looked at her nails, now ragged tips that she had bitten off in angst. Gina knew that she and her daughter had a few days at most of clean clothes and soon she would have to go to the Laundromat.

But that meant soap powder and bleach and dryer sheets, things she did not possess, and she was certain her mother would pitch a fit if she attempted to use any of hers.

Gina was lying on the full bed, staring at the ceiling, waiting for her mother to leave when a warm wetness eased against her thigh. "God damn it," she bellowed, pulling back the sheet and jumping out of bed, eyes fast on the dark pee stain easing along the worn, pale blue sheet.

She could not remember the last time Kanisha had peed the bed, but here her child was wetting the sheets, fast asleep. Gina shook her. "Kanisha, damn you, girl, wake up."

Kanisha came awake, eyes mirroring Rick's with decimating clarity. It took a second or two to realize she was wet. She looked away from her mother, sleepiness shifting into apprehension as she felt the rage in her mother building.

Whop! The impact of her mother's hand on her thigh stung like fire. Kanisha yelped, was up on her knees in a flash, scrambling to the corner. Instinct made her tuck her head, cover it with her arms.

Gina caught herself. Saw her self, strung tight as violin wire, hand raised, hovering over the bed like a maelstrom. She felt the familiarity in the picture, down to the faded pink walls, the pee-stained bed and the little girl cowering in the corner.

"Damn you," was all she could mutter in a hushed whisper. "Damn you," the sound of the gas-guzzling Lincoln revving filling the bedroom briny with the smell of pee.

Careful.

Gina took the old coffee-grind measuring cup and leveled it out. She added it to the seven-inch-deep hot bath water and swished it around, hoped it would be enough. Her mother would have a fit if she knew Gina had used even that little bit.

Doreen Alexander had made clear what Gina could and couldn't use in the house. She could use the phone, but only for local calls. She could watch television, have use of the kitchen, but had to buy her own food.

Gina had to provide her own bath soap, her own toothpaste, deodorant and other toiletries, including toilet paper. She and her daughter could use the room, but clean sheets and towels were on her.

So Gina took the bedsheets, her and Kanisha's wet pajamas and a few dirty underwear for safe measure and began washing them by hand.

It had been a while since Gina had done laundry in such a fashion, but with just a few bucks in her pocketbook, there was no other choice. She prayed that the day would remain hot and sunny long enough to have the items line-dried before her mother came home from work.

Doreen Alexander would demand to see the box of soap powder Gina bought. Would rag her incessantly if Gina could not produce it, which she couldn't. So Gina was extra careful to only use a fourth of a cup of the washing powder, taking care to place the box back in the same position under the kitchen sink.

Laundry done, Gina found herself hungry. She took a shower, threw on some clothes and headed to the corner store. She bought fifty cents worth of bologna, fifty cents worth of cheese and a loaf of bread. She bought two packs of Kool-Aid, a pound box of sugar and a small jar of mayonnaise, then went home and made her and Kanisha breakfast.

She called Tarika but nobody answered. Found herself wanting some malt liquor about two that afternoon. Counting her change, she discovered she didn't have enough. She searched her mother's sofa, coat pockets and pocketbooks. She told Kanisha she was going to the store and would be right back.

Gina was gone for over an hour.

It was her intention to go to the store and come right back. But she ran into Ce-lo, a childhood friend, as she made her way to the beer case.

"Yo, Gina, how you been hanging, girl?"

"What's up, Ce-lo?"

"Nutten. You back home now?"

"Yeah, for a little while."

"You finally leave that old man?"

"Nigga, please." She reached into the cold case, and grabbed a malt liquor.

"Where you headed now?"

"Back home."

"Got some serious tree. You down?"

Tree. Marijuana. It would go great with her beer. Wouldn't take her but a few minutes to get her high on. Gina debated.

"We can go back to my place. You know I'm back home."

No, Gina hadn't known. She hadn't been paying much attention to who was and wasn't back "home." It was enough that she was.

"It's the shit, I'm telling you, girl," he added.

His mother lived right around the corner. A five-minute walk. She'd take another ten to smoke, drink her beer, be back home in no time. "Yeah, aw-right."

Ce-lo smiled. Followed her to the register. When Gina starting laying out her collection of coins, he stepped up. "Put that shit away, girl. I got you." Paid.

It had never been that way between them, and though they both had a nice buzz, Gina wasn't that high. She shoved Ce-lo away. "What you doing?' she asked.

"Come on, girl, you know I always had a thing for you."

"Well, I sure ain't had no thing for you. You know it ain't even like that."

"Shared my shit, least you can do is give a brother some play."

Gina laughed. "Nigga, you is crazy. I came here to smoke, not fuck."

"Can't blame a man for trying, right?"

Gina looked at him, saw sincerity in his eyes. "Whatever." She finished off the last of her malt. Put the bottle on the coffee table. Reached for another joint. Smoked it, eyes closed. Gina drifted, the radio just loud enough not to be invasive.

Seconds became minutes, minutes rolled into segments of ten. Gina opened her eyes. Looked around at the heavy baroque furniture, the walls full of elementary school photos, boasting hopes and dreams that never materialized.

She looked away. Saw Ce-lo rolling another joint.

He waved it her way. "Another?"

Gina took it, lit it, inhaled. Held her breath, let it go, the smoke a white curl leaving her lips like a python.

Kanisha knew all the do's and don'ts when her mother left her alone. She wasn't supposed to answer the phone, answer the door or go near the stove. She was not to drag chairs to cabinets to get stuff, play with lighters or mess with her mother's things.

But when the doorbell rang, her little heart leaped and she forget the rules. Maybe it was her daddy. Maybe he had come back to get her.

She went to the door, the peephole too high for her to look out, and unlocked it. She swung it open wide, expecting to see her daddy there. But it wasn't. Just some old man.

"Hey, Doreen here?"

Kanisha looked up to the lanky man's pecan-brown face. Frowned. She didn't know who Doreen was. It wasn't her daddy, and she was home alone.

"Doreen here?" he asked again.

"Who's Doreen?"

"Alexander, Doreen Alexander. This is her house, right?"

It took a moment for her to understand that Doreen was her grandmother. Kanisha nodded her head yes.

"Who are you?" Curiosity danced in his eyes.

Some part of her wanted to tell him, but the bigger part would not let her. Kanisha stepped back and closed the door. Locked it. Sat back against the heavy wood as the doorbell rang and rang.

The pork chops had stayed a day too long in the refrigerator as leftovers, and the red rice didn't have nearly enough spice, but Gina sat at Ce-lo's kitchen table wolfing it down. Across from her Ce-lo was up to the same, the marijuana they had smoked sending them on a serious food binge.

"You got something to drink?"

"Water."

"That's it?"

In truth there was one can of Pepsi all the way in the back of the refrigerator, but suddenly Ce-lo wasn't up to sharing another thing. He was still stinging over Gina's refusal. He had always thought she was fine, had heard through the grapevine the sweet meat she was. Certain that he'd get a go, he was mad that he hadn't.

"My momma coming home soon. You better go," Ce-lo decided, pork shop bones littering Gina's plate.

Gina belched, wiped her hands and mouth with the paper towel and stood up. "See you later." She made her way through the house, out the front door, the afternoon sun bright against her dilated pupils. Gina squinted, picked bits of tough meat from her teeth. Headed home.

She looked toward the house, saw an old man standing on the stoop ringing the bell and broke into a sprint. In the seventeen seconds it took to reach the walkway, she tried to remember just how long she'd been gone. Couldn't.

"What you want?" she insisted, catching her breath as she headed for the steps.

"Gina?"

"Who the hell are you and what you doing here?"

"I'm Jefferson. Jefferson Carter. You remember me?"

In truth Gina didn't. There had been so many men who had come and gone from her mother's front door, it was hard for her to distinguish one from the other.

"'Course you was just a little-bitty thing back then, maybe you don't." Gina gave him a blank look. "Yeah, it's been a while. Was looking for your momma. A little girl answered the door."

"She ain't here and you got to go."

"Well you tell her I came by here?"

"You in my way."

He stepped back and Gina moved around him. She put her key into the lock, gave it a twist and pushed. The door barely budged. Gina pushed again, tried to peer around the tiny crack to see what was blocking her way. Caught a glimpse of a leg. "Kanisha?"

A scramble of feet, a tiny hand easing around the thick wood, and then Kanisha was standing before her, wide-eyed, scared. "Didn't mean to, Mommy," she muttered. Gina looked her daughter over carefully, her head turning as she gazed hard at Jefferson. Stepping inside, she closed the door, fingers trembling as she locked it.

* * *

"You sure?" She was asking Kanisha half a minute later, her questions producing the same answer.

"Uh-huh. He stayed outside. I stayed in."

"And he didn't touch you nowhere, did he?"

Her head shook no. "Just asked about Granny 'Zander.'"

"You not lying, are you?"

"No."

"He didn't tell you not to tell something, did he?"

Kanisha shook her head no again, waiting for the punishment to come. For the feel of that hand against a thigh, an arm, her face. But her mother didn't do any of that. Gina simply brought Kanisha to her chest so hard and fast, Kanisha felt her mother was trying to smother her.

They sat at the kitchen table, mother, daughter and granddaughter. Gina didn't plan on eating with her mother, but the smell of her mother's take-out Chinese stirred up a hunger in her, and outside of eating in the backyard, the only place a meal was allowed to be consumed was at the kitchen table.

Gina had kicked Kanisha in the shin so many times, she was certain that the child now had a permanent bruise, but despite the silent warning, Kanisha could not stop staring at the fried rice and chicken wings her grandmother was eating, the bologna and cheese sandwich tasteless in her mouth.

It was torture, pure and simple. Doreen Alexander knew it, and Gina and Kanisha were feeling it. But Doreen Alexander was trying to teach her wild child a lesson. Doreen was trying to show Gina that in life there were consequences, good and bad, based on your choices. That you were responsible for your own situation and any bed you made, you had to lie in it.

Doreen's hope was that Gina would grow tired of going without and that weariness would force her to do what she had never done in her entire life—became responsible. Get a job, take care of her own. Do something more than lie around and get high.

Though Doreen sat there eating stoned-face, she did feel for her granddaughter. She had to stop herself a hundred times from taking a chicken wing from her plate and handing it to Kanisha, who was staring at her fried pieces of poultry so hard, she could strip it to the bone with just a look.

In truth she didn't want to see her blood having nothing more than cheap sandwich meat and watery Kool-Aid for dinner. Doreen knew that there should have been some vegetables and a hearty starch on their plates, but Gina needed to get her act together, and if being stingy and mean and cruel would make her, so be it.

Doreen finished half her take-out and put the rest in the refrigerator. She made a show of counting the number of wings left to ensure no one would take one when she wasn't looking. She sipped from her can of soda and dumped it into the trash. "You looking for a job, right?" she asked before she headed out of the kitchen and made her way to her bedroom.

Her words swirled around Gina's head until it was all she could hear. A job. Doing what? And who would watch Kanisha? She didn't feel comfortable with strangers watching her child. It was the main reason why Kanisha wasn't in preschool.

For the first time ever, Gina thought about getting on welfare but she had never been on it and could not see herself doing so now. On the other hand, she had two dollars to her name and had no idea where the next dollar was coming from, so she had to do something.

Call Rick.

Pride said hell no. Reality said she had little choice. She was looking after his child. He would not deny her.

It was difficult seeing a man who worked from four in the afternoon to midnight, with his days off being mid-week, but Dajah got used to the late-night phone calls, the waking from her sleep to let him in.

Rick's hours were unconventional, but they made the best of what time they had. Sometimes they did manage a few minutes of conversation before they got into her bed. This night was one of them.

They were in her living room, Rick unwinding from a too-hard day. "I don't see how you do it," Dajah confessed. "Being around criminals all day, day in, day out."

"It's a job but a good one. And yeah, every now and then there's some static, but most of the time it's okay."

"I worry for you."

"Don't. I'll be okay."

"You ask them about taking the day?"

"Well, you don't ask. You have to find someone to switch with."

"Did you?" her soul wide open, hopeful.

"Yeah. Jimmy owes me a favor. So we're on."

"Me and Frieda go back a ways."

"I kind of sensed that. You were pleading hard."

"I wasn't pleading. Just asking."

"Oh, yeah. You should have seen yourself. You'd have thought the world was going to come to an end if I couldn't make it."

"Only because I want you there, with me."

He looked at her, reading her emotions. "I kind of wanted to be there my—" His cell phone burred. Rick picked it up and looked at the number, his heart missing a beat. "Gina," he said before he hit receive and stood, the phone to his ear. "Hello?"

Without thought, he turned his back to Dajah and walked out of the room.

"I need some serious money, Rick. My momma ain't feeding us or nothing and I'm down to like nothing. Clothes need to be washed. We don't have food."

"Kanisha okay?"

"Yeah, she fine for now. But I need some money, bad."

"How much?"

"Enough to carry us a while."

"A hundred?"

"A hun*dred*? We got to buy our own food, our own damn toilet paper. My hair is about to fall out. Hundred ain't going to get it."

"I can come by in the morning."

"Where you at now?"

"What do you mean?"

"I called your house and all I got was the machine. Where you at?"

"Look, I can come by in the morning, all right?"

"Yeah, but get here early. We don't even have nothing for breakfast."

"See you then." Rick hung up, stared at nothing, feeling so much. He came back to the living room, Dajah's emotions rushing him the moment he stepped in, a fast brew of anxiety and concern, a "why" dancing in her eyes. He gave an abbreviated answer. "I have to drop her off some money."

"So you get to see her."

"Who?"

"Your daughter."

"Yeah," a pleasing thought coming into him. "I do, don't I?"

Chapter 8

Her game face was what Dajah wore the next morning as she stood in the bathroom brushing her teeth. Her lips moved to accommodate the brush, her eyes followed the motion, but everything else about her was stone.

Last night when she and Rick made love, she had felt a shift in him, a drawing away; a part of him gone from her even as he held her close, moved skin to skin. She hadn't wanted to think about why. Did not want to take her mind through the maze in search of a final answer. But a reason had arrived like breathing—*because he's going to see his daughter.*

She understood his need to do that, but there was the other side of the coin. Seeing his daughter meant seeing his baby's momma, and even though it was supposed to be about just a cash transaction, Dajah knew how deep ties could manipulate a situation. Knew that Rick had been with Gina for all those years, and though a man might walk away, it was often difficult to stay gone.

Dajah worked the toothbrush, foamy paste full in her mouth, about her lips. She was trying hard not to think at all when Rick popped his head in, eyes dazzling with expectancy. "Gotta run. Call you later." He didn't wait for a reply. Gave no time for her mouth to be rinsed, receive a parting kiss. He simply dashed off, the front door closing quick.

Rick stood on the front stoop, eyes hungry at the partially cracked door. The money was still in his hand, and Gina had hers extended, but they had reached a stalemate.

"You giving it to me or what?"

"Where's Kanisha?"

"I told you. She's asleep."

"I want to see her."

"She's sleeping, Rick."

"I still want to see her."

"You see her some other time."

"Some other time when?"

"I don't know, the next time. Can I have the money now?"

"Can I see my daughter?"

"I already told you no." Exasperation moved through her. "You know, forget this shit. We'll just starve." She turned and headed into the house, the warped screen door yawning open with a squeak.

"Gina, wait."

She about-faced. "What?"

His hand extended out, something vital loosening for him. "Here."

She took it almost as if she was reluctant, but quickly counted the roll. "You know we going to have to do something regularly."

"Regularly?"

"Child support. She is your kid." Gina looked at the money. "Four hundred is fine for now, but it won't last a month . . . six-fifty."

"Six-fifty what?"

But Gina didn't answer, the door closing on his asking eyes.

Where did it hurt?

Nowhere really, just a random flicker of emptiness that drifted through her, making random pit stops along the way.

Day ten was too soon for that emotion. Day ten should have been still marveling at the newness of day one. Day ten should have found Dajah exhausted with euphoric giddiness; overwhelmed with the sweetness. Just tingly all over.

But all Dajah could feel was the change, the rules broken and scattered in bits about her feet. All Dajah could experience was the jeopardy. The jeopardy of being with a man who had a child somewhere else with someone else.

There was more to being a couple then hitting the sheets. There were supposed to be dates and outings, exact moments that moved toward a deeper connection. Dajah and Rick hadn't had that yet.

Beyond his late-night visits and sunrise good-byes, their life was an incomplete pie—all filling and not a drop of crust. There were no specific boundaries to them. Nothing to keep them together, keep them from slipping and sliding all over the place.

Off to see his baby's momma first thing that morning didn't help.

Even as Dajah sat in her office, filing old paperwork, answering phones, working numbers on the calculator, her mind was fixed squarely in the unease of it. She had picked up the phone and started to dial his cell a dozen times, but things stopped her.

Pride, wisdom, gut feeling, they were strong stances that would not let her do it. Would not allow her need to show that way. Trust him, something suggested as 2 P.M. moved into 3 P.M. But how could she if those boundaries were already missing?

Suspicion was never a part of her game. Dajah would rather walk away than be a party to it. But here she was thick inside of it, unable to take two steps back or a single one forward.

She had Rick's word that she was the one he wanted, but Dajah was in a brand-new place called share. She was sharing Rick with his daughter, and with the daughter, came the mother. As far as Dajah could see, Rick was too good a man for any woman just to let go of. The fact that he hadn't called all day just stirred up her pot of worry.

Her mind in full battle with her heart, when 5 P.M. arrived and her co-workers begin filing out of the office, Dajah knew she would have to make a stop before she reached home.

The soles of her high heels mashed against the grains of sand that littered the boardwalk, the boardwalk's edge, her final destination. She didn't have to touch the rail to know it was hot. Fingertips first, she took her time wrapping her palms around it, fixing the fit of her sunglasses and gazing toward the blazing sun.

Hours from setting, she knew she would not be at Jones Beach long enough to watch the wonder this day. She should have gone home first, changed her clothes, her shoes, and come back more suited for the excursion.

As it was now, the polyester of her dress was a heat magnet, the fit of her leather shoes a sauna about her feet. Dajah hadn't stood there three minutes before sweat began gathering on her brow with a swiftness the ocean breeze couldn't keep at bay.

She abandoned her watch and headed for the snack bar, a few customers before her. She wiped the sweat off her forehead with the fingers of her hand, pulled a few times at the tight fit of her dress about her neck.

A shout of *"Next!"* propelled her to the dented shiny metal counter.

"A root beer."

"We have Barq's," the counterman said.

"That's fine."

"Cup or can?"

"Cup . . . lots of ice."

The counterman turned away, coming back with her tall, cold drink. Soda in hand, Dajah moved to the boardwalk railing, drinking her root beer as if she hadn't had a drop of liquid in weeks. She stood, hot and sticky, searching for peace within her soul.

By the time she took her last sip, it still had not come. Pitching the cup into the garbage, she headed toward her car, her healing, unarrived.

Burnt.

That was how Rick felt. All the juices were gone from him and he was dried out to the marrow. He'd hoped that by the time he started his shift, the impact of his failed morning would have lessened. But he could not stop kicking himself for handing that money over without so much as a peek at his daughter. Could not forgive himself for caving in.

Least they won't starve. But it was little compensation. By the time he took his meal break, it was all he could consider, his daughter's absence a freshly inflicted wound.

Two leaves, yellow as a buttercup, lay half curled on her hardwood floor. Above it, the five-foot ficus tree stood, innocent, unwavering.

"Oh," was all Dajah could manage at the sight, mouth opened in deep surprise, unable to recall her tree ever losing leaves.

Energetic and encompassing, her house tree had been like a four-year-old on a playground; unhindered, boundless. Its fronds pressed against the wall, hung in soft slopes over the window sill and seemed bent on reaching the wicker trunk three feet below it.

A happy little tree, it was as much a part of Dajah as the double pierced lobes of her ears. A tree so joyful, Dajah had given it a name—Baby. From the moment it had arrived home from the nursery, Baby had been nothing but lush and green. Now it was losing leaves.

Dajah moved across her living room, face pinched, hand extended. She gathered a handful of tender shoots into her palm, brought her lips to them and kissed them. "What, Baby? What?" She bent down, dug a middle finger into the soil, found it crumbly moist.

She began a careful inspection, looking over each leaf. Green. Green. Green. Green. Green. Green. *Yellow/green.* That stopped her. Made her heart ache a bit. With care she grabbed the minute stalk and attempted a gentle tug. The yellowing leaf held steady.

She eased it over, searched the back for black dots, indicating spider mites, but saw none. She calculated the last time she had given her tree Miracle Grow and knew it was not time for another feeding. She continued her troubled leaf search.

When the count reached twenty, she stopped counting. One wasn't bad. Two could be overlooked. Five meant trouble. Twenty? She dropped back down and began testing other areas of the soil. Everywhere she probed was moist.

It didn't need water. There were no spider mites. What then? All she wanted to know as she tried to conjure her tree to reveal its mysteries and another dead leaf hit the floor.

Some people had the ability to divide themselves, giving each half to separate issues. Some people had the nuance to juggle daily dramas with keen insight and skill. Rick wasn't one of those people. He could not consider Dajah, only the absence of Kanisha. Could not begin to contemplate what she was thinking or wasn't, only the willful hurtfulness of Gina.

This was the reason he called his friend Nelson instead of dialing Dajah's house when his shift was through.

Nelson had always been the level-headed one. As a child, when the rest of his friends were looking for danger and excitement, Nelson was the one who held back, gave reasons why they shouldn't climb Old Man Smitty's garage, why it wasn't a good idea to throw rocks at the junkyard dogs.

Nelson had been the scholarship kid, garnering enough to go to just about any school of his choosing. But as the only child of a widowed mother, he felt obligated to stay close to home. He chose a local college, moved into his mother's basement and had been down there since.

Nelson had had it refurbished. He installed white oak paneling on the walls, a thick, sturdy carpet on the floor and new insulated windows. The formerly dark, dank, basement was now cheery, dry and comfortable. There was a kitchenette, an eating area, a living room and his bedroom off in the back.

"Watch your head," Nelson warned as Rick aimed his foot toward the last step. Rick ducked, the angle of ceiling hanging over the steps deadly.

A dehumidifier hummed in one corner; the large-screen TV played softly in the other. Rick took a seat on the cream leather couch, throwing one leg along its length. Headache receding, he knew a brewski could whittle back the rest of the pain. "Got a Heinie, man?"

"Is my name Nelson?" Nelson shot back.

That's how it was at Nelson's place. Refrigerator always stocked, comfort always easy.

Rick went and got his beer. Nelson got comfortable in his love seat, his feet landing on the weathered trunk he used as a coffee table. "So what's going on?"

"She won't let me see Kanisha."

"Gina?"

Rick closed the refrigerator door. "Yeah."

"Why?"

"I broke up with her."

"Say what?"

"Broke things off. Put her out. Now she won't let me see Kanisha."

"When?"

"Almost two weeks ago."

"I know this may seem like a dumb question, but why now?"

"I met this woman."

"Woman?"

"Yeah, like my age, good job, good head and a serious loving-heart woman."

" 'Bout time."

Rick ignored the remark. "Met her and wanted to get with her. Leaving Gina has been on my mind for a while. Meeting Dajah just made me like Nike."

"You just did it."

"Right."

"And now you regretting that move."

"Not regretting, but damn, you know Kanisha is my heart."

"Don't you know, more than anything else Kanisha needs a father who's happy. And I know for a fact that you haven't been in years. Maybe you got a shot at it now, with this Asia."

"Day-zah. D-A-J-A-H."

"Yeah, her, but you hear what I'm saying? Gina pulling rank, let her pull the hell on. She can't keep Kanisha from you forever."

"I guess you right."

"So tell me about this Dajah."

Rick smiled for the first time, the memory of her filling him. "Fine. Smart. Sexy. All that."

"Yeah?'

"Oh, yeah. Looks a lot like Bridget."

"High school Bridget?'

"Yeah."

"Thought you got over that skeezer."

"I did."

"So it's just a coincidence that the one woman you were willing to leave a bad situation for just happens to look like her?"

"Yeah . . . no." A small smile dusted Rick's face. "What difference does it make? I like her. I want to be with her."

"But Gina's rocking the boat, right?"

"Exactly."

It was Nelson's turn to chuckle. "What do you expect? You were her suga daddy. She's not going to let you go without trying to make your life miserable. It's up to you if you let her succeed or not."

"But she's keeping Kanisha from me."

"You're her daddy, right?"

"You know I am."

"Then you got the right to see her. Take her to court if you have to. They have laws."

"I don't want to go that route," Rick said, thinking. "Got something else in mind, but it's going to take a little time to set it in motion."

"Rick, always the planner. But be forewarned, bro, the greatest plans of mice and men—"

"Often go astray. Yeah, I know. But I think this one's gonna work."

Nelson considered him for a long time. "For your sake, I hope so. But the bottom line is this. You have choices in life. You can choose happiness or turmoil. Just be clear about which one you really want."

Rick looked over at Nelson, saw a deep meaning burning in his eyes. Looked away. "It's not even a question, chief."

"I hope not. Now pick up that phone and call Dajah. From the looks of you, you in need of some healing."

Rick did just that, the phone ringing unanswered.

Her head had won.

Sometime after she had gotten into bed and her phone had remained silent, the battle was over.

She was going to walk away. Dajah was cutting her losses and leaving Rick and the drama behind. It wasn't too late to kiss their brief life together good-bye. It wasn't too late to step away.

This was what Dajah fell asleep with. A few hours later the ringing phone woke her. Instinct made her reach for it, but her newfound decision would not allow her to pick up.

Dajah lay in the darkness, the *brring* of her phone echoing. She lay there, imagining Rick on the other end, phone pressed to his ear, waiting for her to pick up. She imagined worry along his brow, a battered defeat in his eyes as her voice mail clicked on. Knew he was thinking what any man would be thinking: Where was she?

I'm right here, she had thought. *Right here listening to the phone ring and refusing to answer. It's over, don't you know? I'm finished with you.*

Yet she could not deny the comfort in the sound. A kind of warmth had settled in her spine and drifted along her arms, legs and heart, a strange peace filling her that she did still matter to him. Even though she was leaving him, that knowledge was important. It became something she could tuck away for later, when life allowed her to step back from it all and analyze.

She would need that memory when she sat with Frieda at some later date, speaking bravely of how she had gotten out before it was too late. Dajah would use this last act of Rick's as a banner that said their quick time together had held some merit.

But the euphoria was short-lived as the ringing stopped, then faded. In the silence a different angle came into view. Dajah found herself expecting a second attempt, remaining wide-eyed for fifteen minutes before accepting that a second try wasn't in him.

Chapter 9

Go away, Rick, Dajah was thinking as she listened to her doorbell chime the next morning. *I'm not answering, so just go away.*

But Rick was not going away as he stood on the stoop, the soft haze of morning around him, pressing the slip of white plastic as if the house was on fire. He knew she was inside and ignoring him. Knew because her Mitsubishi was parked at the curb. He also knew that she would have to come out soon if she was going to make it to work on time.

But mainly he knew he had pissed her off, even if he wasn't certain why.

After he had left Nelson's place, Rick had come by Dajah's and seen her car out front even though she hadn't answered the phone earlier. For a hot second he almost got out of his car, but decided to swing by in the morning.

Morning was here and so was he, but she was not answering her door.

He stepped back. Peered up to a second-floor window. He was certain he saw the blinds move. He brought his hands to his mouth and was about to shout her name when he remembered where he was.

Rick rang the bell some more, the *ding-dongs* insistent. Dajah grabbed the window and was about to hoist it up when she caught herself.

She was about to raise the window and yell. Was about to perform an act reserved for uncouth people, folks with poor upbringing. She was about to put her business in the street, wipe away the perfect-tenant history she had with Mr. and Mrs. Merriweather, the old couple who owned the house and lived on the first floor.

All because of *Rick.*

That pissed her off. Made her turn away from the window, snatch up her pocketbook and keys. It moved her through her apartment door and down the hallway, steps quick. It forced her to fumble with locks and snatch the door open.

"Don't you get it?" she said, stepping past him, pulling the door close.

"Get what?"

"I'm finished."

His hand fastened around her arm quick, tight. "Wait, hold up."

Dajah snatched her arm back, took the steps. "For what? I don't have time for you and your nonsense." She headed for her car.

"Dajah, wait." But they were empty words that held no power as she rounded the driver's side and slipped her key into the lock. "Dajah," Rick said exasperated as he hustled after her, reaching her just as she slid into her car seat. He blocked the door with his body. "Can you tell me what I did wrong?"

It was the first real look she gave him. There in the depths of her eyes brewed a maelstrom of hurt, anger and bitterness. "Nothing, Rick, you did nothing, okay? Now I got to get to work."

"So why are you so mad at me?"

She reached for the car door. "I have to go."

"I know you do, I know. But I really need to know what's going on."

Clueless. He was absolutely, positively clueless. Everything about him, in him, around him told her so. It was in the bewilderment in his eyes and the way his hands were fixed slightly from his body as if waiting for an answer to land upon them.

He really doesn't know. Has no idea that I needed him to call me earlier than past midnight. That I needed reassurance that we were still okay after seeing his baby's momma. Dajah sighed. "Call me later."

"Dajah—"

She held up a hand. "No, Rick. Later. Just call me later. I got to go."

He stepped away. She closed her car door, started her engine and peeled away from the curb.

She cursed him all the way to work. Cursed him through her morning coffee and her lunch break. Dajah cursed Rick and his ignorance as she took her fifteen-minute afternoon break in the break room and went on to curse him on the commute home.

Men were from Mars.

How many times had she heard that? A trillion? But until today she had never given it much thought, for most of the men in her life had been in tune with her. They had possessed the ability to read her correctly, gauge her needs.

Not Rick.

He was tunnel-visioned and single-minded, an idiosyncrasy over which he had little control. Could she really hold the shortcoming against him? She couldn't walk away because of his ignorance. That would be blaming him for something he had no knowledge of.

Still, she would not make him faultless. *Strike one*, she summarized, a Rick tally starting. *Three and you're going to be out.*

Don't you get it? I'm finished.

No, Rick didn't get it. Had no idea why in twenty-four hours she had gone from sweet and loving to handing in her walking papers.

He had never expected that from Dajah.

Never anticipated that she would be like a sheet in the wind, emotions dependent on which way the breeze was blowing. Rick could not even begin to imagine what had come into her mind that made her flip like that.

He had given up his whole world for her. A woman of her intelligence had to have known that by doing so, he was serious about her. But for reasons unknown, Dajah didn't, or she forgot, or *something*.

Rick just wanted to know what that something was. He didn't need any additional puzzles in his life right now. What he needed was for Dajah to be there for him the way she had been, willing, with open arms. Hours from solving that mystery, the day moved by at a snail's pace; evening dragged in slow and unhurried.

"I'm calling," he offered at eight o'clock during his lunch break. "Calling to find out what this morning was about."

"You have to understand something, Rick. You have understand how I see things, what it looks like from where I'm standing."

"Shoot."

"Night before last when we were making love, you felt a million miles away from me. The next morning you're up and gone before I could even rinse the toothpaste from my mouth. You were off to see your baby's momma, and I needed you to call me sooner than past midnight. That's what it was about."

But the huge gaps in her summary did little to help him understand the why. "I'm not getting you."

"It was like you drifted away from me, and I felt like maybe you weren't coming back."

"I just went to see my daughter, Dajah."

"Yes, I know that. But you and her mother have a history . . . stuff happens all the time. And when you didn't call me, I started putting two and two together."

"You mean like me and Gina?"

This was the part Dajah didn't want to confess to. She felt she had already said too much. But it was truth-telling time. "Yeah."

"I told you I left her."

"What people say and what people do are two separate things."

"I'm not even like that."

"You didn't call me."

"I did call you."

"Past midnight?"

Silence, the sound of loud voices, hard-sole shoes on metal steps and slamming gates filtering into the mix. Prison life at its noisiest. Rick swallowed. "It went bad."

"What?"

"The visit. She wouldn't let me see Kanisha. Took my cash, yeah, but wouldn't let me get a peek at her . . . just messed up my head all day. After work, I went by my boy Nelson's house, rapped a little. That's when I called you. I couldn't before then. It was like I was just filled to the brim with Gina and her nonsense."

"So you didn't see her."

"No."

"Sorry to hear that."

"Yeah, me too, but you know you can't jump to conclusions like that. If you ever have a question or some issue, you should at least let me address it before you decide you're finished. I know my situation ain't easy or pretty, but I chose you, Dajah, remember?"

Yes, she did. "I know."

"So we okay now?"

"Yeah."

"What you wearing to the party?"

"What party?"

"Your friends? This Saturday? Don't tell me you forgot. I took the day, remember?"

"Something that'll have you looking twice."

"Is that a fact?"

"You can take it to the bank."

Frieda had it all planned.

Friday at five to five she would cut off her computer and lock up her files, then head off to the ladies' room for a bathroom stop before her trip to Costco. Depending on traffic, she would be pulling up to the huge warehouse on Rockaway Turnpike no later than ten to six. Would have her cart loaded with sodas, snacks, whole chickens, pork ribs, paper plates, cups, charcoal lighter, charcoal, onions, potatoes and mayonnaise no later than six-thirty.

By seven she would be dropping off everything except the onions, potatoes and mayonnaise at her parents' house. By seven-thirty, she'd be home, the large pot spitting and boiling about ten pounds of potatoes.

By nine-thirty that night the potato salad would be done and she'd be off to a beauty appointment to get her nails and hair done. Salon Suites did a booming business, their doors open past midnight on Friday and Saturdays. Getting a late appointment wasn't a problem at all.

This was what Frieda had decided, but her boss had other plans.

At exactly seven minutes to five he came into her office. "I need an update on accounts receivable for the last quarter."

Frieda looked up at him, stared two seconds and shook her head. "No can do."

"What do you mean, no can do?"

She reached out a finger and hit the Start button on her keyboard. "I'm not staying."

"But you won't be in on Monday."

"I know that." She grabbed the mouse and clicked Shut down.

"I can't wait until Tuesday."

Her computer screen gave her four choices: Shut down. Restart. Restart in DOS. Close program and log in as a different user. She dragged the arrow to Shut down. "Then you'll have to do it yourself," she answered with a click.

County Hospital had denied her sleep, healthy hair, R&R and quality time with the man she loved. It had denied her overtime pay, getting up at a decent hour and the life she used to have. There was no way it was going to deny her a great birthday barbecue.

Her screen went blank, her boss watching the action. "I'm serious, Frieda."

She grabbed a file off her desk. "So am I." She opened the file drawer and slipped it inside. She pushed the lock and reached for her bag. "I've given everything I had and then some in the last few months. Today I'm leaving on time."

She stood and moved past her boss, his words lost to a newfound determination.

Dajah was fussing over nonessentials. She knew this even as she took off the pale yellow sleeveless blouse and picked up the skin-tight cream one. She had spent too much time at her mirror as it was. She was supposed to have left twenty minutes ago. But it was almost July and she was trying to do justice to the season and keep her promise to Rick.

She took a long, hard look at herself in the mirror.

The tight top gave emphasis to her generous breasts and showed off the sexy curve that lay midway down her lower back and the rounding of her behind. It looked like a winner to her.

She reached for her white short-shorts and eased them over her lotioned legs, synthetic hair swinging in the emotion. Braids had been her mainstay for years, and she refused to use the real stuff. Synthetic was proof positive that it didn't come off some dead Asian woman's head. Dajah wasn't about to risking bad mojo for the sake of fashion.

She turned sideways in her mirror. Liked the look of the mile of thigh her booty cutters afforded. *Don't bend over, girl,* she thought, peering over her shoulder, the edge of the white denim less than two inches below her panty line.

She picked up her gold sienna lipstick, filled in her lips and outlined them in a soft brown pencil. Smoothing it together, Dajah put on her hoops, a gold bracelet on one arm, her watch on the other. She spritzed herself with Versace Jeans cologne and gave herself the once-over. Her promise to Rick had been kept.

Jamaica, Queens, had its ups and downs, but today the negatives were on vacation. The sound of lawn mowers and the smell of clipped grass filled the air, and the sunshine was summertime perfect. The breeze was constant, keeping the humidity at bay, and the whole world shimmered.

It was a day for easing away from the stresses of daily life and enjoying all that outdoor leisure could allow. Not a single cloud could be seen in the periwinkle-blue sky as Dajah got out of her car and glanced upward, the warmth of summer finding her.

She walked down the drive, entered the backyard, spotted Frieda dumping ice into a large metal garbage can. The first thing she noticed was the difference in her friend. The hair was cut and styled to perfection, and the bags seemed less visible. Frieda look happy and on her way to healthy again, making Dajah's heart sing. "Well, look at you. Hey, birthday girl."

"Hey yourself. Just in time. Go in the house and get an apron from my momma."

Molasses, tomato sauce and fresh-cut onions drifted in the hot kitchen air as Mrs. Wilkes stood stirring up a pot. "Hi, Dajah." Her smile was bright as she placed the wooden spoon on a plate and opened her arms wide.

"Hello, Mrs. Wilkes." The fan in the window sent a hot breeze her way, not a drop of cool in it. "Is it hot today, or is it hot?"

"From the day that girl was born, I've never known this time of year to be anything but."

"Frieda said there was an apron for me."

Mrs. Wilkes indicated a kitchen chair. "Right there and you're just in time. This sauce needs to be stirred for about five more minutes, and I need to hop into the shower."

"Consider it done. Where Daddy Wilkes?"

"Ran out to get more charcoal."

Mrs. Wilkes headed toward the stairs. Dajah picked up the wooden spoon, resisting the urge to sample the spicy coating.

The back screen door yawned open, Frieda toting empty ice bags. "Momma got you watching the sauce?"

"Yeah. Good as it smells, you know I don't mind."

"Where's Rick?"

"He'll be here later. Told him around two."

"So things going good?"

"No complaints."

"Well, I'm happy to hear that."

"Weren't we like eighteen just yesterday?" Dajah asked, subject switching.

Frieda laughed. "I was just thinking the same thing."

"What happened?"

"Time . . . speaking of which . . ." Frieda glanced at the wall clock. "At one-thirty, please tell me to get changed."

"You look fabulous already."

"Yeah, Salon Suites works magic."

"It's a great day for a party."

"Hot day. But I'd take a heat wave over rain any day of the week."

"It's never rained on your party, Frieda."

"First time for everything," she answered, dumping the wet plastic bags into the garbage, thinking of her own showdown. It still scared her. Scared her and amazed her, fear and fearlessness rolling through her like a river.

Frieda hadn't told a soul about her brave stance against her boss. Had not shared how in that moment enough had become enough because she knew whomever she revealed that declaration to, they would expect more. They would think she was on the right path after months of being on the wrong.

Frieda didn't want that pressure. Didn't want anyone watching her with hawk eyes for her next move—because she wasn't ready to pack up her toys and go home yet. She wasn't ready to kiss that job goodbye, start all over again.

All she wanted was time and space to enjoy the celebration of her thirty-first birthday. She had wanted enough time to get food items and get her hair and nails done. She wanted the affair to be free of other responsibilities, like work.

She couldn't begin to consider what would happen when she returned to work on Tuesday. Could not decide if she'd be written up or if her boss would allow her the one lapse. For the moment life would be about her party. Tuesday morning would come soon enough.

Dajah sat at the picnic table, burger slathered with cooked onions to her mouth, barbecue sauce about her mouth. "Still got it, Daddy Wilkes."

"And you know that," he answered, turning chicken legs over the smoky fire.

Dajah looked around her, the backyard full of familiar faces and some not so familiar. She took a glance at her watch, saw it was three minutes after two. Could not stop herself from glancing at the driveway.

"Clock watch. Must be special," Barry teased.

"I'm not on a watch, and he's okay." But there was no denying she wanted what she had been sitting up there witnessing for the last ten minutes. There was no denying she wanted the closeness, the intimacy, the bone-deep connection she'd seen as Frieda and Barry sat close, eating their chop-barbecue sandwiches, something special between them.

At first look Dajah had thought Barry too mild mannered for her friend. There was a fire in Frieda and Dajah just knew it would take a special man to be by her side. But the temperament of Barry was a perfect fit to the domineering Frieda. Together they made a good couple.

"It's just a little after two. He's coming," Barry offered, putting the last bit of chopped barbecue and hamburger bun into his mouth.

"I never said he wasn't." But she had been entertaining the idea and as three minutes after two rolled into ten after, it was all Dajah knew as Frieda wiped the edge of Barry's mouth with a napkin and moved them to the patio for a fast dance.

Michael Jackson was singing about a girl rocking his world, and it was a song that made Dajah want to get up and boogie too. A few guys drifted over to ask her, but Dajah turned them down.

David had never been late. David had never made her wait. But she wasn't with David anymore, was she? No, she was with a man with deep ties elsewhere. A man who was clueless and ignorant of how she expected things to go.

Would she have to produce a manual for him, with Chapters and sub-Chapters on how he was supposed to proceed? Would she have to enroll him into the Dajah Moore School of Being With Her, make him take a final and drop him if he failed?

What was difficult about getting somewhere on time? His lateness was just feeding the fire, stoking the cooling embers that had been burning just days ago.

Laughter reached her. She turned her eyes toward the sound. Saw two men standing, beers in their hands, eyes her way. Dajah was certain they knew all her business. Was certain they were standing around talking about her. Maybe even pitying her.

She got up from the table, her half-finished plate in hand. She was heading for the garbage, no longer hungry, in need of movement, when a flicker of energy caressed her check. She turned and saw Rick standing at the driveway's end, looking like all that and then some.

It was in the way his navy cotton shorts kissed the edges of his knees, hiding the full muscles of his thighs. It was in the fit of the white sleeveless cotton shirt loose at the waist and the sculpted slopes of his arms.

It was in the sunglasses that hid his eyes, filling his whole being with seductive mystery. But mostly it was in the lips spreading wide with a Colgate smile.

The paper plate and burger hit the trash, forgotten. Her legs took her toward him, her body moving into the arms opened wide for an embrace. Her nose found a shoulder blade, cologne and heat circling her heart. "You smell good."

"And I'm looking twice."

"You're late," Dajah said, pulling back from him.

"Had a flat." He looked around. "I'm starving—what's on the menu?"

"What's not?" she answered, taking his hand and leading him toward Daddy Wilkes and the grill he was manning.

"Young man," Daddy Wilkes said deeply.

"Sir?" a stunned Rick answered back, searching the lines of Daddy Wilke's face for an indication he had done something.

Daddy Wilkes ignored the perplexed look, his smile blossoming wide as he considered Dajah. "You hear that? Now, that's home training. Called me sir, like he was supposed to do." Daddy Wilkes wiped a hand on his sauce-stained apron and extended it Rick's way. "I'm Leonard Wilkes."

"Nice to meet you, Mr. Wilkes. I'm—"

"Rick. Yeah, I know. Heard all about you." From who? Dajah hadn't said a word to Daddy Wilkes. "What be your pleasure, son?"

It was hard choosing, so much of everything and every bit of it looked good. "Is that chopped barbecue?"

"Sure is. Buns over there. Slaw on that table. We have baked beans, corn on the cob and potato salad for backup."

"Well, I think I'll try some of the chopped barbecue first."

"Don't wait too long. My bourbon chicken is famous. It's always the first to go." Daddy Wilkes turned and called over his shoulder. "Frieda? You got company over here." Then he went back to his grilling.

Frieda liked him.

Dajah could tell. As hard as she tried to keep the smile off her face, be cutting with her tongue, Frieda could not stop the pleasure of meeting Rick from showing. "I knew it had to be something special about you," she went on to admit as the two girlfriends and their mates sat around the table. "And now I'm seeing."

It made Rick blush, which was so much better than the tense moment he had when Dajah introduced them. He had seen it all in Frieda's eyes: the leeriness, the mistrust, initial dislike. Women talked, and best friends talked even more. He had wondered just what Dajah had told her friend about him.

But the ill start faded, went away forever as he remembered Barry from his freshman year in college. They had not been great friends, but they had shared the same Lit and Math class. It stung a little bit that Barry had graduated and he had dropped out.

"Overrated anyway," Barry said. "College, I mean. Yeah, I have my degree in Earth Science but working for the water company isn't quite what I had planned on graduation day."

"You're a technical supervisor," Frieda insisted.

"Yeah, and when the lead and minerals get too high, I get to sign off on a 'fix it' sheet. I just saw myself as doing something more down in the trenches."

"I hear you," Rick added, without thought.

Frieda saw it differently. "A degree is a good thing. So don't even try and front like it's not. You can't really say you would have the position you have as a black man at your age if you didn't have that sheepskin hanging on your wall."

Barry smiled and placed a hand over hers. "Babe, first off, it's not sheepskin. Hasn't been in a long time. Second of all, I started at the bottom to get that gig. And yeah, the degree helped, but in truth it was my hard work and determination that got me there."

"It was both, Barry."

"I do believe this is a dead issue, and this is a party." He found Rick's eye. "You ready, man?"

"For?"

"Get this jimmy-jam started," he answered, standing from the table and taking Frieda's hand.

"I like the brother," Rick was saying minutes later as he and Dajah moved their feet on the cement patio.

"What about the sister?"

"She all right."

"She likes you."

"Really? How can you tell because I sure couldn't."

"The way she was smiling at me. The things she could have said, but didn't."

"Oh, like a man not being valid unless he had a degree behind his name?"

"She never said that."

"Not in so many words, she didn't."

"She was talking about Barry."

"Then how come I felt like it was being directed at me."

"Because you're too serious sometimes."

"Oh, I'm the too-serious one?" He opened his mouth. Closed it. Shook his head.

"What?"

"Nothing."

"No, really, what?"

"Just thinking, that's all."

"About?"

"You," a half-truth he decided to follow through with. "Remember when I said I looked twice? Truth was I haven't stopped looking."

"You like?" Dajah teased.

"Like ain't the word. I'm waiting for some slow jams, give me a reason to pull you close."

"Who says you need a reason?" Her arm snaked around his neck, claiming him, faults and all, in a single hold.

Tarika leaned back against the booth, the oversized plate before her scattered with broken crab legs and the husk of two lobster tails. She picked up her drink, took a long sip and put it down. "The lobster was kickin'."

"It was all right."

She didn't expect any more sentiment than that from Gina anyway. She had been moody for days. "You ready?"

Gina looked over the food that had yet to be eaten. Glanced at Kanisha's plate that was completely empty. "Yeah." She flagged the waitress with her newly manicured nails, asked for the check and paid. She stopped at the pay phone, dialed a number. Heard a strange little melody, a voice that said the cell customer she was calling was not answering.

It was the eighth time today she had gotten that message. Rick was somewhere. Gina just wished she knew where.

They stood at the bus stop, the traffic along Sunrise Highway brisk. Kanisha stood on the grass twirling a plucked dandelion, sleepy but wired in the same breath.

"You think he seeing somebody?" Gina asked.

"Rick?"

"Yeah. You think that's it?"

"I don't know. All he do is work all the time. When he got time to hook up with someone?"

"So if he's not, how come he won't answer his phone?"

"Maybe he's not home."

"Talking about his cell, fool. He ain't answering."

"Maybe he went to visit his momma or somebody."

"Yeah, maybe." The bus appeared. Gina got her Metrocard ready, Tarika plucked a piece of food from a front tooth, and Kanisha blew a fast breath, setting the dandelion seeds free.

Chapter 10

When Felipe Rodriguez left his small hometown of Via de Rios in Mexico years ago in pursuit of his American dream, he had never seen himself becoming a super.

He had envisioned his own small business, a painting company like his childhood friend Jorge had, or perhaps masonry work like his cousin Juan. But not once had the idea of looking after one hundred and forty-four apartment units ever passed his mind.

It was not an easy occupation, but Felipe didn't mind hard work. What he did mind were the bad tenants who disrespected both him and the property under his care. Now, as he scrubbed furiously at the fresh scrawl of graffiti on the lobby glass panel, he wished the annoying señorita would just go away.

"No. No. No," he insisted to Gina.

"Come on, Felipe. It'll take me two seconds."

"I not gonna let you up. Señor Rick, he tell me you gone. He have me change the locks. Tell me don't let you inside."

"He wasn't serious."

"No. Señor was very serious. You go away now or I call the cops!"

Gina had known Felipe for as long as she had known Rick. A

somber man of small stature, he was a by-the-book type of guy. Still, everyone had a weakness. Gina wasn't sure what his was, but she was willing to find out. She pulled out a twenty-dollar bill. "Will this do?"

Felipe Rodriguez looked at Gina. "I no take your money. You go away."

But Gina didn't want to go away. Couldn't. She was in deep need of answers, like, was Rick really seeing somebody else? Access to his apartment would give her some clue.

She had dropped Kanisha at Tarika's place and waited until Rick had left for work to come over. Gina couldn't believe it when her key didn't work. She didn't think Rick was that smart, but he was, making her seek out Felipe. "What? Twenty ain't enough? You want fifty?"

While he lived rent free, he had a growing family of six. His youngest daughter was in need of new shoes and his oldest, going on thirteen, was no longer happy wearing hand-me-downs. "*New clothes, Poppi. I'm tired of these rags,*" she'd whine.

Fifty dollars could get her a pair of those jeans, with enough left over to get his youngest shoes.

"A hundred, but that's as high as I'm going," Gina insisted, gathering up five twenties. "Here, take it."

One hundred dollars. Fancy sparkly pants for his oldest, shoes for his niña. Maybe a dress for his wife. Who would know?

God would, came the answer, so swift and clear that Felipe crossed himself. He dropped the scrub brush into the bucket, snatched up the bottle of paint thinner. "You go away," he said and hurried inside the building.

Tarika never thought she would get tired of seeing Gina, but in the weeks since Gina had moved back home, it seemed every time Tarika breathed, there Gina was inhaling. Today Tarika had plans of her own.

She had not seen Sha-Keem in two weeks, and though there had really been nothing regular to them since he got out of jail, she still considered him her man. Tarika had planned to do her hair, hook up her nails and wear that new outfit she had fleeced from Dr. Jay's Tick-Tock.

She had planned to saddle up to the corner with enough *umph* in her walk to at least get his attention. She wanted to show him what he had been missing by staying away.

But Gina showed up, Kanisha in tow. Said she had to go somewhere and she'd be back. Tarika had turned on the cartoons for Kanisha and taken a quick nap. By the time she'd awakened, Gina was rapping at the window, carrying the infamous brown bag.

Tarika didn't mind smoking marijuana and drinking forties with Gina, but she didn't feel comfortable with Kanisha sitting around not only watching, but breathing in the smoke. The little girl was just four, which was way too young.

But if Tarika was concerned, it was obvious Gina wasn't. "You got paper?" she wanted to know. Tarika reached over and tossed her the pack of Bamboo. Like a pro, Gina separated the seeds from the dried weed and produced a joint that was nearly a perfect cylinder.

She lit it, inhaled, taking it from her mouth to inspect it, then going in for a second, third and fourth puff before she passed it to Tarika. Tarika shook her head no. She still planned to make it to Sha-Keem's corner and wanted to be both clear-eyed and clear-headed. Sha-Keem may have sold drugs, but he didn't have time for anyone who used any form, marijuana included.

"No?" Gina asked, perplexed.

"Naw, not today."

Gina considered her. "What's wrong with you?"

"Nuttin. Just don't feel like smoking."

"Since when?"

Since Tarika decided maybe smoking all the time and sucking down forties wasn't the way she wanted to go. Or maybe it was because it was all Gina seemed interested in these days. She wasn't sure. She shrugged.

"Well, the hell with you. Shit, just more for me." She took a few more puffs, flicking ashes. "Your cousin, she still work for the phone company?'

"Who?"

"You know, that one. Work for AT&T, down south somewhere?"

"Oh, you mean Cassandra? I think she do. Why?"

"Can she, like, access people's phone records?"

"She work for the cable company, not the phone company."

"No shit? Can she give us a free hookup then?"

"Got to be living in Georgia or somewhere. Won't work in New York. Whose records you want to get to?"

"Rick's."

"Why?"

" 'Cause there's stuff I need to know. Figure if I check the phone records, I can find out."

"Stuff like what?"

But Gina didn't answer. Tarika couldn't help. It didn't even make sense talking to her about it. She searched her brain for another plan.

Life and death.

Those were the only messages that came through the main NYC Corrections switchboard that were passed on to to the various correctional staff. When Rick received one on his shift from Gina, he called her right away. "She okay?" were his first words.

"Kanisha? She just fine."

"Whew," he said finding the breath he hadn't even known he'd lost. "I was thinking the worst."

"Yeah . . . look, I know I'm not supposed to call you at work and shit, but your cell been off and all I get is your machine. Now, I don't know what kind of game you playing, but as Kanisha's father, I need to be able to reach you."

"You can leave a message, Gina."

"Message might get to you too late. No, I need to reach you when I need to reach you . . . where you been anyway?"

A pause. Barely two seconds of silence, it said all that Rick wouldn't. "Been nowhere."

"Stop lying to me, Rick. I ain't stupid, okay? Out of the clear blue you turning off your cell and ain't answering your phone. Like I said, where you been?"

"Living my life."

"Oh, you kick me out and suddenly you living?"

"I got a right."

"Who is she?"

"Who's who?"

"The heifer you been messing around with, 'cause I know it got to be somebody."

"I'm not messing around with nobody."

"Oh, you think I am a fool, huh. Well, let me tell your black ass this. You can't be on the up-and-up with me, then I sure ain't gonna be on the up-and-up with you."

"What you trying to say?"

"You want to see your daughter?"

"You know I do."

"Then you better come straight, hear? Now . . . I'm going to ask one more time, who is she?"

Rick swallowed, then swallowed again. Felt the power and its loss behind one name. He tried to weigh the consequences of saying it now or letting her find out later. Remembered his daughter. "Dajah."

"Who-jah?"

"Day-jah."

"Where you meet her?"

"Don't matter where. I did, okay. Can I speak to Kanisha?"

Gina did the unthinkable. She put her on the phone.

Rick didn't know where the time went, only that one minute he was listening to his daughter talking about living away from him and the next his supervisor was tapping him on the shoulder.

Rick knew what the action meant, but the last thing he wanted to do was disconnect. "I gotta go, baby. But Daddy coming to see you real soon, okay?" He hung up, Kanisha's words with him. September was the month his Plan would come together; the month when he would be back with his child. But in that moment September seemed far, far away.

She was trying not to stumble, trying not to pinch up her face, but the hard wooden platforms she had swiped were half a size too small and they were pinching her toes in the worst way.

Tarika had known they would hurt her the moment she slipped them on her feet. But she had stood before the old mirror, taking in her silky halter top, the low-riding capri pants, and not even Jesus Christ himself could make her take the shoes off.

Yes, her big toe hung over the edge just a bit, but she had given herself a pedicure and it emphasized the bright red of her toenail polish. Her belly was flat and smooth, her hips just round enough, and though her breasts were on the small side, she had great shoulders and not a single mark on her arms.

Though her feet hurt, burned and ached with every step she took, she was on a mission, her destination half a block away.

"Yo, here come your girl," Little Ned said, tugging at the edge of Sha-keem's jersey. "And day-um, she looking good."

Sha-Keem gazed up the block and saw Tarika heading his way. He turned his back.

"You still hittin' it?" Sha-Keem didn't answer. "Well, shit, if you ain't, I'm more than willing."

Sha-Keem had shared things with Little Ned in the past. There was that time that they had crack whores give them blow jobs on the corner underneath the illumination of the street lamp, cars and pedestrians moving by as they stood, pants to their ankles, desperate mouths on their dicks in public display.

It had been a surreal moment for Sha-Keem. He had felt both powerful and powerless in that same breath, so much so that when he came, it rocked his soul with an emptiness that ached while Little Ned chuckled like a banshee, talking about how *on* that shit was.

"You believe that?" he had gone on to say, the two women, crack in hand, off to smoke their ill-gotten elixir. "Right fucking here, sucking our dicks down on their knees, bro, for every got damn body to see."

Sha-Keem hadn't believed that a woman could go so low. Even as the one name Hootch unzipped his jeans and fell to her knees, he didn't think she would do it. But she had, her ravaged friend taking on Little Ned. It was in that moment that Sha-Keem understood the power of crack.

But Tarika was a different matter. Tarika wasn't a crack whore and never would be. Tarika had been his girl, and letting Little Ned have a chance at her wasn't even a consideration. The fact that Little Ned even voiced such a thing raised his ire.

"You 'bout ready?" Sha-Keem asked. "'Bout ready to do what, nigga?" Sha-keem moved up on Little Ned, his lips inches from his face. "'Bout ready to get my foot up yo ass?" He jabbed him with a finger. "Asked you a question."

"Nutten Nigga."

"Thought so."

The sound of feet drifted near. Sha-keem faced the brick wall, pulled out his roll, counted his money. Not because he had to, but because he could not look at Tarika. To look at her that close with her looking that good would break the promise he had made.

She was a good girl. A little banged up, a little beat down, but he realized long ago just how special she was. When she told him she was having his baby, he prayed that she would lose it. She had. And though he never made it once to the hospital to see her after she'd miscarried, he was the first person she sought when she was released.

When Sha-Keem got arrested, she had been the one at his hearing. Not his momma, not his grandmother, just Tarika, crying out when he was sentenced. And when he started serving his year at Riker's Island, she came every single day to visit, rain or shine.

It was during his prison time that he realized Tarika was special. That with a little effort she could become something, and being with a going-nowhere young thug like him would never give her the chance. When Sha-Keem was released, he started pulling away.

Footsteps drifted past his back, did not cease the way he expected but kept on their tap-*schlip* rhythm. He shifted his gaze, watched the shake of her behind, how her taut calf muscles gleamed above those too-high shoes.

"Hey, girl," he found himself calling out. "Since when you walk by me and don't speak?"

Tarika took another step, her heart beating fast in her chest, the smile she had held on to leaving her like sunshine, lightening up his world. "Since when you ain't found time to come see me?"

Sha-keem dug into the deep pockets of his jeans, passed items over to Little Ned. Headed towards Tarika, his arm fast around her shoulders. "Damn, girl, you look good. Where you headed?"

"Where you headed?"

"With you, where else?" Sha-Keem answered as they turned and headed back up the street.

"You still playing that old shit?" Sha-Keem asked twenty-two minutes later as he lay on the mattress on the floor, sweaty, spent, heart open and in turmoil.

"Jill Scott ain't old."

"From like two years ago? Hell, yeah."

Tarika shrugged, snuggled close to him, wondering how much longer he would stay. "I like what she has to say."

"What? Walks in the park and some dude banging the chick in the grocery store?"

"No, not that."

He shifted, looked at her. "Then school a brother." This was why he dug her so much. She talked about things most girls wouldn't. Tarika showed him her true heart every time they were together. She was vulnerable and didn't mind letting people know.

"I play it 'cause it reminds me of you."

He chuckled. "Me?"

"Yeah. Like that song about taking a walk around the park. Sometimes I lay here listening to it and I see us doing something like that."

"Since when we ever walk around no park?"

"Since never, but that don't mean I don't want to or we can't."

"You trippin'."

"I ain't tripping. Taking a walk is a nice thing."

"Oh, yeah?"

"Yeah."

Sha-Keem looked away. "So what other song remind you of me?"

"'Exclusively.'"

Sha-Keem sat up, shaking his head. "Oh, you really are trippin' now, ain't you."

"Why, 'cause of Angie?"

"Who?"

"Nigga, don't play me. I know all about the little stink-bitch ho." Tarika's voice grew soft, painful. "What I don't know is why? Why you drop me for her?"

"I didn't drop you for her."

"Then why?"

Sha-Keem shifted around on the mattress. Found her eyes again. Reached for her hand. "For you. I did it for you. Last thing you need is a no-good nigga like me. You deserve someone better."

"How you gonna tell me what I deserve?"

"'Cause I've seen your soul. Know all about what you've gone through. I know I'm not the one."

"How can you say that, after all we been through?"

"That's exactly why I can. Shit, you did for me, nobody else ever did and I doubt anybody ever would. You worthy of a good man and that ain't me." He stood, found his boxers, his pants, his jersey.

"You leaving already?"

"You know I'm on the clock. Stupid-ass Little Ned can't be out there alone too long."

"You coming back?"

"Yeah." But Sha-Keem knew better. He dug in his pocket, produced a roll of fives. Laid it on the mattress, left.

"How long will you be working this shift?"

"What do you mean?"

"I mean, will you be having Wednesdays and Thursdays off forever?"

Rick laughed. Reeled in his smile. "A few years up the road."

"Years?"

"Something like that."

"Why?"

"Seniority. All the old guys got the weekends. The rest of rookies take whatever left over."

"So if we wanted to do something, say, on a Saturday night, we couldn't?"

"Not unless I arrange for a day. Why?"

"Take a wild guess."

"We still have Wednesday and Thursday."

"Yeah, but everything happens on the weekend."

"What can I say, Dajah. It's just how it goes for now."

"I'm tired of doing nothing, going nowhere."

They had just gone to Frieda's party, but he caught her drift. "Oh, so you want to go somewhere, do something."

"That would be nice."

"Where you want to go?"

"There is the rest of the Ailey summer series I haven't seen."

"You mean like a dance concert?"

"Something wrong with that?" Some men had an aversion to men in tights. The Alvin Ailey Dance Theatre was infamous for its scantily clad male dancers. She was waiting for his ignorance and his homophobia to show. But it never did.

"Wednesday sounds good?"

"For?"

"The concert?"

"This Wednesday?"

"Sure, if that works for you?"

Dajah could not hold her smile. "Works for me."

Tuesday morning Frieda pulled up to her designated spot and took a moment to take a deep breath. She had spent a sleepless night conjuring up all types of scenarios about how this morning would start. But none of them seemed to match the deep fear in the back of her throat.

She slipped her magnetic card into the slot and pushed the heavy metal door open. She saw Tom, the security guard at his post, his eyes moving over her with interest. He seemed to take his time this morning checking her out from head to toe as if she had had on mismatched shoes, or her clothes were on backward.

Frieda forced a smile. "Morning, Tom." When he did not toss the greeting back, she just knew he was going to tell her she had been transferred. That she had to hand in her pass key.

"Look like somebody stuck your finger in an electric socket, girl," was what came out of his mouth. "Never known you to look so bugged-out scared. What's going on?"

Frieda laughed, a nervous titter that released the adrenaline that had built up inside of her. It flooded her system like an open dam, making her feel woozy, light-headed. "Nothing wrong with me," she said, with a rapid blink of her eyes.

"Could have fooled me." He went back to his coffee and morning paper. Frieda headed up the hall to the elevator.

The piles were so high, she could not see her chair or the personal mementos that were laid out on the lateral files behind it. There on her desk were mountains of files, four in all. Her mouth dropped open as she stared at them; a note on legal-pad paper affixed to each stack.

Frieda rounded her desk and put her pocketbook inside. With a sigh that took much out of her, she shifted three of the four piles to the space behind her, leaving one mountain to tackle. It would take her all week, but at least she still had a job, all the compensation she needed as she got down to work.

* * *

In a deep sleep, it took a moment for Rick to come to, understand what that sound was. It was his intercom and someone was laying on it heavy.

He sat up, swung his legs out of bed and headed down the hall. Eyes half shut, he pushed the intercom button. "Who?"

"It's us."

Rick swallowed, wetting his dry mouth. "Us who?"

"Gina. Kanisha."

Kanisha, the magic word, whipping away the last remnant of sleep, sending his hand to the open-door button. Rick went to the door and opened it wide, waiting for the sound of the elevator, the first look in weeks at his daughter.

It seemed forever, but was just a few minutes as the sum of his world stepped off the elevator and came running his way, her face overrun with a sweet joy. He bent down low to grab her, hoist her up.

"Daddy," she breathed against his ear, kissing his cheek and holding tight, as if she never wanted to let go.

"You been okay?" he asked, pulling back, searching her carefully. Her hair was neatly done, her eyes wide and bright. He saw no marks or bruises beneath the fit of her shorts or on her bare arms.

"Been okay, Daddy. We came to surprise you. You surprised?"

It was in that moment that Rick found Gina's eyes, fixing on them as the words left him. "More than you can know."

It was Kanisha's idea to go for breakfast, McDonald's her choice. " 'Cause I'm hungry, and McDonald's got the best pancakes." He would have argued that point, but he was just too happy to be with his daughter again.

"Let me take a quick shower and we can be on our way."

Rick left them in the living room, surprise still with him, Gina saying few words. Kanisha had done most of the talking, the sound of her voice filling the apartment again, sweet. When he came out of the bathroom, he found Gina in the bedroom going through his nightstand.

She didn't stop her searching. "You remember that silver fingernail polish I use? I think I left it. You seen it?"

"It wouldn't be on my side," he said, tempered.

"Well, I checked mine and it wasn't there. Guess I'll have to buy some more."

"Guess you will." They stared at each other. Gina closed the drawer. Headed back to the living room, waited for Rick to finish dressing.

They sat in the hard plastic booth, Kanisha swirling bits of pancake around in the puddle of syrup. She bought it to her mouth, a drop of syrup landing on her chin. She lapped at it with her tongue.

"Use your napkin," Rick suggested, his Big Breakfast, half eaten, no longer wanted.

"You gonna eat the hash brown?" Gina asked, plastic knife and fork working quickly over her own meal.

"No. You can have it."

She reached over, took it from his plate, put it on hers. Added three packs of ketchup and continued her chowdown.

Rick took the moment to look at her. He found himself looking at her as he had never looked at her before. Too much fake hair on her head. Acrylic nails too long to ever be deemed real. One too many holes in her ears. Everything about her—excessive.

Not like Dajah.

The name made him smile. Dajah, possessing such a beauty and self-awareness that she didn't need a whole lot of trappings to make her shine. Dajah, whose world went beyond hip-hop and street life. She was someone he could take to Broadway, a nice restaurant, and not worry about her showing out.

He had it all planned.

They'd arrive in the city early. Do a little strolling before the concert. After the performance they would go to a nice place to eat. Maybe go over to Stuyvesant Town, find one of those park benches near the river. Take in the majestic Queensboro Bridge at night.

Fingers fluttered in his face. Rick came back to himself, Gina getting his attention. "Can you?" she wanted to know.

"Can I what?"

"Drop us back home. We took a cab over, but if you can drive us back . . ."

He looked at his watch. He had another five hours before he had to head off for work. "Maybe we can go to the park for a little while."

Gina considered him. Saw things in his eyes. "Got plans for today.

Tomorrow would be better. We could go somewhere really nice, like Rye or somewhere."

Rye, New York. They had the amusement park up there. He hadn't taken Kanisha in a while. They could leave early, be back in time for his date with Dajah. "Yeah, I guess we could do that."

Like a mouse going after the cheese, Gina thought as she picked up her ketchup-slathered hash brown. Took a big bite.

Rick might have another woman in his life, but Gina was not about to give up her hold. She'd make it her business to spend as much time with Rick as she could. He would not refuse her that. Kanisha made it so. And then when the time was right, she'd make her move.

Miss Dajah wouldn't know what hit her.

Chapter 11

Long, soft and made of silk, the layered earth-colored skirt kissed her ankles every time she took a step. The sleeveless top in the matching shade played hide-and-seek with her navel. A strand of delicate gold circled a left ankle above the three-inch wedge of her leather open-toe shoes.

Dajah stood at her bathroom mirror, gathering up her braids into a thick black rubberband midway up the back of her head. She turned sideways, checking the effect and saw three inches of braids sprouting out like porcupine quills.

She slipped her large hoop earrings on, added rich red lipstick to her mouth. Lined her eyes with a black kohl pencil. Dusted her face, shoulders and neck in a shimmery powder. She stepped back and checked herself. Summer-evening perfect.

Dajah left the bathroom and went to her bedroom. She stood before the full-length mirror, checking for flaws in her flawlessness, daring her image not to reveal perfection.

She had been looking for somewhere to wear the soft layered silk and knew the Alvin Ailey dance concert was it. The audience would be a mix of wannabe dancers, used-to-be dancers, hoped-to-be dancers and people like herself—appreciative of the art form but possessing neither the opportunity nor the desire to attempt it.

Such a mix would lend itself to the silent competition of who could be the most ethnically chic, what ensemble would turn the most heads. A mud cloth, cowree beads, one-of-a-kind Afro-fabulous fashion show, the patrons would parade and saunter, haughty and coutured, heads held high, backs straight, sipping dry wine like reincarnated kings and queens of a lost dynasty.

While it was not Dajah's intention to be a part of that competition, it was her intention to look nice for Rick and their first real going-out date, a date that would commence in less than half an hour.

She went to her living room window. Peered out. Hoped he would be on time. Silk wrinkled easily and she would not even consider sitting down until she was getting inside his Navigator.

The hum of tires was all the sound inside Rick's SUV. Kanisha was in the back seat, dead to the world, but not even her slight snores could disturb the reverberation of rubber moving quick over the asphalt highway.

"Speed limit's fifty-five, Rick. You trying to get a ticket?"

No, he was trying to strike a bargain with time. He looked at his digital clock on his dash for the twenty-seventh time since they had left Rye, New York, and his stomach ached. He was supposed to be picking up Dajah in less than half an hour. It would take that long to reach the Throgs Neck Bridge. While the flow of heavy traffic was now on the other side, it would switch to his side when he hit the Cross Island Expressway.

Rick could not even ask himself where the time went because he knew. It had become lost while he and Kanisha rode rides and ate everything her heart desired. It had been forgotten sitting on the rocks that edged the lake and pitching stones into its murky depth. Time was abandoned to picture-taking and bumper cars. That second go-round on the roller-coaster. Before he knew it, it was five-thirty, two hours beyond what he had wanted to stay.

Rick had wanted to be home by four-thirty. He wanted to go to the barbershop on Hillside and get a haircut and a close shave. He wanted to run by Hack's, an exclusive men's clothing store on 164th Street and pick up the shirt and slacks he had picked out. As it stood now, Hack's would be closed, and there would be no time for either a close shave or that haircut. There'd be no stroll along Broadway either.

He fingered his cell phone. Glanced at Gina, who was looking back at him. Rick itched to dial Dajah's number, a tingling, in that moment, he could not scratch.

The digital clock on the cable box read six-thirty-eight. Dajah looked at it with apprehension. Phone in hand, she took a breath and dialed Rick's number, hating every unanswered ring. As soon as his voice mail came on, she disconnected. She dialed his cell. Was told the customer she was calling was not answering at this time. Put the phone down.

Dajah went to the window, her legs beginning a mild protest. She had been standing and waiting for twenty-three minutes. *Almost half an hour.* Angry was what she told herself she was feeling, but disappointment sprinkled with hurt was what it really was.

Where is he? I'm standing up here trying not to wrinkle my slamming outfit, waiting on him and he hasn't even called me to say boo. Why?

Because she had put all her eggs in one basket. Because she had been so certain he was going to get there fifteen minutes before he said he would, she had gotten dolled up early. *Because you chose to put yourself in this dilemma,* she could hear Frieda saying, wanting to call her so bad in that moment she didn't know what to do.

But such moments had never been shared with Frieda. Dajah had never lived a life that called for it. Every man she had real interest in was always on time or at least called to say they were going to be late and why. *Not Rick.*

Her feet began to ache. Frustration swelled inside of her like a balloon. Dajah took off her shoes. Looked at the swollen comfort of her chair. Looked down at her top, the long, still straight, without-a-wrinkle skirt. Went back to her window watch.

"Why can't you drop us?" Gina wanted to know as Rick reached behind him, shaking his daughter awake. "Don't make sense, taking a cab."

"Come on, Kanisha. Wake up . . . time to go." He was in a bus stop; a slew of buses were waiting out a red light behind him. No doubt one of them would be pulling up into the spot his SUV occupied, and there wasn't a single available parking space for a block and half. "Come on. Wake up. You got to wake up. Now."

A police cruiser rolled up behind him, whooped its siren. Rick turned back around to the steering wheel, put on his turn signal, eased back into traffic. Came to a halt a block away from Red Cap Car Services.

Rick pulled out his wallet and forced a twenty into the pocket of Gina's T-shirt. He hopped out of the vehicle and hurried around to the passenger side. Opening the back door, he unhooked Kanisha's seat belt. "Let's go." Slowly she scooted out of the seat, her father's arms lifting her and putting her on the sidewalk. "I'll see you soon," he said, kissing her forehead, and then hurried around to the driver's seat.

Gina hadn't moved. Like a queen on her throne, she appeared glued to her seat. "I ain't taking no cab," she said, arms folded.

"Then take a damn bus, I don't care, but you're getting out of my car, now."

She glared at him, saw the fire. Reluctantly she undid her seat belt and opened the door. Got out, slamming the car door hard. Rick pulled away from the curb as if his wheels were on fire and speed would put them out.

The front door opened with a quiver. Dajah stepped out, her face a mask of bitterness and anger. Rick was halfway to her, words ready on his tongue when her hand shot up toward him. "Don't," she warned, heading for his vehicle.

She opened the door, closed it hard. Putting on her seat belt, her eyes and face were a mask of stone. Her nostrils were flaring by the time he got behind the wheel, the tips fluttering like a sail in the wind as he headed for the 150th Street entrance ramp.

"Can I explain?" Rick managed as he raced his car onto the Van Wyck, a line of slow-moving cars coming up fast in the near distance.

"No."

"So we're going to be like this for the whole evening? Because if we are, then I might as well turn around and take you home."

"The hell you will. You promised Ailey and I want it."

"Even though you aren't talking to me."

"You hearing words coming out my mouth, right?"

"Angry ones, yeah."

"Then okay. I'm talking." She folded her arms, forgetting the delicate silk. Looked out the window. Muttered, "Two for two."

"Excuse me?"

Dajah didn't answer. Just kept up her silence the whole too-long, too-slow ride. Traffic was at its worst as they headed into the City.

She did not let him hold her hand on the walk from the parking garage to the theater. Refused the door he held open for her. Rick didn't have to worry about her refusing a bought drink because there was no time. The curtain was rising when they got to their seats.

For all that she was thinking and feeling, she could have stayed home. But for all the grief he had given her, she was due this evening even if she wasn't feeling him. And Dajah wasn't. Mentally she had gone through all the dresser drawers of her heart, the closet and the basement of her mind, and packed her bags. After this night was through, she would never see him again.

It was this knowledge that cooled the fire. This secret weapon that allowed her to accept his offer for an after-the-show meal, she ordering the most expensive meal on the menu, slipping into new, bitter shoes, the fit strangely comforting.

If Dajah wasn't willing to share five words with him during the whole evening, a flood of them left her as he pulled up to her place.

"You know, Frieda warned me about getting involved with a man who had a child somewhere, and from the looks of things I should have listened. But I didn't, did I? No, because I thought you were different, special. I thought you wanted to be with me. Well, guess what, Rick? Guess what I've discovered in the weeks we've been together? I've discovered that what you had is obviously more important than what we got. I've discovered that you rap a good game but you don't come through . . . a damn phone call, couldn't even give me that. I'm standing up there waiting for you almost an hour and you couldn't even call me?"

She took her first breath, blazing fire from her eyes, expecting words from him, none of which she would consider. There was no defense. None. Not a single word Rick could speak would change it or make it better.

Dajah stared at him, not because she wanted a comeback, but because she wanted him to remember this moment, forever. She wanted the lay of silk across her breast to invade his dreams, the smell of her perfume to haunt his senses. She wanted the fire in her eyes to scald his soul. She wanted Rick to go to his grave regretting all that he didn't give her, all that she never got a chance to give.

What Dajah wanted wasn't what she got as Rick came back swinging. "You talk about calling you. How could I with Gina sitting right there next to me in the front seat? I literally kicked my daughter out my ride to be with you and you can't hear nothing I have to say?" He looked away, head shaking. "You want me twenty-four-seven? Well, guess what, I can't give you that. My daughter always comes first."

There it was. His bottom line. Like it, or lump it.

Dajah lumped it. "I'm not going to be second to anyone." She reached for the car handle. Opened the door. "Good-bye, Rick." Got out. The echo of it closing was still fading in the air when Rick got out behind her.

He grabbed her shoulders, turning her so hard, her ankle jarred. "You love me?"

She did not expect that question. Dajah couldn't even begin to see how he could even ask at such an early time in their life, especially with her closing the door on with them. "What?"

"I said, do you love me?"

She didn't even have to think about it. "No."

"But she does. My little girl Kanisha loves me. She loves me totally and unconditionally. In her world, I am all that and more. Nobody has ever given me that. No one. And if you think I'm just going to shut my heart down to be with you, then you're crazy."

Rick took a breath. "Was I late today? Yeah, I was. Why? Because I was having big fun with my heart up at Rye Playland. Having fun with the one true thing in my life, my daughter. Just basking in being her daddy. So yeah, for a hot minute I forgot we had plans. But the moment I remembered, I busted my ass to get to you, and all you had to say to me was 'Don't.' After all I've been through to be with you?"

His head shook. The deepness in his eyes swelled. "You think you the only one going through shit? You think you're the only one upset, hurt and disappointed? Well, news flash."

He turned and headed for his SUV, while Dajah, rooted to the spot, could only stand and watch as he pulled off.

Confused.

That was all Dajah was as she stuffed her silk outfit into a plastic bag, making a mental note to drop it off at the cleaner's. Her line in the sand had vanished. Her "I'm not going there anymore" proclamation was fading fast as she realized the deep relationship between fathers and daughters.

She had never had a child. Had never given a mother's love, but knew, like breathing, about a father's. Dajah knew that hell or high water, her father would lay down his life for her. That even though he had been married to her mother for decades, whom he loved more wasn't even a question.

Rick had it right. A child was supposed to come first. In Hank Moore's life she certainly did. So how could she expect Rick to feel any less? She couldn't. *But how can I become a second fiddle?* The same way mothers of daughters and the fathers who loved them did.

She picked up her phone, dialed Rick's cell. "Sometimes you don't know something until somebody says it out loud."

"Like?" Rick asked, relieved that she was calling.

"Like, what you and your daughter have is something that I not only should respect but know. I got a daddy too. But you got to do better, Rick. Before you left Rye, you knew you were running late. I know Gina was there and all, but you could have ducked into the men's room and called."

"You're right."

"So, okay," she said, taking a long needed breath. "We both messed up. I know it happens sometimes, but it can't be happening all the time."

"I hear you, I hear you . . ." He paused. "You know, right before you called I was just thinking about what happened. I kept on telling myself it can't be. As much as I want to be with you, how could this happen? But then I was like, 'Well, Rick, it did. What you gonna do next?' Thing was, there was no 'next'. I couldn't even see the next second of my life without you."

"You mean that?"

"Have I lied yet?"

She took a second to think. Tried to find one single lie he had ever told. Came up blank. "No."

"So is the coast clear?"

"Clear."

"Then is it safe for a brotha to make a U-turn? 'Cause I mean a brotha take a sista to a concert and buy her the most expensive thing on the menu, a brotha might feel he due a little sumptin' sumptin'."

"Is that right?"

"Most definitely."

"Well supposen a sista ain't up to it tonight?"

"Then a brotha is going to be mighty disappointed."

"I guess I wouldn't want to disappoint a brotha."

"I'm on my way."

Hugging never felt so good. Standing in her hall foyer, her arms around Rick, his arms around her, Nirvana.

Snuggled up tight, he poised a question. "How come you didn't even blink when I asked if you loved me?"

"Because I didn't have to think about it."

"Not even a little bit?"

"No, not even a little."

"Not impossible?"

"No, not impossible."

"Just not now, right?"

She nodded a yes, unwilling to show herself for a liar.

Half an hour ago, her heart had given her a firm no. Now the vortex of the entire evening settled down into this moment of her body close to his and pertinent words shared.

Love came in baby steps. Not quick, not immediate, but some so soft, so barely there, you missed them. This was not one of those baby steps, but a heart felt flicker of the possibility.

Thursday morning arrived hot and sullen. Not a breeze stirred, and even the birds seemed more content to give in to languor than give up their sunrise song. There were two windows in the back bedroom Gina and Kanisha now called home. And though two window fans were fixed squarely inside of them, they only filled the room with a hot breeze.

Gina lay on top of the sheet, sweaty, fatigued. It was not so much that her body was wearied, it was her soul that was. Deep inside resided a listlessness she could not locate or even attempt to adjust. All she knew was she was just tired.

She was tired of the mundane routine of her life. Tired of waking up five days a week waiting for her mother to go to work so she could get up and have uninterrupted access to the kitchen, the bathroom, the living room space.

She was tired of hanging with Tarika all the time, having Kanisha up under her almost every minute. She wanted something else, something more, but she could not put her finger on just what.

Her mind rewound to yesterday. Recalled the day out with Rick. Though they had not shared a lot of words, they had shared the same space, finding a peaceful compromise. She lay there seeking answers and had a heart-shaking revelation.

After doing the frantic, indecisive thing for years, it no longer suited her.

She found herself looking for something else, something more. Gina was trying to put together the pieces, make her way through the muck. Create a new determination. But she couldn't reach it; her head was too muddled.

She reached over into the ashtray and picked up the half-smoked joint. She had just flicked on the lighter, the flame hungrily reaching for the marijuana perched in her mouth, when her bedroom door opened.

"You clean the house today, hear? I want the floors scrubbed, the carpets vacuumed, the bathroom done and the furniture dusted. And don't you dare light that in my house."

Gina released the tab on the lighter, the flame going out with a poof. She pitched it onto the nightstand, took the joint from her mouth and placed it back into the ashtray, refusing to find her mother's eyes as she waited for the bedroom door to close.

"Why I got to clean her damn house?" Gina asked no one, wringing out the stringy mop and running it over the kitchen floor. "Who the fuck she think she is?" she went on to say, pausing to wipe sweat from her brow.

But even as she muttered the questions to herself, she knew. *She's Doreen Alexander, and she can kick me out in a heartbeat.* And there was no other place to go.

This was the reason Gina was washing the kitchen floor and Kanisha was in the living room dusting. The same reason she had already cleaned the bathroom, getting pee stains from under the toilet seat, the scummy ring from the bathtub, and her mind was on the vacuum cleaner that would make her acquaintance real soon.

If Gina didn't know it two days ago, she knew it now. Her mother's house was her only option, and if her mother said jump, she'd better ask how high.

There had been a time weeks ago when she was certain Rick would change his mind and take her back. Gina had been certain that he had been just feeling the heat of the moment and would soon regret his choice.

Yesterday told her different.

Yesterday he had literally kicked both her and his daughter to the curb. In finding somebody new, he had discovered a new will power, and Gina's sure fire-plan to resecure herself back into his life wasn't sure-fire at all.

Gina's mother stepped into her house at exactly five minute to six, eyes over everything, nose sniffing the air. A cornucopia of smells came to her: Lysol, furniture polish, carpet freshener. But something else arrived too.

Hot oil. Seasoned, crispy-fried meat. Cheese and noodles. It took a moment for her to understand that it was dinner she was smelling. It took her no time to head toward the kitchen, her granddaughter by the kitchen table laying out silverware, her daughter wiping grease pops off the stove.

"I made dinner," Gina said carefully, spying the bag of take-out in her mother's hand.

"Since when you cook?"

"You know I've always cooked." Which was a true statement. There had been a point in their lives when Gina made dinner more often then her mother.

Her mother rattled the bag. "Well, I bought take-out."

But Gina could hear in her voice that the fried pork chops, the cooked cabbage and the macaroni and cheese had more appeal. "You can save it for tomorrow."

"Where you get the money?"

"From Rick."

"Rick? Thought he kicked you to the curb."

"Table is set and the food is done. You want a plate?"

Gina's mother turned her attention to Kanisha. "Here, go put this in the fridge for me." She looked toward the stove. "Not too much cabbage, but I'll take two chops."

Cleaning her mother's house had done more for Gina than make her break out in a sweat. It gave her thinking time, and as she ran mops over floors, rags over dusty furniture, paper towels over mirrors, she found her mind traipsing along all kinds of terrain.

For the first time Gina saw all the deficiencies in her life. Coming back home forced it. Coming back to a life she'd sworn she'd never be stuck in again had peeled back the layers, exposed the roots. In the midst of her self-analysis, others came into the fold.

She thought about her mother; she thought about Rick. But mostly she found herself thinking about her daughter and the life she had given her.

She knew she was a little too heavy-handed. Knew she had a patience level of zero. Gina understood her parenting skills bordered on terror, something she herself had been subjected to. But she didn't want that for her daughter and made a promise to herself to work on that.

Kanisha was the innocent in this mess Gina called her life. Gina found herself wanting to make it better, to give her child a little ray of sunshine. She remembered that Kanisha had a birthday coming up.

In previous years, Gina had always insisted that they go to Red Lobster to celebrate. In the passing years, it had become a tradition. But this year, with things being the way they were between herself and Rick, she knew the tradition was going to be broken. She thought of something else they could do.

She came up with a birthday party. A real sheet cake, party streamers and balloons, party. Her child deserved that much even if it meant going to the two people who could deny her and had.

Now as she sat at the kitchen table, it was hard swallowing when the question Gina was burning to ask jammed in her throat. She reached for the glass of Kool-Aid more times than not, trying to wash the food down past the lump.

"Next time don't use so much season salt. You know my pressure's high."

The fact of the matter was that Gina had known no such thing. Her mother had never discussed her physical well-being or lack of with her. But she mumbled an "okay" anyway.

She glanced at her daughter, conjuring up some resolve. Forking up some macaroni and cheese, she kept her eyes to her plate. "I was thinking about giving Kanisha a party."

"A party? For what?"

"Her birthday's coming up. She's gonna be five. There's a few kids in the neighborhood. Figured we can have it outside in the backyard."

"I don't want a bunch of wild-ass kids running over my grass."

What grass? Gina wanted to ask, but didn't. "We could do it in the driveway."

"I'm gonna have a party, Mommy?" The awe and surprise in Kanisha's voice drew both her mother and her grandmother's attention. "Am I?"

"I ain't paying for it," Doreen said quickly.

Gina looked at her daughter, enthralled with the rapture she saw in those eyes. "You sure are, Kanisha. You sure are."

Cloud Nine.

That's where Dajah found herself, with Rick in her life the way he was supposed to be. She felt good. She felt free. She felt connected and a part of his world. The dramas had been laid to rest, and they were coasting down the open highway, cruise control on, sitting back and enjoying the view.

They had gone to a comedy club out in Hempstead, Long Island, sitting in the back and laughing hard. Making a stop at White Castle for a late-night snack, they headed to his place, a first for her. She had never been to his apartment. She was curious about how he lived.

They rode the elevator up, her anticipation mounting. Rick fitted his key into the lock and swung open the door, turned on a light. The short hall showed a gleaming hardwood floor. "Give you a tour." A few steps took them to the kitchen. He clicked on a light and stuck his head in. "My kitchen."

Though it was a small space just big enough to accommodate a small table and three chairs, the vinyl floor was shiny, the stove scrubbed clean and everything was neat and in its place. He clicked off the light, continued.

Darkness moved to a soft brilliance as he turned the knob on the dimmer. The navy leather sofa and love seat were a nice match to the creamy beige walls. Dajah looked around, taking in the Persian area rug, the large-screen TV. Her eyes latched onto a sixteen-by-twenty photo that could have been no one but Rick's little girl.

"Kanisha?"

"Yep, that's her. That's my baby."

She was pretty, with shoulder-length thick braids and a rabbit-tooth smile. Dajah stared at the photo, saw the eyes that were Rick's, the same shape face, the same prominent forehead. "She looks just like you."

The assumption pleased him, his lips unable to contain his teeth as his mouth widened his smile. "Everybody says that."

"It's true." Dajah looked around, saw more photographs, mostly of Kanisha, a few of Kanisha and Rick. She spotted a smaller one on an end table, the two adults and a baby moving her closer. She picked it up, curious about the woman in the frame.

But before she could get a really good look, Rick took it from her hands. "Ignore that one."

"I want to see what she looks like."

He laid the frame facedown. "No need."

"She looks young."

"She is."

"How young?"

Embarrassment and discomfort filled his eyes. "Let's just say too young."

"Seriously, Rick. How young?"

He looked away, not wanting to share the truth of it. Rick didn't want to reveal how poor his choice from a long time ago had been. "It's not important, Dajah."

"Yeah, it is. I didn't get a hard look, but she looks like a kid."

"That picture's from almost five years ago," he said, defensive.

"And you were what, twenty-six? She looked about sixteen."

"Eighteen."

Her eyebrows shot up.

"Yeah . . . it's a long story, and I really don't want to get into it right now."

But Dajah did. It was a news flash. An unnerving, unsettling major piece of information that she should have known about weeks ago. She wanted to get into it *right now* because there was something freaky about a man that age getting involved with someone *that* age.

"You were a grown man and you got involved with a teenager and you don't want to get into it."

"Don't look at me like that."

"How am I supposed to look . . . She was a kid."

"She was seventeen when we met. Seventeen going on thirty, okay?"

Dajah looked away, Rick changed in her eyes. She tried to find a middle ground. Couldn't. "She was jail bait, and I really need to know why."

Their eyes met. With a sigh that hurt, Rick nodded. Took a seat on the sofa. Patted the space next to him. Shared his journey.

"You loved her that much, this Bridget?" Dajah was asking minutes later.

"Yeah, I did. Too much."

"So when you met Gina?"

"I was all twisted inside." He looked off. "And she was like this great big wave of comfort, you know? I knew it wasn't the right way to go, but I needed somebody and she was there."

"And Kanisha?"

"She wanted a baby, and it sounded like a good idea."

"Did you want one?"

"Yeah, I did. At the time things between me and Gina were good. I saw no reason not to. Then when Kanisha came, everything got changed. But it was too late. I couldn't abandon my kid like that."

"Or Gina, right?"

"I loved her, or least I thought I did."

"Do you still?"

He looked off. "That's a hard question to answer. Sometimes I think I do, other times . . ." His head shook.

"Could you go back to her?"

His eyes found hers, disbelief full in them. "Never."

"You sure?"

"I was with her for all the wrong reasons. How would I go back . . . especially now?"

"Stuff happens all the time."

"Not to me it doesn't."

"So this Bridget. Is that the one I reminded you of that night we met?"

That Dajah not only remembered but had managed to put two and two together surprised him. "You got a mind like an elephant, don't you?" But he said it with a smile, and it was the tension breaker needed in that moment.

"I'm an Aries by birth, but a Scorpio by nature. We forget nothing and remember everything."

"Yeah, I noticed."

"And for the record, we hold serious grudges."

"So I've heard. Anything else I need to know about you?"

"That's it for now." She got up from the couch. Looked towards the hall. "You're going to finish giving me the tour?"

"Guess I am." He stood too. "Bedroom's this way."

Rick waited until Dajah had fallen asleep to pick up the phone and head into the kitchen. He entered his voice-mail number, heard that he had a message. Punching in his code, he stood in the darkness of his kitchen and listened.

"Rick, this is Gina. I'm giving Kanisha a birthday party. Call me back when you get this."

He looked at the calendar. Flipped the page. July ninth, next week. July ninth, his daughter's birthday. Rick could not believe he had forgotten.

We see what we want to see, pick and choose emotions that suit us in the moment. Dajah was no different.

Last night the notion that Rick's baby's momma was so young got pushed back in the moment. But morning brought it to the forefront again, and it was all that was on Dajah's mind the moment the alarm woke her.

It was early. Not quite six and sunrise was just a sprinkle of blue fairy dust on the horizon. Rick had gone off to use the bathroom, and Dajah was putting on her pants when he got back.

"Almost ready?" he asked. He could feel her thoughts, the implications that surrounded her like mist. He tried to find her eyes, but the look in them made him look away.

"Yeah," she replied as she zipped up her zipper. She found her blouse and put it on. She went to the mirror, tousled her braids. Put on her shoes. Got her pocketbook. Looked around her. "I'm ready."

Without any additional words, they headed out of his apartment, the early morning strip of 89th Avenue barren as a wasteland.

Dajah sat in her cubicle at work feeling like a drowning woman. She was filled to the brim with Rick, who he was and who he wasn't. She wanted to unload her burden, wanted to spill her guts, share his latest secret.

She had kept so much of Rick's story to herself, telling no one, holding it all in. But the cup was running over now, slipping down the sides, forming a pool of worry around her, and Dajah had to let it all out.

When her phone rang around two that afternoon, the last voice she had expected was Frieda's. But it was, Frieda telling her that she was on vacation. "Two weeks away from that madhouse. Girl, I don't know what to do with myself. Haven't seen you since my party. Thought you might want to come over after work."

It was all Dajah wanted. She wanted her friend's ears, heart and mind, open and alert to the burdens that had claimed her. Dajah wanted the sage, clipped, to-the-punch advice her friend could offer. Dajah needed a critical ear to dissect and exam up close the man she had fallen for, wanting to make sure she wasn't about to bite off more than she could chew.

"You just made my day. Your timing is absolutely perfect."

"What's going on?"

"Rick."

"Oh."

"Yeah, oh. I can come over straight from work."

"I'll be here."

"Good. See you then."

Dajah hung up the phone, relieved. She would go to Frieda's house, where they would talk, drink wine and share until the late-night hour. When she had her fill, she would leave with the ease she was deeply in need of.

* * *

"You chose to be with that man, troubles and all, remember? I tried to talk you out of it, but you wouldn't listen. He left his baby's momma to be with you. Just walked away from a relationship he had for all those years and *now* you want to change your mind?"

Dajah looked at her friend, puzzled. "I can't believe this is you talking."

"I *was* totally against it at first, but then I met the brother. I seen he's got a head on his shoulders."

"He impressed you," Dajah stated, needing confirmation. She needed to know that the worth she'd first seen in Rick actually existed.

"Yeah, but more than that. I watched you watch him. Saw all kinds of things in your eyes. Good things. I can't be breaking his balls about having a baby somewhere else. A lot of men do."

"But she was so young."

"And from what you told me, he had been badly hurt. Hurt and fear makes you do strange things."

"So I shouldn't worry."

"Don't be blind stupid or nothing, but yeah, just try and enjoy it and don't try and worry too much about the bad times. They're going to come anyway. But if there is more good then bad, then roll on."

Queen Frieda had deemed him worthy. Dajah took her friend's advice. Ran with it.

Chapter 12

The phone was ringing as Rick let himself into the apartment. He looked at the display and saw Dajah's number. Picked up. "Hello?"

"Hey," one word sung sweet and complete.

"Dajah?"

"Sorry to call so late, but I just got in."

"I just got in myself. Where were you?"

"Over to Frieda's . . ." She sighed. "It's no secret that you threw me for a loop yesterday. The whole thing's just a bad taste in my mouth. But I realized nobody's perfect, and I just wanted to say sorry for the way I acted."

"Baby girl, you don't know how happy you've just made me."

"Baby girl?"

Even though he could not see her, he could sense the turning up of her lip, felt the nerve touched in her expression. "Just a saying, Dajah. Just a 'you've-just-made-my-world-go-round' expression, that's all."

"You can call me Dajah. You can call me Ms. Moore. You can even call me Day. But please, don't ever call me that again."

Rick didn't have to ask why. He moved on. "I'm on for tomorrow, but maybe we can get together during the day."

"It'll be a short day. You have to be back home by three."

"Yeah, I know. But there must be something we can do."

"The beach. Jones," Dajah decided without a second thought.

It was not the best day the summer season had to offer. The sun was out, but the morning temps clung stubbornly to the mid-seventies and the breeze off the water was a bit too brisk, but Dajah and Rick made the most of it.

They sat near the shore, ate fried chicken and potato salad and water-gazed. They tried a game of Spades, but the wind kept flipping the cards. Giving up, they watched brave souls splash in the chilly water. Talked.

"You know how many times I was leaving you?" Dajah confessed.

"You were leaving me?"

"Oh, yeah," Dajah said with a flip of her hand. "Mind made up, heart ready for takeoff. The whole nine yards." She looked at him through the tint of her sunglasses. "But something always happened to change my mind."

"Something or someone?"

"Oh, you fishing big time, aren't you?"

"A brotha like to know how a sista feel about him, that's all."

"Why do you do that?"

"Do what?"

"Whenever there's something deep or really important you want to know from me, you always come out with what 'a brotha' wants, needs? How come you don't just say 'I'?"

Rick shrugged. "I don't know. I didn't even realize it."

"Well, I just told you. So ask me again, the right way."

But the words were hard. They did not want to leave his throat with 'I' attached. His head dropped a little.

"If you want an answer, then *you* have to ask me."

He gazed up at her. "I"—he tried to find her eyes behind the glasses—"would like to know how you feel . . . about me?"

She smiled and took off her shades, giving him the benefit of her eyes "How do I feel about you? First look in the diner, I was checking out your body. Then when it was time for me to go, and I was scared as anything, I was checking out your gun."

"My gun?"

"Yeah. You were an officer of the law, and I knew that gun would keep me safe."

"Only fired it at the shooting range. Can't say I would be much of a shot."

"But that wasn't the point. The point was you were some great protector of the law. You could keep me safe."

He chuckled. "Go on."

"Then, when we were at the bus stop . . ."

"Wait, hold up. I didn't mean a second-by-second play."

"No, no. You asked and I'm going to tell it. Where was I? Oh, yeah. The bus stop. When the bus was starting to take a long time, I was like, man, maybe he shouldn't have walked me because you had stopped talking and I figured suddenly you didn't want to be there."

"You were the one who went all mute."

"Because you stopped talking. You just like pulled back from me. But then you were taking off your Mace and handing it to me and I was like, wow, he serious about me being safe. I guess you can say that's when I started to really like what I was seeing."

"And when I told you about my situation?"

"That was drop number one."

"Drop? What drop? We weren't even together."

"Yeah, but we were both feeling each other. The possibility did exist."

"Go on."

"So you come and get the Mace and I had already made up my mind that I was going to give it to you and send you on your way. But when I opened the door and saw you all beat up . . ."

"I wasn't beat up."

"Yeah, Rick. You were. Shirt torn, scratches, looking like your momma died. Looked pretty bad. Anyway, I felt sorry for you *and* concerned. That's when I invited you in. Just wanted you to stay." Her eyes moved carefully over his. "That's why I said the thing about you being free."

"Okay, let's get to drop number two."

"Hmm, let's see. Drop number two? When you called me and I'm thinking you left her and you told me you hadn't yet. I was like, Negro, who you think you messing with?"

"But you waited, right?"

Dajah looked away. "I wasn't like *waiting* waiting."

"You did, right?"

She heard his deep need to know. Gave up her truth. "I wouldn't call it waiting, more like a 'maybe' I toted around."

He reached out and took up her hand. "I'm glad you did." He considered her. "Were there any more drops?"

"Most definitely. One of them was the other night."

"When I told you about Gina."

"Yeah. I was like, this guy has issues."

"So what changed your mind?"

"A lot of things. But all that really matters is we're here now, right?"

Rick smiled. "Aw, sukie, she fallen, y'all. She fallin' hard."

Was she? Dajah didn't want to know. She did not want to spend another second analyzing. She just wanted to feel what she was feeling and how she was feeling it in the moment. She didn't want to ask herself if they would reach Love Town or something would cause them to fall short of that journey.

She just wanted to be Dajah, a woman who had found someone new, he entering her heart a baby step at a time.

Gina didn't expect Rick to call her just to see how she was doing, but she did expect him to return the message she'd left about Kanisha's party. The money he had given her was all but gone. Down to coins, she had Kanisha make the call, understanding just how deep their connection went when he answered.

"Hi, Daddy, I'm having a birthday party, and we need some money."

"Kanisha?"

"Who you think? Mommy's giving me party, and we need money to get stuff."

"How you been, baby?"

"I've been okay."

"Your mommy there?"

"Uh-huh."

"Let me talk to her."

"Hello?"

"Gina?"

"Yeah. Her birthday's coming up, and I figured I give her something in the yard. But you know my momma ain't giving me a dime, and the money you gave me is gone."

"What day?"

"Saturday, when else?"

"What time?"

"I figured around three."

"Can't you make it earlier?"

"Why?"

"I have to work. You know that."

"I don't know nothing since you kicked us out."

"Can you, Gina?"

"I don't know. I have to think about it."

"Well, maybe I'll have to think about giving you money for the party." He had been suckered once. He wasn't about to become a victim again.

"Oh, you threatening me?"

"No, I'm stating fact. As far as I'm seeing, without me, there isn't going to be a party."

"Two o'clock," she said after a while.

"Twelve," he countered.

"Negro, you is crazy. People just getting out of bed at that time on a Saturday."

"Well, I guess they're going to have to get up early."

"One o'clock, but that's it."

"Works for me."

"When you bringing the money by?"

"Thursday."

"Late or early."

"Early."

"She wants a Jeep. One of those motorized ones. And I have a bunch of stuff to pick up. I ain't got no ride or nothing, so maybe you can take me out to Valley Stream. Toys "R" Us is there. You can get the jeep and I can pick up stuff for the party."

Rick hesitated. The idea of Gina being back in the passenger seat didn't sit well with him.

"You know they have the best party decorations out there. I can't be taking no bus, bringing home toys and all that stuff. This is her first real party. We should try and make it nice."

"All right. We'll do that Thursday."

"And don't even think about bringing her to the birthday."

"Who?"

Gina didn't answer. She just hung up the phone.

Nelson was Kanisha's godfather, but it was a role he had little opportunity to perform. Beyond her christening when she was a baby and toys dropped off at Christmas time, Nelson hardly got to see the child he was deemed to be spiritual counsel to.

In the scheme of his life it wasn't so much a deficiency as a fact, but it still caught him off guard when Rick called to tell him about the upcoming birthday party.

"What? Red Lobster burned down?" he asked with a chuckle.

"Forget you, man."

"I'm sorry, bro. But Gina has never wanted to give Kanisha a party so you have to excuse me if I seem a little perplexed. I mean, why?"

The question hadn't occured to Rick until that moment. He found himself seeking out his own answers. "I guess because," he began, but nothing would come after it.

"Exactly. See, Rick, you treading uncharted waters here and you have to be careful of a great big old shark called Gina."

"You cold, man."

"But right on target. So, tell me. What's been going on with you two?"

"Nothing much. I took them up to Rye Playland."

"That's it?"

"That's about the size of it."

"And how does she like being kicked to curb and you being with someone else?"

"She's cool with it."

There was a pause on the other end of the phone. "We talking about the same Gina?"

"Yeah."

"And you telling me she's 'cool' with it?"

"Yeah. She hasn't said anything except I can't bring Dajah to the party. But I hadn't planned on that anyway."

"Smart move. So what time is it and where is it?"

"Saturday at one. At her mom's."

"That place still standing? I thought the bad boy got condemned years ago."

"Hey, my kid lives there."

"But not for long, right?" It was Rick's turn to be silent. "Yeah, you thought I forgot. But I haven't forgotten a thing. I still say your plan is crazy, but I wish you much success."

"Thanks, means a lot."

"September, right?"

"That's the plan."

"This is what, July?"

"Yeah, it is."

"Got a pen and paper?"

"For?"

"I told you when you were ready, I would hook you up. I know who you need to go to. And if you plan to make that move in two months, you better get on the ball now."

Sometimes you dream a moment for so long that when the time comes to take that first step, it scares you. The 'why nots' pop up and won't go away. This was what Rick was feeling as he held the phone to his ear jotting down names and numbers of people he had never met, but would meet soon.

It was the reason why fear was beating down the anticipation. Why his mouth went dry when Nelson asked him to repeat it back to him.

"That's it. Today's what, Sunday? Make sure you give them both a call first thing Monday morning. It should run smooth, but you know how life always likes to throw you that monkey wrench."

"I hear you, man."

"So Kanisha's party. Should I come packing?"

"I'm warning you."

"Just teasing. You know Kanisha is my girl. She's the only one, and I mean the only one who gets to call me that—*Uncle Nel*, like I'm a woman or something."

"She could never say Nelson."

"Yeah I know, but she is going to be what, five? I think it's time we worked on it. Anyway, chief, I'll catch you Saturday. She want anything in particular?"

Yeah, me, Rick thought. "A Jeep, but Daddy got that covered."

"Maybe I'll get her a little boom box she could put in the trunk," Nelson offered, laughter in his voice.

The next call Rick placed was to his parents. He wasn't sure if they would come, or how long they would stay, but the idea of all of Kanisha's family surrounding her as she blew out the candles on her cake was more than enough incentive to invite them.

Gina stood in the doorway of her mother's bedroom, taking in the flat-on-her-back, mouth-open-wide snoring woman before her. The last thing she wanted to do was ask her mother for anything, but with her money gone and she and Kanisha hungry, she had little choice.

She had called Rick but he wasn't answering. She had called Tarika, but Tarika wasn't home. She had gone to the corner store and asked Lucco for credit, but she already owed him twenty dollars and she couldn't get another penny of credit until she paid him back.

That left her mother to appease the hunger in her stomach, one Gina herself had heard rumbling in the hollow of her child's. Gina swallowed. Opened her mouth. "Mommy," she whispered. "Mommy," her voice gaining a little more intensity.

But the eyes stayed closed, the mouth continuing to issue snores.

Gina stepped into the room, looking away from the bra and girdle slung over a chair, the panty hose and party dress in a heap on the floor. Her mother had gone out last night and hadn't returned until late.

"Mommy, you awake?" Gina half whispered, knowing she wasn't. She spied the pocketbook on the dresser. Knew her mother had gotten paid on Friday. Working for the Department of Motor Vehicles for the last twenty years had earned her a decent salary. Gina also knew that if she tried to take so much as a dollar, her mother would know.

"Mommy, we hungry." Her voice was too soft to hear over the snores. Gina knew that, but she could not get it to go any higher. She also knew she would have to walk over to the bed and touch the fleshy shoulder. That she would have to touch her mother and shake her. Force her from the deep slumber.

"We hungry, and I ain't got no money. There's bacon and eggs and bread in the fridge," her words more plea than question. Her mother mumbled something in her sleep. "What you say?" But no answer came as Doreen Alexander turned on her side, lips coming together twice before they parted like the red sea, a rumble of snores issuing out of it.

Five feet separated Gina from her mother. Five feet. Ten steps and she could not move. She could not will her feet to go forward, feeling an antsy need to beat a fast retreat.

Maybe it was her stillness, her statued presence; maybe it was her fear and need that swirled around her like a maelstrom that sent some sort of shock wave through the room. Gina wasn't sure. Only that one second she was still trying to get her feet to move and the next her mother was sitting straight up in her bed, red-tinged eyes settling on her with utter surprise.

That surprise turned to confusion. Confusion turned to anger. "What you doing in my room?"

"We're hungry, and I don't have any more money. Rick bringing some, but not till Thursday."

"What you doing just standing there?" Gina's mother asked.

"You was sleeping."

"So you stand there, staring at me sleeping?"

"I didn't want to wake you."

"What the hell you think you just done?"

"Can we?"

"Can we what?"

"Eat?"

"You woke me about some damn food?"

"We're hungry."

"Girl, you ain't got a damn bit of sense in your head, do you? All that food in there, and you come and ask me about it?"

"But you said—"

"Get out of my face."

Gina went. Went straight to the kitchen and pulled out pots and pans. She made grits; she cooked up bacon. She scrambled eggs and added slices of cheese. She made toast, pulled out the butter and jelly, poured glasses of orange juice, then called Kanisha to the table, the both of them wolfing it down like they would never have another bite to eat ever again.

Her mother never said a word about the food. But Gina had felt her thoughts the moment they had crossed paths in the living room.

Damn twenty-three years old, and you still can't take care of yourself. There was no real need to verbalize it. Gina's mother had always thought badly of her, and over the years it was apparent every time Gina looked her mother's way.

For the second time, the idea of public assistance arrived. This time it stayed, and Gina knew just who to ask.

Monique Winterthur had been the great black hope of 104th Avenue. Born in 1979, she had been the clear shining star of that particular generation. As a child she had been a Girl Scout, took music lessons and got straight A's. Neighbors would smile at her approach, warmed by her mild-mannered politeness and the good English that flowed through her mouth like water.

Parents and grandparents alike held her up as the one to be like; the other children on the block were spoon-fed her name over the breakfast table and at backyard barbecues. "Try and be like Monique." "Now there's a child who's gonna be something." "You know she won the spelling bee for the third year in a row?"

While Monique had been mentioned in the households up and down 104th Avenue, it was a fame she neither wanted nor asked for. They had raised up an unwilling hero, and when she reached high school, she rebelled.

The straight-A student started bringing in D's and F's. The mild-mannered adolescent became a self-involved teenager who cut school, smoked marijuana and snuck boys into her bedroom.

When the school counselor could not help and a private psychiatrist could make no headway, her parents' dream of having a child who went to Spelman College got whittled down to "Just let her graduate high school on time."

Monique did. But two months later she had a child. A year later, she had a second one. She would have gone on and had a third had not her parents had her tubes tied.

Neighbors stopped smiling when she walked by. Instead they talked about how much of a waste she was and had long conversations about the lost generation. Her parents had their basement redone into a two-bedroom apartment, encouraged Monique to go to a junior college and paid for her children to go to day care.

But Monique had no interest in that. She had no interest in keeping a job. After years of being perfect, she had found her niche. Had become all that she wanted to be—a mother. She was certain she could be just that, until the rules for getting welfare changed.

No longer could she sit around and wait for her monthly stipend. She had to get out and work. She did her twenty-five hours a week at the local cleaner's and spent the rest of her time being a mother to her children.

Gina had seen her often since her return back home. And though their exchanges had not gone beyond "hey", she knew Monique could give her some insight. Gina would use Kanisha's party as an excuse to ring her bell. Ask about public assistance when the time came.

They had never been close, but as Gina stood at the side door of Monique's house, the delightful surprise on Monique spoke of possibility.

"Gina?"

"Hi, Monique. How you doing?"

"Living. What's up?"

It took a moment for Gina to put the woman before her with the stuck-up, snobby little girl she used to torment whenever the chance hit.

"I'm giving my daughter a party this Saturday. I've seen your kids around. I wanted to invite them."

"Well, ain't that sweet."

Ain't? Gina didn't even know Monique knew the word. She looked at her, seeing her in a new light. "Can I come in for a minute?"

"Sure, come on." She looked around her. "Where's Kanisha?"

Gina didn't think Monique even knew her daughter's name. "Oh, I left her home watching cartoons."

"Well, next time bring her," Monique answered, opening the screen door wide. "People on this block is so damn funny."

"I know what you mean," Gina answered, stepping into the house. "I sent Kanisha over to Miss Mason's house, figuring she could play with her grandchildren. Kanisha wasn't back home in ten seconds."

"Girl, these old folks are a trip."

Gina knew she had just made a new friend.

* * *

It was late. Past noon. Sunday. Frieda lay in Barry's bed hearing him banging pots in his kitchen. She knew he was cooking her up a breakfast. She also knew she should at least get up, brush her teeth, wash her face before she ate. But the feeling of lying in bed, late on a Sunday, with not a drop of work ahead of her for the next eight days was intoxicating.

She didn't want to move anything more than her leg that was gliding along the cool, tight space on Barry's side.

She could not remember the last time she had stayed the night at his place. Could not remember the last time she had roamed around the three-bedroom house with the nice backyard and the in-ground pool.

That she couldn't recall the last time she had taken a dip in the pool, felt him close to her as they skinny-dipped, was a real crime. But she had, last night. Music playing on the CD player and backyard lights off, she had stripped down to her birthday suit and jumped in, Barry a heartbeat behind her.

The night swim felt good. The feel of cool, crisp water moving along every inch of her body, even better. There had been such a freedom in that motion as she swam beneath the surface, the glow of the underwater pool lights making everything soft, surreal.

She didn't mind that anyone with good vision or a pair of binoculars could see all that her mommy and daddy gave her. She had laughed hard and loud when she spied the blind of a window behind the house move a few times when they got out of the water.

"You like?" Barry had shouted toward it, his own body bare, penis halfway to a hard-on. "Well, I sure damn do."

"You're bad," Frieda had warned, unable to keep her eyes off him. Pool water clung to him in sparkly drips, his penis growing longer, thicker with every beat of his heart.

"Let me show you how bad I am," Barry had decided, reaching for her, pulling her back into the water, easing her back against the cement edge as he went down. Down under the water, down on her, first contact pulling such a moan from her throat she was certain her own momma heard five miles away.

Frieda tried to be quiet. Tried to keep the sighs and the pleasure from leaving her throat, but she couldn't. And as she came under the night stars, half a dozen blinds and curtains flickering and moving, opening and closing, she didn't care one bit.

Now huddled under the sheet, Frieda was lost to the memory when she felt the bed shake.

"Wake up, sleepyhead. Breakfast is served." She forced an eye open, saw the breakfast tray laden with French toast sprinkled with powdered sugar. Bacon fried up crisp. She didn't see the coffee, but she could smell it as a hunger she didn't even know she had awakened.

"Can I eat now?" she asked.

"That's the idea."

"I haven't brushed my teeth, or showered or anything."

"Don't you know breakfast in bed doesn't require that?"

She sat up, the sheet falling away from her shoulders, pooling at her waist. She reached for the tray, brought it to her lap, picked up a fork and saw the French toast already cut into squares. "You really know how to do it up right, don't you?"

"Well, when you're with El Excelente, there's not much choice."

She speared a piece of French toast. "Am I that bad, Barry?"

"Nah. But for a hot minute, you had me really worried. I was about to change your name to the B word."

"Work."

He put a finger to her lip, hushing her. "Not here and not now, okay? I got you for a whole eight days. I want this time to be about us."

Good times were meant for sharing. Frieda gave Dajah a call, inviting her and Rick over Thursday night after work. "I remember it's his day off, and I'm telling you there is nothing like swimming at night. Barry's going to heat up the grill. He's gonna do steak, shrimp. And if you get here before dark, you know he gets an incredible view of the sunset."

Which was an absolute truth.

Barry lived near the wide-open spaces of JFK Airport. There was a huge space between the houses on the next block behind him, and the view was all sky. Cookout. Hanging with her best friend. Chilling in the pool with Rick. There was no way Dajah could say no.

"I'll get right on it," she told Frieda. Hanging up, she called Rick. "Hey, Frieda and Barry invited us for an late-afternoon cookout on

Thursday. In-ground pool. Shrimps on the barbie, the whole nine yards, what do you say?"

Thursday he was taking Gina shopping. If he got there early, it wouldn't be a problem. "Sounds good. What time?"

"You can pick me up at six?"

"Six is good."

"And I do mean six, Rick. Not a minute after, not quarter after, but six."

"I'm going to surprise you. I'm going to get there early. In fact I am going to get there so early, I will be sitting in front of your house when you get in from work."

"Really?"

"You can take it to the bank."

He called Gina when he got off the phone with Dajah. "We have to change the shopping to Wednesday."

Gina would have asked why, but she was broke. The sooner she saw Rick and got her hands on that money, the better. "Around noon?"

"Works for me. How's Kanisha?"

"She fine."

"She awake?"

"Right here. Hold on."

"They ain't got shit," Gina was saying days later as she stood in the party aisle of Toys "R" Us, looking over the decorations.

"What are you talking about? They have a ton of stuff."

"Yeah, but she wants Harry Potter and they don't have any."

"Kanisha, how about the Little Mermaid?" Rick asked.

"Dat's old. I want Harry Potter."

He could see the wheels in Gina's head turning. She would want to go someplace else. Someplace that would take more time from his day, and he had a very important appointment in an hour and a half.

"There's this other place out in Hempstead."

Rick shook his head. "No."

"But they don't have the Potter stuff."

"I understand all that, but I have someplace to be and soon."

"Since when some bitch becomes more important than your own child?"

Her words stung so hard and so deep that Rick felt the hairs rise on the back of his neck. He checked himself. Remembered where he was. Felt his daughter beside him. Her gaze. Swallowed down his anger. "Number one, she's not a bitch and number two, it has nothing to do with her."

"So where you got to be then?"

Rick thought about telling. Decided against it. It had to be played right. "Somewhere, all you need to know."

"So what am I suppose to do about decorations?"

"Buy what's here or don't get nothing."

"I want Harry Potter, Daddy."

He looked at his daughter, eyes plaintive. "We don't always get what we want. Sometimes we have to make do with what we have, understand?" She nodded her head, but solemnly and reluctant. "Look, you're getting a big old party and a very special surprise."

Her eyes lit up. "I am?"

"Sure are. But the only way you can get it is if you pick what's here."

She looked at the available decorations. Looked at her father. Went back to the decorations. Decided on the Power Puff Girls. "These," she said, handing the party pack to her mother.

"Power Puff Girls it is," Rick said, grabbing extra packs of cups and cake plates.

After Toys "R" Us they made a stop by the bakery to order the cake. They purchased packages of hot dogs, buns, soda, potato chips, pretzels, napkins and forks. Rick slipped away and paid for the Jeep. He would pick it up early Saturday morning, keeping it a surprise.

They went to Gap Kids to get Kanisha a new outfit. Stopped at Foot Locker and bought her a new pair of sneakers and summer sandals. Gina tried to get Rick to buy her something, but he flatly refused.

They were nearing her house when she asked about money.

"I just gave you a couple hundred a few weeks ago."

"I know, but I'm broke."

He shook his head. "Me too. Spent all I had today."

"Ni—" She caught herself. Swallowed the rest of the word, angry. On fire. "You ain't even broke. You got money."

"I don't have any on me."

"Well stop at the ATM."

"I don't have time." Which was the truth. He had just enough time to drop them and run home. Shower and change his clothes for his appointment.

"So what are we suppose to do?"

"Daddy, I'm hungry," Kanisha piped from the back.

"I'll take you to the drive thru at McDonald's."

Errands over, appointment done, Rick eased out of his dress shirt and nice slacks and sat on the edge of his bed in his boxers.

He looked around the room that had witnessed so much in his life, some good, most bad. But he was about to turn a new page, get a new lease on life. The thought brought a smile to his lips.

He had taken his whole existence and tossed it into the air. Now that the pieces had settled, they weren't presenting a bad picture at all. There had been some rough moments, but what would life be without them? You had to have some bad to appreciate the good. Needed a little rain to appreciate those sunny days. His life with Gina had prepared him for the one he was having with Dajah.

Dajah, sweet, sweet Dajah.

Tomorrow they were going to Barry's house for that afternoon of poolside fun. Rick wondered how she'd look in a bikini. Couldn't wait to find out.

Chapter 13

When Dajah had talked about an in-ground pool and a slamming view of the sunset, Rick had envisioned a stately two-story colonial with columns that ran from the first floor to the second. But what he thought and what he saw were two separate things.

Barry's house turned out to be a ranch, an okay-looking ranch with grass that needed cutting and hedges that needed pruning. The aluminum of the gate had faded to a dull gray, and the sidewalk leading up to his house had more than a few cracks. At first glance it just looked regular.

But when Barry opened the door, Frieda at his side and a blast of cool air rushed Rick, he'd had his first indication that looks could be deceiving. No doubt there was central air conditioning blowing about.

The layout of the house was simple. There was a small foyer, a bedroom/study off to the left with dark wood bookshelves and an overstuffed reading chair. The living room had a coffee table made from a tree limb, an area rug of sheep's wool and a extra-long brown leather couch.

Railroad tracked behind it was the dining room that housed a glass tabletop and four wrought-iron chairs. Off to the left of that was the kitchen, painted in black and white, two bedrooms and a bathroom.

The walls were done in a clayish-white with a smattering of lithographs in oversized frames. Sunlight pouring in from the front and back gave the whole house an open, airy feel.

But the real delight was the backyard. Inlaid river stones, flat and smoothed at the top, made a wandering lane to the in-ground pool. The diving board told Rick it had a deep end.

Planted palms swayed along the walkway, keeping sentry over a four-foot edging of grass. Torch lamps with blackened tips sat unlit in the corners. The grill was brick, complete with what looked like a smoking box.

The patio furniture had lush padded seats and not an inch of gathered dirt in any of its crevices. "Mi casa," Barry said, watching the amazement in Rick's eyes.

"I had no idea all this was back here."

"That's the point. You drive by the front of my house, and folks think it's nothing special. Got to be careful these days, you know, so many player-haters. So I keep the front looking on the down low. But inside and beyond?"

"I hear you," Rick uttered as the four of them settled into chairs and began filling their plates. Rick's steak was a little too rare for his liking, but as he took a bite, then another, he could not deny it was some of the best seared beef he had had in a while.

As the meal settled in their stomachs and they were bringing glasses of Chardonnay to their lips, Rick couldn't help but ask, "How did you get this?"

Barry wiped his mouth, his fingers. Tossed the napkin aside. "Hard work and some serious planning. The house I got it for little or nothing. It was just a run-down ranch that needed a ton of love. It had been vandalized. Copper pipes gone, radiators ripped out. You name it and it had been stolen. But that"—he pointed toward the pool— "now that was a king's ransom and then some. I had to get all kind of permits. Between my water bill and the pool taxes, I could finance a car. But you know, after a hard day at work, there is nothing like coming back here and seeing what all my hard work is for."

"I hear you," Rick said again with a nod of his head.

A slice of brilliance filled the background, hot, orange and bright. Everyone squinted as it surrounded them. Everyone except Dajah.

She closed her eyes, lifted her face and breathed deeply, as if the golden rays could be inhaled.

"There she go, y'all," Frieda joked, watching her friend take her moment, privately, personally, uncaring that no one else got it the way she did. They didn't. But there was such a reverence in her, such a soft, sweet energy buzzing through her, they had no choice but to respect it.

It didn't last long, the brilliance fading soft but swift. Dajah smiled, opening her eyes. She picked up her wine and raised it high. She looked at the three faces around her, nodded and drank deep.

It was hard telling that the four people in the pool were over twenty-one. Hard to tell by the giggles, the splashing, the screams, the dunking. What gave them away was the subtle body language, the expressions that over faces as hands brushed buttocks, feet slid across a thigh; a gentle fire came into the mix as the group broke off into twos, each pair heading into the opposite end of the pool.

Dajah rested against Rick's chest, feet in front of her, treading the water lightly. She could hear Frieda's giddy, surprised whispers of "Don't you dare" and "We got company" coming from the deep end. Dajah wondered just how far they would go.

There was no doubt the backyard was filled with sexual tension. Warm, wet, near humid, it hung in the air about them, entering Dajah's lungs with every breath she took.

She could feel Rick hard behind her. Allowed the motion of her legs to make and break contact with him. His hands were up under her breasts, holding her steady, but she could feel them tingling for one real good touch.

Rushing water met her ears. Voices made both her and Rick turn their heads. They saw Frieda and Barry standing, water turning the stones beneath their feet dark. "We are going to head into the house. You two just stay back here and chill as long as you like," Barry offered.

Frieda gave a goofy grin, adding a wave as they moved past them.

"Just us," Rick whispered into her ear as the back door closed.

"Yeah. Just us."

One thumb made contact with her nipple, a slow drag of finger across its hard, gnarly surface. She opened her mouth to protest, but none came, allowing him to turn her toward him, his mouth finding hers.

Still Dajah had never done it outside. Certainly not in her friend's boyfriend's pool. As much as she wanted to, as much as a yes seemed just a heartbeat away, she broke away when Rick's fingers found the waistband of her Tankini.

"Uh-uh," she warned, water seducing every nerve ending she owned.

"What do you think they're doing?"

"I don't care what they're doing. We're not doing it here."

"Even if I said I want you so bad, just the sight of you—"

"Even." She looked around her. "Anybody could see and nobody needs to."

"So what am I supposed to do?"

Her smile came quick. "Some laps." Then she disappeared under the water, reemerging at the opposite side.

Frieda and Barry didn't know what to expect as they peeked out the bedroom window fifteen minutes after they came inside, but the last thing they expected was to see Rick and Dajah having lap races.

"Are they racing?" she asked.

"Looks like they are."

She gave Barry a smile full of conspiracy. "They don't know what they missed." They left the bedroom and went through the kitchen, Frieda picking up the key lime pie. "Anybody for dessert?" She asked as she stepped down onto the flagstones, the creamy delight in her hands.

It was hard to say good night.

Rick started by getting up from the table, saying he'd had a great time, which began a three-minute conversation about how they needed to do it again. Then there was a stop in the kitchen for leftovers, which led to conversations about what Barry used in his marinade.

They made it as far as the living room, but track trophies halted the journey as Rick asked Barry about his track history and Barry was all too happy to share it. Ten minutes after that, they moved down the front steps and headed to Rick's SUV.

It took another two minutes of hugging and late-night chatting before Rick and Dajah got inside and put on their seat belts. Twenty more seconds of praise for the wonderful evening before Frieda and Barry stepped back, gave a wave and Rick was able to pull away.

"I should be dead tired," Dajah decided, the digital clock on the dash saying quarter to one. She looked at him. "But I'm not."

"Because the night's not finished."

Dajah knew Rick was absolutely right.

They barely got the upstairs door closed before they were removing shirts and shorts, over each other as if they were both new discoveries. They were hot, on fire, determined to quench every thirst. Rick was inside of her less than two minutes before she was coming, he right behind her.

It wasn't enough.

They both knew it. Rick headed to the bathroom to dispose of the condom. He reappeared at the bedroom door, a strange look on his face. "Think you better go to the bathroom."

"Why?"

"Either you've just turned into a virgin, or you just got your period."

Dajah got up.

Friday morning Gina sat on her bed going through her Coach bag looking for a miracle. She had served herself and Kanisha some of the hot dogs for the party yesterday but could not stand the thought that hot dogs were all they had to eat.

While her mother had silently changed the rules about eating whatever food was in the house, Gina couldn't bring herself to do that anymore because every time she did, it felt as if every bad thing her mother thought of her was true.

There had been times when she found five or ten dollars in the ripped lining of her pocketbook. But that had been when money was never really an issue. When the search yielded forty-seven cents, she decided to go through her wallet again.

She pulled out her Blockbuster card, old phone numbers and her picture ID. She was about to put it all back when another card caught her attention. Blue and white, with the funny little logo in the corner, she couldn't believe she had forgotten about it.

Or that Rick had.

She laughed, high pitched and loud. Jumped and did a dance, the ATM card in her hand. Gina brought it to her lips and kissed it twice, then slipped it back into her wallet and told Kanisha to go put on some clothes.

Gina stood in the alcove of the bank, card in hand, hesitant.

What if the machine ate it? What if Rick had reported the card stolen, or it had been deactivated. Though she had a card, the account was in his name. He had given it to her so long ago that she had forgotten she even possessed it.

She could feel a line of people behind her. Mentally remembered the code. Zero seven zero nine, a numeric for Kanisha's birthday. Gina swallowed. Slipped in the card. Watched the screen, certain it would implicate her.

But it didn't. It asked for her PIN number. She put it in. It gave her choices in increments of twenty. She knew she had to be careful. Couldn't take too much. She requested forty, a weight coming off her shoulders as two twenties zipped out her way.

"No, girl," Frieda was saying that evening on the phone.

"Yes. Talk about embarrassed? Went to the bathroom. Wiped myself and all this blood."

"He used a condom, right?"

"No one gets entrance without it."

"You didn't know it was coming?"

"I knew it was coming, but it wasn't due for a few more days."

"Guess things got so hot last night, it stirred it up."

"Guess it did."

"Me and Barry have had some of the wildest times in that pool."

"So I saw. I really thought you two were going to do it right in front of us."

"If Barry had his way, he would of. He's a little freak, you know. But he's my freak. And as long as he's all mine, we cool."

"A part of me wanted to. Right there in the pool. Under the stars. You and Barry in the house. I know if I had said yes, Rick would have been all in it."

"We thought you two were."

"No, you didn't."

"Yes, we did. We were finished in a minute and we took showers to give you more time. We peeked out the window to see if it was safe to come out, and I see you and Rick having a lap race."

"Now, Frieda. As long as you've known me, did you really think I'd do something like that, there?"

"Me and Barry do all the time."

"All the time?"

"His yard. His water. His pool. Folks want to look, we say let them."

"Girl, you are wicked."

"No, I'm just trying to enjoy the rest of this vacation. I can't believe how much I've been missing out on. And the idea that I only have a few more days hurts."

"You can change it."

"We not going there."

"All right. I'll shut up. Thanks again for a great evening. Rick and I had a ball."

"Ain't no thing. We'll do it again."

"Hope so."

Tired from her previous evening out, Dajah called it an early night and went to bed around nine. Hours later the sound of her doorbell ringing woke her and she got up, went downstairs and let Rick in.

She wasn't certain if he would come by tonight but was very glad he had. Ice cream was the last thing Dajah expected, but she took the bag from him, spying the Baskin-Robbins logo. "Ice cream?"

"Figured it would help. That maybe you might have cramps."

He considered her discomfort, had not stayed away during her menses, and that touched her deeply. The fact that he thought ice cream would help menstrual cramps made her smile. "Ice cream, Rick?"

"My mother and sister swore by it. I can't tell you how many late-night runs my father used to make."

"Midol, sure. Pamprin, definitely. But I never heard of ice cream." She looked at the bag. "But I appreciate the thought." Looked inside. "Butter Pecan. How did you know?"

"You have a kind of butter-pecan personality, that's why. Caramel. Sweet, with a few nuts tossed in."

"Oh, you are funny." She headed toward the kitchen. "One spoon or two?"

"One. I like my ice cream real basic."

"What? Vanilla?"

"Keep it simple, I say."

Dajah laughed as she searched a drawer for a spoon. "Somehow I'm not surprised." Found one. "Well, for the record I don't have cramps. At least not anymore, but I'm sure going to do justice to this ice cream. Baskin-Robbins? You're definitely after my heart."

Magic word sprinkled with fairy dust, her proclamation warmed Rick all over. They had been together on a regular basis, but it was the first indication that Dajah was willing to take things as far as they could go.

He took a seat on her sofa, Dajah going to the opposite end. "Why are you all the way over there?"

"No reason."

"Well, come on over here and keep a bro—I mean, keep me company."

She went. Snuggled into the crook of his arm. Took the lid off the ice cream as he picked up the remote and turned on the TV.

"Kanisha's party is tomorrow," he said softly. "I can't bring you."

"Oh."

"I would if I could, but the last thing I need is more static."

"I understand. I will get to meet her one day, won't I?"

Rick's face turned up, surprised that Dajah was even asking. "Of course you will."

"No idea when, right?"

"Soon enough," he answered with a yawn, one hand landing softly on her thigh. "So am I going or staying?"

"If you don't mind, I don't mind."

"Don't mind," he answered, slipping off his shoes.

* * *

"Hold still, Kanisha." Gina was saying the next day, trying to keep her voice even. She was trying hard not to wrench the fistful of hair she was holding, but Kanisha couldn't keep still and stillness was required for the perfect part.

This day required that her daughter looked perfect.

Gina was determined to show people that she could handle her business and did. She was determined to make Kanisha the prettiest little five-year-old that ever had a birthday party. She had bought a disposable camera and everything to capture the moment, and Kanisha's antsiness was starting to work on her nerves.

"Look, girl," Gina found herself warning as the edge of the comb slipped off Kanisha's forehead. "You want to look nice today or sloppy?"

"Nice."

"Then sit still and let me do this hair, damn."

Kanisha did and when the hair was done, she stood before her mother for a final inspection. Gina adjusted a pink ruffled-lace sock, the fit of the front of the denim halter. She slicked down a bit of unruly eyebrow with spit and her finger. Nodded.

"Okay, let's go outside and take some pictures."

The party Gina had imagined in her head did not quite meet the reality. While she had purchased quite a few rolls of party streamers, she discovered that there was no place to stream them from and had to make do along the wooden fence.

There was an art to laying them, and Gina's effort looked sad to her as she took in loops of various sizes. She had purchased a helium balloon kit, but half of them had escaped to the sky when she tried to fasten the ribbons on the end.

The mismatched chairs pulled from the basement looked skuzzy, and the handful of plastic lawn chairs were permanently stained in the seat. Nothing could get out the gray. The card tables leaned to one side, and the legs on them were rusty.

Gina didn't think to rent tables and chairs. She never thought that her mother would only let her use the raggedy ones, but her mother had given a firm no when Gina asked for use of the ones from the kitchen.

Outside of the tablecloth, the large sheet cake and the Power Puff cups, plates and napkins, the driveway looked cheesy. Not what she had in mind at all. *Got to do better*, she was thinking when Monique came through the gate, her two children in tow.

While her neighbors never allowed their children and grandchildren to play with Kanisha, the sound of an outdoor birthday party changed the rules. It started with two little faces standing at the gate, staring, taking in the balloons, the music and the smell of grilling hot dogs.

"Y'all want to come in?" Gina asked.

"I got to go ask my Nana," the oldest of the two said.

"Well, go ahead. Tell her it's outside. A birthday for Kanisha."

They took off and came back within three minutes, with three additional kids. "My Nana say we can come in, and my friends Asia, Deon and Jamal, said their mommas said they can come in too, if it's all right with you?"

"It's all right. Come on in."

The five little bodies entered the yard, slowly, leery. They stopped five feet from the huge sheet cake, eyes dancing over the potato chips and cheese doodles.

"Go ahead, help yourself and introduce yourself to the birthday girl."

Kanisha, who had been blowing bubbles with Monique's two children, glanced upon the new arrivals like a home invasion. She stared, defiant at their presence. "Kanisha, come on and say hello to your guests," Gina insisted.

But in Kanisha's eyes they weren't guests. They were the children who had told her no, they couldn't come out and play, only to be running out and about three minutes after she had left their front doors. They were the ones who whispered behind her back and giggled to themselves whenever she passed. They were enemies. Kanisha would not move.

Besides, she liked Elliot and Claire just fine. Claire was the same age as she was and Elliot just a year younger, and their momma liked her momma.

"Go on, Kanisha, go introduce yourself." The wine cooler in Gina's mother's hand had taken off the hard edge she had had earlier that day, and Kanisha saw some gray area in which she could possibility get defiant.

"Why?"

The simple word coming from her daughter's mouth made Gina turn all the way around in her chair. She stared, mouth opened, in utter surprise, seeing the hostility in her child's eyes. She understood it and with every bone in her body wanted to respect it. But she had been raising Kanisha slackly long enough. It was time to instill some home training.

"Because they came to your party, that's why, and you can't be having strangers at your birthday party."

Kanisha lifted one palm, flipped it their way. "Hey."

"Hey," came the chorus.

"You got any more of them bubbles?" asked the oldest.

Gina put her wine cooler down, got up and reached into the Toys "R" Us bag, pulling out bottles in the colors of the rainbow. "Help yourself," she insisted, turning away, her eyes fast on Monique's with a knowing smirk.

Rick's mother and father had never been to Gina's mother's house, but Gina had been to theirs. She knew they would not be impressed with the wooden fence with spokes missing, or the washboard-gray color the unpainted boards had turned.

She knew the scrubby weeds running down the middle of the drive would not win her any brownie points nor would the mismatched chairs she had gathered for the occasion. What she hoped would impress them was how cute Kanisha looked in her tiny denim skirt and matching halter top.

On a twenty-year-old, it looked fine. On a five-year-old, it looked too grown. That was what Rick's mother and father thought as they spied their only grandchild munching a hot dog at the lopsided table, Gina drawing a long sip off a wine cooler.

They were disappointed that Rick hadn't arrived yet. They needed him to be an icebreaker, the usual go-between between themselves and the woman he chose to mother his child.

Gina put the bottle down and got up, a fake smile filling her lips that could never touch her eyes. "Hi, Mr. and Mrs. Trimmons. Come on in." She turned her head. "Kanisha, come say hello to your granny and granddaddy."

Kanisha turned, mustard smearing a cheek. She dropped the hot dog, got up from her chair and raced to her grandparents, her eyes on the four presents in their hand. "What you get me?"

"Kanisha. Is that anyway to say hello?" Mrs. Trimmons wanted to know.

"Sorry, Granny. Hello."

"Better." Mrs. Trimmons bent down and gave her grandchild a kiss. Mr. Trimmons' eyes were on the battered fence, the poorly hung decorations. "Now did you say hello to granddaddy?"

She tugged a hand, getting his attention. "Hello, Granddaddy."

"Well, hello, baby. Happy birthday," he answered, extending the gifts her way. "Your father here?"

"Not yet. He'll be here soon." Mouth of babes, Mr. Trimmons thought when the SUV pulled up to the curb a minute later.

"Skeezer got a friend?" Nelson asked Rick from the passenger seat, taking in Gina and Monique.

"Guess so." Rick looked at his watch. Whistled. It was already twenty after one. He had planned to get there early, but Nelson had called needing a ride. "Benz in the shop," he told him. So he had to go by and pick up Nelson plus the mini Jeep.

They got out, both of them calling out to Rick's parents as they rounded the back and together took out the gift.

"This bad boy weighs a ton."

"And it cost a small fortune," Rick shared. But the sight of his daughter racing toward him with a thousand stars in her eyes made every penny worthwhile.

"That's mine?" was all Kanisha wanted to know.

"Sure is."

"Can I ride it?" Rick looked at the gathering of children. Did the math. One Jeep, eight kids. He smiled softly as he shook his head and told a white lie. "Battery has to be charged. We'll take it for a spin tomorrow."

"Can I sit in it?"

"You sure can." Rick watched as the thin little legs climbed in, joy filling him as Kanisha sat tall behind the wheel.

"Let me get a picture," Gina called, getting the camera. Without thought Rick dropped down beside Kanisha and looped his arm around her shoulder, a Kodak moment in the making.

It took a minute for Rick to realize something was wrong. Tarika, Gina's main girl, was missing in action. He looked around him. "Where's Tarika?"

Gina rolled her eyes. "Hell if I know." But the truth was Tarika had flipped the switch on her. Suddenly the things they used to do—get high and listen to music, no longer suited Tarika. She was changing, and Gina wasn't happy with the transition.

Monique filled the gap. More times than not Gina found herself down at her place, sharing forties and smoking weed. Now as she took in her newfound friend trying to make headway with Nelson, Gina wanted to tell her not to waste her time.

In her opinion Nelson was as phony as a three-dollar bill. He'd never have any use for a woman as real as Monique. But she smiled at her friend's attempt, gave her kudos for trying.

Rick sipped his soda and finished off the rest of his hot dog. Saw the curtain in the side window move for the fifth time since he had sat down. He knew it was Gina's mother and could only surmise why she hadn't come out to join the party. He noticed his father standing by the fence. "Dad, you can have a seat."

"I'm all right, son," his father answered.

Rick looked at his watch. Saw more time had slipped away. "Gina, we're going to have to do the cake. I got to go."

"Ain't no rush here."

"You know I have to go to work."

"Well boo-hoo on you. The cake get done when I say it get done."

Rick glared at her, embarrassed and hot. He was embarrassed because both his mother and Nelson were sitting in earshot. He was hot because he wanted to be by Kanisha's side when she blew out the candles.

Then he remembered his Plan, the idea a bit of sunshine in the quick gloom. Gina may have won this battle, but Rick was certain that in a few months he would have won the war.

Kanisha didn't want him to leave. Rick didn't want to go either, but he was on the clock and beyond dropping Nelson back home, he had to get to work. Still, he didn't try too hard to pry her small arms from around his neck, held her as tight as she held him when it was time to say good-bye.

"I'll come by tomorrow and we'll take your new ride to the park, all right?"

Kanisha nodded and let her father go.

Chapter 14

The wandering Jew plant had started out as a seven-inch cutting, half the width of a pencil and too flexible to stand up on its own. Now it was a waterfall of green, rushing and spilling three feet across the hardwood with thick strands inching atop the double window.

It had birthed a dozen other clippings Dajah had given away, becoming plants with new homes in different parts of Queens and even in Long island. She had been stepping over the wandering trail along the floor for weeks, resisting the urge to cut it. But the time had come.

Shears in hand, she grabbed the end, found the niche between the leaf and the stalk and snipped. It hurt that the cutting would go into the garbage, but she had no more room for another plant and knew no one else who would want it.

What didn't hurt, bother her or mess with her head was the fact that at that very moment Rick was with his daughter and Gina at the party. No angst visited her, no concern claimed her. Dajah was okay.

A part of her did want to be invited, but Dajah understood that such moments would take time to occur. No doubt next year she'd be there, or if not, the year after. Dajah had finally settled into where she fitted in Rick's life.

She felt good about him. Good about them being together. Dragons slain, she was certain that they would be just fine. Last night, proved it. Last night, when he had held her until she fell asleep, she knew it was more than a sex thing. That it was a heart thing.

Her life had hit a balance, and it freed up those parts she had put in restraints. She hadn't called her folks just to say hey, unable to risk disclosure of how her life had been. But she could now and did.

She called home, her mother coming on the line. "Hi, Mom."

"Dajah?"

"Yeah, it's me."

"Everything okay? Haven't heard from you in a while."

"Everything's fine."

"That's what your father said, but I felt like something was wrong."

"Just fine. How have you been doing?"

"Oh, I've been okay."

"Good. Daddy there?"

"He's in the basement. Hold on. I'll get him."

"I told your mother you were still living and breathing," her father said half a minute later. "Told her no, don't be calling her up. When she ready to talk, she'll call us."

Her father had always understood her best, something that Dajah appreciated over the years. She had worked hard to gain an independence from her parents, and while her mother had been reluctant to let the apron strings go, her father never tried to stop it.

"So, how have you been?" she asked.

"Question is, how have you been? Haven't heard from you in a while."

"Been living, I guess."

"Living, living or *living?*"

This was the part she was happy to reveal, the sweet icing on her cake. "*Living.* I met somebody new. His name's Rick."

"Rick?"

"His real name is Reynaldo, Reynaldo Trimmons."

"Trimmons. That name sounds familiar. Where is he from?"

Truth was, she didn't know. She only knew where he lived now. Told her father so.

"So, you haven't met his folks."

"No, Daddy. We just started seeing each other."

"But we're going to get a chance to meet him, right?"

"Sure."

"Looking forward to it. I know it's been a while since David. Have to admit I was a little concerned."

"Well, there's no need to be. Life is treating me good."

"Glad to hear it. Looking forward to meeting him. Don't keep us waiting too long."

"I won't. Talk to you soon." Dajah hung up and dialed David. She got the answering machine but didn't leave a message. For over a year they had been cool like that, but a final end had come to them. He was off living his life and she, finally, was living hers.

She made a call to Frieda to see what she was up to, but Frieda was gone too. There was a ton of other things she could do this day, all of it labor-intensive. With a sigh she headed for her laundry hamper and began sorting clothes for the Laundromat.

The bus lumbered down Liberty Avenue, full of mothers in their Sunday finest and antsy children in bow ties that scratched and lace-edged dresses that itched. Along the route various storefront churches were opening their doors to their congregation, organs, snare drums and amplified gospel singing slipping through.

Tarika sat on the bus, the heavy New York Times against her legs. She looked down at her fingers and saw the ink smears, realizing too late that she should have asked for a bag. The fact that she had to take two buses just to get the Sunday Times spoke volumes about not only how she lived but where.

Her neighborhood did not boast the rolling-lawn lushness of Valley Stream, nor could it hold a candle to the idyllic splendor of Forest Hills. Still, there were people in her neighborhood who made enough to live in those places. Tarika wanted to be one of them.

With an education that stopped at the tenth grade, she possessed neither a high school diploma nor a GED. But she was good with numbers and had possessed a secret love for science. At fifteen she hadn't seen the need for a good education, but at twenty-three suddenly it was all she knew.

She wanted better; she wanted different. She wanted out of the gloom of her uncle's basement and into the bright sunshine of a place of her own, Sha-Keem's words haunting her. She did love him with all her heart, but a drug-dealing thug did not fit into the picture she was conjuring up for a new life.

She did deserve someone better than him. Did deserve something better for herself. Lying around smoking tree and guzzling forties with Gina wasn't going to make it happen. Spending her days watching talk shows in the dismal darkness of her uncle's basement wasn't going to do it either.

That was the reason Tarika had awakened early Sunday morning, took a shower, pressed her clothes and got dressed. It was the reason she hopped the bus to the main bus terminal, paying two dollars for the Sunday Times.

She had seen the ads on television. Knew the Times was full of jobs. Even without a high school degree, she was sure she could find something somewhere. The first step was to start looking.

She got off the bus and headed home. Let herself into the side door and down the stairs. She clicked on the table lamp and sat on her bed. Found a pen and a piece of paper, started her search.

She wasn't even a fourth of the way through the thousands of ads, most of which she didn't qualify for, when there was a knock on her window. She stared at the two pair of legs outside the dirty pane and debated about answering. She did.

"How come you didn't show?" Gina asked, the famous brown bag in her hand.

"Show where?"

"Kanisha's party? You knew it was yesterday."

"I forgot."

"What you mean, you forgot?" Gina asked, moving past Tarika, Kanisha behind her.

"Just like I said. I forgot."

Tarika realized the Times was spread across her bed. Knew Gina would see it, ask her about it.

She had learned early in life that some dreams weren't meant to be shared. That there were people out there ready to cut any effort off at the knees before you could take a first step, Gina was one of them.

Tarika glided past Kanisha, slid past Gina. She made it to her bed, but Gina was right behind her. Even though Gina never read the

paper, she recognized the oversized sheets of newsprint. Gave Tarika
a bewildered look.

"Since when you read the Times?"

"Delivery boy made a mistake. Dropped it at our front door. I was
just going through it."

"Why?"

"Ain't nothing else to do."

Gina took a seat. Kanisha went to the old unused stove. Turning
the knobs, she began making imaginary food. "You got paper?" Gina
asked, glancing up from her pocketbook search.

Tarika shook her head no. She had run out the last time Gina had
been there. Saw no need to buy more.

"You ain't got no damn paper?"

"Uh-unh."

"Go bum a cigarette from your uncle."

"He's not home."

"His car's outside."

"He took a bus trip to Atlantic City."

Gina looked at the package of marijuana she had pulled out of her
bag. "Damn." Put it back. She picked up the malt liquor and un-
screwed the cap. Took a long pull. Urged it Tarika's way. Tarika de-
clined.

"What is up with you?" Gina asked, hostile. "Just what the fuck is
up?" She had tried to make it unimportant when Tarika didn't show
for Kanisha's party. Tried to act as if she didn't care. But she did care,
deep inside where all the important things mattered. She and Tarika
had been tight since forever.

"I'm just not down with that anymore. I want more than getting
high and laying around doing nothing."

Gina looked at her, stunned. The initial surprise went to disbelief,
a crumpled laugh left her mouth. "Since when?"

"I just don't want to live like this no more. I want to do something
with my life."

"Oh, so I guess what I do ain't good enough for you no more?"
When Tarika looked away, Gina knew the answer. "Well, fuck you,
Tarika. Fuck you, talking all this shit about what you don't want. After
all the shit we been through, all I've done for your broke, ignorant
ass, and you telling me you ain't down with me no more. How many

times I fed your ass, clothed your ass? Sharing my shit with you like you my sister?"

Tarika said nothing. Just sat, watching Gina, her tirade. She felt the hurt beneath it all and the anger, two dangerous emotions. Gina had never swung at her, but she knew the power of those hands. Decided then that she would fight back, if it came to it.

"How you gonna tell me that? Mother-fucker, I should beat you down for even considering it." She had moved closer, a mere four feet separating them.

Tarika swallowed. She had taken the first step. Nothing, not even Gina, was going to prevent her from taking a second. "You want to fight me, Gina? Go ahead. Take your best shot, but it's not going to change a thing. It's not going to change me finding a job and getting out of this hellhole. It's not going to make me smoke tree with you, or drink that damn forty. So go ahead, beat me. I've been beat before."

Gina blinked, coming back to herself, confusion and anger falling away. She stared at Tarika, trying to find herself. Saw she was nowhere within her friend. Nowhere. She stepped back, looked off, a tear slipping from her eye. She wiped at it emphatically, her head shaking, the anger in her voice a memory. "You my girl, Tarika. You my girl. How you just gonna abandon me like this?"

In the corner, Kanisha stood wide-eyed and watchful, sensing the answers her mother sought.

Gina was in a foul mood by the time she got back home. She sat in her room, slugging down the forty, smoking the second of two joints. Her mother wasn't home, and Gina had no idea when she would return. But the wrath of Doreen Alexander couldn't hold a match to the hurt she was already feeling.

Tarika had plans, big plans, that did not include her. Tarika, her best friend, who had always had less than nothing, determined to take that nothing and make something. Odds against her, not a drop of backup, she was going for a new life. She had found goals and dreams when Gina wasn't looking and was leaving her by the wayside.

The doorbell rang.

Gina got up angry, bitter and not the least bit mellow. Looking out of the window pane, she saw Rick. Whipped the door open. "What the fuck you want?"

He could smell the malt liquor, the scent of burnt weed. Even without those signs, he could tell she wasn't straight by the glassiness of her eyes. "I came to get Kanisha. Take her Jeep for a spin."

"She ain't going," Gina decided, stepping back and closing the door.

Rick blocked it with his hand. "Wait, hold up."

But Gina wouldn't. She pushed her whole body against the wood until the cylinder met the metal. Turning the knob, she locked it. Staggered away.

Rick raised his hand to knock, but knew it would be futile. He stared at the wood door for a hot second before he turned, walked away too.

It took a while to get it, to understand, accept that Gina was back on her warpath. It took three phone calls and another visit before Rick came to the conclusion. But in the process of that discovery, Rick made another one.

He had found duality.

While he was upset with his inability to see his daughter, he had learned not to let that dismay show around Dajah. Every time he rang her doorbell, called her on the phone, he made an extra effort to show that everything was all right with his world.

His Plan helped. His Plan, feeling more surefire every day.

The only problem he foresaw was sharing it with Dajah. Rick tried to prepare himself for the uphill battle it no doubt would be. He hoped she saw the merit in it, that she would believe it was doable.

Hurt and betrayal made Gina depressed. Anger at Rick made her vengeful.

She hadn't figured out all the specifics, only that Rick had changed everything about her life. Because of him, she was stuck at home with her mother and she had lost her best friend. Until Rick had kicked her to the curb, life had been fine.

For four days she simmered. For four days she stewed, until an idea came into her head and stayed.

Every other Thursday of the month, Rick got paid. Every other

Thursday of the month, a total of thirteen hundred and twelve dollars and four cents was automatically deposited into his account.

Today was Thursday.

Gina had been making small withdrawals with the ATM card for over a week, twenty dollars here, ten dollars there. She knew he didn't pay much attention to his monthly statements, and the money she'd taken would hardly be missed.

But now as she stood at the ATM, she was defiant.

She checked the balance and withdrew nearly all of it; eighteen hundred dollars, hers. She had no real idea what she would do with all the money but that didn't stop her from slipping the bills into her bag. It did not stop her from turning toward her daughter and asking if she was hungry. It did not stop her from catching a gypsy cab and going out to Hillside Avenue for a meal at IHOP, then on to Jamaica Avenue for a shopping spree.

Gina was unstoppable.

The ATM was taking too long.

Rick stood at the machine, mindful of Dajah in the car and the movie that would be starting in fifteen minutes.

A few flashes on the screen and normally the money would be sliding out the little slot. But the green light was flickering as if it had the hiccups, and Rick knew it wasn't good. His thoughts were confirmed as words appeared on the screen. Insufficient Funds. Request Denied.

"What?" Rick stared at the terminal. His card zipped out at him, and he immediately stuck it back in. Punching in his code as if he was killing ants, he requested fifty dollars, refusing to believe that the money wasn't there. Again, the message: Insufficient Funds.

Insufficient Funds, hell. Today was payday.

The screen asked if he wanted another transaction. He punched the yes button. Asked for his balance. Could not believe the digits that came up. He could not believe the system was saying he had exactly three dollars and twelve cents.

Picking up the phone, he waited for an operator. Gave his account number, his PIN and Social Security number. He asked about transactions, nearly fainting when he was told a withdrawal for eighteen hundred had been made earlier that day.

"If you are not aware of this transaction, we can investigate it for you, sir."

But there was no need. He knew who had taken his money. Rick could not believe he had forgotten about that ATM card Gina had. He sighed hard. "No, that's all right. Thank you."

He hung up, the ten bucks he had in his wallet all he had.

Rick's parents didn't believe in credit cards. Every purchase they had ever made had been done with cash or a bank loan. Rick had taken their example and made it his own. Every time a credit application came in the mail, he tossed it into the garbage. But in this moment, he wished he had had at least one.

Heading back to the car, he plopped into the driver's seat and slammed the door so hard it made Dajah wince. "Something wrong?"

"Yeah."

"What?"

"She cleaned me out."

"Who?"

"Who you think?"

"Gina?"

Rick took a deep breath, let it go. "Had eighteen hundred, and now I don't have four bucks."

"I have money," was what Dajah supplied.

"What?"

"I said I have money, for the movies."

"The movies? You can't be serious."

"Isn't that what we're supposed to be doing, going to the movies?"

"Fuck the movies, Dajah. Didn't you hear? I was just ripped off."

Her neck swerved. "Who you think you talking to?"

"What?"

"I said who do you think you talking to?"

It took a second or two for Rick to understand. Get it. Concede. "I'm sorry." He shook his head. "Didn't mean to jump all over you like that."

"But you did."

"I'm sorry, but damn, how could she do this to me?"

Dajah had an answer. Wouldn't supply it. "So what do you want to do now?"

"Go over there and wring her freaking neck."

"Besides that, what do you want to do? Press charges?"

"How can I? She had an authorized card . . . I forgot about it. I gave it to her like four years ago and she never once used it." His hand hit the steering wheel. "Damn."

"Well, I guess you better drop me off so you can go handle your business," she said, wearied.

It was her second indication of just what type of woman Gina was. The second eye-opener to the type of woman Rick had once wanted in his life. Dajah had understood the circumstances, and she now understood the pitfalls. Rick may have been finished with Gina, but by no means was Gina finished with Rick.

"Don't do nothing stupid," she warned when he pulled up to her place.

"I'm not."

"I mean it, Rick. I know it's everything you had, but it's not worth ending up in the same place you work, you getting my drift?" Dajah took his hand, pressed twenty dollars in it. "Not much, but maybe it will help."

"I can't take your money."

She stared at him, indignant. "You can when you don't have any."

But Rick was not having it. He could always borrow from Nelson. He gave the money back. "I'll be all right, really."

"You call me later," she demanded, leaning over, giving him a kiss. "And I meant what I said. Don't be stupid, Rick. It's not worth it."

But Dajah's advice wasn't getting anywhere close to his brain. First Gina denied him his child, then she stole his money. Two things that mattered to him most. She was in a whole heap of trouble.

Rick stared at the warped, flaking screen door, and it seemed to be looking back at him just as hard, daring him to touch, try to open it. Get inside. The old Lincoln was gone from the drive, which meant Gina's mother wasn't home, but Rick sensed Gina inside somewhere.

Rick stood there in the dying afternoon sun waiting for the slightest quiver of the door, the subtle shift of a curtain. But he got nothing for his patience, not even a tremble of the cheap mini-blinds.

Hot, bothered, just all-out mad, Rick tromped down the steps and rounded the side of the house. He heard a TV playing and tried to peek in a window. But it was too high, and beyond the sound of a commercial there was no other noise.

Rick headed for the back of the house. Tried the back screen door and found it unlocked, but the wood one behind it was tightly secured. He rapped on it until the bones of his knuckles began to ache. He banged on it, his fist replacing his knuckles.

Rick banged as if his life depended on it, and when he got no response, he gave it one final kick. Turned and headed toward his car.

"He mad, Momma?" Kanisha whispered as the hand that had been fastened to her mouth slid away.

"No, your daddy ain't mad. He just paying the piper."

Kanisha looked up confused. "Who da piper?"

"Me."

"No answer," Rick was telling Dajah over his cell phone five minutes later.

"So what are you going to do?"

"Confront her."

"Is it worth it, Rick? I know the money was no drop in the bucket, but is it worth it?"

To Rick that wasn't even a question. Gina had taken so much from him, and he had let her slide for so long, this was a final straw. "Yeah, Dajah, it's worth it . . . I'm going to head on home. We'll hook up tomorrow."

"Okay . . . just be careful, okay?"

"Boy Scout honor," Rick said, wearied to his soul.

Money to burn, Gina had gone shopping that Thursday, that Friday, and on Saturday she left Kanisha with Monique and hit the stores early. By noon she was on her way back home. Hands full of packages, mind on the new clothes she had purchased, she didn't even consider that Rick would be waiting in ambush for her, but he was.

He popped out from behind the hedges as she came through the gate.

She jumped, startled, grip loosening on her bags. "Damn, Rick," she said carefully, reaching down to get her packages.

"Why you do it, Gina?"

She considered the man who had given her much and then in a heartbeat had taken it all away. "You ain't that damn stupid."

"You could have asked me."

"I did, remember? You told me you spent it all on Kanisha's party."

It was then that she noticed the tears. Not falling, but those eyes she had once been drawn to were glistening. Rick didn't mean to show his pain, but it had caught him by surprise, arriving without warning.

The anger he had felt two days ago had moved into sorrow. "I never did a bad thing against you. Why you treating me like this?" he said softly.

She forced herself away from it. "Monkey see, monkey do. You through with me, I'm through with you."

"But not my money, right?"

"Damn straight. I'm raising your daughter, remember? We need shit, and you haven't given me a dime but one time."

"You won't even let me see her."

"You kicked us to the curb."

They stood there, silent, staring, trying to find the good times they had shared, pain all they uncovered.

"I didn't need all that money, I know that. But I wanted you to feel what I was going through. Wanted to give you a taste of how life been for me."

"But you cleaned me out."

" 'Cause I was mad."

"What was I supposed to use?"

"Don't even play yourself, Rick. I know about that money you got stockpiled in that other account. I seen the statements."

The stockpile. One he had been garnering for three years. The dream money, the one that he swore he would never touch until it was time. The money that would allow him to still be a part of his daughter's world without really having Gina in it.

"I was buying us a house."

"What?"

"I said, I was buying us a house."

"A house?"

Outside of Nelson, Gina was now the only other person who knew this. "Yeah. One of those two-families. Figured you'd be upstairs with Kanisha, I'd be down. You'd be free to come and go, and I'd still get to see her."

Something danced in Gina's eyes. "You fucking with me?"

"No, I'm telling the truth."

"And I'd be free to come and go."

Rick nodded.

Out from under her mother's rule. Her real first place of her own. Nobody telling her what to do, when to do it or how. She looked at Rick with brand-new eyes. "She up the street at my friend's."

Together they headed up the block. Gina rang the bell, Monique coming to the door. She turned, yelled down the steps, "Kanisha, your momma's here." A few seconds later Kanisha appeared.

If Rick was missing his daughter, it was obvious that his daughter was missing Rick. She flew to him, feet barely touching the ground, sprouting wings, a fast breeze shifting love his way.

Rick bent down low. Opened his arms wide. Snatched her up like he was feeling her, never wanting to let her go. He held her tightly, unburdened. The long-held secret revealed.

"Guess what, Kanisha?" he said, his voice cracking.

"What?"

"Remember when I said we'd be together again?"

"Uh-huh?"

"We are. Real soon."

"Soon soon, Daddy?"

He nodded, unable to speak, throat locked up tight.

Gina took in the scene, feeling something loosen from her. Rick got on her last nerve regularly, but there was no denying he brought stability to her life. She wasn't looking to be all tied down to him, but having him there behind her had its merit.

"Thanks, girl," she said to Monique.

"Not a problem, you know that."

Father, daughter and mother headed up the side of the house, Monique taking in the scene.

As always, Rick was on the clock. "I better get to work."

"Daddy, you leaving already?" Kanisha asked from the sanctity of his arms.

"Yeah. I have to go."

Gina considered father and daughter. "He'll be back, Kanisha. Don't worry, he'll be back." Then she did something Rick never expected her to. She went into her pocketbook and pulled out the ATM card, a roll of bills. Peeling off two hundred for herself, she gave him the rest along with the bank card. "Should be about five hundred left."

Rick looked at the money, looked at her, a new wonderment in his eyes.

The late summer night moved Rick and Nelson outdoors. They sat in white metal chairs, insects buzzing in the near darkness. Nelson was used to Rick's late-night visits. Understood his role as counselor in his friend's life.

"I know you've had this planned for a while, but do you really think having Gina over your head is going to give you peace?"

But that was exactly what Rick thought, especially with the memory of Kanisha fast in his arms. "Her life and my life, she knows that."

"And you seriously think she's going to let some other woman be in your life and not cause problems?"

"Gina don't want me." It was a confession he had felt years ago but never had the will to say out loud.

"No, not now, but you let some other woman come sniffing around you, and I guarantee she's going to have a change of heart." Nelson tried to find his eyes in the dimness. "Serious, Rick, I know it's sounding like a master plan, but in reality it's not going to go like that at all."

Maybe it was the two beers Rick had downed, or the hope now crushed under Nelson's words. Whatever the reason, there were tears in his voice as he swallowed, spoke. "Just want to be able to see my daughter, y'know? Give the world to be with her."

"You tell Dajah?"

Rick shook his head no, looked out into the fuzzy darkness.

"You going to, right?"

"I don't have a choice."

But he couldn't do it. Could not disturb the rainbow that was her face the next day when he showed up at her apartment, a summer breakfast drifting past her, her smile wider than two moons. Rick couldn't tell her over the omelets she made, his toast that she buttered.

He could not tell her as he left for his shift, or the next day. So he put it on the back burner. Turned off the flame.

Chapter 15

"Only two years old," the real estate agent was saying, fitting the key into the lock and giving it a twist. But Lynette Kincaid could have saved her praise, her hype and her pitch. Rick liked the house at first glance.

"As you can see, you have a wonderful eating area here," words not quite hitting their mark as she walked. Rick was off in some other place, seeing a world he had longed for.

There was Kanisha at the dining room table, doing kindergarten homework, enjoying a real sit-down dinner. Rick saw her in the living room on the newly cleaned carpet watching television.

In the kitchen he imagined her helping herself to a glass of water from the dispenser, saw her down the short hall sleeping under a pink comforter inside a pink bedroom with a canopy bed. Rick envisioned her legs as flashes of brown in the summer air as she swung to and fro from a swing set in the backyard. He imagined her noisy and cheerful with newfound friends downstairs in the unfinished basement on rainy days.

"Let's go upstairs."

The visions stopped the moment they hit the second-floor apartment, Rick's mind unable to fathom what Kanisha's life would be with Gina. It didn't matter, though, because she would always have a haven downstairs with him. She would always be able to find love and comfort there.

Twenty percent down had been the goal that pushed him to work all those extra hours. Rick had saved up a lot of money, but even with a loan from his pension, he would not reach it.

"It's still doable, Mr. Trimmons. Five percent can qualify you."

Sitting in the clutter of the tiny real estate office, dying plants in the dusty window, Rick realized just where he was, what he was about to achieve.

Home ownership. It had never been a plan until Gina forced him to seek a solution, never considered until his back was pushed to the wall. But here he was not quite thirty-two years old and about to become a homeowner. The thought made him smile.

Rick watched as Miss Kincaid worked the calculator, extending the slip of receipt toward him. The figure wasn't scary, his proposed mortgage payments would be six hundred more then he was paying in rent.

"That's before rental income. Rent the upstairs, and you're cutting the payment in half."

Half was sweet. Half made it less than what he was dishing out for his two-bedroom now. Rick relaxed, picked up the dream where he left it, eager to make it complete. "What happens next?"

"You've got your pre-qualification letter, am I correct?" Thanks to the people Nelson knew, he did. Sitting down with the Mortgage Rep at First National had not been as painful as he thought. His credit was good, and his work history was long with steady raises.

Rick smiled. "Right here." He slipped the envelope toward her.

Miss Kincaid put on glasses, took up a form. "Well you've prequalified for more than this house, so I don't see the problem." She picked up the mortgage credit report. "And your credit rating is excellent."

His parents had shown him the worthiness of good credit. When the boiler broke, the car needed a new transmission, there had been no mad dash scrambling for cash. Money came from the savings account or a loan from Household Finance. Though he didn't have credit cards, he had had quite a few auto loans and personal loans from his credit union, proving his credit-worthiness.

"I've always understood the power of good credit."

It was Miss Kincaid's time to smile.

It wasn't the ringing phone that was so unusual, it was the question the caller on the other end asked.

"When you coming by?"

It took a moment for Rick to realize who was speaking. Another second to understand what was being asked. "Gina?"

"Yeah . . . ain't seen you in days. When you coming by?"

Rick hadn't thought about it, his life a whirlwind of overtime and getting documents to the real estate broker.

It was a little past noon and he normally slept to one, but Gina had zapped the last bit of sleep from his eyes. "I can be by in an hour."

"You get the house yet?"

"Working on it."

"Can we see it?"

"Yeah, I can pick up the key."

"Day-yum," Gina said, getting out of the car.

Rick understood. Before them was more than a detached two-family of red brick and black wood shingles. Before them was more than the front yard that needed weeding and the awning of glossy black. Before them were his hard work and determination. A piece of the pie.

"This your house, Daddy?" Kanisha asked, getting out of the back seat.

"It sure is."

"I like this house, Daddy."

Maybe if the day hadn't been so sunny and bright, people moving down the street eyeing them with soon-to-be-neighbors and "are-they-decent?" eyes, Rick would have let the surge in his heart go. He would have let that single tear of joy escape the corner of his eye, but such pleasures were not allowed him.

Gina stood on the top stoop, doing a little jig, as if she had to use the bathroom. "Hurry up, negro. I want to see inside." The remark went right over his head because he was feeling the anticipation too.

He took up Kanisha into his arms and moved down the walkway. He didn't put her down until the door was opened and they stood in the foyer, the empty silence a soft balm to the hot, sunny day.

"Day-um, this is tight," Gina said, moving through the rooms, her joy mounting. "Look at that kitchen . . . new shit," she admonished, running her fingers over the sheen of the stove, the soft gloss of the refrigerator.

She moved her hand to the ice dispenser on the door, disappointed that nothing happened. "It broke?" she asked, pushing the water button.

"No. Just disconnected."

It was one of those raw moments where her lack of knowledge made her feel belittled and small. Gina turned away. "Let me see the rest of this joint." She moved down the hall toward the bathroom.

She marveled over bedroom size. Ooh and ahhed over the backyard. Flicked light switches off and on. Upstairs she danced in the living room, lay flat on what would be her bedroom floor. Checked the closest for size and accommodation. Looked upon Rick with new eyes.

"You know you got to go to Social Services," Rick was telling Gina as they sat in IHOP, eating lunch.

"Why?"

"How else are you going to get the rent?"

"Rent?"

"You didn't expect me to pay . . . besides, you are a single mother and unemployed. My name's not on Kanisha's birth certificate. All you have to do is go down there and say you need assistance."

But the idea of going there depressed Gina. It showed in her eyes.

"You have to, Gina. It's the only way it can be done."

She took up her Coke, drained it. Knew Rick was right. "Yeah, Aw right." She considered him. "What you been up to?"

"Working."

"Yeah, working, what's her name? Daisy?"

Rick swallowed. "Dajah."

"Yeah, that's her. So y'all like bread and butter, huh?"

"We're doing okay."

"What kind of name is that anyway?"

Rick didn't answer.

"I know that's where you been."

"When?"

"Those times I called and got no answer. You were with her, right?"

Something flitted in his eyes, some bright spot of joy at the mention of her. "Yeah."

Gina wiped her hands on a napkin. "Can we drop by your place before you take us home?"

"Why?"

"I was going through my CD's and some are missing." Which Rick knew was true. She had left quite a few behind. But a glance at his watch said he didn't have time.

"I can't. I got to get you home, head to work."

"We can take the bus from there."

Rick looked at Gina a long time. Didn't see the harm. Nodded his head yes.

Gina entered Rick's apartment, went to the kitchen and got a plastic bag. She went to the CD rack and began going through them. Rick left her and got his duffel bag. Came back. "Almost done?"

"Almost," she answered, not looking up. She grabbed a handful of CDs, went through them quickly and suddenly clutched her stomach, a small "ooh" leaving her lips. She paused for a hot second and then went back to her CD search.

Suddenly two CD's dropped to the floor as she clutched her stomach. "Damn," she said, surprised. She got up, hurried to the bathroom. Slammed the door. Rick heard the toilet flush, then heard it flush again. He looked at his watch. It was time to go.

"Gina."

"What?"

"You almost done?"

"No . . . I knew I shouldn't have gotten that shrimp salad. My stomach is tore up."

Rick looked at the closed bathroom door. Looked at his watch. He had to leave right then or be late. "Gina, I got to go."

"And I got diarrhea."

His door was self-locking. He was getting them a house. She wouldn't do anything stupid. "Look, I got to go. Just close the door behind you." Rick called out to Kanisha, "Come give Daddy a hug good-bye." Soon after Rick was leaving, the toilet flushing a third time.

Gina stayed in the bathroom for ten minutes for good measure. She went into Rick's bedroom and opened the closet door. She went into the file cabinet and grabbed a handful of paid bills.

The one from Sprint was the one she was looking for.

She pulled out a statement, her eyes scanning numbers, looking for one that repeated itself over and over again, found it. She got a piece of a paper, a pen and jotted it down. Putting the old bills back, she closed the cabinet drawer, the closet door and went to the living room, gathering up Kanisha.

Gina couldn't remember the last time she had gotten up at six in the morning, but the next day she did just that.

She left her house at twenty-five after six, Kanisha still fast asleep and the sky still dark. She had told Kanisha the night before she had to watch herself, going over the list of do's and don'ts.

Leaving early, Gina figured she'd be back home by nine, a half-hour window between when her mother left for work and Gina would be returning. She had been certain that by leaving so early, she'd be in and out of the Family Independent Administration in a flash.

She had taken two buses, getting off on Jamaica Avenue, hitting the corner at exactly ten minutes to seven. Gina thought she was seeing things when she saw the line of people before her.

She waited an hour and a half just to get inside and nearly two hours later she was still waiting. Her legs hurt, her back ached and her stomach was so empty it grumbled. The whole thing just made her feel weary as she looked around the crowded room. Various dialects rose into the air; children entertained themselves with information brochures and empty coffee containers. Young mothers absently rocked newborns.

To the passerby Gina knew she looked like just another person trying to get over on the system, but that had never been her plan. Getting that second-floor apartment was. She didn't want to lean against the wall, but she had been standing for three hours and her body was tired. She looked around for the thousandth time, wishing she could be somewhere else.

For the first time in a long time, shame was on her like a plague. Suddenly she had become all those things people thought about her—lazy, under achieving and out for a free ride.

"Eighty-nine."

It had been so long since she had been handed the number that for a minute Gina forgot it was hers. The voice was calling out again when she snapped to and looked at the minute slip of green to confirm the digits.

"Coming," she shouted, making sure she was heard. She had seen the lack of mercy given to others who had slept through their numbers. No way was that going to happen to her.

Gina sat before her counselor, unsure if her story about "Joe Jenkins," the proposed father of her child, who disappeared when she was six month pregnant, would fly.

"Nigga skipped," she said with a roll of her eyes. "Ain't seen him since." Gina claimed she had been living with her mother and had found a nice apartment for her and her child. That she had never graduated high school or held a job, that her mother had supported both her and her daughter.

Her Job Opportunity Specialist, formerly known as an Eligibility Specialist, told her that the first thing she had to do was get a new birth certificate for Kanisha listing "Joe Jenkins" as the father and supplying a last-known address for him.

Secondly, she would have to get a letter from her mother stating that Gina did in fact live there and she had been supplying means of support for Gina and her child.

"We don't play that anymore," her Job Opportunity Specialist had told her. She went on to say that if approved, Gina would have to work a minimum of twenty hours a week and her benefits would include child care for Kanisha, a food allowance and a housing stipend.

"Housing?" Gina had asked, her mouth going dry.

"You'd have to supply the owner's name and address for where you will be staying and proof that they are the owners, which, for now, would be your mother."

Gina knew getting those documents from Doreen would be like pulling teeth. But she wasn't about to be deterred. She would forge them if she had to, and if she was found out, she was found out. If not? She'd find some other way.

Her Job Opportunity Specialist looked at her paperwork for a minute. "Your daughter just turned five, right?"

Gina nodded.

"She should be in kindergarten." Gina knew that and had been resisting the notion. She didn't want strangers watching her child, and she had gotten away with not sending Kanisha to preschool. But now that Kanisha was five, she knew she no longer had a choice.

"Who's going to watch her when I work?"

"There are after-school centers she can go to. They have van service and everything, so that won't be a problem." After school sounded better than having her child staying in somebody's house.

By the time Gina left, she had no indication whether she would qualify or wouldn't. All she had was an intake appointment in two weeks. She stopped at a pay phone and called home. Asked Kanisha if everything was okay and told her she'd be there soon. Stopping at a diner, she ordered two hot breakfasts to go, her mind on that phone call she would make later that evening.

"Hello, can I speak to Dajah."

"This is her." Dajah didn't know the voice, only that from the range and the accent on the word *speak,* the caller was young.

"This is Gina."

"Kanisha's mother," was all she could manage. "Just wanted to set the record straight."

"About what?"

"Rick."

Dajah swallowed. "What about him?"

"You know he's buying us a house, right?"

"What?"

"Oh, you ain't know? Guess he ain't told you yet."

Yet? Dajah's head swam. "What do you mean, 'yet'?"

"Just like I said. He's been working on it for weeks now. I figured you didn't know."

Gina had figured right. Dajah felt the anger sizzling through her, words jamming her throat. She was on the verge of releasing them when she caught herself. She understood that fighting back wasn't the best way to handle the situation. Hanging up was. "Don't call here anymore."

Dajah disconnected, trying to find the lost beat of her heart. Without thought she started dialing another number. Rick was on the job, and his cell would be in his locker. But she left a message: "You need to come straight here when you get off."

Four hours later, he called her from the road, wanting to know what was wrong. But Dajah wouldn't speak of it until he was face-to-face. The moment they got upstairs, she did.

"How dare you give her my number? How dare you?"

"Who?"

She spat the name out. "Gina. She called me. Today. Talking about some damn house you getting."

Dajah was waiting for his denial, waiting for him to say Gina had been lying. It was what she'd been waiting to hear since the call, the part she expected. But it never came. Nothing did for a hot minute as Rick looked away.

"She was telling the truth?"

Rick tried to get his mouth to work, but couldn't. He was trying to figure out how Gina got the number. When he did, it knocked the wind out of him. He moved to the couch. Plopped down. "Damn . . ."

"Damn? That's all you got to say is damn?"

He looked up. Tried to implore her with his hands, his eyes, his heart. "Dajah, I—"

"I what? Been lying to me? Trying to fucking play me?"

"No. No."

"Then how she get my number, huh, Rick? I sure as hell ain't give it to her. And what about this house? When did you plan on telling me?" He got up to reach for her, but his attempt was like gasoline on the fire. "You touch me and I swear, I'll hurt you."

Rick backed away. "It's not like she makes it sound. It's a two-family. She's gonna live upstairs and I'm going to have the apartment downstairs. We won't be living together."

Dajah looked at Rick just as he was—someone who clearly had lost his mind. "Get out."

"No, Dajah, wait."

"Fuck wait. Get out."

"You don't understand."

"Yes, I do and I want you gone."

"For my daughter," he pleaded.

But Dajah wasn't trying to hear that. Wasn't trying to hear anything but the tom-tom of her heart, the blood pounding too fast in her head. She could not consider anything except how she felt on the verge of a stroke because of him and his nonsense. "I have to call the cops?"

Rick ignored her warning. "To keep my baby, that's why I did it. It was the only way I could be with her."

"Last time I'm asking, Rick."

"I know it sounds crazy, but you know what Kanisha means to me, and if buying a damn house says I get to see her like I have the right to, well then, I'm just a crazy fuck."

A crazy fuck. Yes, that's just what she was thinking. That Rick was stone-cold insane and he didn't even know it.

Rick kept talking. "I know all this seems like it's just insanity. I mean, I leave a woman and then turn about and buy a house so she can live there too . . . but the real world ain't that simple. Rules change and sometimes you got to do what you don't want to get what you need."

There were tears in his eyes now. "And I need my daughter. More than the air I breathe, I need her. Need her here, with me, by my side. I'm not going to ask you to like it or even understand it. I'm not asking you to go along with me, because it just seems crazy. But my daughter is everything to me. I did what I had to do. Not because of Gina, that shit's finished. Because of my daughter, my flesh, my blood, *my* responsibility, and it was the only way I could have it.

"So you want me gone, then I'm out of here. I'm not even going to try and put that burden on you. Being with you has been the best thing that has happened to me in a long time, but I'm not going to force you to stay."

Dajah swallowed, conflicted. Felt the truth in every word Rick had spoken. "That's because you can't force me to do anything," she insisted, her heart heavy, emotions in a tangle.

He nodded solemnly "Yeah, I know."

"But why does Gina have to live there? Can't you get custody?"

"The day Kanisha was born, I decided she belonged to both of us. She belongs to Gina, she belongs to me. I admit, every time Gina did something stupid I thought about it. Thought about going to court to get full custody. But it wasn't how I was raised. I had a mother *and* a father, and I promised myself Kanisha would have both too."

Dajah looked at him, sighed as if life would never be all right again. And nodded.

Torn and twisted, that was how Dajah went to bed that night, not even giving Rick a hug good-bye. Torn and twisted was how she woke up the next morning, his presence still with her.

Dajah went to work, put in a full day and then headed for the beach.

So certain that she would be there after work, Dajah had packed shorts, a T-shirt and sandals. She took the blanket from her trunk, bought a snack from the snack stand, making the sausage on a roll and root beer her dinner, and headed down to the shore.

Laying out the blanket, she sat on its lumpy surface, ate, leaned back on her elbows, closed her eyes to the sun. She allowed the breeze to find her, the sound of the rushing waves to soothe her, soul open to what was and wasn't.

She didn't fight a single emotion. Allowed every heartaching thought to roam as long and hard and fast as it wanted to. When tears welled up in her eyes, she wiped them unashamed, her heart a land mine.

She didn't need to confer with Frieda. Didn't need the counsel of her father. She didn't need a mind reading, a psychic or Tarot cards to know that life with Rick was about to get messy. That there would be incidents, dramas and tangles.

What she needed she could not grasp. What she desired most, she could not undo. She could not cut herself loose, could not pack her bags and walk away. She was connected to him now. Calling herself stupid, calling herself crazy, insisting that she leave while she could, did not change a thing for her.

Dajah opened her eyes and stared into the blinding ball in the sky, trapped in its fiery blaze.

Chapter 16

Dr. Alvin Kay, born and raised in Macon, Georgia, had a simple approach to the medical profession he practiced. Healing was more than pills and prescriptions. Healing involved a state of mind, and beyond determining the effects of any given affliction, he always tried to get the patient to determine the cause.

Like a detective, he took time to go through all that was and wasn't happening in his patient's life, often going step by step through everything that occurred prior to any given illness. The majority of sicknesses had a starting point, and it was important for anyone coming into his examination room to understand that.

Frieda Wilkes was no different.

She sat on the examination table, dressing gown about her, eyes shifty, weariness apparent. She was a new patient, and even though Dr. Kay had gone through her medical history, it was obvious to him that the woman before him was suffering from exhaustion and stress.

If Dr. Kay were back home in Georgia, he would have taken her vitals and told her straight off the bat that whatever she was doing, she was doing way too much of it and she needed to slow down and get more rest. But he wasn't in Georgia, he was in Forest Hills, Queens, and the laid-back lifestyle of the South had no merits in fast-paced New York.

"So tell me, Ms. Wilkes, why are you here today?"

"Isn't it in my chart?"

"Yes, it is. But I like to hear my patients tell me. Sometimes you get more hearing it said than reading it off a paper."

Frieda swallowed, studying the top of his head. She did not expect him to be black or young or from the South. When Barry had suggested she go to see his doctor, he had never mentioned his age or his race or his accent, only that he was very good.

"I'm not really sure."

Dr. Kay looked up, surprised at her answer, his face somewhere between a smile and a frown. "You're not really sure?"

Frieda shook her head, looked away. "I mean, I know something's going on with me, but I don't know what. My boyfriend said you were good, that I should come see you."

"Your boyfriend?"

"Barry Knowles."

"Ah, yes, Barry. How is he?"

"Fine."

"Good. Good. Okay, now, what has changed so much that you felt the need to seek medical attention?"

His question surprised her, but it made her think. Without thought, the word "Work" came from her mouth.

"I see. What about work has changed?"

"Everything."

"Meaning?"

"My staff got cut."

His eyes raised to hers. "Staff?"

"Yeah. I'm an accountant at County Hospital."

"How many staff did you have?"

"Two."

"How many do you have now?"

"None."

"So, it's just you?"

"Yeah."

He looked at her chart. "Your chart says you're complaining of dizziness?"

"Yeah, a couple of times."

"And where did these episodes occur?"

"Twice when I was driving home, once when I was on my way to my office."

"Did you feel you were on the verge of passing out?"

"Yes."

"What do you think prevented you from doing so?"

"Well, when I was driving, I just pulled over and closed my eyes until it passed. When I was on my way to my office, I just sort of leaned against the wall."

"Now, before any of these incidents occurred, can you remember what you were thinking or feeling? Had anything important or different happened right before?"

"Nothing in particular."

"Nothing comes to mind?"

"No."

"During the weekday, what time do you get up?"

"Around six."

"And what time do you go to bed?'

"These days? It's hard to stay awake past nine."

"During an average week, let's say, how many hours do you put in at work?"

"Between fifty-five and sixty." Frieda expected him to stop writing then. Expected him to cast condemning eyes at her. But he didn't.

"So, that's what, about eleven to twelve hours a day?"

"Something like that."

"And how often do you take a break?"

"Break?"

"You know, get up, get some water, a cup of coffee, move around?"

"Maybe about three times."

"So for most of your workday, you're sitting?"

"I guess you can say that."

"Why do you say that?"

"Because even though physically I'm sitting, I'm always doing something: typing, filing, reading, writing, on the phone."

He looked at her. "Do you take lunch?" He wore glasses, but despite the glare of the lens, she could see the scope of his eyes—concern filled.

"You mean do I eat?"

"No, I mean take lunch. Leave the office for a meal?"

Frieda laughed. "You kidding me?"

Dr. Kay nodded, went back to his note-taking. He filled up half a page with a script she could not decipher before he put the pen down and turned toward her. "You don't need me to tell you what's going on, Ms. Wilkes. But you took the time to come and see me, so I'll say it out loud for both of us . . . it's your life, pure and simple, and it's taking a toll on you. The feeling dizzy? Stress. Will it go away? No, not until you do things to alleviate that stress. Do you understand?"

"Yes, doctor, I do."

"So, what are you going to do about it?"

"Nothing I can do right now."

"You don't believe that, Ms. Wilkes, because if you did you would have never taken the time to come and see me." He opened a drawer and pulled out a paper bag. "I could prescribe medicine, but I won't because that will just treat the symptoms and not the illness." He opened the bag and brought it close to his mouth and nose. "When you start to feel dizzy, put it over your nose and mouth, take deep breaths in and out. You'll be breathing in carbon dioxide, which helps ease the dizziness. It's a temporary fix, but in a pinch it will work."

Frieda took the plain brown bag, looked at it and looked at Dr. Kay "That's it?"

"You are a smart young woman, Ms. Wilkes. You want to start feeling better, stop these dizzy attacks, then you're going to have to make some changes in your life."

He closed her chart and stood. "I want you to come back and see me in two weeks. In the meantime, let's see if we can get that pressure down. Watch your salt, drink lots of water and try to get some exercise. If there's another bathroom on another floor at your job, start using that one. If there's stairs, try taking them instead of using the elevator. See you in two weeks." Dr. Kay left the examination room.

Frieda left the doctor's office, went back to work, finished her too-long shift, came home and for the first time in months, she wasn't tired. She was pissed.

Taking precious time away from her workday, she had gone to Dr.

Kay expecting real help. All she got in return was a paper bag, and seventy-five dollars gone from her. She wasn't inside her apartment five minutes before she was on the phone blasting Barry. "A damn paper bag, that's all he gave me. No prescription, no medication, just a damn paper bag."

"What did he say?"

"What do you think? I work too damn hard, have too much stress. I need to cut back, exercise. Drink water. That kind of nonsense."

"It's not nonsense, Frieda."

"And it's not anything I didn't already know." She paused, a hurt coming into her voice. "I was looking for him to help me, Barry." The fire was going from her. " I don't like having to worry about blacking out anytime, anywhere."

"Then do something about it, Free. Do something."

"I'll be all right," she decided.

"Will you really?"

Frieda had no idea. She didn't try to convince him.

Like fashion and music, architecture changed with the times. Where once people desired the seclusion of closed-off rooms, wide open and airy had become the way.

Even though Dajah knew this, she was not prepared for the welcoming she felt when Rick opened his soon-to-be-home front door and ushered her in. She had not been looking forward to the trip. Felt no need to spy in the soon-to-be den of iniquity that Rick was so eager to move into.

She did not try to hide her feelings. She wore her reservations like a shawl about her on the ride over. Rick knew it and respected it, glad that, despite her doubts, she was still there by his side.

"Oh," was all she could manage as she took in the soft, off-white walls, the carpet showing steamer tracks and footprints.

"You like?"

She sought his eyes for the first time since he had come to pick her up. "Yeah," she said, her voice soft, "I do." She hadn't expected to be touched this way, had no premonition that walls, doors and windows could be so mood altering. But it was, lifting doubt, unease and concern from her, shifting the gloom she'd felt, far far away.

In that moment, she realized it was a brave thing Rick had done, a different stand against the inequities of his life. Not only was he trying to level the playing field, he was securing something vital and important in his life—a real home to call his own.

Feeling the shift in her, the change in her mood, Rick closed the distance between them, his arms going around her waist, her tense back against his fast-beating heart. Close. "We'll be okay, Dajah."

"Will we?"

"Yeah, we will."

Dajah felt it then, the surrender; the "damned if I do, damned if I don't" of it all. Options were all gone now. She was standing firmly in the middle of the long haul. Having never handed the reins of her life to any one person so completely, she needed confirmation that he would not let her down, allow her to fall. "You promise?"

"Promise."

Dajah turned to accept the fullness of his embrace and his lips found hers. The hug became hot, intense, near desperate and soon hands were finding inappropriate places to delve, explore, touch, as buttons got undone, zippers unzipped, lovemaking coming quick, intense and unprotected on the freshly shampooed carpeted floor.

In the aftermath, neither moved, unwilling to talk about what had just occurred. The moment had been a needed one, a salve against still-fresh wounds, against the future that no longer shined so bright.

Dajah shifted from his embrace, but Rick pulled her back. "No, don't move." His eyes closed, body spent.

"You know what we've just done, are doing, don't you?"

"Yeah."

"What?"

"We just made the sweetest love bareback . . . and we're lying here butt-naked in a house I don't own yet."

She swallowed. "Bingo."

He sat up. "We got carried away."

"We sure did. No need to worry about babies . . . it's the other stuff."

"I always came to Gina protected."

"Not always," she said with a tense laugh. "Kanisha, remember?"

"Yeah, but since then I have. It's condoms or nothing."

"Me too . . . you were the first."

"Ever?"

"Ever." She grabbed her underwear, scooted into it. "You ever been tested?"

"Once a year."

Dajah nodded. "Me too." It came to her then, the foolish risk they had just engaged in, what-ifs dancing in her mind. But mostly what she found herself thinking was how far Rick had taken her, how far she had allowed herself to be led. She considered the man beside her with curious eyes.

"What?"

Dajah shook her head, keeping her comments to herself.

Gina watched as Monique wrote and wrote her mother's signature on the legal pad. Thirteen was suppose to be an unlucky number, but that was the number of tries when Monique aced it.

"Damn, you good," Gina muttered, taking in her mother's original signature on the court entered house deed and the one Monique scripted. Finding the document hadn't been hard. Doreen Alexander kept all her important papers in an old dented metal box inside her bedroom closet.

Monique went to her Dell desktop computer and began typing fast and quickly. She stared at the screen, typed in a few more keys, then sat back. Five seconds later, the letter was coming off her printer.

"You know how to type?"

"Yeah, girl. I've gotten better since I started working at the cleaner's. Everything's on computer these days."

"So how you like it?"

"It's all right."

"I mean working."

"Like I said, it's all right." It was the first time Gina had ever seen Monique get tense since they became reacquainted. "But my benefits will be getting cut off soon."

"What you mean?"

"Your Job Specialist didn't tell you?"

"Tell me what?"

"Five years, girl, that's all you get and then they boot you off. I loved President Clinton, but damn, did he jack us up or what?"

"You mean they only allow you five years?"

"Isn't that what I said? Those old days of a free ride is over. And what they give you isn't enough to do nothing with."

"Well, she said they would give me food and housing."

Monique looked up at her. "Yeah, but she tell you how much?"

In truth the Job Specialist hadn't. Gina told her so.

"You get two hundred and fifty bucks toward your housing. And about two and change for your food and other monthly expenses, and you have to get out and work."

"You lying."

"I'm lying if I'm flying."

"That ain't nothing."

"Yeah, but it's better than zip."

"So what you gonna do?"

"When my benefits run out? I guess I'll keep on working at the cleaner's. My folks aren't about to kick me out, so I'll be all right." Monique took the letter from the printer bay. With care, she executed the name of Doreen Alexander under the word 'Respectfully'.

She folded it up nice and neat and slipped it into the envelope. Handed it to Gina. "Now, the next thing you need to do is find some old abandoned building around here, one that's been empty for at least six years or so."

"Why?"

"Because you're going to have to supply an address for 'Joe Jenkins', that's why."

"Do they really check?"

"Do they? Girl, you'd think with all the clients they have to handle, they don't have time, but computers have changed everything. Whatever address you give they will put into the system to verify that it exists. Using an abandoned house makes it legit, but there's nobody there to ask. And you better get that address soon. You have, what, two weeks to get that birth certificate? You're going to have to go down to Worth Street real quick."

"Worth Street, that's where?"

"Down by City Hall. Go there with the right info, they give it to you right away. Now, you sure Rick's name don't appear nowhere for Kanisha? That he hadn't been claiming you or her on his income tax or nothing?"

"I don't know."

"Well you better find out, because if he has, the State going to know, and there goes your benefits."

Gina called Rick when she got back in, surprised that he answered. "You ever claim me or Kanisha on your income tax or anything?"

"Gina?'

"Yeah."

"I know how you got her number, and that was a damn sneaky thing to do. But I swear, you ever call her again, you won't be moving in."

Silence. Then. "I ain't gonna call her no more. I just wanted to make sure she knew."

"It was my place to tell her."

"I'm sorry, all right? Damn . . ." But she wasn't, and in that moment it wasn't her biggest concern. Finding out if Rick had claimed Kanisha was. "So did you?'

"What?"

"Claim Kanisha."

"Yeah."

"Day-yum."

"Why?"

"Nothing," she said solemnly, refusing to speak it out loud. If her mother taught her anything, it was the power of words. All her life her mother had said she would amount to nothing. Hadn't it come true? Gina wasn't about to give defeat the same chance.

Monique said everything was computerized, but computers weren't foolproof. Forging ahead, Gina decided to let the cards fall where they might.

It was something that needed to be done, but still the sight of Joe Jenkins being named as Kanisha's father stung Gina in the worst way. She could not stop looking at the official document, kept pulling it out of her bag and putting it back, on the subway and bus ride home.

Later, when her life got straight, when she found a way to live without the assistance of Family Independent Administration, she would correct it. But for now, Joe Jenkins was Kanisha's daddy.

The night before her appointment, Gina tossed and turned, waking up weary, and red eyed. She had approached Mrs. Mason, who lived two doors down and cared for three grandchildren about watching Kanisha for her. Since Kanisha's birthday party, she played with the kids often enough for Mrs. Mason to agree.

Her appointment at ten in the morning, she and Kanisha got up the moment her mother headed for work. Gina retrieved the house deed while Kanisha took a bath, checking her pocketbook three times to make sure all the required documents were inside.

Giving Kanisha a breakfast of cold cereal and milk, they headed out. Mrs. Mason answered the door with something between a smile and a frown. "Now, how long you gonna be gone?"

"No more than two hours."

"You got a cell phone?"

"No."

"Well, here, take my number, in case you get *delayed.*"

Gina took the piece of paper and slipped it into her bag. Kissed her daughter good-bye and headed for the bus stop.

If there had been any doubts her Job Opportunity Specialist doubted her story, Gina had none now as she sat before her, watching her closely scan everything Gina had presented.

"And I guess you don't have a Social Security number for Joe."

Gina almost asked "Who?" "No. It wasn't that type of relationship."

"Do you know if he was employed anywhere?"

"Not that I know of."

"Can you give a physical description?"

"About five-seven, a hundred and fifty pounds. Brown skin, short hair," which fit the profile of about a couple of thousand black males living in New York City.

Her Job Opportunity Specialist handed back the papers, copies in her file. "It will take about two weeks to process this, at which time we will get back in contact with you."

Gina stood, nodded, left.

The Family Independent Administration called the house three times asking to speak to Doreen Alexander. Fate had it that all three times Doreen wasn't home. After the third call, Gina sought Monique's advice.

"We'll go down to your house, and I'll call and be your mother."

"Why down there?"

"Caller ID, girl?"

Monique called, using the perfect pitch to act the part of an older black woman. She stated that she was Doreen Alexander and understood they had been trying to reach her. Apologizing for not being home, she verified all the information Gina had supplied. "You in like Flynn, girl," Monique told her, hanging up.

"How you know?'

"Because if they had found one little thing that they thought was wrong, they would not have been calling up your momma, that's how."

But it did not feel like a victory. It felt like what it was, the greatest lie. A lie so omnipotent, so soul-stealing, it had, in that moment, become true.

Mother Nature was having a party.

She had invited the brightest sunshine, the softest breeze and the most prolific of birds' songs. She had allowed everything green to be bright and shiny and had offered every flower the opportunity to display its best bloom. The whole world was swollen with the promise of August, but beneath the veneer lay the whisper of fall.

Dajah felt it deep inside of her. Felt the falling away of the hot season like beats inside her heart, each measure a lessening of its intensity, each measure a drawing to the cooler days ahead.

As her car raced along the Southern State Parkway, her destination work, she witnessed trees yearning for the turning, leaves sporadically sprinkled yellow at their tips. She could sense a cooling down within the hot, intense brightness. Found herself wondering if her fall would reap the benefits of her not-too-kind summer.

There had been moments that shined brighter than the rest— going to see Alvin Ailey twice and hanging out with Rick at Barry's house poolside. But as she revisited those moments, she made a new discovery in the process—that the last time she and Rick had gone out had been nearly a month ago.

"Listen for the song of the day, 'A Long Walk'," the DJ on the radio announced. *"Be caller number one hundred and seven and you got yourself two front-row tickets to the Jill Scott Concert at the Nassau Coliseum. That's right,*

Jill Scott, in concert, for one night only. Thursday, August fifteenth, eight p.m. Be slow, you blow."

Jill Scott. A Thursday night. Rick's day off. Dajah made a mental note to call him when she got to work.

"I can't. I'm working that night," Rick was telling her a few hours later.

"But it's your night off."

"Overtime, Dajah. I'm getting this house. I need all the money I can get."

"But we haven't been anywhere in weeks." Spoken out loud, it became a thorn in her side, pricking with intensity.

"Just a little while longer. Few more weeks, then I'll cut back."

"So we can't go see Jill Scott."

"Not this time around."

"And tonight?"

"Working my regular."

"So I guess I'll see you later."

"I'll be there straight from work."

But for Dajah the idea held little promise.

Two weeks after submitting the documents, Gina received her notification in the mail, along with a type of debit card. Gone were the days of paper checks arriving on the first of the month and coupon booklets of food stamps. Now the total sum of benefits were magnetically available, one swipe offering cash in a single shot or increments.

There were other papers as well. Documents listing names and addresses of child-care providers and an appointment at a Training Center. The letter went on to state that Gina needed to ensure her child was enrolled in an authorized center prior to her appointment at the Training Center, that failure to show up would mean termination of her benefits.

She had taken everything down to Monique, who gave her the ins and outs on how things worked. "The Little Red Robin is where my kids go. Claire's in kindergarten too. A van picks her up afterward and takes her. It's like four blocks from here, and my kids like it. They can go together."

The idea that Kanisha would be with strangers for six hours a day did not settle well with Gina. The idea that she would at least have two friends there did.

"They do background checks?"

"Hell, yeah. They don't play that there. Everyone, and I mean everyone is thoroughly checked out, from the teachers to the janitor. You're lucky. My Training Center was all the way in East Elmhurst. Took me forever to get there. Yours is right up on the Ave."

"What do they do there?"

"Train you."

"In what?"

"Well, they give you a bunch of tests to determine what your strengths and weaknesses are, and then they put you into a six-week training course. Then they help you find a job."

"Help?"

"Yeah."

"I thought they gave you a job?"

"No, nobody's giving you nothing. They have a listing of openings, but you have to go and fill out applications. Have an interview and stuff."

"I didn't know I'd have to do all that."

"It's not so bad."

"Not for you. You were a brainiac. You know how to talk and act like somebody. Me . . ." Her voice trailed off.

"Gina, stop it. Stop it right now. You aren't as dumb as you like people to think you are. Hard, yeah, but you are far from stupid. And what, we about the same size, right? I got a ton of clothes for interviewing. We'll hook you up, have some practice sessions. You'll be fine. Soon you are going to be working, having a nice apartment for you and yours. Life's about to get good."

It had never been verbally discussed, but as the refrigerator began being stocked with fresh meats and root vegetables and the pantry shelves became crowded with Jiffy Corn Bread, canned green beans and boxes of macaroni, the unspoken rule became apparent. Doreen Alexander bought the food, and Gina was expected to cook it.

The menu this afternoon was whiting fish, cucumber salad and corn bread. Gina, Kanisha and her mother were sitting down eating when Gina spoke what she had been longing to say.

"I'm moving."

"Moving where?" Doreen Alexander wanted to know.

"With Rick."

Her mother choked on her food, coughed loose a piece of fish stuck in her throat. "Rick?"

"Yeah, Rick. He's buying a house, one them newer two-families. Me and Kanisha gonna have our own apartment upstairs."

"And how you gonna pay the rent? I know you ain't about to get no job."

"Yes, I am. I start in two weeks."

"Working where?"

"Don't know yet, but I'm in this program."

Her mother gave her a hard look. "What kind of program?"

"The kind that trains you and help you get a job."

"Welfare."

"Ain't called that no more."

"So when did this happen?"

"Couple days ago."

"I knew you'd be on it sooner or later."

"What should it matter to you? I'm gonna be out of your hair, right? Figured you be glad to see us gone."

"You, working? This I got to see."

But if Gina had it her way, once she left her mother's house, her mother would never see her face again.

Chapter 17

A body needs what a body needs. There was no getting around that fact. More than food, water or shelter, what Rick's body needed was sleep. He was working on a deficiency, and the overtime he had endured doubled his exhaustion, something he was fully aware of as he climbed into his bed, the sixteen-hour shift behind him, another eight coming up fast.

He set the alarm to "radio", turned the volume up as high as it could go and allowed the compounded weariness to have its way. It felt like half a second, but in truth two hours had passed when the ringing phone woke him.

He fumbled for the cordless on his nightstand. Swallowed a few times, bringing the receiver to his ear. "Hello?"

"Rick? It's me. I need you to come over. We have to talk about my benefits."

"Benefits?"

"Yeah. I went down and applied. I need to see you so I can tell you what they said."

He hadn't opened his eyes yet. Hoped that he wouldn't have to, that the call would be quick, brief, demanding little of him. The last thing he wanted was to get up out of bed.

"Rick?"

"Yeah."

"You hear me? I need you to come over."

"Can't you just tell me on the phone?"

"Figured you could see Kanisha. It's been a while."

Kanisha, opening his eyes, boosting him with extra energy. "On my way."

They sat in Gina's mother's living room, Rick listening attentively as Gina gave him the lowdown, his heart sinking when she told him two hundred and fifty was all she could pay.

"Two-fifty? That won't even cover the utilities."

"I know, but I will be working and so I could give you a little more."

He looked at her sideways. "You sure you ready for that?"

"It's not like I got a choice. If I don't work, I don't get benefits."

"They tell you how much you'll be making?"

"I won't know that until I know where I'm working."

Numbers ran through Rick's head. His mortgage would be about sixteen hundred a month. Utilities upstairs and downstairs would probably run him another four hundred. That was two grand by itself. Every month he brought home at least thirty-six hundred, and with Gina's part, that raised it to about thirty-eight.

Thirty-eight hundred minus two thousand left him with eighteen hundred. After he covered his car note, food, cable, phone, that would give him about five hundred a month. Five hundred divided by four weeks came to a hundred and twenty-five dollars a week.

Not much.

"So can we still do this?"

It wasn't so much the question Gina asked, but the way she asked that caught him, the "we" vibrant, clear.

"Yeah, *I* can do it."

"Ain't no *I*, Rick, it's *we*. *We* the ones that will be living in the house. We the ones who will be covering the mortgage."

"But *I'm* the one whose name will be on the deed. It's going to be my house, understand?"

"Mine's too, right, Daddy?" Kanisha asked quickly.

For a second Rick had forgotten Kanisha was there, discussion with Gina all consuming. He fixed his eyes on her, smile bright. "Yours too, Kanisha, yours too."

Something in Rick's voice caused Gina concern. "Wait, hold up. You not putting her name on the mortgage or nothing, are you?"

"No, but it will be deeded to her. Anything happen to me, it's hers."

"You can't do that."

"Why not?"

"If you want me to keep my benefits, you can't."

Questions popped into Rick's mind, but quickly left. He had never been a liar. Didn't want to start.

Fourteen hours and nineteen minutes later, coming off another eight-hour shift, the blare of a car horn jolted Rick awake, precious seconds coming before he could register that he had fallen asleep behind the wheel. He blinked and blinked again, rolling down all the windows on his SUV, the hot summer night air muggy and thick about him, its impact fading by the time he drove past the Main Street exit.

His head was dipping again, his eyes nearly shut before another series of horns erupted beside him. Rick sat further up in his seat, shook his head. Home wasn't even four miles away, but it felt like a hundred.

He could not stop the yawns once they started, could not close his mouth a second before it was ready to close. Leaning up against the elevator, bleary-eyed, he watched the light flicker above him, number fourteen as infinite as space.

The elevator came to a hard stop, the door sliding back syrupy-slow. Rick dragged himself out and headed for his apartment. Getting the door opened, he scrounged up enough energy to lock it.

His destination was his bedroom, but the couch called his name. Falling onto the sofa, Rick gave in to the exhaustion, not stirring until one the next afternoon.

He got up, mind on a shower, a late breakfast and a phone call to Dajah. Time had lost all meaning for him, and as he turned on the hot and cold water, he tried to remember the last time he had seen her, talked to her. Couldn't.

Clean, stomach growling, Rick went to the kitchen to make some breakfast. Fire under the pan, he whipped up three eggs, chopped onion and red bell pepper and added a dash of salt. Eggs met grease as he reached for the phone and dialed Dajah's job. She answered on the third ring.

"Dajah Moore."

"Hi. It's me."

She was aware of the two days Rick had been MIA, but she was not going to ask him why. Her voice came cool and unaffected as she asked, "What's up?" with no anticipation about getting an answer.

"Work, work and more work. Working so much, Dajah, I don't know if I'm coming or going." She didn't say a word. "Everything cool with you?"

"Everything's cool."

"Missing you like crazy."

Dajah had no intention of getting into it. She had no intention of having a battle of words about his two days of non-contact. But his statement fired up her defenses, and she exploded. "So much so I haven't heard from you in days?"

"You know what that's about."

"If I'm asking, it's obvious I don't. So please school me."

"Dajah, there's so much going on now, and I know you can't understand it, but I'm asking you, please, just give me a little more time."

"And if I do, then what? Are you going to have real time for me, or am I still going to be sitting on the sidelines as you find something else that needs to be done?" She took a breath, then another. "You know, from the moment we met, I've been hedging myself, on the lookout, on guard. That's not how it's supposed to be, but here I am, doing it anyway, and I'm tired of it."

"So stop. Stop hedging yourself, stop being on the lookout. Trust me enough to do this."

"How can I when every time I turn around it's something."

"Have I ever lied to you?"

"We've had that conversation."

"Don't matter. Have I?"

It took a while for her answer to come. "No."

"So if I say I want to be with you, that I'm trying to make a life that will work for us, is that the truth?"

"I really don't know."

"Yes, you do, because if you didn't you would have been long gone.

So I'm saying whatever it was that made you hold on this long, can you use it to hold on a little longer . . . to us?"

"Us? Where's the 'us,' Rick? I haven't talked to you in days. I can't tell you the last time we've done anything or gone anywhere. Where's the 'us'?"

"Look, I don't like how things are going either, but I'm determined to make it better. If it means working sixteen-hour shifts, then so be it, because I'm going to do what I have to do. And if you don't know what you mean to me, *how much* you mean to me by now, then I guess you never will. So you wanna walk, Dajah, then fine, walk. But it won't change how I feel about you or what I have to do. So decide, one way or the other."

But Dajah didn't. Just told him she had to go. Hung up the phone.

At five o'clock, as her co-workers poured out of her office building, Dajah remained. At six, she called the local pizzeria and had them deliver two slices and a root beer, eating it at her desk as she played endless games of solitaire, surfed the Net. Logged into chat rooms.

Waiting. She was waiting for ten minutes to eight, the right time to head for Jones Beach and watch the sun set.

When she tired of net-surfing and her wrist began to hurt from using the mouse so much, Dajah turned off the computer and did some long-needed filing. By the time she was done, it was a little after seven and she was getting a bit tired.

On a whim she called Frieda at home and got no answer. She tried her job and got no answer either. Depression slipped up a notch. *Better to be depressed than to be desperate.* She looked at the clock on her wall, saw she had another twenty minutes to go and knew she could not sit at her desk another minute.

She got up, bypassing the empty cubicles, and went to the ladies' room. She used the toilet, checked her face in the mirror and ran her fingers through her braids. She took a close look at her edges and knew it was time to make an appointment soon. Four hours of sitting in a chair while fake hair was interwoven into her own depressed her more.

"Just a depressed ol' mess," she told her reflection. "Look at ya. All sad and torn up over some man? Since when? Since when you let a man just mess with your head like this?" It took a hot second to realize she was talking to her reflection.

She didn't know whether to laugh or cry.

She got to the beach around quarter to eight. Stayed there on the boardwalk until the lights began to twinkle on. Then she went home and popped a Lean Cuisine into the microwave. Curling up on her sofa, she watched television, unable to connect to anything rolling across the screen.

She went to bed that night around eleven. At quarter to one in the morning, she came fast awake. She sat up, straining to hear some noise she thought she heard. It took a couple of seconds to realize she wasn't listening for something. She was waiting to *hear* something.

The doorbell.

Quarter to one, the magic hour. Quarter to one, the time Rick always showed up. She lay back down. Looked at the phone, uncertain if she wanted it to ring. Uncertain of what she would say if it did.

Had despair made her latch on to the first man who came her way, or was there really something to Rick, something worth fighting for, holding on to?

He had never lied. Had never cheated. He had shown up late a few times and had missed a few phone calls, the total sum. In hindsight it wasn't a lot, but it felt like a mountain because somewhere out there was another woman, who had been with Rick for almost seven years. A woman he had felt a deep enough connection with to have a child together. A woman Rick had once loved and Dajah felt incapable of competing with if it ever came down to that.

That was the thorn in her side, the one Rick could not talk away. No matter how many times he confessed his intentions, his heart, to her, the possibility of backsliding existed. It hung in a glass case on the wall; one good swing with the hammer, and bingo.

Outside of the situation she could see the solution clearly—walk. But she was inside of it, and an exit couldn't be gleaned. Despite her reservations, she knew Rick's commitment was real. The problem was, she could not hammer it into an absolute.

Rick had asked her to choose. And though she had made the choice half a dozen times in the past, this time around wasn't so easy.

*   *   *

The Dream didn't hold so much magic now. The Dream, born of The Plan, had a major player missing. Rick wasn't certain if Dajah was AWOL or had become a full-fledged deserter, but he did know that he could not force her hand or her decision, that he had to wait until she spoke it.

Maybe that was the reason why, when he got the call about his closing date being set, the thrill he expected was only partially fulfilling. Why, when he went with his agent to do a walk-through of the home he would soon claim, he didn't notice a single thing that needed to be corrected, and Ms. Kincaid walked away with a whole legal pad full.

What Rick did know was that the last thing he wanted was for Dajah to be away from him even if she had every right to.

He conferred with Nelson about it, Nelson offering a little ray of sunshine. "The fact that she's taking some time means she's thinking about it. And if she's thinking, then she's not sure. And if she's not sure, then there's hope."

Herman Drake, in need of an afternoon pick-me-up, was heading down the hall toward the break room for a hot cup of coffee. He was nearly beyond Frieda's office when he decided to see if she wanted a cup too.

He knew the strain she had been under and both privately and openly had applauded her commitment. But there was no denying that she was slowly crumbling under the weight of her job, and he was worried.

He rapped once, grabbed the knob and swung the door open, unprepared for the sight of Frieda leaned back in her chair, a paper bag to her face, breathing hard. He had heard of snifters, but they were kids, teenagers, mostly white, inhaling cleaning fluids. He never suspected Frieda was one.

Their eyes met, the paper bag expanding, caving in, expanding, caving in. "Frieda?"

She held up her hand, eyes closing, knowing what it looked like, too dizzy to explain. She went on breathing into her paper bag, trying to lift the dark curtain she'd felt claiming her. Her vision grew sharper, her mind clearer. She took the bag away.

"Carbon dioxide," she finally managed.

"Carbon who?"

"Dioxide. We exhale it. The bag puts it back. Stops the dizziness."

"What dizziness?"

Frieda paused, unsure of how her disclosure would be greeted. "The ones I've been having."

Herman stepped in, closing the door. "Having?"

"For a while, Herman." She neatly folded the pleats back into the bag and pressed it flat with her hand. "I went to the doctor about it. Said it's—guess what?—stress. He told me they would not stop until I make changes in my life. He gave me this paper bag to carry with me."

Frieda looked at the simple device in anger and awe. "I've used it quite a few times since then. More times then I want to think about. Like I said, it stops the dizziness, but it doesn't treat it."

She stopped talking. Waited for her boss, the man who had taken a liking to her and had shown her the ropes, to guide her.

"I'll see what I can do."

Frieda had heard those words before, and they had failed her. She had no faith in them now. "You asked me to hold on, and I'm holding on. It's killing me, but I am. The last thing I want to do is quit, but it's getting to that point. So you tell them when you talk to them. Tell them that I've hung in this long, but I don't know how much longer."

She did not realize she was trembling until the door closed and she went to reach for her can of flat Mountain Dew. She stared at her hand, amazed at its quivering, awed at its defiant display of free will.

Frieda had taken a stand. She wanted to share with the ones who mattered most. She called Barry, but he was out in the field. She moved on to Dajah.

"Guess what?" she began.

"What?"

"I did it. I took a stand."

"No, you didn't."

"Yes, I did. Those dizz"—she stopped herself—"long hours are hurting me bad. I told Herman to let the department manager know that just because I'm still here doesn't mean I going to stay here."

"So what did Herman say?"

"He said he'd tell them."

"And if they don't do anything?"

"I'm leaving."

"Well, let's hope they do something."

"Let's hope." Frieda sighed. "You know, I'm looking around this office, stacked high with a ton of work to do, and I've just decided that I'm leaving on time today. Five o'clock and I am out of here. It's Thursday—you and Rick have plans? Maybe we could meet up over at Barry's later."

She wasn't about to tell Frieda she was in the middle of deciding to leave Rick or stay, that she had been trying to decide for days if it was the end. So she told a lie. "He's working."

"I thought Thursday was his day off."

Dajah had not told Frieda about the house. Had not disclosed any of the recent bad news. "Overtime."

"Well, maybe next time. You know, I never realized just how right you and Barry were. I can't believe I went on for as long as I did. I must have been—" A knock interrupted her. "Hold on." She put her hand over the receiver, looking up.

The eyes that found hers said a war had been waged and lost. "I told them, Frieda," Herman said solemnly. "They say there's nothing that can be done now." He stepped back out, the door closing gently. Frieda held her forehead in her hand, the sound of Dajah calling her name tiny, faraway.

Rick sat on the edge of his bed, letter in hand. It was his official notification of closing, and it was set for tomorrow. He wasn't sure how to feel, some part lacking, near empty. Yes, he would have his house, with his daughter right upstairs, but no one to really share it with.

He did not expect five days to go by without Dajah calling to tell him something. Rick did not expect her pondering to take so long. While Nelson said that wasn't a bad sign, it felt like one, *because either way, she should know.*

She should have known if he was as honest as he presented himself, or considered him a low-down lying dog. Dajah should have been able to decide if he was worth a try or not worthy of her time.

He had come to Dajah as he had approached all the women in his life, up front with his intent and honest about his emotions. He had not tried to run a game on her, had not tried to play with her mind.

He had been straight in a way a lot of men in his situation wouldn't have been, and still he was in the doghouse.

Rick folded up the paper and put it on his nightstand. Picked up the phone, paused, then made a call.

Doreen Alexander answered. "Yes?"

"Hi, Miss Alexander. It's Rick. Can I speak to Kanisha?"

"Gina say you buying a house—that true?"

"Yes, it is."

"And she talking about getting a job. Is that true too?"

"Yes, that's true."

"You know, Rick, I ain't never liked the business between you and Gina. Always knew that child was too young and immature for you, but I got to tell you, it's the first time in her life she ever talked about being responsible."

"Yes, Miss Alexander, I know."

"Now, I don't know if this is just a phase, if it's gonna last or anything, but at least she done found some real drive, you hear what I'm saying?"

Thank you. Doreen Alexander was saying thank you. "Yes, Miss Alexander, I'm hearing."

"Hold on, let me get Kanisha. She outside playing rope in the front."

Forty seconds later she was on the line, breathing hard. Excited. "Hi, Daddy."

"Hi, baby. How you doing?'

"Fine. You get the house yet?"

"Tomorrow."

"You gonna buy it?"

"Yeah, Kanisha, I am."

"And we moving in, right?"

"Absolutely."

"Momma say we gonna live upstairs, but can I sleep over with you?"

There it was, his one true thing. No, life wasn't perfect, but even within the turmoil, his absolute could still shine bright. "Sure you can, anytime you want."

Tarika didn't mind the looks and stares she got on the first day of her new life. She could even understand the snickers, the shaking of heads as she made her way to the bus stop, the polyester pants sticky in the heat, the polo-styled shirt too big and drooping from her shoulders. In some ways she expected it; after all, she had only had one previous job for a hot second in all her twenty-three years of life.

What hurt the most had been running into Sha-Keem and Little Ned, Little Ned hooting and howling at her uniform and Sha-Keem letting him.

"McDonald's?" he had asked, nonplussed. "Oh, hell no, Tarika, hell no," as if scrubbing bathrooms and cleaning up mashed French fries from the floor was too beneath her. "You need money that bad? Shit, girl, you can come work for me."

She had looked to Sha-Keem, wide-eyed, watchful, waiting for him to put Little Ned in his place or at least defend her choice. But Sha-Keem hadn't said a word, not to the heckling Little Ned or even to her.

He had not smiled, nodded, given a thumbs-up. He had simply stood there stoned-faced and eyes away from her.

Tarika did manage a comeback—"Work for you, Little Ned? You got to be joking"—but it had not been sharp enough or cutting enough. It had not taken the sting out of either Little Ned's words or the moment. The whole incident stayed with her as she boarded the bus and headed toward Jamaica Avenue, her first day of work before her.

It was still there when she went to the employees' door, knocked and was greeted by the manager who looked barely older than she was. Still with her as she was quickly shown where the time clock was located and how it worked, seasoned workers drifting by her with stares both critical and indifferent.

It magnified as she was shown the janitorial closet with dirty mops, shabby brooms, smelly rags and cleaning supplies. It was not the vision she had had for herself, and certainly eight dollars and seventy-five cents an hour with a forty-hour week wasn't about to make it materialize.

Tarika's dream did not include the overwhelming smell of grease, little toddlers who could not keep their lunch down, or their mothers who tossed dirty pampers in the corner of the bathroom instead of the waste disposal.

It did not include cleaning shit stains off the toilets, pee puddles off the floors or emptying the personal hygiene containers full of bloody sanitary napkins and used condoms. It wasn't supposed to be about aching arms from washing windows that loomed five feet taller than she was, or the soreness that claimed her whole body after her first shift finished.

But it was.

Tarika came home, opening a folder of ragged-edged glossy pages pulled from magazines from the public library. Before her were three-thousand-dollar sofas and eight-hundred-dollar coffee tables, carefully arranged on Persian rugs over carpeting that cost forty dollars a yard.

On those pages were sparse bedrooms done in natural light fabrics of muslin and silk, with huge French doors leading to balconies that overlooked oceans, mountains, forest. There were kitchens with Mexican tiles, center aisles with indoor grills, shiny plates, delicate etched glassware, stoves and refrigerators of buff aluminum.

Within those pages, Tarika placed herself, moving from the gathered rooms before her, a symmetry of air, light and classic grace. Within those pages Tarika held fast to her dream, making a way, if only in her head.

The three keys, shiny, brass, never used, landed in Rick's hand delicate and unexpected. "Congratulations, Mr. Trimmons, you are now a homeowner."

The closing had been long, a hundred papers pushed before him, the attorney speaking words that Rick's brain could not comprehend, but his head agreed with, nodding in a constant motion as he was asked over and over, "Do you have any questions? Do you understand what was just read to you?"

After a while Rick had no idea what had been read to him, only that he had muttered yes too many times to count, placing his initials, RRT, on the required spaces. By the time the last document had been signed, Rick had forgotten why he was even there, the procedure draining.

So when those keys were placed into his hands, and those words were spoken, he could not stop the sting of wetness that raced to the edge of his eyes. "I'm a homeowner," he found himself muttering, the long-awaited moment arriving, a glass half full.

* * *

Seven days was a time frame that meant different things to different people. Seven days late for women who awaited their menses held life-changing complications. Seven days for someone going on vacation was a godsend.

For Dajah, seven days was six days too long.

She had never considered herself a chicken—cautious, yes, but not chicken. Still, she could not bring herself to call Rick. Every time she tried to deliver the words "I can't," she found she couldn't dial past the fourth digit.

By day four she had convinced herself the call wasn't even needed. That his silence said he not only knew her choice, but respected it. It had suited her because it saved her from putting the final nail in their coffin, but more importantly it saved her from later turning out to be a fraud.

But day seven arrived with a different agenda, she coming face-to-face with the truth. No, she wasn't ready to walk away. No, they weren't done yet. So she called him, surprised when the automatic operator said, "I'm sorry. The number you have called has been disconnected. There is no further information."

Dajah called him on his cell. He didn't pick up. She couldn't bring herself to leave a message.

Chapter 18

Living so close to the shopping mecca of Jamaica, Queens, Rick was used to seeing former Riker's Island inmates. Strolling down the main shopping strip filled with discount stores, jewelry shops and fast-food places, it was a surefire guarantee, Saturday no different as he made his way, Gina on the other side, Kanisha in the middle.

What was different about spying the former lockups was how he noticed the look they got in their eyes when they saw he was with Gina. Maybe he had always gotten that look, disbelief and an unsettling knowing, but for the first time Rick became aware of it. Still, it couldn't be helped. They had to buy furniture for her apartment.

Jamaica Furniture in its former life was known as Mullins. As a child, Rick's parents had bought him his bedroom furniture there. Coming up to the swinging glass door, he held it open, allowing Gina and Kanisha to enter, Gina drawn to a gaudy, oversized bedroom set done in shiny black and swirls of gold. "Yeah," she breathed, going to touch its rippled headboard, sliding open a drawer on the attached nightstand.

"No," Rick countered, spotting the thousand-dollar price tag. "We're on a budget, Gina."

"I know, Rick," Gina said, flinging herself onto the bed, "but you got to admit, this here is the shit." She rolled over onto her side, then rolled over to the other. "Feels good."

"Too much, come on."

They headed down the aisle, furniture as far as the eye could see. An eager salesman was shooed away. "Just looking," Rick said curtly.

Last night he had slept for the first time in his new home. He had tossed and turned against the unfamiliar shadows, thought he heard noises from the apartment above. Gun drawn, he found himself creeping up the stairs, doing a room-by-room check. Rick found the apartment as it was supposed to be—empty.

He had hoped this time of being moved in and Gina not arriving until a couple of days later would be filled with quiet moments for him and Dajah. But she had not called him yet, and as hard as it was, he was respecting her choice.

Gina drifted off in one direction, while Rick followed Kanisha toward the back, where the juvenile furniture beckoned. He watched her climb up on a very high canopy bed that looked just like the one he had envisioned for her, full of white eyelets and delicately embroidered flowers in pink and yellow.

"Can I get it, Daddy? Can I?"

He went over and grabbed a post, gave it a good shake. Lifting the comforter, he studied the construction of the iron slats, the make of the headboard, pleasing. He took up the price tag, saw the amount was one hundred more than he wanted to spend, as was the dresser and the bureau. But when he looked into Kanisha's face, the anticipation was compelling.

"It's yours."

He was flagging down a salesman when Gina reappeared. "I'm getting a king, right?"

"No, a full."

"A full, Rick? I should at least have a queen."

"See something you like?" the salesman asked, jumping in.

"Yeah. I'll take that bed, the dresser and the bureau, so you can get started. I have a few more things to buy, so it'll be a minute." He turned to Gina. "Let's go look at dinette tables."

* * *

Three thousand, nine hundred and seventy-three dollars later, including a bed set for Rick's second bedroom, they left out and headed to the McDonald's next door. Rick went to place the order. Gina took Kanisha to the bathroom, her mouth falling open as Tarika came out, pushing a bucket and a mop.

"Tarika?" Her friend looked up at her. "You working here?"

"Yeah."

"Since when?"

"Started last week."

"McDonald's?"

"Yeah. I can't stand around and talk. Have to get the other bathroom done." She edged the wheeled bucket forward four paces and knocked on the men's room door. Opening it, she shouted "Maintenance," slipping inside, two unflushed urinals awaiting her attention.

"McDonald's, Rick?" Gina was saying three minutes later over their meal. "We used to joke about that shit, how we'd never work there."

Rick took a bite of his Filet of Fish. "It's a job, Gina."

"Ain't no real job . . . I can't believe she doing this."

"Doing what? Trying to make a decent living?"

"Nah, I ain't saying that, just that, shit, I know there got to be better places to work."

"You can't always land the great job first time out. Sometimes it takes time." He was looking at her, deep, intense. It took a hot second before Gina understood why.

Her head shook. "Unh-uh, not me. I'm going to be in an office or something."

"Doing what?"

"Typing, answering phones."

"You have to be able to type."

"They gonna train me."

Rick said nothing. Everyone was entitled to their dreams.

Dajah eased up the street, steeling her nerves for the moment before her. She pulled up to the house, Rick's car nowhere to be seen. She hadn't been certain if he had moved until she took a trip to 89th Avenue, rang his apartment and received no answer. She looked at his mailbox and saw it had been stripped of his name. She decided to head over to the house he had shown her, hoping.

His car wasn't out front, but there were blinds on the window, confirming, if nothing else, that somebody had moved in. A split-second decision came, and Dajah went with it. She picked up her cell and called him on his, surprised when he answered.

"I've made my decision," she began.

"Where are you at?"

"In front of that house you showed me . . . you moved?"

"Yeah."

"Oh." It stung a little that he hadn't told her. But in an instant she understood why. *Because he was giving me the space to choose, and calling me would have denied me that.*

"A few days ago," Rick went on to say. "I was out buying stuff. Can you wait for me? It'll take about fifteen minutes?"

She had given herself eight days; fifteen minutes wasn't anything but a heartbeat.

Car doors opened and closed, two bodies became one. Hugging, kissing, feeling each other's absence like a tender wound, it became a never-let-go moment. But they did. Rick and Dajah broke apart, he taking her hand and leading her up his stairs.

"Still unpacking. It's a mess."

"Don't matter. I don't mind helping."

They entered, navigating around boxes in the middle of the floor, taking another tour, Rick showing the little he had accomplished.

"I'm making the third bedroom like a game room. Set up my games systems, stuff like that."

"And the other?"

"For Kanisha . . . when she spends the night, y'know."

Dajah nodded.

He turned, reached for her again. "I just knew you were gone."

"I thought so myself for a hot minute . . . had a lot of soul-searching to do, and I realized just what the problem is."

"So?"

"Gina," Dajah said, pulling away. "You might not feel for her the way you did before, but once upon a time those feelings existed, and

I'm afraid that somewhere down the line they're going to return, and it keeps me on edge."

He started to say something, but she quieted him. "No, let me speak. Let me just say this while I still can . . . You say that you won't go back, but see, you're not a woman. You don't know what we are capable of, and after what she did with your money, I know she's not ready to let you go yet . . . she's going to be upstairs. Right over your head. That's tricky at best."

"Yes, she's going to be over my head, but she better be cool and she knows that. I already gave her the riot act about letting me live my life. She cause too much drama, she's gone."

"Things change; people change. You've shown me that. How they feel today isn't always how they're going to feel tomorrow. All I'm saying is *you* have to be careful."

"You mean with Gina."

"Exactly."

Frieda was certain the pack of brown paper bags were in the broom closet where she stored her plastic bags. She was certain she had slipped them on the shelf. But when she looked up, she couldn't see them. She went to the hall closet and got her footstool.

Muttering to herself, "I know they're here," she stood on the second rung and began searching the top shelf. Pulling out every item until she was staring at the bare wall, she concluded the bags were still missing in action.

She retraced her steps, trying to visualize just where she had stuck them, going back to the moment she had come in from the store. She saw herself with the package in hand and was certain she had slipped them up on the shelf. The empty space told her she had remembered wrong.

Getting off the ladder, she went to the kitchen drawer where she kept her foil, freezer bags and Saran Wrap. She didn't find them either. Next she went to her junk drawer, filled with various sauces from the Chinese restaurant, take-out menus, cutting shears, rubber bands, extension cords, Christmas light bulbs, packs of salt and hastily jotted phone numbers. No luck.

She stooped down and looked under her kitchen sink, moving cleaners, spray bottles, boxes of Brillo pads and a can of paint. She went through her cutlery drawer, checked the cabinets over the re-frigerator. Moved to her bedroom and did a thorough search.

Frieda checked her bathroom cabinet, feeling downright stupid when she looked in her medicine cabinet, fear making her desperate, her heart beginning to race. She closed it, took two steps and felt the edge of that scary curtain hovering.

She lumbered to her bedroom, her bed looking a million miles away as another blackout began, claiming her by the time her head reached the mattress.

The ringing phone bought her to.

She wasn't certain how long she had lain there, passed out, ethere-ally gone from the world, only that she came to slowly, as if drugged, disoriented and a bit queasy. She reached for the phone, brought it to her mouth. Whispered, "Hello?"

"You okay?"

"Herman?"

"Yeah. It's nine o'clock. What are you still doing home?"

She felt weak all over again. "Passed out."

"Out out?"

"Yeah. I was getting ready to go work, and I just passed out."

"Are you hurt?"

"No." She sat up slowly. "I'm okay."

"You're well enough to come to work?"

"Yeah."

"So I'll see you soon, right?"

She could hear the fear in Herman's voice, a mixture of worry and need. Yes, he was concerned for her, but he needed her there at her desk. "Yeah, Herman, soon."

Frieda disconnected, put her feet over the edge of the bed. Tried to remember where the paper bags were. Couldn't. She sought out another option. Found one. Snatching up a freezer bag, she headed for work.

On the drive to work, Frieda came to understand the world of the abused. She saw clearly for the first time that no matter how bad things were, there were always reasons, no matter how insane, to stay.

As crazy as it was, she needed her job. As much as it was hurting her, she could not find the key to walk.

Stepping outside of her shoes, she looked at her situation, all the reasons for leaving coming quickly. But just as quickly she found reasons to stay, things like, if she left now, the work would fall on Herman, the one person who had made possible her position of Accountant.

Not junior, not assistant, but Accountant with a capital A, a dream she had wanted when she had discovered a love for math. Leaving meant private sector. Private sector meant she would be at the whim of others, where downsizing occurred every day.

County Hospital couldn't do that. They could transfer her, but they couldn't fire her as long as she did her job. And if nothing else, Frieda did her job.

This was why she didn't call her doctor about her nearly three-hour blackout. Why she didn't mention a word to Barry. This was why Frieda went to work and put in her ten hours, not leaving until near eight p.m. that night.

Guarantees were guarantees.

The roadside greenhouse had been there a while. Dajah had been passing it for weeks, wanting to stop, buy something, but her apartment didn't have room for another plant.

For weeks she had eyed the cactus plants, some as tall as she was, refusing to pull over. For weeks she had glanced longingly as the swaying palms, huge lush leaves blowing in the curbside breeze.

She had been resisting pulling over, parking her car, getting out and exploring. But now she had an excuse. Rick's new place was crying out for greenery.

Dajah got out of her car, the smell of creation itself thick in the air, the coolness beneath the tent rainforest-moist. Drawn to the ficus, she fingered the leaves even though she knew they were the wrong choice for Rick. She spotted potted palms. Three feet in height, they were young enough to adapt to their new surroundings and small enough not to take up too much space.

Perfect.

Dajah was supposed to call before she came over, but calling meant no surprise. She wanted Rick surprised.

She spotted the SUV out front and pulled up behind it. Taking the plant in her arms, she headed up the walk. Loud music seeped from the opened windows, and she hoped the bell could be heard as she rang, waited and rang again.

The music stopped, seconds passing before the front door opened. Face peeking between the fauna, Dajah shouted, "Surprise!"

Rick looked stunned.

"House gift. Kinda of heavy—can you take it?"

He stared at the plant as if it was from Mars. Stared at her as if she was from Venus. "You didn't have to."

"I know I didn't, but I did." The pot slipped to her thighs. "If you don't take the thing, it's gonna fall."

Reluctantly, Rick took it. Placed it at his feet. His body filled the doorway, blocking off her view. "Gina's here." Dajah wanted to meet her. Rick didn't, something that was obvious as his face went through various expressions. "It's not a good time."

Dajah had declared her commitment, understood and was willing to accept the road bumps along the way. She nodded, about to leave, when someone appeared over Rick's shoulder.

"You must be Dajah."

She knew Gina was young, but she looked even younger standing there in a halter top made of a handkerchief and hip-hugging shorts. She reminded Dajah of the high school students that crammed the bus stops and slunk around the malls, their rainbow hair connected to too-black roots, comedic.

Gina pushed past Rick. "Move outta my way." Her eyes cut into Rick's. "No damn manners." A smile blossomed with wicked intent. "I'm Gina."

Dajah looked at the hand with the Dragon-lady nails, took it reluctantly, afraid she'd get sliced. "Nice to meet you."

Gina looked down at the plant. Rolled her eyes. "He don't know nothing about no plants. Shit, it'll be dead in a week." She glanced over her shoulder. "We got the furniture today. You want to see?"

Dajah heard the "we" and for the first time noticed what Rick had on, or what he didn't. A pair of basketball shorts was all. No shirt, just shorts, clinging to the seductive V of muscles that bordered his stomach.

"No, maybe another day." She looked at Rick. "Call me later." She headed back down the steps.

* * *

"She was messing with you," Rick was saying hours later.

"Yeah, well, she sure succeeded."

"Don't let her."

"Too late, Rick."

"She was helping me arrange the furniture. That's all she was doing, Dajah."

"I didn't say a word."

"But I felt your thoughts."

"You were half dressed."

"About ninety degrees inside, and I had two apartments to do. Mine and hers."

"So how is that working out?"

"So far, so good. See my baby all the time."

"That's a good thing."

"It is. But I want some time with you too. Tonight's my last night of vacation. I thought maybe we could catch a movie. Dinner or something."

"Movie would be good."

"Great. Check the papers and let me know."

The movie, a comedy, was just what the doctor ordered, the laughter freeing up Dajah's soul. They left the theater, Rick asking the one question she wasn't certain she had an answer for. "Want to head back to my house?"

A part of her did, but another part of her didn't. The idea of that foul-mouthed pushy heifer over their heads was a lot to swallow. "I was thinking about going to mine."

"Yeah, but I'm looking to some good old-fashioned christening of the place. Every house needs one."

If he hadn't been looking at her the way he was supposed to, as if she was his alpha and omega, with no in-between, Dajah might have said no. But he was.

"A christening it is," she decided.

They had just settled into bed, their arms finding each other, when the walls began to tremble with the sound of the bass guitar. It was such an unexpected sound, such a soul-stealing intrusion, that both

Rick and Dajah sat up, staring at the ceiling, the plastic comb on his dresser trembling across the shiny surface.

"Oh, hell, no." Rick swung his feet out of bed and went charging down the hall. Dajah's mouth moved to call him back but closed. Wrong was wrong.

She sat there for four seconds and then got out of bed too. Strained to hear noises above the pump of the too-loud music. She moved to the open foyer door, the one that accessed the stairs. She listened to Rick's feet heavy upon the steps.

The music raged on for what seemed like a lifetime, and just when Dajah thought it would never stop, it did. In the silence she tried to hear shouts or screams, but nothing drifted from the ceiling above.

Gathering up nerve, she edged her head around the doorway and took a look up the long set of steps. She saw a leg shoot out—Rick's— and stepped back. Like a child about to be caught with the cookie jar, Dajah scampered back to the bedroom, Rick appearing ten seconds later.

"Sorry about that," he said wearily, getting into bed. He turned off his bed lamp, reached for her and Dajah moved into his arms, the passion between them doused.

Knocks awoke them, Dajah and Rick coming to, both searching out the time on the cable box: 7:20 A.M.

Rick got up and lugged toward the door. Opened it with sleepy eyes. Kanisha stood before him. "Hi, Daddy."

"Hey. Everything okay?"

"Yeah. I was hungry, and we ain't got no milk." She shook a box of Froot Loops his way. "Momma said to come ask you."

"Go look in the refrigerator." He watched his daughter pull out the milk and looked around for a bowl. He got one from the cabinet. Taking up the cereal, he poured her a serving. Adding milk, he took it to the dining room area. Pulling out a chair, he waited until she was settled in it. "Somebody I want you to meet."

"Who?" she asked with curious eyes.

"My friend. Miss Dajah. I'll be right back."

Rick went to the bedroom, closed the door. "Kanisha. She's eating breakfast. Get dressed, and I'll introduce you."

Dajah rose, the hour still too early for her liking, and began finding her clothes, wanting a shower. Dressed, she ran her fingers through her braids, took one last look at herself in the mirror and headed for the dining room.

Kanisha.

A cute red-brown little girl with eyes that matched her father's. She stared at Dajah, and Dajah made herself smile, extending her hand with a hello.

Kanisha stared at the hand, looked back up at Dajah, seconds stretching out.

"Take her hand, Kanisha. Say hello." But Kanisha didn't want to. "Go ahead."

"My momma say you ain't nothing. That you trying to steal my daddy." Dajah blinked, then blinked again, stunned. "She say you ain't nothing but an ugly old stink-heifer."

"Kanisha!" She looked up at her father, her turn to be surprised. There was a fire in her father's eyes. "Now you apologize right this minute."

"Sorry."

"And you take Miss Dajah's hand and tell her how nice it is to meet her."

"Nice to meet you." But both of them knew it wasn't.

It didn't seem appropriate to return to the bedroom, so Dajah took a seat in the dining room, but even with her back turned she could feel Kanisha's gaze as she ate her breakfast. Five minutes later, she was gone. Dajah was ready to go too.

"I'm sorry,"

"Yeah, I know. I still can't believe she said that."

"Because she doesn't know any better. She was just repeating what Gina said."

"Which makes it worse."

"You know none of it's true."

"Yeah, but it doesn't make it hurt any less. I didn't expect her to like me right away, but I did expect her to give herself time to know me."

"I'll talk to her."

"Yeah, you do that," Dajah decided. "I'll catch you later." She left.

* * *

Rick waited until Dajah pulled off, then made his way upstairs. "Gina!" he called, entering her apartment. He heard the shower going. Went to the door. Knocked. "Gina, you in there?"

"I'm in the shower."

"I need to talk to you."

"About what?"

"You know what."

"Kanisha was hungry. We didn't have any milk."

"That's not what I'm talking about, and I need to talk to you."

"I'm taking a shower—can't it wait?"

Rick opened the door and stepped inside. Gina was sitting on the toilet, pajamas on.

"You coming out, or are we talking here?" was all Rick wanted to know.

Gina got up. Turned the water off.

"I'm not going to play these games, Gina. Now, I told you the deal, how it's going to be, and you agreed. My life is my life, and yours is yours."

"She was hungry, Rick."

"Well, you should have gone to the store like you used to do, that's number one. Number two, you told Kanisha that Dajah was an ugly old stink heifer? You better start telling her different."

"That's what she is."

"You think I'm playing?"

The look in his eyes said he wasn't, but Gina wasn't going to admit it to anyone, not even herself.

Chapter 19

"How come you ain't got no man?"

Monique looked off as if searching for the right answer, time passing before it came. "My children are my life."

They were at Monique's place, the kids outside playing in the front of the house, drifts of their voices filtering through the open window.

"But don't you miss it?"

"Miss what, the sex?"

"Hell, yeah. Shit, I know I do." To Gina's disbelief it had been months, her last encounter with the pathetic Mustapha.

"You don't need anyone to have sex. I have all the sex I want."

"Not talking alone. I'm talking with somebody."

"Can't be bothered."

"Bothered? Girl, I know you crazy now."

A small smile raised the edges of Monique's lips. "Everybody's not into everything."

She was talking that mystery talk, something Gina had discovered Monique did from time to time, full of vague notions with no specific points. Just a whole lot of filling in the blanks.

"What about your kids' father?"

"What about him?"

"Where he at?"

"Gone from here."

"How come?"

"How come what? How come he's gone?"

"Yeah."

"It wasn't what he wanted. He said he was too young to be tied down to children." Her eyes searched the horizon again. "After him, there wasn't anybody else."

"So you still love him?"

"I never stopped."

"So why don't you do something about it?"

"What's there to do? You can't make somebody who don't want you want you. Besides . . ." her voice trailed off.

"Besides what?"

Monique shook her head. "Nothing."

"Well, I'm going to do something about mine."

"Meaning?"

"That stank heifer. I fixed her last night, fixed her good."

"What did you do?"

"Last night her and Rick went somewhere. I stayed up purposely until they got back in. Gave them like four minutes, and then I blasted my music. Rick came up stairs all huffing and puffing and shit, and I was like, 'Oh, was it that loud?'" Gina laughed. "I was like, 'Oh, I'm sorry, I'll turn it off.' Then first thing in the morning I sent Kanisha downstairs. Kanisha don't like her either, so that meeting didn't go good. Then Rick comes upstairs, all in my face, talking all this yang-yang like he was suppose to be scaring somebody." The truth was, he had scared Gina. "But I wasn't even caring 'cause I know that heifer be thinking twice about the next time she stay over."

"Before you start trying to get Rick back, don't you think you better first find out if he even wants to come back?"

"I know he does."

"How? Have you asked him?"

"Course not. He wouldn't tell me the truth anyway."

"Gina, I was right where you are now. Planning and scheming to win my baby's father back. All I got was another baby."

"Rick's different."

Monique could only hope Gina was right.

The next stop wasn't so pleasant, but it was necessary. Gina put the key into the lock, turned it and let herself in. She saw her mother's car in the drive but knew that on a Saturday morning her mother would still be asleep.

She made her way into the living room and headed for the kitchen. The wooden rack on the wall was where her mother kept Gina's mail, and she was expecting her papers from the Family Independent Administration.

What she wasn't expecting was for a man to be sitting at the kitchen table in a thin navy robe and beat-up leather slippers on his feet.

"Who you?" she asked, something familiar in his face.

"I'm Jefferson Carter. Came by here a while ago. You answered. Said your momma wasn't home."

Gina turned away, went to the wall, saw the envelope with her name on it.

"Your momma, she still sleeping. Me, I like to get up early. Course, you probably don't remember that either." She didn't, but the image made her uneasy. "Yep, back then, it be me and you sitting right at this table. I'd make you all your favorites—pancakes, grits—and you sit up here and eat like you was starved."

Gina shook her head. "I don't know you." She left the kitchen, then the living room, quickly pulling the front door shut.

Monday was coming too fast.

Like a train on well-oiled wheels, Gina could feel it drawing closer and closer with every remaining minute Sunday offered. She tried to imagine getting up at seven in the morning, getting both herself and Kanisha dressed and heading out of the door by seven-thirty.

Gina tried to imagine leaving Kanisha in the company of strangers. She had enrolled Kanisha in school near her old neighborhood, and then it would be off to the day care after. Beyond trying to imagine her daughter's first day, Gina was trying to imagine what hers would be like at the Training Center.

She found herself wondering if they would treat her like a real person or something she had become—a high school dropout without skills or visions, living off the welfare system.

Gina wasn't looking forward to Monday at all.

"Name." It wasn't a question, just some requirement to get Gina to where she had to be, or at least that was what it felt like as Gina stood there, studying the top of the receptionist's head, the micro-braids in need of serious redoing.

"Gina."

The head looked up, annoyed. "Gina who?"

"Alexander," she found herself saying softer, uncertain of exactly what she'd done wrong to get on the woman's bad side. Gina found herself unsure if it was the borrowed clothes on her back or the way she put her weave into a French bun, only that it was something about her, or a lack of, that this woman sensed as a problem.

The head went back down; a brown, greasy clipboard with a stack of papers attached landed on the chipped, ink-stained Formica counter. "Fill these out and bring them back."

Gina took up the board, turning to survey the room full of hard aqua-blue chairs with flip-up desks. Most of them were occupied. She sought a seat that gave her some breathing room, one in the corner.

With care she filled out the first couple of lines, taking her time, making it neat. Beyond gathering information, they would use how she filled out the application as part of her skills.

On the bus ride Gina had decided that if she had to do this, get out and work every day, she should at least go for an office job; McDonald's or some neighborhood cleaner's would never claim her.

She couldn't remember the exact address of her high school and had no clue what type of diploma she had been enrolled for. She had to do the math in her head to determine when she had left, "year graduated" making her put down "didn't."

She looked at the word, somehow sensing it was the wrong word, and before she could reconsider, she scratched it out with the pen. She had never gone to college. Had never taken any technical classes. She had never worked and didn't belong to any clubs. The activities she participated in were basically illegal, so most of the application was left blank.

There was a basic English test, a math quiz that went from simple to math that used letters along with the numbers. Then there was the questionnaire that had no clear right or wrong answers. She took her time filling that out, giving what she perceived as the "best" answer, as opposed to the one she actually felt.

Half an hour later she returned the form to the receptionist. She stood there, awaiting further direction. The head shot up from what Gina saw was a Vibe magazine. "Have a seat till your name is called."

Gina sat.

Her counselor made up for the rude receptionist, smile genuine as she welcomed Gina into her office that looked just the way an office should look, filled with personal pictures, plants and nicely framed artwork.

Her counselor, Ms. Mackie, explained the program to her, emphasizing promptness, best behavior and consideration of others. "The first time you're late, that's one demerit. The second time that's two. The third time, you're out."

"Out?"

"Out. We are preparing you for the workplace, and it's important that everyone who walks through these doors understands the importance of becoming regulated."

"Regulated?"

"Yes, you know—structured. On a real timetable. The workplace demands your best, and we want to ensure that when you leave here, you have the tools necessary to give them just that." Ms. Mackie pulled open a drawer, removing manicure scissors. "The first thing we're going to have to do it get rid of the nails."

Gina blinked. "Excuse me?"

"You're excused. Those nails will make it nearly impossible to train on the word processor." She extended her hand. "I can cut one and then you can do the rest, or I can do all ten. Your choice."

Gina looked down at her manicure not even three days old, complete with rhinestones in a powdery shade of blue. She looked back at Ms. Mackie. Debated.

"I gave you the choice of who will cut them, but cutting them isn't a choice. So who's going to do it?"

"Me," Gina decided, taking the scissors and going for her middle finger.

"Here. Let me cut the first to show you the acceptable length. Then you can do the rest." The first cut took off half the length of her entire nail. It was all Gina could do not to say a swear word.

Everything about her was tired. So weary was she from her first eight-hour day locked inside the Training Center that she swore even the edges of her hair hurt, and it wasn't even hers. Gina bypassed a corner store on the way to pick up Kanisha and nearly stopped for a forty, common sense telling her she could not go pick up her child from day care with a great big telling brown bag in her hand.

Kanisha came out, smiling, happy and all too excited, her mouth non-stop about her day, Gina's mind on an ice-cold malt. Spending the last thirteen hours without a single buzz was showing by the time she and Kanisha caught the bus that would take them back up to the Avenue, only to catch another bus home.

By the time they got in, it was after six. Gina knew she'd have to find Kanisha a day care close to home. She went straight to her room and stripped to her underwear. Sitting on the bed Indian style, she rolled two joints. Smoking them back to back, she fell asleep.

"Momma, I'm hungry."

Gina came to, Kanisha hovering over her. Still exhausted, she closed her eyes.

"I am, Momma, I am."

"Go get some cereal or something, damn."

"We ain't got no more."

"Well, make yourself a sandwich. Just leave me the hell alone."

Kanisha left. Headed to the kitchen. The peanut butter was in a cabinet too far up to reach. She dragged a chair, climbed up onto the counter. Sorting through the canned goods, she spied the Jiffy. With care, she grabbed it and placed it on the counter, eased back on the chair and closed the cabinet door.

She went to the refrigerator, looking for the bread. Found none. Closing the door, she got a spoon out of the sink, ran water over it and opened the jar of peanut butter. Sitting at the dining room table, she ate spoonfuls until she couldn't stand the taste of it in her mouth.

Putting the jar on the counter, she turned off the light and went to watch television.

* * *

It took a lot of convincing to get Dajah back over to Rick's place. As far as she was concerned, her first time would be her last. But he had convinced her that coming over was not only the best thing to do, but the right thing.

A part of Dajah wanted to go. She didn't want some little girl running her off like that, so if nothing else, she went to prove a point.

Rick greeted her at the door with a generous hug and a soft kiss. He told her he had the grill going, that he had bought fresh shrimp, a couple of steaks and had concocted a pitcher of sangria. "Can't see the sunset from my backyard or anything like that, but I thought it would be nice."

Engaged and hopeful, Dajah got right into the spirit of things, spearing the shrimp onto soaked bamboo sticks and adding her special seasoning to the steaks. She poured them glasses of the sangria and sucked on a slice of orange seductively as they shared the kitchen space.

They were in the middle of some irrelevant laughter when a knock came on the door. Rick looked at Dajah. Dajah nodded. He went to answer.

"Daddy, Momma said to give her some money."

From the kitchen Dajah could see her. Could see pretty little honey-dipped Kanisha in the cutest, littlest denim skirt and top she ever saw, standing there, palm out, leaned to the side, waiting for Rick to give her what her mother wanted.

She caught Dajah looking and stared back at her in defiance, making Dajah look away, the ire in those eyes too deep to belong to the tiny body.

Gina had just gotten her money. Rick knew because she had paid him her rent portion that past Saturday. "No. Tell her I said no."

Kanisha turned around and went upstairs. Twenty seconds later, Gina was coming through the door.

"What the fuck you mean, no?"

Dajah slinked back toward the sink, out of view.

"Just like I said, Gina. You just got your money."

"And the shit's gone. Taking four buses all week, buying lunch. My benefits are shot, I ain't got a drop of food upstairs, and you playing Big Willie for that stank-ass ho? What the fuck is that, Rick?"

"Number one, watch your language. Number two, I ain't got it. You have to wait till tomorrow."

"So how am I supposed to get to the center? What the fuck we supposed to eat tonight?"

"I'll send you up something later. Drive you in the morning."

"Yeah, you do that. In the meantime, you need to get your fucking priorities straight, cause that bitch hiding in the kitchen ain't it."

Gina turned and walked away, Kanisha fast on her heels.

A trillion dollars could not make her stay.

Dajah waited exactly forty-five seconds after the door closed before she was getting her pocketbook. "I got to go."

"You can't."

"Watch me."

"What about all this food?"

It was not what she had bargained for. Things weren't supposed to be this funky. Gina wasn't supposed to intrude on them like that.

"Give it to them. Me, I'm out of here." Dajah started for the door, got as far as opening it, then paused, turning. "This isn't going to work, Rick. She's never going to give us a minute's rest, never."

There were tears in her eyes, wetness that surprised her, burning with their intensity. But Dajah was hurt, hurting and torn in a thousand directions. And scared. So scared, she had stood hiding in the kitchen while another woman called her foul things. Hiding because she knew if Gina saw her face, she would come after her, her rage was that deep. The whole thing was beginning to feel like madness.

"This is my house, and she has to live by my rules."

"But is she?"

Rick looked away, knowing the answer, knowing things Dajah didn't. Things like he could have jumped in Gina's face, but it would only have made matters worse. The best course of action had been the one he'd taken—letting her have her say and dealing with her later, which he planned to do after his evening with Dajah was over.

As far as Dajah was concerned, the evening *was* over. They were too. "I can't do this anymore."

"So that's it, Dajah?"

"Yeah, that's it."

"Even if I say I don't want it to be?"

The sound of heavy footsteps tromped over their head. Dajah looked up at the ceiling, seeing things Rick never would. "Saying and doing is two separate things."

Rick stood in the silence of his living room, no noise upstairs, none seeping from outside. He stood, the past two minutes a whirlwind.

He felt like a hurricane victim who found himself still living, still breathing, but destruction everywhere he looked. It took a while to gather his thoughts, move from Point A to Point B. Understand the nature and origin of it all, but mostly, the aftermath.

She's gone, Rick. Dajah is gone, *for good.*

The thought hurt, then angered him, making him snatch up keys and head up the stairs. He unlocked the upstairs apartment door, sweeping past Kanisha with barely a glance. Rick moved down the short hall, came face-to-face with the closed bedroom door. Opening it quickly, his voice arrived outraged.

"You listen to me, Gina, and you listen good." She blinked, eyes wide. Went to say something, but Rick hushed her. "Shut up. Don't say a fucking word, hear? There will not be any more stunts like you've been pulling. No more blasting your music in the middle of the night, and don't you even think about coming and knocking on my door for a damn thing when I got company.

"I know your game, and we ain't playing no more, understand? I'm going to live my life, and you're not going to stop me. One more stunt, and I promise you, your ass will be gone so quick, your head'll spin. You got me?"

She had sort of gotten it before, but this time was different. Twice she had sent Dajah scurrying, but the fire in Rick's eyes said there wouldn't be a third. She looked away, an avalanche of emotions zipping through her. "Yeah. I got you."

"Good. And if you thinking I'm playing, try me."

Rick headed back downstairs, feeling his daughter's eyes burning question marks in his back, understanding he had just done the easy part.

The hard part was Dajah.

* * *

"You ready?"

That was all Rick had to say to Gina the next morning as he turned and headed down the steps.

Gina expected more. Expected the angry Rick from last night to still be putting in an appearance this morning. But she thought wrong because Rick was done with her. He wasn't going to speak another word about it. His mind was made up. She try something else, and she was gone.

She and Kanisha followed out behind him, everyone piling into the SUV.

"Hi, Daddy," Kanisha said cheerfully.

"Hi, Baby," Rick answered, timing his next words, waiting until a true lull had arrived. "I'm going to give you three hundred dollars, not a dime more. Now you make that last for the next few weeks or starve, you understand?"

Gina did.

When Gina left the Training Center that Friday afternoon, for the first time ever she understood the saying, "Thank God it's Friday." A hard week, neither her body nor her soul had been prepared for the journey.

"Regulated," that was what her counselor, Ms. Mackie, had called it, but it was kicking her butt. Getting up early, readying herself and Kanisha. Day in, day out, every day she came home exhausted.

But tired or not, it was Friday and she had plans, minute as they were. She would go pick up Kanisha from day care, then stop by the Chinese restaurant and the corner store. From there they would head to Monique's place, downtime from her too-hard week.

"I think he means the shit," Gina was confessing to Monique as they sat at the dinette table, chicken bones and bits of fried rice littering their plates. "I think he would kick me out, Kanisha or no Kanisha."

"Well, at least you know."

"What the fuck that suppose to mean?"

"Just like I said. At least you know. You want to stay there, you got to stop."

Gina got up from the table, went to her bag, pulled out her rolling paper, the marijuana. Rolled a joint. She took a few puffs and passed it.

"You have to decide what's important," Monique advised between tokes. "You have to make up your mind what matters the most. Have the apartment or try and mess up what Rick has. You can't do both."

But Gina wasn't in the mood for advice, not the kind that gave no easy answer. "I ain't come here for no fucking lectures, okay? My week's been rough enough."

"I'm trying to help you, Gina."

But Gina didn't want help, she wanted ease and bold-faced lies. All Monique could offer was what she didn't want. Suddenly the great friend didn't seem so great. Whatever ties she had had with Monique began to crumble as she took her in, not seeing a hip hanging buddy, but the smarty-pants know-it-all Monique used to be.

"You trying to help me?" Gina asked, a sudden rage in her voice. "How? By always trying to tell me what the fuck to do? Who the hell are you anyway?"

Monique stood and took up Gina's pocketbook. "Get your stuff and go."

Gina snatched it. "Bitch, I am already gone." She called out toward the back bedroom, "Kanisha! Kanisha. Come on, we leaving."

Tarika unlocked the huge gate enclosing the dumpster and stepped back. Sometimes rats would scurry out, and she had no intention of getting in their way. Seeing nothing, she hoisted up the heavy metal lid and began pitching plastic bags of uneaten food, paper cups and dirty napkins inside.

She had gotten good at it. She had learned to control the force of her swing and had determined the right moment to release the bag from her hand. Too many times in the past the bags had over-swung the bin, forcing her to squeeze her way to the back of the giant container to retrieve them, water bugs and rodents scurrying in her wake.

Like everything else about her job, she had learned to get a handle on dumping the garbage. In no time all ten bags were inside, and she stepped up on the platform and lowered the lid. Wiping her hands on sheets of rough paper towel, she headed back into the eatery.

She still had two hours on the clock, but the hard labor was done. The bathrooms had been cleaned, the floors swept and mopped and the windows washed. All that was left to her day was counting inventory and wiping down the tables.

Despite the labor-intensive work, it began to feel good having somewhere to go and something to do six days a week. Tarika didn't mind putting in an extra day, and her manager certainly didn't either. He had taken notice of her hard work and had told her often that he was looking to promote her.

Tarika was fitting into the scheme of things and it felt good.

Sorry had never been a word that existed in Gina's vocabulary. Just the thought of speaking it out loud made the word freeze on her tongue, but she knew she had to speak that word to Tarika even if she didn't know just what she'd done to make Tarika back out of her life the way she had.

If nothing else, Monique had showed her what a real friend was and wasn't.

Monique had fronted real good. She had sucked Gina up like she had her back, was down with her. But even living off welfare with two kids and no real job in sight, she still liked to act as if she was so much better, giving her advice like she was God Almighty.

Tarika would never have done that. Tarika would spoon her a big gulp full of lies just to make her feel better. That was what Gina needed. Someone to make her feel better.

This was the reason she walked, Kanisha a half pace behind, toward Tarika's uncle house. She opened the squeaky gate and headed for the side of the house. Bending down, she rapped on the window, waiting, hoping Tarika was home. Getting no answer, three seconds later she rapped again.

"Tarika?" Gina called. "Hey, Tarika?" She peered into the dusty window trying to see inside. But the room was full of shadows too murky to distinguish anything. Gina rapped some more, calling out to her friend, a dread moving through her.

A window flew up from the first floor, Tarika's uncle appearing. "She ain't here."

"You know where she at?"

"No."

"She didn't move or nothing, did she?"

"Move? Where she gonna go?"

Gina didn't answer, just turned, told Kanisha to "Come on" and headed out of the yard.

Chapter 20

What do you do when a man wants to be with you and his ready-made family too? How do you deflect the dramas, pretending everything about you is made of Teflon and none of it sticks?

You don't. You walk.

You walk and spend sleepless nights trying to fully separate your soul from what could have been. You design plans and formulate situations that will take you outside of your pitiful self and start living again.

You tell yourself a hundred times a day that it was for the best, that it couldn't work out. That in truth it never had. A journey neither painless nor simple, it was racked with pitfalls, backslides, and unexpected consequences. Like missing him.

That was the only reason Dajah opened her door to Rick, his face full of a pain she could touch. A want within it so deep, she could swear it was love.

"You look good," he offered.

"You too."

"Can I come in?"

Her head shook softly. "No, Rick. You can't."

He nodded, unwilling to deny her wishes. "I called, left a few messages. Guess you got them."

"I did."

"I figured I'd just drop by to see how you were doing."

"At quarter to one in the morning just to see how I was doing? I don't think so."

"You have to know I've missed you."

"I've missed you too, but it doesn't matter."

"Why?"

"We were both there. Me hiding in the kitchen . . ." Her voice trailed off.

"The last thing I want to do is to be coming around here like this."

"So don't."

"I just want to make it better."

"Your better doesn't work . . . look, it's late and I'm tired."

He nodded again. "Yeah, you're right." He took her hand, gave it a squeeze. "You've given up on me, but I'm not giving up on you."

"You should."

But somehow both of them knew better.

Out.

That's all Gina knew, felt, thought, as she sat in her living room, flipping channels, another Friday night surrounding her. She had had another hard-ass week, Monique was out of her life and she couldn't find Tarika. Gina needed to unwind.

Sitting at home wasn't going to do it.

She glanced at the clock. Saw it was close to one in the morning and knew of more than a few places that were just getting started. She imagined herself inside one of them, music pumping, drinks flowing. Rick would be home soon, and Kanisha would sleep to morning. It would be okay.

Gina went to her bedroom, took a shower, changed her clothes and fixed her hair. She snatched up her keys, placing money into her tight jeans pocket. She left the kitchen and the living room light burning and hurried down the stairs when she heard the cab's horn honk. Getting into the back seat, she gave an address on Farmer's Boulevard and sat back, tension leaving her for the first time in weeks.

* * *

Rick pulled up to the house, saw the upstairs lights burning and let himself in. He opened the hallway door, listening for the sound of music, television, but upstairs was tomb-silent. No doubt Gina had fallen asleep with the lights burning, something she did from time to time. He headed up the stairs.

Three knocks went unanswered. He called out Gina's name and got no response. Rapping a few more times, he thought maybe she might have company. Cursing under his breath, he headed downstairs. Picked up the phone. Called her. If there was some other cat in her bed, he didn't want to know about it. Rick just wanted those lights off.

The phone rang until her machine clicked on. Rick hung up and got his keys. Her electricity was on a separate meter, but he paid that bill and there was no way he was going to let those lights burn all night.

Back upstairs, he let himself in, walking carefully inside, seeing her bedroom door wide open. He called out once more, still getting no answer. Moving through the apartment, the rooms turned up empty.

Gina's bed was unmade, but she wasn't in it. Heart racing, he went to check on Kanisha.

He saw his daughter fast asleep. *Just ran to the store,* he told himself. Settling on the sofa, Rick waited for the sound of her key in the door.

"Daddy. Wake up."

Rick opened his eyes, morning sunshine filling the room, his body stiff. It took a moment to piece it all together, understand why he wasn't in his bed. A moment to remember Gina's disappearance. "Mommy home?"

Kanisha shook her head no.

Rick got up slowly, muscles stiff, headed for Gina's bedroom. Found it as he had left it, fear turning to worry.

"She call?"

"Uh-uh."

"What time did she go out yesterday?"

Kanisha shrugged.

"She tell you where she was going?"

"Nope. You got cereal?"

*   *   *

The hours moved by quickly. Eight in the morning became past noon. Past noon became a little after two, time for him to get ready for work.

He had called Gina's mother, but Doreen hadn't seen her. He called Tarika, but her uncle said she wasn't home. The last phone call Rick made was to his mother, apologetic, but in a bind again. "I have to get to work and Gina's not here."

His mother agreed to watch Kanisha, the disappointment in her voice thick. "She needs to get her act together, Reynaldo, that child really does."

He had not told his mother the worst part, could not bring himself to share how Gina had left Kanisha alone. He could not speak out loud how grateful he was that Dajah had turned him away. If she hadn't, Kanisha would have been in the house all night all by herself.

He hadn't spoken it, but it was all he could think about. Suddenly the idea of going to work became something else. Something he had refused to consider; something that was dramatic and full of impact. Something that would change his life forever.

Rick called his job, told them he would not be in. Getting Kanisha dressed, he took her over to his mother's. Like a snowball down a powdery slope, courage gained inside of him—too late to stop, too late to take back.

Technically, the 113th Precinct was in the same business as Rick was, upholding the law and protecting the innocent from the guilty, but he felt as if he had landed on some strange planet as he stood at the desk sergeant's desk, waiting not only to be heard, but seen.

The uniformed officer before him seemed more interested in the *New York Post* he was reading than in Rick. He had glanced up when Rick came through the doors, but looked back down at his newspaper as Rick headed his way.

With deft slowness, the beefy, red-faced sergeant wet a thumb with a thick tongue and turned a page, Rick invisible as black eyes scanned the print. Seconds began to tick by as the bent head stayed down, yesterday's scores more important in that moment.

"Excuse me," Rick said tersely, three seconds passing before the eyes meet his.

"What can I do for you?"

"I want to file a report."

"What kind of report?"

"Abandonment of a minor."

Black eyes blinked. The newspaper was pushed out of the way. A form was grabbed, as was a pen. "Name of the offender?"

"Gina Alexander."

"Address of the offender." Rick gave his address. "And the minor?" Rick carefully spelled out Kanisha's full name. "And you are?"

"The father."

"Your name?" Rick gave it. "And when did the incident occur?" Rick told him. "Where is the minor now?"

"With her paternal grandmother."

"Your mother, then?" Rick nodded. More questions were asked, and Rick carefully answered them, the moment surreal. He never thought it would come to this.

"Where is the offender now?"

"I don't know."

"You think she's home?" Rick shrugged. The sergeant slid a phone his way. "Give her a call. See if she's there. If she is, make up an excuse so she'll stay."

The caravan was slow, silent. Rick's SUV and the two additional cars, unmarked, took the less-than-quarter-mile trip from the precinct back to Rick's house. Rick parked, the two other cars a few doors away. Rick headed up the steps and waited for the two officers and two Administration for Child Services workers to join him.

He rang Gina's bell and waited until she came down to answer, looking what she was—a young mother who didn't have a care. She came to the door in a pair of wrinkled shorts, a washed-out T-shirt and her hair uncombed. Her face was full of the sleep she had not gotten, and she looked as if she was suffering from a hangover.

"Gina Alexander?" one of the officers asked.

"Yeah, that's me."

A badge was flipped open her way. "I'm Officer McDonald, this is my partner, Officer Scalli, and this is Mr. Whitaker and Ms. Morrison from the Administration for Child Services. We'd like to talk to you about Kanisha. Can we come in?"

Gina nodded and held the door open, Rick disappearing into his apartment.

They weren't up there long. When they finished, Gina was escorted downstairs in handcuffs and was put into the back of the unmarked squad car. Mr. Whitaker rang Rick's bell. Peering out of his window, he answered before the *ding* could meet the *dong*.

"Mr. Trimmons, we need to go and retrieve Kanisha. Can you call your mother and let her know we are on our way?"

"Why?"

"Because Ms. Alexander has been arrested, and according to the birth certificate, the father's name is Joe Jenkins, and that, sir, is not you."

Spots appeared before Rick's eyes. "What?"

"It seems that Ms. Alexander has listed Joe Jenkins as the natural father of Kanisha and, accordingly, you are not Kanisha's father. Until we can locate Mr. Jenkins, Kanisha must be remanded to the state."

"Foster care?"

"Yes, sir."

"But that's crazy. I am her father. She looks just like me."

"I understand that, sir, but this document"—the birth certificate was waved under his face—"says you're not. And until such time as a true determination is made, you have no claim to her."

"True determination?"

Mr. Whitaker leaned in a bit. "Off the record? Women do it all the time, putting down some fake man so they can collect benefits, and though Gina didn't admit to it, it was all in her face. What you need to do is contact a family lawyer. They can get what needs to be done into motion. Schedule a DNA testing, have the birth certificate corrected. The sooner you do, the easier it will be for you and Kanisha."

Mr. Whitaker straightened up, back into his child-protector mode. "Now I need you to call your mother and let her know we're coming, let her try and prepare Kanisha for our arrival. Please, sir, go make the call."

"Can I come with you?"

"Legally, we don't advise it, but we cannot stop you from visiting your own mother's home."

Rick nodded, went to make the call.

* * *

But nothing could prepare Kanisha, Rick or his mother for the moment. Rick tried to explain the best way he could why she had to go with those people, promising with all his heart that she'd be back with him as soon as possible.

But Kanisha didn't understand. She kicked and howled as she was lifted and put inside the van, the door shutting off her "daddy" in mid-howl.

"Sweet Jesus," Mrs. Trimmons murmured, one hand slipping around the shoulder of her son, the other moving away tears sliding past the corner of her eyes.

It was the last place Gina expected to be. She had friends who had gone to jail, mostly men, and it scared her to find herself under lockup.

You just act hard, act like you a crazy fuck, someone had once told her. *Act like you'll kill a mutherfucker if they look at you wrong.* Even though toughness had been a part of Gina's game since she could remember, prison humbled her.

When she was arrested and taken to the holding cell, another detainee asked her for her gold earrings. Gina handed them over. After that she sat in the corner and just held herself.

She didn't know what she'd done. Yes, she had left Kanisha alone, but she had done it many times. Besides, Rick *had* come home. It wasn't like Kanisha had been by herself all night. She tried to explain that to the Administration for Child Services, but they weren't hearing any of it.

A few hours for herself, that was all she'd wanted. And after that hard-ass week at the Training Center, she deserved it. But they got it all twisted and wrong. Accused her of a terrible crime. Now she was in jail, and her daughter was in the system. Worse yet, her lie had been found out.

She never thought using a fake name would come back to haunt her. She had every intention of correcting it when the time came. Now everything was jacked up because of it, she in lockdown, her daughter God knew where.

Tears were not common to Gina, but now that she had started, she couldn't stop the flow. "Bitch, shut the fuck up," she heard from somewhere across the room. Gina couldn't shut up if she wanted to, and for the first time, she didn't.

"Rick?"

"Can I come in?" There were tears in his eyes.

"What happened?"

He swallowed, the words hard in his tongue. "Can I come in? Please, Dajah, can I?"

She opened her door, closed it behind him, ascending the steps. "Everything okay?"

"No."

She stopped midway. "Can you tell me what's going on?"

"Soon as we get upstairs, okay? I just need to sit down."

It took a while before Rick could get himself to speak, his throat tight, tears sprinkling his eyes. "ACS has Kanisha."

"What?"

"I didn't know," he said softly. "Didn't know."

"Know what?"

"What Gina had done."

Dajah swallowed. "What did she do?"

"She put some other man's name on Kanisha's birth certificate, not mine, but some man's name—Joe Jenkins."

"Why?"

"To get benefits . . . welfare." Rick chuckled, but there was only sorrow in the sound. "I should have been smarter, should have known, but I was too busy wanting *The Plan* to work." He looked at her. "People tried to tell me it was crazy, but I just knew in my heart it would work. I just knew my Plan could fix things."

"What plan?"

"The one I've been working on for years now. Getting the house. Being downstairs, Kanisha up. Never thought that Gina would have to lie to make it work. I never thought that it would land my baby in foster care, that I'd have to prove that I'm her father."

"I'm not getting you."

Rick sighed "Gina has never worked. Never finished school. None of that. I couldn't afford to have her living upstairs rent-free, so I told her to go down to Social Services and apply for welfare. But they've changed stuff around so much, and now you have to have all kinds of documents to apply."

"Like a birth certificate."

"Yeah. My name was never put on Kanisha's, Gina's choosing. Never thought much about it, 'cause I'm her daddy, everybody knows that. So when she goes to apply, I guess she had to give a name and she made one up."

"Because if she put your name, she couldn't qualify?"

"Right."

"So how did she end up with ACS?"

"After I left here, I went home and saw all the lights upstairs on, Gina's got a bad habit of going to bed with lights on, and I'm not trying to support Con Ed. So I go upstairs and she's not there, but Kanisha is."

"She left Kanisha alone?"

Rick nodded. "I'm telling myself, she just ran to the store. She does that sometimes. Runs to the store and leaves Kanisha in the house. So I figured I'd wait until she came back. Next thing I know, it's morning and she's not back. All I can think is, what if. What if you had let me in last night? Kanisha would have been all by herself the whole night."

"How could she do that?"

"Exactly. I mean, anything could have happened. Somebody could have broken in. A fire could have started, anything. I knew then that I had to go for custody of my child, so I go to the precinct and file an abandonment charge, all the while thinking that they'd arrest Gina, she'd get probation as a first offender and I could just get Kanisha."

"But the birth certificate."

"Bingo. Kanisha was at my mother's and ACS went over there . . ." Rick took a deep breath. "She was crying and screaming for me, and I couldn't do a damn thing. My child is in the system, and I can't do jack until I can prove I'm her father."

He broke down. Dajah offered her shoulder. She didn't speak because there were no words to make it better. Just held him in silence, the moment slow in passing. Dajah held him, her heart opening to his grief, and when he was all cried out, she told him he needed to find a lawyer and quick.

Rick didn't know of any, but he knew somebody who might. He

used Dajah's phone and called Nelson. Twenty minutes later Nelson was calling him back.

"His name is Jacob Maitlin, and he can see you this afternoon. He's not cheap, but he's the best."

Jacob Maitlin was short, white, balding, with intense black eyes and bushy salt-and-pepper brows. His office was located in Massapequa, Long Island, and more than once he reiterated how "not many people can pull me off the golf course."

"Nelson knows the right people," was all Rick could offer as he sat upright in the leather wing back chair.

"I guess he does. Okay, Rick—can I call you Rick?"

"Please do."

"Okay, Rick, now the one thing I not only ask but absolutely demand is complete, total honesty. I am your lawyer. I am on your side and I need to know the truth, the whole truth and nothing but the truth, so help you God, okay?"

"Okay."

"Great. Second, I am good, but I am not cheap. Yes, I do pro bono, but I limit those cases to three a year and I just did number three two months ago, so you are out of luck. I have a retainer of five thousand dollars, and I bill two hundred and fifty dollars an hour. Is that a problem?"

Rick swallowed. "That much?"

"Yes, that much. Again, I ask you, is that a problem?"

There was his pension fund, his parents. Nelson, if it came to it. "No."

"Great. Do you have your checkbook?"

"Left it home."

"Never come to see an attorney without money. It's a turn-off." A smile dusted the old man's face. "But since you are a good friend of a good friend of a good friend of mine, we can handle that part later. Okay, now. From what I gathered, Gina Alexander had an illegal birth certificate issued for your daughter, correct?"

"Yes."

The dark eyes honed into him. "And at any time did you have any knowledge that she committed this crime?" Rick went to answer, but Jacob stopped him. "No, I want you to think before you answer. I want you to search your brain for every conversation you had with her and make sure."

But Rick didn't need to. "No, Mr. Maitlin, I did not."

"Not even the slightest hint?"

"No."

"Not even when she applied for welfare so she could move into your house?"

"I suggested she go apply, but I wasn't there when she did. She didn't give me the details."

"So she didn't come to you and share how she needed to forge a name on Kankita's—"

"Kanisha," Rick said pointedly.

"I am sorry. In my day, little girls were named Mary and Ellen. These new names mangle the brain. Kanisha. Okay. Kanisha's birth certificate."

"No."

"Did she discuss with you at all anything about her applying?"

"Yes. She told me she would only get two-hundred and fifty dollars a month toward rent."

"Aha."

"Aha?"

"Rick, you have just shot yourself in the foot. You have just become an accomplice to her crime."

"Why?

"Because not only did you direct Gina to go and apply, you have just acknowledged to me and, if we were in the courtroom, to the entire jury, that you knowingly and willingly became a part of the fraud perpetrated by one Gina Alexander in an effort to obtain state funds that she legally was not entitled to."

"I don't get you."

"As Kanisha's father, it is your responsibility to handle the financial obligations, right?"

"Yes."

"But you yourself have just admitted that you were anticipating receiving monies from the state that you yourself should have been providing in the first place."

"Mr. Maitlin, I've never been on welfare. Not myself, my parents or anyone I have regular contact with. All I knew was that they help single parents make ends meet. All this other stuff you're talking, I don't know about."

Mr. Maitlin pointed a finger his way. "Good answer. And that will be our defense."

"Defense?"

"Rick, Rick, did you not hear me just seconds ago? From the moment you told Gina to go apply, you were a part of this defrauding, whether you realized it or not. Now, my job is to prove to the court that you were innocent of the process."

"I was."

"I know it, you know it. Now we have to make sure the courts know it."

Jacob made notes on a legal pad. "I will arrange for a DNA specialist to take samples of you and Kah . . . Kah . . ."

"Kanisha."

"Yes, Kanisha, on Monday. I will use my contacts to get a hearing as soon as possible. In the meantime, Rick, you start making a list of people who are in your circle, a list of people who, as you claim, never utilized the welfare system, therefore allowing you ignorance of it."

"This sounds like it will take forever."

Jacob shrugged. "Forever? No. A while, maybe. With Gina arrested for abandonment, it might make it easier, unless of course she has family who are willing to take your daughter in."

Rick thought about Doreen Alexander. Shook his head no.

Rick arrived home, exhausted and weary. He knew he should call Dajah, call Nelson, his parents, even Gina's mother, but he was too tired.

Yet beneath his weariness lay a nest of snakes. He could be found guilty too. Could lose everything he had worked so hard for. He could shame his family. Go to jail.

That was the deepest fear. Rick could not imagine himself locked up in the place he had worked for so long. He couldn't block out the stories of what had happened to former corrections officers who become inmates. No doubt he could survive it, but he would be a man forever changed by it.

Once upon a time, the Plan had been a garden of hope, filled with visions of peace and serenity. Now it was a monster, taking biting chunks out of his world, just a heartbeat away from gobbling him whole.

His phone rang.

He didn't answer, just waited for it to stop. When he looked at the display and saw "number unknown," he knew in his heart it was Gina calling from lockup. In that moment, he couldn't think of a better place for her to be. She had cost him that much.

His doorbell rang. Rick didn't answer that either. Then his phone began to ring again, and he saw on the display Dajah's cell phone number. Rick didn't pick up. But when the raps came on his bedroom window, Dajah calling him through the thermoglass, he knew he had to let her in.

"Last thing you need to be is alone," she said as she came inside, take-out in her hand. "I know you haven't eaten all day, so I stopped, got you something." But Rick wasn't hungry. Rick was tired and afraid.

"Chinese. Chicken and broccoli, some soup, nothing heavy," she was saying as she laid out containers on the dining room table. "Kanisha still needs you. You got to keep your strength."

Rick moved toward the table, appetite missing. Stared at the take-out. Did not touch it. "I could go to jail, did you know that?" he said softly.

"You? Why?"

"'Cause I'm an accomplice. By telling Gina to go apply for welfare, I committed a crime too."

"No, Rick, no."

His head nodded furiously. "Oh, yeah. I can end up in the same damn place I work." His fist hit the table hard. "Why? Because I'm a stupid fuck."

"No. You're not. So you stop it right now. There's no time for a pity party, and I'll be damned if I let you." Dajah looked at him, her whole being trembling. "Loving your daughter doesn't make you stupid. Wanting something better doesn't make you stupid. You did what you did because you are a great father wanting the best for your child. That's why you did it and don't you ever doubt the why."

"Oh, yeah? What did it cost me, Dajah, huh? What did it cost? Kanisha in the system, both her parents facing lockup?"

But Dajah wasn't going to join his condemnation. She moved past it, searching for the hope. "What does the attorney say?"

"Mr. I-charge-a-trillion-dollars-an-hour-but-I'm-the-best?" Rick sighed, sarcasm leaving him fast. "He says we have a chance, if we can convince the jury that I had no real knowledge of how the welfare system works."

"Did you?"

He had not considered it while he was sitting in the attorney's office, even though Jacob Maitlin had specifically asked him to think long and hard. But the drive home gave him plenty of thinking time, and one thing came to mind. "Kinda."

"What do you mean 'kinda'?"

"Well, when I was talking about getting the house, I said something about it being deeded to Kanisha if something happened to me."

"And?"

"Gina said I couldn't. That it would mess up her benefits."

"Did she say why?"

"No, and I didn't ask either."

"So you didn't know."

"I guess not. I mean, I don't even know people on welfare, except Gina."

"Right, and the attorney, he's the best. So there's hope, Rick."

"I need more than hope, Dajah."

She didn't answer, just slipped her arms around him, a new journey begun.

Across town, Doreen Alexander's phone rang. She picked up. Heard "This is a collect call from the Department of Corrections, Riker's Island Facility. To accept this call, please press one."

Doreen didn't know anybody in prison and would not take the call. She simply hung up. Receiving eight such calls by the time Jefferson arrived, she told him about it. "I don't know who's calling, but I sure as hell wished they'd stop."

The phone rang again while Doreen was in the bathroom. Jefferson answered and, on a hunch, accepted. A part of him had expected this day, but there was still some disappointment when it arrived.

"Who's this?" the voice asked.

"Jefferson . . . Gina?"

"Yeah. Where my momma?"

"In the bathroom."

"Can you tell her to come to the phone?"

"She can't right now. But I can take a message."

There was a pause. "I'm in jail. They charged me with abandoning Kanisha. They set my bail, five thousand dollars. Five hundred will get me out, and I need to get out of here."

"Which jail?"

"Riker's."

'When did this happen?"

"Yesterday."

"You okay?"

"What the fuck you think . . . been calling my mother all day, but she ain't taking the calls."

"I'll let her know, hear? We'll get you out." A sob came through the wire. "No, baby girl, you dry them tears. Everything's going to be fine." The call disconnected. Jefferson hung up. Sitting down, wearied, he waited for Doreen to come out of the bathroom.

"Gina's in jail," Jefferson told her.

"Who Gina?"

"Your Gina. My Gina."

"Don't be starting that nonsense in my house, Jefferson."

"It ain't nonsense, Doreen, and you know it."

"What she in jail for?"

"She say abandonment of her little girl."

"When this happen?"

"Yesterday."

"Where she at?"

"Riker's. She say her bail is five hundred dollars."

Doreen's head shook. "Always knew she'd end up there one day."

"So you gonna bail her out?"

"Hell, no, her ass can stay right there. I tried to tell that ignorant ass she don't need to be no mother, now look at her. Jail just where she need to be."

But Jefferson wasn't convinced.

Neither was Dajah.

She wasn't certain when the plight of Gina slipped into her consciousness. Wasn't certain when Rick and his dilemma got pushed aside. All Dajah knew was that suddenly she was speaking the words: "She doesn't need to be there."

"Who where?"

"Gina. She doesn't need to be in jail."

"The hell she doesn't."

"I know she did some bad things, but she is Kanisha's mother. Think about how it will affect her."

"Kanisha doesn't know."

"But she will one day. She at Riker's?"

"Yeah. Got transferred this morning."

"Did they give her bail?"

"So I heard."

"How much?"

"How much what?"

"Is the bail?"

"Five hundred, and why do you care?"

"I'm just thinking about your daughter, that's all. Eventually Gina is going to be around Kanisha again, and what does and doesn't happen to Gina is going to matter down that road."

"So you saying I should bail her out."

"Somebody should."

"This lawyer is already costing me a fortune."

"I can loan it to you. You can pay me back later."

"You're serious, aren't you?"

Gina was facing major charges. Rick would get full custody, pushing her further out of the mix. Dajah couldn't see making a bad situation worse. Besides, Gina had lost more than enough. "She may be a lot of things, but I don't think jail is where she belongs."

The next morning Rick bailed Gina out.

He could tell she had been scared to her teeth by the way her eyes skittered around her, uncertain if she had really been released.

"Thought I'd never see outside again." Her eyes found his. "Thanks, Rick."

"Don't thank me. Thank Dajah."

"What you mean?"

"It wasn't my idea to bail you out. It was hers."

"You lying?"

"Does it look like I'm lying?"

"She paid?"

"No, I did. But it was her idea."

Gina nodded. Moved on. "How's Kanisha?"

"Thanks to you, I don't have any idea."

They headed toward his SUV. "My lawyer wants me to pin the fraud thing on you," Gina said. "She says if I make it seem like you forced me to do it, I can get the charges dropped."

Rick's heart double-beat in his chest.

"You know, being in that damn place gave me a lot of thinking time and shit. And I was like, damn, but all Rick tried to do was the right thing." She paused, looked off. "I told her no. I wouldn't do it. Not to you."

Rick swallowed, swallowed again. "I'll take you back to the apartment to get your stuff, but you can't stay there."

Somehow she knew that.

Gina entered her apartment, seeing things as if for the first time. She saw her new couch, her dinette set, the pictures of Kanisha that lined the wall, and she broke down and cried.

She cried softly, not wanting Rick to hear. Held herself because there was no one else to hold her. She thought back to the night that brought her to this moment. How her need to hang out took away everything she had.

She did not want to be the way she was. Gina didn't want to be short-tempered and foul-mouthed. She wanted something better for herself, her daughter. But life had never given her the breathing room to figure out what.

Lockup did.

It allowed her some thinking space, enough room in her heart to clear away some of the clutter. As she packed up her belongings, facing the next seconds of her life, she knew one thing if not anything else: If she managed to stay out of jail, she would make a real change. Find new roads to travel.

* * *

Rick was heading around the back of his SUV getting boxes when Gina came hurriedly out of her mother's house. "She says I can't stay here."

"What?"

"She told me no. I can't stay."

He put the box down. "Did you tell her you had no place to go?"

"Of course I did. Said she didn't care. I couldn't come back."

"Maybe I can help."

They turned at the sound of the voice, spying an elderly-looking black man on the top step. Rick didn't know who he was, but Gina did. It was that man, Jefferson Carter.

"I got a big old house with nobody in it but me. Gina, you more than welcome to stay."

"I don't even know you." But there was less conviction in her voice, and absolutely none in her heart. She *had* remembered those breakfasts he had spoken about. Had remembered how he had sat her at her mother's kitchen decades ago, making her scrumptious things, delighted when she gobbled them up.

Jefferson Carter smiled. "I would have thought, after all these years, your momma would have told you. Guess not."

"Told me what?" But a part of Gina knew, images of joy and pain flooding her. Images of tenderness and scorn mixed up in the same pot.

Jefferson Carter moved down the steps, his words, a private matter, meant directly for her. "I'm your daddy."

Gina blinked, and blinked again, the old man, closer to seventy than fifty, swirling in her vision. "My what?"

"Daddy. Me and your momma, we had you."

"Jefferson, you stop it. You stop your lies right now," Doreen Alexander shouted, coming out the front door, moving down the front steps like a hurricane of black fury. She hurried, arms in the air as she lumbered, as if to do battle. She stopped, her large body settled between them. She turned to Gina, eyes intense. "He ain't your daddy, Gina. Never was. Wanted to be, but he ain't."

Gina looked past her mother's face to Jefferson. "Then why he saying he is? Why do I have memories of him being there when I was little?"

"Oh, he was there all right, but you wasn't his. And the more I tried to tell him you wasn't, the more he insisted you was. Got so, every time I turned around, there he was, taking you places, doing things with you. I ain't loved him, and he was cramping my style. I sent him away."

Something danced in Doreen's Alexander's eyes, something foreign but exact—compassion. "I ain't loved him, but he loved *me*. I treated him bad, real bad, and he just went away. Then, a few weeks ago, he shows up, still loving me. Ain't no man loved me that long, but he did. I got second thoughts. But he ain't nothing to you. I don't know who your daddy is, but Jefferson ain't."

"How do you know?" Gina asked, some part of her in need of a connection she'd missed all her life.

"Because I always made him use something, that's how. The other men—" Doreen's head shook. "But Jefferson, I wasn't taking no chances, being as he was married and all. His wife dead now, but back then she wasn't."

"So he's not my daddy."

"No."

Her eyes sought Jefferson's. "But you treated me like I was yours anyway?"

" 'Cause in my mind, you were, still are. And you are more than welcome to come stay with me."

Gina looked at her mother, Jefferson and lastly turned toward Rick. Rick shrugged, offered, "Your choice, Gina."

She had to live somewhere. "Okay."

Jefferson smiled. "We can go right now."

Gina turned, was heading toward Rick's SUV when her mother's voice came. "I know it seem like a cruel thing to do, Gina, but you can't be here anymore. I been taking you back and taking you back, but now it's time to find your own way."

Gina didn't answer, but she understood.

Chapter 21

Three weeks after Gina's initial arrest, Kanisha was still in the foster-care system and Rick had not seen her face or heard her voice. This was the day that it could all change. This was the day he could be found guilty and face jail time, or be deemed innocent, allowing him to go on to the custody hearing scheduled for later that afternoon.

Rick sat at the defense table, hands folded, heart beating fast. Not once in his entire life had he seen himself being in the middle of a court proceeding, but there he sat, awaiting the verdict.

He had gotten on the stand, testifying about his knowledge, or lack of, one Gina's Alexander's intention to defraud the State of New York. Gina herself had been called to the stand, testifying that "Rick didn't know jack. It was me, all me."

"All rise." Chairs scraped as the defense, defendant and prosecutor stood.

A small case, there were neither spectators nor a jury. Judge Harrison was presiding and deciding. "Having heard the case of The State of New York versus Reynaldo Reginald Trimmons, et al, I hereby find Reynaldo Reginald Trimmons innocent of all charges and he is free to go."

Rick let go a breath. Hugged his attorney.

"We get lunch and then head over to the civil court," Jacob Maitlin offered. "This was the hard one, Rick. The worst is over."

His parents and Dajah wanted to attend the first hearing, but Rick had asked that they didn't. He could not stand the thought of them being there if he were found guilty. As he and his attorney made their way out of the courtroom, he pulled out his cell phone and made two calls, each more excited than the last as he told first his parents, then Dajah, that he was a free man.

For the second time that day, Rick sat stiffly in another courthouse, awaiting a life-changing decision.

The DNA testing had been submitted showing he was at a 99.99 percent certaint the father of Kanisha Adera Alexander. Testimony from his parents, friends and his supervisor at Riker's Island had been heard, and the criminal court proceding finding Rick innocent had been submitted. Now it was up to the judge.

Rick felt his parents, his brother, his sister and Dajah sitting behind him. Rick's family had not known of the new woman in his life, but knew at first look that she was the type he needed and welcomed her.

It had been a bit of joy in an otherwise dreary afternoon, one that was drawing to a quick close as the judge entered the courtroom, Rick and his attorney standing.

Judge Alberts was known for favoring the mother except in the most extreme circumstances, feeling that no child should be denied one. So while Jacob Maitlin had insisted the worst was over, that certainty was missing as the judge's eyes scanned the courtroom, coming to fall directly on Rick.

"Mr. Trimmons, I have reviewed all the documents submitted to this court and heard what I must say is stellar testimony on your behalf. It is no secret that I feel a mother is the most important person in any child's life, and having heard the evidence today, that opinion has not changed."

Rick blinked, then blinked again, acid filling his gut. Behind him he could feel his parents' sorrow, Dajah's concern. It lay across his shoulders like wet blankets too heavy to endure, too numerous to count.

"While Gina Alexander did not perform her duties as well as can be expected, and made some dire wrong choices, including the defrauding of the State of New York, I have considered the psychological reports ordered by the court, and as we know, bad choices are not plucked out of thin air. There is a basis for all our behaviors, good and bad, and I am under the impression that Ms. Alexander has not only seen the wrong of her ways, but is ready to change them."

Mrs. Trimmons moaned.

The gavel hit the wood hard. "I will have silence in this courtroom." The judge's eyes found Mrs. Trimmons. "Any further outbursts and I will have you removed." The eyes left her and went back to Rick. " Now, having said that, by law, I cannot ignore the severity of Ms. Gina Alexander's charges, nor the deep love and concern, Mr. Trimmons, you have exhibited toward your daughter. Therefore, I hereby order that you, Reynaldo Reginald Trimmons, be granted sole custody of Kanisha Adera Alexander until further notice and stipulate that Gina Alexander be allowed visiting rights after completion of parenting and behavioral classes." The gavel hit the wood again. "This court is adjourned."

Rick collapsed into his chair, overwhelmed with relief. He felt arms surround him, shouts echoing about him, words coming that he could not distinguish, the nightmare over. Rick remained sprawled across the table, the promise made to his child—kept.

Gina's court date wasn't so exuberant. Beyond her court-appointed attorney and Jefferson Carter, no one was there for her. She was found guilty on abandonment of a child and intent to defraud the State. Being non-violent crimes and first-time offenses, she was given five years' probation on both counts to run consecutively.

She was ordered to repay the State the sum of nine hundred and forty dollars, her two months' worth of benefits, and directed to begin her parenting and behavioral classes. She was ordered not to get within two-hundred and fifty feet of Kanisha until completion and warned that failure to attend her court-ordered classes meant she would be sent to jail.

She no longer qualified for benefits, her training classes or custody. All her life Gina had longed for freedom from something. But now that she had it, it felt like anything but.

* * *

Rick stood at the gate as Kanisha appeared at the front door. Time seemed to stand still as father took in daughter, daughter took in father. He wanted to run to her, throw his arms around her, but in the distance that separated them, he could sense a new emotion.

Bitterness.

It was in her eyes, blatant in a way no five-year-old should ever know. Her anger, hot and steely, was directed at him.

"No, Baby," Rick murmured, his feet rooted to the sidewalk, his daughter feeling far away.

"Go ahead, Rick," his mother urged, a gentle nudge in his spine. "Go hug her, tell her you love her, that you're sorry."

It had never dawned on him that his daughter would need an apology. Never dawned on him that in his struggle to make her life better, he had in fact made it worse. It never dawned on Rick that he needed to express regret for his actions, but as he moved forward, reached her and took her up, the way she fought to get away told him different.

"I'm sorry, Baby, I'm so sorry this happened. Forgive me. Please forgive me."

Kanisha didn't speak, only lessened her fight, a split second of utter stillness coming before she collapsed against him, weeping, clinging, his sorrows hers.

Rick awoke the morning after Kanisha was returned to him, his body unused to the early-morning rising, a list of things to do jamming his brain.

He went to the second bedroom, now Kanisha's, and opened the door. "Kanisha," he uttered through a yawn. "Kanisha, come on. Time to get up." She mumbled something Rick could not understand, eyes closed, cover up to her neck. "Come on. We have to get a move on."

He went, pulled back the covers, took her wrist, tugged gently. "Up."

She opened her eyes, sleepy eyes. Closed them. "I'm sleepy."

"Yeah, me too. But I have to get you dressed and me dressed. Come on. Go take a shower, brush your teeth while I get your clothes ready."

Kanisha in the bathroom, Rick pulled out the ironing board, the outside sky pitch black. He knew it was six in the morning, but it felt more like midnight and his body was hungry for sleep.

He knew it would take time to adjust to the schedule change, to get used to working when he was normally sleeping and sleeping when he normally was at work. Rick knew it was incidental in all that had occurred in the last month of his life, but his body didn't know that or care. His body just wanted to crawl back into bed.

He pressed a work shirt, jeans and a top for Kanisha and went to check on her. Rapping on the bathroom door, he opened it and found her, sitting on the toilet, fast asleep. That she had managed the feat told him just how tired she was, which he could sympathize with, but her catnap was throwing off their schedule.

"Kanisha, wake up."

She snapped to, letting go a huge yawn. "Come on, clothes off and into the shower." Rick turned on the spray, waited for her to undress and then watched as she got into the tub. "Make sure you don't wet your hair." Doing it was not a task he was looking forward to.

Raps on the door woke her. Gina sat up, unsure for a minute where she was.

"I'm heading out now—you need anything?" Gina shook her head no. "You have change for your pocket?"

"Yeah." She waved a hand. "I'm cool." She lay back against the pillow.

"Well, have a—"

"Yeah, I know, good day," She rolled away, giving Jefferson her back, annoyed with his niceness, his unending willingness to make her happy. The first couple of days, it was cute. Now it was just annoying.

He asked nothing of her, not even to keep her own room clean. More times than not Gina had left it like a hurricane had come through, only to come home and find everything neatly in its place.

Gina didn't have to cook, didn't have to shop, didn't have to do anything but live. He left money for her nearly every day and never asked where she was going and when she was coming back.

Her days moved without structure or design, a routine she was quickly growing tired of. Gina found herself actually looking forward to those court-ordered classes that would start next week. At least they would give her something to do.

She was tired of getting high with Ce-lo, occasional nights with Mustapha. Tarika was still missing in action—and Monique?

Her thoughts wandered to Kanisha, to Rick. Dajah. She saw the three of them together in a way she never saw for herself. Could not stop the tears that flowed, the understanding that her heart was broken. That it had been for a while.

Having gone through so much, Gina just wanted a sympathetic shoulder. Tarika and all they had been to each other popped back into her head and would not go away.

Hours later, Gina found herself on Jamaica Avenue—McDonald's, her destination.

Tarika didn't know what made her stop pouring fries into the fryer and turn her head toward the doors. But when she did and saw who was coming in, she quickly tapped Will on the shoulder, handing him the oversized brown bag. "Handle this for me. I have to run to the bathroom."

"But I'm clocking out."

Tarika acted as if she didn't hear him and hurried to the back of the kitchen. Opening a fire door, she made her way to the basement and took refuge on an oversized box of prepackaged salt. She sat there, looking at her watch, waiting for the seconds to roll by.

She had been dodging Gina on purpose. She had no use for her now. Life was hard enough without a naysayer in it, and that's all Gina was.

When her uncle told her Gina was dropping by, Tarika began to expect Gina to show up at her job. She didn't think she would run like a chicken when Gina did, but she had, because in the split second after their eyes had met, the joy in Gina's had vanished into anger and hurt—a volatile combination. Tarika wasn't about to have an argument with Gina across the counter at her job.

Her job had become her whole world, her salvation, her saving grace. Her job had become her confidant, her best friend. Had became everything Gina no longer was.

She had just gotten her promotion and had a perfect work record. No way was she going to allow Gina to ruin it for her.

Staying down in the basement for twelve minutes, Tarika came back up, scanning the eating area. Seeing the coast was clear, she made her way back to the fryer.

Life had gotten ugly for Dajah, and like a miser with gold, she had held on to the misery tightly and in secret. But now that the end of the nightmare had arrived, she felt the need to connect and share with Frieda. Felt it was safe to play catch-up and tell all of it.

Frieda sounded tired when she answered the phone and just as tired when Dajah went by to see her. Dajah hadn't thought Frieda could look much worse, but in truth Frieda did.

Dajah didn't comment on how bad her friend looked, just gave her a big hug. "I've missed you."

"I've missed you too."

They went to the living room and settled on the sofa. Dajah took a breath. Let it go. "I have so much to tell you, Frieda."

"Good or bad?"

"A whole lot of both," Dajah decided. When the story was over, Frieda reached over and hugged her.

"Didn't I tell you loving somebody isn't easy?"

"Who said anything about love?"

"All the drama in Rick's life, and you're still there—what do you call it?"

"Baby steps," Dajah offered with a smile, getting a real close look at her friend, hurt by all she saw. Her hand snuck out on its own accord, touching the back of Frieda's hair, barely an inch of it there.

Frieda pulled away. "Don't."

"I'm worried about you."

"I know." Frieda sighed. "I'm under a doctor's care now."

Dajah didn't expect that. "Doctor?"

"Yeah. I started blacking out."

"No, Frieda, no."

"Yeah."

"Why didn't you tell me?"

"Because I didn't want you to worry."

"You're my girl, I'm supposed to worry."

"I'll be okay."

But Dajah wasn't so sure. Still, she knew Frieda didn't want to talk about it anymore. She changed the subject. "One good thing has come out of the mess with Rick and Gina."

"What's that?"

"With Gina gone, maybe me and Kanisha can get to know each other better."

"I'm sure once she does, she'll adore you."

Dajah looked off, seeking vistas unseen. "I hope so."

Rick always tried to prepare his daughter for whatever changes were coming into their lives, and the afternoon before Dajah's visit, he prepared Kanisha for that too.

"You remember my friend?" he asked carefully, the two of them eating ice cream cones in the park like old times.

"What friend, Daddy?"

"Remember? She was there that time your momma sent you downstairs."

"The one Momma said wasn't nothing but a stank heifer?"

"Kanisha."

"Yeah?"

"Do you even know what a stank heifer is?"

It took her a moment to think about it, form pictures in her mind, words accurate enough to describe it. Came up blank. "No."

"Exactly. Now, how can you call somebody something that you don't even know what it is?"

"Dat's what Momma said."

"Your mother said a lot of things. It doesn't mean everything she says is true."

"So she's not?" Rick shook his head no. "Why Momma call her that?"

Rick looked off. "For a lot of reasons. But the point is, Ms. Dajah is a very nice person, and she wants the chance to get to know you again."

"How come?"

"Because you're my number one, and I like her."

"You mean like momma?"

"No, not like that."

"Like how?"

"I like her, a lot."

"She like you?" Rick nodded. "A whole lot?"

"Yeah."

"She gonna take you away?"

"From where?"

"Me?"

"Don't you know nobody can do that? That me and you are forever?"

"She got kids?" Kanisha asked, in need of an angle that suited her.

"No, no kids."

"Oh." She seemed disappointed.

"Why?"

" 'Cause if she had kids, then me and her kids could play."

"You play at after-care, don't you?"

"That's different. When we was living at Granny 'Zander's house, I had friends."

"There's kids on our block. Why don't you play with them?"

"They don't want to."

"Well, maybe you just need to introduce yourself. Just go up to them and say, 'Hi, my name's Kanisha.' "

"I did, and they told me they couldn't play with me."

"How come?"

Her eyes grew wide, wounded. "Cause my momma went to jail. That's what they said. They said, 'Your momma got arrested. She went to jail.' "

"For a hot minute, but she's out now."

"They say she's a jailbird, so I'm a jailbird too. Are we jailbirds, Daddy?"

"No."

"Am I ever going to see her?"

"Of course you are."

"When?"

"In a little while."

"That's why I got to wait, 'cause she went to jail, right?"

"Something like that."

"Think she'll forget about me?"

"No, Kanisha, I don't." Ice cream slid along his hand. Rick made a big show of licking it up. "Umm, nothing like skin-flavored ice cream."

Kanisha giggled. "No such thing, Daddy."

"No?" He took another lick of his hand. "Taste like it to me." Rick looked into the brief burst of sunshine full on her face. "So, you think you want to see Ms. Dajah again?"

Her smile faded. "I guess."

"Good. Later on this afternoon, she's coming by."

"She gonna spend the night?"

"No."

That answer seemed to please her.

"Hi, Kanisha."

"Hi." Kanisha turned toward her father. "Can I go to my room?"

Rick nodded. "Sure." He looked at Dajah, shrugged as Kanisha walked away.

"Well, at least she didn't call me those awful names."

"She's having a rough time. Kids on the block won't play with her because they know Gina got arrested and went to jail. And she's worried about Gina forgetting about her."

"Poor kid, she's been through a lot."

Rick looked at the woman who had been there for him even when she wanted to walk away. Wanted her.

He wanted to take off every piece of clothing she wore and lead her to his bed. Wanted her naked and wanting beside him, but understood that until Kanisha grew comfortable with Dajah, such moments were put on hold.

He took up her hand, kissed it. "All I can do for now."

"Yeah, I know. Kind of cramping our style. What time does she go to sleep?"

"You kidding me? She be tucking me in . . . being with Gina."

"When I was that age, I was going to bed at eight."

"Yeah, right? Sun still be up and you be in the bed, just thinking how not tired you are, and the next thing you know it's morning."

"Missing all the good shows on TV."

"The other kids outside playing. You be in bed, hearing them having all that fun."

"Exactly, and you couldn't wait until summer, because then at least you got to stay up to nine."

"Ten, if you were lucky."

"Eleven if your folks were throwing a party."

"Where some uncle got wasted and your daddy had to kick them out before the party was half way over."

"And you be stealing sips from his glass."

"Throat be all burning, eyes watering and you're wondering what was the big deal."

"Till you got a buzz . . ." Dajah's head shook. "Childhood. Some of the best times."

"If you're lucky. And that's what I want for Kanisha. A good childhood. I know I've failed a whole lot. But now I just want to make it up to her."

"You will."

"Next week, I'll plan things a little different. I'll send her to my parents." He kissed her hand again. "It'll be me and you."

Dajah liked the sound of that.

The following Thursday Rick sat at his dining room table, phone to his ear. ". . . Your balance is one-thousand, three-hundred, forty-seven dollars and eighty-three cents." Rick jotted down the number, hung up the phone, sighed. The days missed from work, lack of overtime, was rearing its head.

He did not have to check the utility bills or the mortgage statement to know that what he had in his checking account would not cover it. He did not want to think about going to his parents for a loan to tide him over.

Rick didn't want to feel the strange, ego-bruising hurt coursing through him. But for the first time in his life, he did not have enough money. Couldn't handle his business. For the first time Rick was financially strapped.

He had worked so hard for so long, making sure he'd never get into this situation, but he hadn't counted on Gina doing what she'd done. To cover his legal fees, Rick had to take a ten-thousand-dollar loan against his pension. Now he had to swallow his pride and call upon parents he promised he would never call upon that way.

From the moment he had moved out of their house, he had never asked for a single dime. Not one red cent, something that his parents not only appreciated, but marveled at. But in a heartbeat, that was all changed.

He was five hundred dollars short this month. If he didn't correct the situation now, it would only grow worse. Beyond financial help, Rick needed child-care help. Heavy-duty overtime was called for, and with Gina out of the picture, someone had to watch Kanisha.

His parents weren't surprised to see him at their front door. He had brought Kanisha over so that he could spend real time with Dajah. What was surprising was the expression on his face, full of concern and worry.

"Kanisha, go put your stuff up in the bedroom. Then you watch TV in my room," Mrs. Trimmons said. "And no jumping on the bed. Remote's on the night table." She waited until Kanisha went upstairs before she turned to her son. "Everything okay?"

"No, I'm in a slight jam . . . financially." The word, hard off his tongue.

"You know, your father was saying you were going to come to us sooner or later. Looks like later's here, but that's what we're here for. We can only imagine what this whole mess cost you." Rick blinked back tears.

Rick's father spoke up. "I'll be right back."

His father disappeared up the stairs, returning five minutes later, a check in his hand. "I know this won't cover it, but I'm sure it'll help." He handed it to him. "Wish it could be more, but with those repairs on the house . . ."

Rick stopped him. "No, Dad, this is just fine. Thank you." Rick reached for his father, the two men hugging hard. Rick pulled back and looked at the amount, relief filling him. The check was for a thousand dollars, enough to cover this month and a little something for the next. "Can we go sit down? Something else I want to talk to you about."

The sight of Dajah looking summertime perfect though the season was coming to a fast end was pure eye candy as she opened her front door to him. He took in the little white shorts, barely-there T-shirt, glowing brown skin everywhere he looked.

"I think I'm going to be okay" were his first words as he closed the door behind him.

"We. We're going to be okay" was her response as she snaked her arms around him.

"My folks are going to watch Kanisha so I can go back to overtime."

"You need the money that badly?"

"With no money coming in for upstairs, I do."

"I made dinner."

But dinner was the last thing on Rick's mind as he eased her back toward the bedroom, lips meeting in between their laughter.

With care, he took off the cotton shirt, the second-skin shorts, delighted she didn't have a thing on underneath. In one motion he was on his knees, kissing her belly, nuzzling her pubic hair with his nose, the smell of her pungent, strong.

Everything they were to each other, every sorrow they had shared, coursed through him. Words formed in his heart, floated from his lips in the softest of timbres. "I love you, Dajah."

She had never heard him say it, but had felt it. Now, as his face lay flushed against the hollow of her stomach, she knew. A knowing that ran as wildly as a river, coursing over her, drowning her in its intensity. A knowing she had waited for, its arrival allowing her to admit to both herself and to him that she felt the same. "I love you too."

"Do you really?"

She laughed. "I'm still here, right? All that has happened, and here I am."

"I know it wasn't easy."

"But it was worth it," she offered softly. "You here with me, so worth it." She shifted from beneath him. Got down on her knees. Leaned her forehead until it was touching his. Her mouth sought his, and Rick welcomed it.

Mouths and tongues danced, tangoing around the other, fast, slow, with all the rhythms in between. No hands, no arms. Neither chests, breasts or pelvises. Just mouths, joined, rolling, teasing, tasting deeply.

They kissed as if there was nothing more to their lives, as if the motions of their lips were the alpha and the omega. Cocooned in the motion, lost to all else, they went on that way, flesh growing warm and damp, parts of them swelling, a slow-burning fire in the making because there was love now; love, the illusive dream, chased forever, before them.

Arms tingled to embrace, fingers itched to touch, but they resisted the end to this moment of want, desire and love. They staved off embracing, desire overwhelming them, stealing their breath, stirring up their souls because love had come. And to touch, hold, reach out, embrace, would mean an end to the heaven.

A glorious end, a climactic, soul-stirring end, but an end would surely come, leaving them panting and complete. So they resisted. Kept the motion of their mouths until neither thought they could take another second of the soft, syrupy pleasure. Kissing and kissing until they thought they would burst with pleasure, with heat, their need.

They staved off connecting until resistance was gone, then Rick reached for her, the touch of him making her tremble. They held each other, understanding. Held each other, knowing. The mountaintop had been reached, a second journey begun, as their lips found each other, starting anew.

It started innocently: eight-hour shifts becoming sixteen, regular days off becoming extra days on. Dajah started seeing less of Rick and too much of her own four walls. "I could come over, be there when you get there," she found herself saying.

Dajah found herself buying a second toothbrush and toting a gym bag with a change of clothes. When Rick talked about missing home-cooked meals, Dajah started preparing them, sticking them in the freezer when he was too tired to eat.

Life hit a balance for them again until one night Rick received a call on his cell on his way home. "I didn't want to say anything," his mother began. "I know how much you need to work all that extra time, but Kanisha's not happy here with us like this. I know you come and get her as often as you can, and I tried my best to explain it to her, but she misses you."

"Only for a little while."

"To me and you, but to that little girl it's a little while too long. She don't play with the kids outside no more. Don't want to do anything but sit in front of the TV, looking sad."

"I'll talk to her."

"Talking isn't going to help. Now I know she checked out fine with the doctor after she came from foster care, but that was a traumatic experience, and maybe in her mind she's back in foster care."

"What am I supposed to do, Mom?"

"Rick, I don't have any more answers than you, but something has

to be done. It's late . . . past my bedtime. We'll talk some more tomorrow."

"What am I going to do?" Rick was asking Dajah a little while later.
"What about me?"
"What about you?"
"I mean, I'm here almost all the time anyway. This way, at least
she'll be back here with you."
"You mean like watch her?"
"Yeah. Not like she's in Pampers or anything. We could work out
some kind of schedule where you can take her to her day care and I
could pick her up."
"You won't mind?"
"How could I?" It was a dry run of things to come: herself, Rick and
Kanisha.
"You sure about this, Dajah?"
"What else do I do after work? I go home, grab a few things, come
here. I'm not giving up my apartment or anything, and it won't be
every day. But sure, I'll do it."
"You're amazing, you know that?"
She considered the man before her. "Pretty amazing yourself."

Dajah closed Kanisha's bedroom door and went to let the bathwater
out. Then she was off to the kitchen to start the dishwasher. She wiped
down the countertops, as soothing music came from the living room.
    It had not been an easy journey, the business between her and
Kanisha. A difficult road. Kanisha had looked at her sideways, with
obvious discontent. But it became Dajah's very presence that shook
loose those shackles. Dajah gave her stability.
    It was Dajah who got her ready and drove her to school. Dajah who
picked her up at day care after work. It was Dajah who made sure
Kanisha had her favorite snacks. Dajah who helped with the homework, washed and combed her hair.
    She took Kanisha to her apartment a few times a week to check her
mail and water her plants, involving Kanisha in the simple activities.
Fridays became their "Blockbuster night," when they rented movies
and microwaved popcorn and huddled on the couch watching PG
movies.

During the third week of Kanisha's care, a corner was turned. Out of the clear blue sky, Kanisha addressed her as "Auntie Day."

"Auntie Day?" she'd said simply, catching Dajah by surprise.

"Yeah."

"Can I call you that?"

"If you want," Dajah said casually.

Dajah shared the milestone with Rick when he got in from his shift. But cute monikers were the last thing on his mind. His too-heavy work schedule was all he could consider. Financially he was making strides. Physically was a whole different ball game.

"I called up the newspaper, placed the ad for the apartment. It'll run in next Sunday's paper," Dajah went on to say.

"Thanks." Rick answered, getting into bed, fast asleep in no time.

Chapter 22

The trees along the Southern State were beginning their annual turning, hints of yellow, tinges of burgundy, crisps of brown filtered through the green in full color.

Dajah looked through her windshield at the marvel, the scent of damp, fallen leaves filling her car. She inhaled, exhaled, closed her eyes for a second, a part of her wanting to pull over, bask in the festive colors dotting the landscape.

But she had to pick up Kanisha by six, and it was already ten minutes after five. In her heart she knew there was no time. But she did the quick math anyway. Realized a piece of her life was missing.

She couldn't remember the last time she had stood on the boardwalk, the last time she had a good deep breath of ocean air. She was more than an accountant and surrogate mother. But in that moment it didn't feel like it.

Every nerve in her tingled for Jones Beach, two exits away. Every nerve wanted thirty minutes for herself. But there was no time; Kanisha was gobbling it whole. No time for herself and no time with Rick. Work, work and more work had become his mantra.

She was with him, but she had become a backdrop. *He has to make time,* she decided, bypassing the Jones Beach exit. *Just has to find some time for us.*

She searched her brain for something simple and uncomplicated. Came up with a movie date. It was doable, and Friday night would be perfect. She asked him later when he got in. "Think we can go to the movies this Friday?"

"Friday?"

"Yeah. I figured if you don't work that night, your mother could watch Kanisha."

"Friday." No longer a question.

"Yeah, Rick, this Friday. Nine o'clock show."

"I put in for overtime."

"Well, can't you just not work it this once?"

"You know I need the money."

"And I also know that you need time for yourself . . . and me."

"Just a little while longer, Dajah. Ms. Kincaid has a few people lined up for the apartment. She hasn't screened them yet, but she told me they looked hopeful."

"That's what she always says, and then she does the screening and finds out they've been in landlord and tenant court a few times, or can't really afford the place."

"I can't have just anybody living upstairs."

"I understand that, Rick, but we haven't done anything since I don't know when."

"We back to that?"

"Yeah, we're back to that. You know when I said I'd look after Kanisha, it was with the idea that it would free up our time."

"You offered, remember?"

"Yes, I did, but looking after her is all I do. You come dragging in here, too tired to even have a conversation." She shut up then, because that was the part that hurt, the part that showed a neediness she wasn't willing to expose.

"A few more weeks. That's all I need. By then I will have enough saved to see me through until the apartment gets rented."

"And if it doesn't?"

"It will." But Rick had more faith than Dajah could ever possess.

* * *

Tuesday morning Frieda stood in front of her bathroom mirror, running Hot Six oil through her hair—or at least what was left of it.

In need of a touch-up, a deep conditioner, a skilled beautician's hands, the roots were tight and the edges barely there. What used to dust her shoulders in full, shimmery sweeps now struggled along the back of her head. What used to gather willingly into her fist and fall past the grip, now could not contain itself in a scrungee.

But she brushed and brushed, adding thick black gel to the crown, the edges that were nearly nonexistent. Frieda ignored the hollows beneath her eyes, cheeks that looked sunken, the face she no longer knew that haunted her every time she glanced in a mirror.

She rinsed her hands of gel, dried them on the damp bath towel, left the bathroom and got her pocketbook, her keys. Four minutes later she was stepping out of her apartment building, an unforgiving wind finding her, the morning sky still dark.

She had an appointment with Dr. Kay later on that day, her one hope against the pressing gloom. *Doctor, heal me,* she thought as she made her way to work, not a speck of morning light anywhere.

Dr. Kay adjusted the fit of his glasses and looked at Frieda with critical eyes. "What do you want to do, Ms. Wilkes?"

"I'm not getting you, doctor."

"You've been seeing me for a while, and in all that time I've been telling you the same thing. So I am going to tell you what I haven't said. I am going to lay it all out for you."

Frieda swallowed. "I'm listening."

"Your pressure is so high, I should commit you to a hospital for rest, but I know you won't stay there. You are beyond dangerous waters; you are in them. If you do not slow down, you will probably have either a stroke, a heart attack, or both. Now I suggested to you on your first visit that you cut back, and obviously you are not heeding that advice. You can keep coming to see me, but there's nothing I can do for you if you don't do something for yourself."

With that, Dr. Kay stood, picked up the charts and left the room.

Stroke. Heart attack. It was all Frieda could think about. At thirty-one she was too young but was running the risk. She didn't go back to work. She went home and called her boss. "I just came from my doctor, and I can't work the way I've been working and I'm not coming back today, Herman. I'm taking a few days off too."

She didn't wait for an answer. Just hung up the phone. Lay down in the middle of the afternoon, fear keeping her wide awake.

She was trying to bargain with her body, trying to get it to correct itself. Frieda tried to get her heart to lessen its pace, get the nutrients to flow back to her skin and hair.

She was trying to will the circles from her eyes, flesh back onto her bones. But the more she tried, the worse she felt. The harder she tried, the more her heart raced. Then a pain came into her chest, as if a dragon had taken up residence there. She tried to will that away too, but the pain only got worse.

Heart attack.

Frieda reached for the phone, dialed 911, her chest feeling as though it was on the verge of exploding. She gave her name and address between gritted teeth, mewling moans, pain surging. The operator would not let her hang up, insisting that help was on the way.

It arrived five minutes later, but Frieda wasn't able to get up and let them in. Five minutes after that, just as Frieda was certain she was drawing her last painful breath, she heard a commotion at her door, uniformed paramedics racing her way, the building super behind her.

Not dead, she thought, but she'd come too close to count.

"Panic attack, Ms. Wilkes," the attending physician in the ER was saying twenty minutes later, "and hypertension."

"Not a heart attack?"

"Not yet. I've spoken to your doctor, and we both agreed that you need to stay overnight for observation. We're getting a room ready for you now. Is there someone you need to call?"

Frieda nodded her head yes.

No tubes up her nose, no monitors beeping out her vitals. Just an IV, and the daughter who looked as if she had aged twenty years.

"Oh," was all Mrs. Wilkes could say, one hand covering her mouth, keeping back the anguish that wanted to leave her.

Mrs. and Mr. Wilkes moved apart, each taking up one side of the bed. "No, Frieda, No," her father muttered. "This can't go on another day."

"I know, Dad . . . thought I was dying, and all I could think was how I have a whole life to live. So I'm not going back there. I'm finished. Through. Going to take some time, get myself together. Find another job."

"Frieda?" They all looked up. Barry stood in the doorway, holding both sides of the frame, chest heaving. He had raced over to the hospital the moment he had gotten the message, his first real breath coming as he saw her, fear tinging the air around him, charged.

"She's going to be okay," Mr. Wilkes said.

Frieda lifted a hand, summoning him. "I'm quitting, Barry. This is it. I'm done."

He went to her bed, reached for her. "All I want," he said, feeling more bones than skin beneath the gown.

"The scariest thing I ever went through. Just a panic attack, but I thought I was dying." She sighed. "Can you call Dajah, let her know where I am, that I'm all right?"

Barry nodded. "Consider it done."

Dajah let herself into her apartment, eyes scanning the floor beneath her ficus tree. There had been three dead leaves the last time she came home. Now there were too many to count.

Already after six she knew she had to get back to Rick's and soon. There was dinner to be made and homework to be worked through. Kanisha was only in kindergarten, but the agenda went beyond learning how to spell her own name.

She did a fast inspection of her apartment, checking the contents of her refrigerator for spoilage and making sure the windows were tightly shut. Dajah checked the soil on all her plants and then went through her mail, separating junk from bills.

Last she checked her messages. There was only one, and she hoped it wasn't important. It was nearing six-thirty, and she was on the clock. Dinner alone would take nearly half an hour.

"Dajah, this is Barry." *Barry?* "Frieda's in the hospital. She's at Jamaica. Just a panic attack, but they're going to keep her for a few days. She can have visitors up until eight. Call her if you can't get over there."

Frieda was in the hospital. Her favorite plant was dying. Dinner had to be made, and Kanisha had to get her homework done.

"You know your granny's number?" Dajah asked Kanisha, picking door number one.

Steely and determined was how Dajah drove, face hard-edged, every breath urging her to get there. With the same stony expression, she didn't even consider a meter, but drove into the pay parking lot, making her way into the hospital.

She went to Information, the two people ahead of her making her antsy, the thirty-second wait feeling like a lifetime. Armed with a visitor pass and directions, Dajah boarded the elevator, eyes straight ahead.

The doors opened to the sound of chimes, women shuffling by in colorful smocks and white leather shoes. Heart monitors, wheelchairs and IV stands stood sentry and abandoned, forgotten weapons in the battle to heal.

But it was the absence of vibrant life, the hushed whisper of death and dying that she noticed. It was the hospital rooms, doors ajar, curtains drawn, others opened, exposing failed health, death dancing everywhere she looked.

Dajah moved, room numbers going by like road signs. She had promised herself that she would be strong, but by the time she got to Frieda's, all semblance of that determined strength had left her.

The first tear was trickling as she rounded the door, saw Frieda, eyes closed, Barry holding her hand, staring out into space.

He looked up, their eyes locking, an anguished knowing moving between them as Barry blinked and blinked again. He found a smile, sorrowed, pain-filled, and offered it up as he rose and embraced Dajah.

They held each other a long time. Didn't share any words. The silence continued as they broke apart. Dajah wiped a tear, and Barry woke Frieda up.

"Babe, Babe? Hey, Dajah's here."

Frieda came to, squinting against the soft light over her head. Lips dry, she wet them, lifted a hand.

Dajah took it, squeezed it. "Hey, girl."

"Hey," Frieda answered softly.

"You okay?"

"Yeah, I'm okay now. I wasn't earlier, though. Dr. Kay warned me, and I wouldn't listen. Well, I'm listening now. County Hospital has seen the last of me."

"You sure?" Dajah wanted it affirmed.

"As sure as my name is Frieda Maryanne Wilkes."

Thrice spoken, it became deed.

Dajah and Barry sat with Frieda until visiting hours ended, both of them unwilling to leave her even as the nurse insisted they had to. The two of them didn't speak much as they waited for the elevator and rode it down, the day coming to a wearied end.

Best friend and boyfriend walked, neither certain if Frieda was truly over the hump, or if she would give herself real time to heal. Sitting around twiddling her fingers wasn't in her nature. Frieda was always about something, and work was at the top of her list.

Barry broke the silence with a secret confession. "Every day I thought she was just going to drop dead. Every time I kissed her good-bye, I just knew it was the last."

"You love her a lot, don't you?"

"Like I never loved anybody. Frieda is my world."

They stopped at the parking attendant's office, sharing a long hug. "She's going to be okay, Barry."

"In a big way, this was a good thing. She's not going back to that job."

"No, she's not."

"You get home safe."

"I will. Good night." Dajah waited until Barry headed up the street before she handed over her parking ticket, pulled out a ten-dollar bill. Yawning, she was tired as she waited for her car, looking forward to a good hot shower and sleeping with the bedroom windows cracked.

Fall had geared up, and the cool breeze was invigorating. It wasn't until she was on the Van Wyck Expressway that she realized she couldn't go home. Kanisha had to be picked up, homework had to be done and a bath had to be given. Clothes needed ironing, and there was a backpack to inspect.

Dajah thought about the man in her life, too tired to hold simple conversations, and the words Barry had shared with her this night.

She tried to find the silver lining beneath it all, but it refused to show itself.

After nine at night, and it felt like midnight. After nine, and Dajah still had a list of things to do before she could turn in. She dragged the dishcloth over the dining room table, gathering up bits of NY Fried Chicken into her palm.

She was halfway to the kitchen when the doorbell rang. Nobody ever rang the bell so late at night. She ignored it. When the bell began ringing again, urgent and anxious, Dajah decided to at least have a look.

Eye to the peephole, she spied a slice of burgundy hair with thick black roots and knew who it was without seeing the face. She was not supposed to be there, but Dajah opened the door anyway, letting the storm door be a barrier between herself and Gina.

The first thing she noticed was how worn Gina looked. The second was the eyes—puffy, red. Either Gina was high, or she had been crying. She found out the answer when Gina spoke.

Every word was a stumbling block, every word difficult for her to say. "Know I'm not supposed to be here and shit . . . just wanted to see how Kanisha's doing."

"I can't let you in, Gina, you know that."

Gina raised her hand with a weary smile. "I know that. I ain't asking to come in. Just wanted to know if she okay?"

"She's fine."

Gina's eyes glistened. "You tell her I asked for her, all right? You tell her her Mommy asked about her. That I ain't forgot her."

"I will."

Gina turned and headed down the steps. Dajah watched until she disappeared up the block. Later that night when Rick came in, she didn't tell him. Dajah didn't tell Kanisha either. Just kept Gina's visit to herself.

Better, that's how Frieda looked four days later, the hospital stay doing her good, the heavy work load gone.

Dajah hugged her, and Frieda hugged her back. Whispered, "I know, I know."

Frieda pulled back. Took in the cute little girl standing next to Dajah. "This must be Kanisha."

Kanisha stared at her. Dajah urged her to speak up. "Say hello, Kanisha."

"Hello." Her eyes immediately left Frieda, mistrust filling her face as she looked around.

"Well, come on in. I have Cartoon Network—would you like to watch that?"

Kanisha didn't answer, just looked up at Dajah, one tiny hand clasping hers hard. It was then that Dajah saw fear in her eyes. Knew she had to dismantle it. "Me and Ms. Frieda need to talk in private, and she has a big television in her bedroom. You can go in there and watch it. I'll be right out here."

"Promise?"

"I promise."

Kanisha nodded. But she wouldn't move an inch until Dajah did. She took her down the hall, found the remote, clicked on the television and warned about "putting your feet on the bed." Dajah left, closing the door behind her, taking refuge on Frieda's couch, ready to talk, and listen.

"Is she attached to you, or is she attached to you?"

"She's had it rough."

"But she's cute as she wants to be. Looks just like Rick."

"Yeah, right? So, how is it going?"

"Going okay."

"You stir-crazy yet?"

A small smile escaped Frieda's lips. "You know I am. I still wake up at five, every morning like I have somewhere to go. I am managing to go back to sleep, but my whole body is just off."

"Takes time."

"Yeah, I know. But it's hard."

"Most important thing is you're still here."

"It's amazing what a little panic attack can do. Don't you know the money County couldn't find to get me staff has suddenly appeared?"

"You lying."

"You see me sprout wings? Herman called yesterday. Talking about the budget was approved and if I came back—"

"If?"

"Don't even worry. I'm not, but he said that if I came back, I would have two staff employees waiting. I told him it was too late. That I wasn't coming back, not even to clear out my desk." Frieda looked off. "You know, when you all in the middle of something, you really can't see the forest for the trees. Nobody can tell you nothing, because you just know it all. I just knew I was fine. I could handle it. Now? It was just crazy, plain madness. My next gig is going to be a strictly nine-to-five."

"You know General Management is always looking."

"Yeah, but I want to take my time and decide. I have some money socked away, so I'll be okay. But my next job is going to be carefully selected."

"Good for you, Frieda."

"Yeah, good for me. So, how does it feel?'

"What?"

"Having a ready-made family?"

"It's not peaches and cream."

"You are looking a little worn around the edges."

Dajah's voice rose—"because I am"—then lowered. "All I do is go to work and look after Kanisha."

"What about Rick?"

"What about him? Overtime, all he knows, thinks about. We haven't been anywhere, done anything, in I don't know when. And our sex life?" Dajah looked off.

"That bad?"

"Yeah, that bad. I mean, here I am lying next to him every night, and the few times we do manage a little something, it's nowhere near what it used to be."

"You talked to him about it?"

"I tried, but he's always too tired to listen or don't want to talk about it or tells me it's just for a little while longer."

"So what are you going to do?"

"You seen how Kanisha is with me. If I left now . . ."

"Dajah, are you hearing yourself?"

She looked at her friend, caught and surprised. She hadn't heard herself when she'd spoken it, but she did in the aftermath. "But what can I do, really? I can't leave."

"Not just because of Kanisha, right?"

Dajah paused. "He loves me, Frieda."

"And you love him back."

"Yeah, I do . . . never thought I'd end up here," she said after a while.

"Relationships aren't easy, Dajah."

"Yours and Barry's is."

Frieda laughed. "You think? Then you've been thinking wrong. It's a real give and take, and a lot of times I'm just not up to the giving. But then other moments come when I realize just how foolish I was in hesitating. Then something else will pop up, and bingo, I'm like, oh, hell no, it's not what I want. It's a merry-go-round, being with someone. You go up, you go down, but it's never steady. Only thing that is, is the love."

"Well, my ride must be stuck or broke or something because me and Rick's been down for a while."

"You've come this far. I think you owe it to the both of you to go a little further."

"To where? Where are we heading, trying to get to? Because if it's going to be about Kanisha all the time, or him, where's my place?"

"For right now you're the center. Their life revolves around you."

Frieda had found a reason for her to stay in Rick's life, and it lifted Dajah's heart by the time she left there. *They need me* became her new battle cry, but day-to-day living began to wear away the strength of those words, especially when Rick seemed unwilling to talk about anything.

By the next week, *they need me* held no power, and Dajah was back to feeling overwhelmed. The last thing she needed was Gina ringing the doorbell a second time, but she did, with "Just want to check on Kanisha" before Dajah could even say hello.

More visits happened; brief words spoken through the glass pane of the storm door. Gina's questions—"How's Kanisha? You tell her I asked about her?"—and Dajah's answers—"She's fine and I did"—barely wavering until one night Gina asked, "You got a minute?"

For the first time ever, Dajah left the safety of the screen door, coming out to sit on the steps.

"I don't know where to begin, y'know? So much shit happened." Dajah didn't say anything. "Till this fucking day I don't know what I did so wrong. She was only by herself for a little while. I knew Rick would come home soon. But they act like I tried to kill her or something. Now everything is gone. My place, my kid. Benefits . . . Rick." Her eyes found Dajah. "I just knew I could run you off. But shit, you like fucking glue."

She sighed. "Didn't mean that shit. You all right. More than all right. You taking care of my kid. Not many women would do that. I know I wouldn't, that's for damn sure. Rick told me you was the one who said I should be bailed out. That blew my mind. You must really love him."

Dajah didn't answer.

"Must do. All the shit you been through. Can't be for the money 'cause since he bought this house, I know he broke." Gina looked up toward the second-floor window. "He rent it yet?"

"Not yet."

"I liked that apartment. Seemed like all my life I been looking for some space to call my own. I had it and blew it." Dajah saw her shoulders jerk, realized she was crying.

She didn't try to interfere. Did not try to soothe her. Just let her be. Then Gina was looking over at her with wet, sad eyes. "Ever been scared?"

"Yeah, I have."

"When?"

"That day you came down stairs and I was hiding in the kitchen, for one."

Gina smiled. "You right. I couldn't see your face, but the fact that you was hiding out told me you wasn't about to get in my face." She looked off. "Been going to my parenting classes and behavioral thing. Get to see a counselor four times a week. One on one. I talk about everything. Stuff that happened in my life."

"That's good," Dajah offered, the night air cold. She rubbed her arms. "I better get back inside."

"Yeah, I know. And I got to get my ass home. My parenting thing early in the morning. I was already late once this week."

They both stood, Dajah noticing they were the same height. She found herself studying Gina all over again, her eyes lingering on her earlobes. The holes were puffy, black-ringed and empty of her signature oversized hoops.

"Some bitch took them from me in jail," Gina offered, heading down the steps

Chapter 23

Another work day behind her, Dajah was busy in Rick's kitchen when the phone rang.

"Dajah? Nancy Kincaid. Would Rick happen to be home?"

"He's working."

"Listen. I've got a couple. Great jobs, impeccable credit and they are looking to move by the first. I want to come and show the apartment. I need to know when would be a good time?"

"Any day after six."

"Any day?"

"Sure. If Rick can't be here, I can. Just let us know."

"Great. Will do."

Nancy Kincaid hung up, and Dajah thought about all that it meant. No more overtime. No more baby-sitting. She would have her life back, be able to spend real time with Rick.

She couldn't wait to tell him, staying up past midnight to call him on his cell. Dajah repeated verbatim the conversation she'd had with Ms. Kincaid. Waited to hear his joy. But there was no enthusiasm in his voice.

"That's great."

"I call to tell you what I thought we both have been waiting for, and you act like I just told you a weather report . . . y'know, this has gotten beyond tired, this whole thing."

"I know it's not easy."

"Well, good."

"It's just that . . ."

"Just what?" Because she really wanted an answer as to why he wasn't seeing it the way she was—a prayer answered.

"I didn't buy the house with the idea that some strangers would be living over my head."

"It *is* a two-family house."

Rick could feel the tension in her. Didn't have to dig too deep to determine why. The last few weeks had been about work, saving up his money and little else. Dajah had been forced to the sidelines.

He had promised her 'just for a little while," but even he knew that time had come and gone. He thought about what he had saved so far. Realized that if he was careful, he could be okay. Dajah had done more than her part. It was time to do his. "Tonight was my last night," he decided at the last minute.

"Last night for what?"

"Overtime. I got enough saved. I'll be okay."

"You sure?"

"Absolutely. And Friday night, we'll go somewhere."

"Where?"

"Any place you want."

Five seconds ago it had seemed as if they would never get beyond the impasse. Now that the reward was before her, she didn't know what to say.

"Dajah?"

"Yeah, I'm here."

"I know it wasn't easy, all you've done. But I do appreciate it and you. I just wanted to let you know that."

She wanted to say that she did. Dajah wanted to say his words weren't even necessary, but it was too close to a declaration she'd longed for, and its arrival held her tongue.

Lost time could never be reclaimed, lost moments could never be regained, but Rick seemed to be on a mission. At least twice a week he was taking Dajah somewhere, the two of them out and about doing something.

This night found them at an Italian restaurant in Astoria.

Rick ordered spaghetti, and Dajah found herself doing the same. Twelve minutes later their meal was before them and they both began to dig in.

"Good?" Rick asked.

"Yeah."

He nodded, went back to eating. Rick took two more bites. Chewed, swallowed, waiting for Dajah to find his eyes. "I got a call."

"From who?"

"The courts. Gina's finished her parenting and behavior courses. They've scheduled her to come see Kanisha next Wednesday."

"Well, that's a good thing."

"Yeah, it is. I just wanted to let you know."

"You tell Kanisha?"

"Not yet. I want to make sure it's a go before I do." Rick laughed. "You never know with Gina."

"Yeah," Dajah thought, recalling all those visits she'd made, "you never know."

The idea that Gina was coming back into the mix was okay with Dajah right up until Wednesday at two o'clock. Sitting at her desk at work, she longed to be a fly on the wall, wanting to see how Kanisha would react. How Rick would.

She hadn't loved her brief time as surrogate mother, but some part of her wanted what she'd done to remain important. She had made sacrifices and wanted it to matter. Dajah didn't want it forgotten in Gina's return.

Dajah didn't want to have the empty feeling that found her, eyes on the clock, imagined scenes in her head. But there was little choice because the equation had just been changed.

The family unit she had slipped into with opened arms was, at that very moment, welcoming home the true lost daughter, the one who had been there first, the one who had been there longer. The one whose connections ran deepest.

"Cut it." Self-advice formed in her head and made its way to her tongue. "Ain't even that kind of a party." It took a hot second to realize she was talking to herself out loud. Another before relief found her that she hadn't answered back.

Good or bad, Kanisha wasn't sure, only that her heart spoke what her mind couldn't decide, and she went running across the room, arms open, eyes wide with delight. "Momma."

"Kanisha." Gina bent down, and held her daughter kissing every inch of her face. "I missed you, I've missed you. I missed you. Lord knows I've missed my baby." Gina's voice grew choppy. "You been okay? You been all right?"

"Yeah."

"Dajah tell you all them times I came by, asked about you?"

"No."

Gina looked at Rick, but Rick seemed just as puzzled. Gina looked back at Kanisha. "She ain't tell you? She said she did. Every time I came by, I asked and she said yeah, she told you."

"You came by?" Rick's question.

Gina let her daughter go. "At least two, three times a week. Never when you was home 'cause I knew I wasn't supposed to, but yeah. Dajah used to come to the door. Sometimes we sit and talk."

Rick looked at her, trying to determine fact from fiction. "You sure, Gina?"

"Why would I lie about something like that? I've told enough lies already. I'm not trying to tell any mutherfu—any more."

"I'm not saying you lying."

"Well, good." She looked around. "Can I get a seat?"

Rick indicated the couch. Gina took it. She looked at her daughter, patted the space next to her. "Come and sit over here next to me." Kanisha did. "That's right. Right next to your momma. Got to apologize, Baby. Got to apologize for leaving you alone like I did. Like I used to do. I didn't know it was wrong till they told me how wrong it was." She looked at Rick. "They pulled out pictures and stuff of burnt-up little bodies. Women leaving their kids home for just a few minutes. I saw that, and it blew my mind. Kept thinking, what if that had happened to me?"

"They?" Rick asked, taking a seat too.

"Yeah. My parenting classes. Ain't no joke, Rick. It makes you take a hard, long look at a lot of stuff. They gonna help me find a job. I'm ready now. I wasn't really ready before, but I sure am now. I want something for myself, y'know?"

Yes, Rick did. He had known it all his life. Had lived by the creed. What surprised him was that Gina did.

He saw other changes in her, about her. For the first time in years her hair was her own color and all hers. The dragon nails were gone, and even her style of dress had changed. Her khakis weren't skin-tight, and the sweater she had on only showed skin around her neck and her wrists.

Gina talked on. "I'm still living with Jefferson, and I swear most the time he drives me crazy. He like an old woman, fussing over me and stuff, but you know, sometimes it's nice. Nice to be fussed over."

"I guess."

"I know I'm not supposed to leave here with her, but would it be all right if I take her to the corner store, buy her something?"

"I don't know about that."

"You could come with us, make sure she's okay. Just up the street and back."

Rick took a few seconds to think about it. Nodded and went off to get his and Kanisha's jackets.

To the minute, that was how Dajah calculated the time Gina would be leaving and the time Rick would be calling, telling her all about the visit. She predicted no later than four-forty. But four-forty soon became five to five. Then five to five became five o'clock, time to go home.

But Dajah didn't go home. She drove to Rick's house, expecting to see his SUV in the driveway. It wasn't. She rang the doorbell and got no answer. Using her key, she went inside, not really knowing why until she found herself checking the garbage cans.

What am I doing?

Looking for evidence, something told her, evidence that Gina and Rick had done more than share a visit. She was looking for that little ripped foil package, a used condom wrapped in a tissue.

Dajah was looking for hints of perfume on the bed, body fluids on the sheets, except she didn't have time to fully investigate as she heard keys going into the front door lock and the turn of the cylinder.

She dashed to the kitchen as a slight whoosh filled the air, the front door opening, Rick calling out, "Dajah? You here?"

"In the kitchen," she answered back, grabbing a glass out of the cabinet and opening the refrigerator. "I decided to stop by on the way home," she went on to say, pouring herself some ice water. "Just got here, figured I'd wait for you guys." She came out, sipping, a wide, unfeeling smile on her face. "So, how did it go?"

"It went pretty good."

"My momma came by?" Kanisha wanted to know.

"Today, right? Earlier?" Dajah asked, puzzled.

"No. Before. She said she came by lots of times and asked about me."

Dajah looked to Rick, but she could tell Rick had questions of his own. Let go the truth. "Yes, Kanisha, she did."

"How come you didn't tell me?"

"Because she could have gotten in big trouble if anybody found out, and I didn't want her to get into trouble."

"She used to say she miss me?"

"Yeah, she did."

"I missed her too." With that, Kanisha went to her room and closed the door.

But if Kanisha was letting her off the hook, Rick wasn't. "Since when we keep secrets?"

"We don't. But like I said, if anybody knew, she could have gotten into trouble. You know she wasn't supposed to be within two-hundred feet of that child."

"If anybody knew but you, right?"

Dajah was already outdone by her own actions and Rick's lack of. She wasn't willing to go head-to-head over a long-ago decision. Tried to cut to the quick. "We are not going to get into an argument about this."

"But she wasn't supposed to be here, not even outside the house."

"I know that. That's why I didn't say anything . . . Look, she wanted to know how her daughter was, and I took the time to tell her."

"She said sometimes you two talked."

"Yeah, we did."

"And I guess what was said is between you two."

"You want to know what she said? What she talked about? Fine, I'll tell you. She talked about being confused. Talked about having nothing and losing everything: the apartment, Kanisha. You."

"She said that?"

"Yeah."

"I knew she had changed."

"A whole lot from what I could see. I mean, she actually thanked me for taking care of Kanisha."

"That's deep."

"Exactly. So should I have turned her away? Yes, but she was just being a mother, and if telling her about her daughter was what she needed to hear, so be it." Dajah took a deep breath, her mind swirling. A minute ago she had been certain that Gina had been up to no good; now here she was defending her.

"I'm sorry."

But Dajah had no use for his sorry. He had given her too many already. "Forget about it. It's done." She took the glass back to the kitchen, put it in the sink, moving into her caretaker mode. "You guys eat yet?"

"Yeah. Went to IHOP."

"The three of you?"

"It was Kanisha's idea. 'Like before' was how she put it." The delight in Rick's voice, full.

It was then that Dajah felt it, the major corner, turned. One that had happened without her, leaving her somewhere in the background. She tried to put those feelings somewhere less hurting as she came out of the kitchen, but they stuck to the corner of her eyes, the curve of her mouth. "I think I'll head on home." The last place she wanted to be.

"Catch you tomorrow?"

"Sure," Dajah answered, "tomorrow." The words like sand in her throat.

Excuses filled her on the drive home. Dajah came up with a whole bunch of reasons why Rick had not ask her to stay.

He was preoccupied with how well the visit went. The IHOP meal made him tired. He had to get up early in the morning. This was what

Dajah clung to as she made her way down the street. But the farther her car took her, the less sound the excuses became. The closer she got to home, the more lucid other reasons grew.

She opened her apartment door, stared at her dead "Baby," the Ficus looking like a scarecrow, not a single green leaf anywhere. She was supposed to have thrown it out days ago but had forgotten to put it out with the trash.

There were quite a few dead plants about her apartment, their leaves parched and yellowed. They were supposed to have gone out to the trash too, but she'd forgotten. Friday, she told herself as she clicked on more lights and went to check her messages.

Dajah took off her work clothes, put on her pajamas and turned on the television. But nothing held her attention, and she found herself reaching for the phone.

The phone rang four times before he picked up. "Hello?'

"Hey."

"Dajah?"

"Rick?" she volleyed back.

"Everything okay?"

The fact that he didn't have a clue hurt, but he wasn't a mind reader. She hadn't told him, but she could tell him now. "I was doing a lot of thinking on the ride ho—" A split second of dead air came into the line. She knew the words before he spoke them.

"Got another call. Hold on."

But she had been on hold for far too long already. "Nah, go answer. Not important. Catch you later." She hung up, turned off the light, sleep far, far away.

The couple Ms. Kincaid had called about found another apartment before she could show Rick's. Dajah was devastated, but Rick wasn't.

He took it in stride. Put the whole thing out of his mind. Stayed careful with his money and managed.

Occasionally he would go upstairs, wander around the rooms like a ghost. He would vacuum the carpets and dust the furniture. Heading back downstairs, he'd feel better about things.

It was never his intention to be a landlord to strangers; his house was supposed to be a home. When Ms. Kincaid stopped calling about potential tenants, that was fine with him too.

He installed light timers, so that lights would come on at dusk and go off at eleven at night. He had had a few people ring his bell inquiring if it was empty, and the light tricks put a stop to that.

Life settled back into a rhythm, a pattern he could use. Rick had few complaints, had reached the milestone of having the best of both worlds: his daughter and someone to share life with. For him life was complete. For Dajah, it became a compromise.

She'd learned not to make plans on Wednesdays because that was Gina's day to visit. Dajah learned to stop asking about anyone inquiring about the apartment, got used to its pressing emptiness. She'd learned to take the shift in Kanisha with huge grains of salt. Gina was back, but Dajah was still in the running, a running she would continue until the race was finished.

Because he loves me.

It took a while for her to reach that bottom line. A while to wade through the morass of all she'd been through with Rick and without him. It took some time to realize that what she'd wanted, she finally had. That reaching such a milestone was never easy, but it had been reached.

Candy corn.

Big bags of it spilled out of bins in the supermarkets and in the front aisles of drugstores. This was the first sign that Halloween was on its way.

Dajah had been big on it when she was a kid, but it had been decades since she'd given the trick-or-treat days much thought. This year was different.

Dajah had spied the cutest little fairy princess costume in the Eckerd drugstore. She found herself going through plastic-sealed bags looking for the right size. Dajah didn't cringe at the twenty-dollar price tag, just placed it on the counter along with her deodorant, sanitary napkins and toothpaste.

She left it in her car overnight, taking it with her when she went to ring Rick's bell the next day. She held it her behind her back and then thrust it in front of her when he let her in. "Isn't it the cutest thing?"

"A costume?"

"Yeah, for Kanisha. You know, I was thinking. I could leave work early, come on over and the two of us could take her."

"Take her where?" Rick asked, closing the door.

"Trick-or-treating."

Rick's eyes left hers, came back. "Me and Gina was going to take her."

"Oh."

"I didn't think to tell you."

Dajah shook her head, gathering up all the scattered pieces of her heart. "No big deal." She looked at the costume in her hand. "Well, she can still use this."

"She's already picked out who she wants to be. A PowerPuff girl."

Dajah blinked. Looked off. "Batting zero, aren't I?"

"It was the thought that counts."

"I guess I can get a refund. It's not open or anything."

"I'm sor—" Rick stopped himself. Took the costume from her hand. "Tell you what. Keep it here. Who knows, she might change her mind."

"Or maybe she can use it to play dress-up. I know when I was a kid I used to wear my princess costume way past Halloween." She looked around her. "Where is she?"

"With Gina. She's getting unsupervised visits now, so Kanisha's spending the night. Figured it would give us the whole evening to-gether."

"Oh."

Rick headed for the kitchen. "Dinner's done. You ready?"

It was Frieda who called, having not seen her friend in a while. "It's been a while since we got together."

For good reason, Dajah thought. "You're right. We can get to-gether tomorrow."

"Tomorrow it is."

Dajah was happy to see how good Frieda looked. Her hair had got-ten thicker and longer, the hollows of her eyes had filled and she had gained back the ten pounds she'd lost. More importantly, she had found a job that worked.

"It's kind of weird, you know. Having people running around doing stuff for you all day. I swear, Dajah, all I do is assign work and look it over. I feel like I'm cheating somebody with what they're paying me."

"I'm happy for you."

"I'm happy for myself. And you, how are you doing?"

"Doing okay."

"And Rick?" Dajah hesitated. "It's all over your face. What's going on?"

She felt silly even sharing her fears, knew the advice Frieda was going to give before she even gave it.

"Gina is Kanisha's mother, and she's going to be around. You really have to make yourself comfortable with that."

"I know that, Frieda. But you know, knowing something and feeling something is two different things and I'm trying, really I am, just that I didn't expect it to be so hard."

"What hard? Gina being a mother to her child? I know you took up the slack, but it was never really your slot, it's Gina's. And you have to accept it."

"The whole Halloween thing . . . I know it's such a small thing, but I made it into some big deal. I just assumed it would be the three of us. Felt like a fool standing there with a costume I picked out, like I didn't remember that part of the fun was picking out who you wanted to be."

"It's just the beginning, so get ready. There's going to be a whole lot of holidays when you're going to have to step away. Thanksgiving and Christmas, the major ones." Dajah hadn't thought of that. "It's part of what it's like when you are seeing a man with a child by someone else, and to survive it, you have to get your heart right. And trust Rick."

"That's what it's really about, isn't it?"

"That all it's ever been about. It's about Rick and Gina and Kanisha being together, and I know every time they are, some part of you thinks it's going to become a permanent thing. And I can understand that. But you have to concentrate on your relationship with Rick and forget everything else. As long as you feel he's there for you, with you, then you have to let all that other stuff go. Because if you don't, it's going to become like a cancer, eating away at you bit by bit till there's nothing left."

Dajah knew that. Knew because the process had already begun. She felt the nibbles every time Rick mentioned Gina's name. "I just don't know how to handle it."

"Well, you have to find a way—that is, if you want it to work."

Chapter 24

Laughing out loud.

It took a moment for Rick to realize he was and that Gina had been the cause.

"It's the truth, Rick. Look at him. You know his momma took an old sheet and draped it across him. Took some of them fake flowers and told him, boy, put that thing on your head and get out of here."

The days had grown chilly, but Indian summer returned for Halloween. The breeze was soft and warm, and the sunset was luminous as Rick, Gina and Power Puff Kanisha moved through the neighborhood.

They stopped in front of a low-roofed ranch. Rick urged Kanisha toward the front door. "Don't forget to say thank you," he shouted as she rang the bell.

"His momma probably doing the best she can," Gina went on to say. "When I was a kid, my costume was whatever I had on that day. Funny how stuff don't change."

It took a while for Rick to notice it, but in the times he had spent with Gina, he saw it for himself. She had stopped cursing. Rick asked about it.

"Yeah, those behavior classes. I learned that using foul language was a way to show my anger, and every time I said one of them four-letter words, it hurt me, not helped. So I been trying real hard, especially since I got my job. Can't be cursing at work—that's grounds for them firing you, and I like working at the library. They got all them books, and I get to read as many as I want."

"You read?"

"Yeah. Got my favorites too. Octavia Butler. She be creating whole worlds and shi—stuff. Just deep. Makes you think. But I kinda like thinking." She paused. "You still ain't rented the apartment?"

"No."

Kanisha came running back, candy, bag swinging. "I got lots of candy, Daddy," she said, opening her sack for inspection.

"You sure have. Now let's go see if we can get some more."

Dajah pulled away from the window, the night sky complete, her street hushed. Every year the number of kids out ringing doorbells seemed to grow less and less, and this year the downward trend was holding. She knew why.

The streets were no longer as safe as they used to be, and parents began directing their children to houses of people they knew. The days of canvassing a whole neighborhood were over, and running out of treats was a rarity.

She glanced at the clock. A little after eight. No doubt her last little goblin had been half an hour ago. She would take the remainder to work, put it in the break room, let her co-workers indulge themselves till it was all gone.

Dajah went down her steps to get the big plastic bowl of goodies by the front door and was on her way up when her doorbell rang.

The door was only halfway open when she heard an enthusiastic, "Trick or Treat!" Pulling it wider, Dajah saw a Power Puff girl she knew to be no one but Kanisha, Rick behind her.

"Hi, Auntie Day, you got candy?"

"What are you guys doing here?"

"Kanisha wanted to come over."

"Do you, Auntie Day? You got candy?" she asked, opening her too-full bag.

"I sure do. Come on in."

Dajah held the bowl aloft. "Take whatever you want." Kanisha was happy to oblige, digging in with both hands.

"We're talking a stomach ache from now to Christmas," Rick decided, the three of them heading up the stairs.

Christmas. Dajah did not want to think about it. Didn't want to imagine herself at her parents' holiday table and Rick somewhere across town. But she did need to prepare herself for the moment. "What are your plans?'

"For?"

"Christmas."

"Haven't thought that far."

"I mean, where are you going to spend it?"

"At my parents', I guess."

His parents. They liked her. She could go there and feel welcomed, no matter who was there, or wasn't. Mood lifted, her concerns shifted elsewhere. "You guys are out kinda late. It's past her bedtime."

Rick closed the upstairs door behind him. "Yeah, I know. Just wanted you to see our little Power Puff girl." 'Our' magic. 'Our' special. 'Our' reconnecting her.

"Auntie Day?"

"Yeah?"

"Where's Baby?"

"Baby's gone."

"Where did she go?"

Dajah looked at the empty space near her window. "Far, far away."

When Rick stopped working his overtime, he had done so with the idea that he would be careful with his money. But he hadn't counted on the little things. His heating bill for one.

A summertime move did not prepare for winter living. How much it cost to heat a two-family house didn't even cross his mind until the bills started rolling in. October was the forerunner for winter, and he begun turning the heat on in the mornings. When October became November, he kept it on all day, keeping both floors at a comfortable seventy-six.

Rick had promised himself that when he grew up and had a place of his own, he would never go cold. Rick had promised that he would never have to walk around in sweaters and socks the way his parents made him do, the thermostat never pushed higher than seventy, even on the most severe cold days.

He didn't think much about it until he got his heating bill. What had been seventy dollars had bloomed to a hundred and forty. With darkness coming in early, the electric bill went up too. Kanisha had outgrown her winter clothes from last year and needed new ones. Before he knew it, his backup had backslid.

Rick knew what he had to do, but refused to ask Dajah for help this time around. He thought to ask his mother, but it hadn't worked out before. That left door number three. Rick walked though without looking back.

Truth was the moral ground upon which Rick stood. He had not disclosed his financial difficulties to Dajah. But he knew he had to. He also knew she would not like what she would hear and would have to trust him, a risky wager at best.

"I'm going back to my overtime," he told her one night as they watched television.

"When?"

"Starting next week."

"I thought you said you would be okay?"

"Yeah, I thought so too until the utilities bills started coming in, and Kanisha outgrew everything. It'll only be for a little while. I got this guy on my job who'll take the apartment in January."

"So who's going to watch her?"

"Gina."

"Gina?"

"Yeah, Gina."

"She's going to be here like I was?"

"No, not like that. She'll pick her up from after school. Take her to her place. Then on my way home, I'll swing by and pick Kanisha up."

"Oh." But it was a hollow 'oh', filled with doubt and thick with suspicion. "So she won't be here?"

"No, Dajah, she won't."

"And you trust her with Kanisha?"

"Yeah, I do."

"And it's okay—with the courts, I mean?"

"It will be considered unsupervised visits, so it'll be cool. And it won't be every single night. Just a couple of times out of the week."

"There really is a guy who wants the apartment?"

"Isn't that what I said? I don't know why you're still tripping like this."

It was the first time he had said that out loud to her, but it wasn't the first time Rick had felt it. He was getting tired of always reassuring her. After all this time, all he had been through not only to get her in his life, but keep her, she should have known better.

He got up off the couch. "You ready?"

"Ready for what?"

"It's late and I'm tired. Want to go to bed. You ready?"

The look on his face was the type that no lover ever wanted to see— breaking point. And though it was a temporary expression, one that would be gone the next time they crossed paths, it still tugged at her. That and the fact that a little after ten wasn't "late."

"I'm tired, Dajah. Just want to hit the sack early."

Without me, Dajah thought as she got her bag, tossed a good night and headed out his front door.

The last time Gina had decided she was going to go see Tarika, she swore that would be the last time. She was tired of Tarika not answering, tired of her uncle telling her "She ain't here."

Lights would go out in the basement when she rapped on the window. More than once she saw the TV flicker off. If Tarika had let her go, that was fine. Gina just wanted to tell her that she hadn't.

She wanted to tell Tarika that she had had a chance to take a second look at her life and found what had worked no longer did. She wanted to tell Tarika that she had discovered goals and visions too. That she had a job. That she felt in her heart what they had had was worth preserving.

So Gina went by Tarika's and didn't rap on the window. She rang Tarika's Uncle's bell instead. He appeared at the door, and before he could tell her where Tarika wasn't, Gina spoke first.

"Mr. Jones, I need you to do me a favor."

"What kind of favor?"

"I need you tell Tarika something for me."

"She ain't here."

"But she'll be back sooner or later, right?"

"I don't know. She come and go as she please now that she got that job."

"Can you tell her something for me? Can you tell her I ain't given up on her? Can you tell her that even though she done turn her back on me, I ain't never turning my back on her? That I miss her?"

Mr. Jones studied her hard. Like Rick, he saw the changes that had come into Gina's life. Good changes as far as he could see. "That's a whole lot to remember. I don't know if I can remember all that." He opened the door to her, and Gina stepped in. "Go on down. She down there."

He didn't follow her to the kitchen where the basement steps were. Mr. Jones simply went back to what he was doing before he was interrupted—shouting out the answers to *Wheel of Fortune.*

Gina paused at the door off the kitchen, a lifetime coming and going before she could force her hand to the knob. She thought to knock first, but nobody knocked for Tarika on that door. Silently she chided herself for even considering it.

She took a deep breath, grabbed it, gave it a twist. She was grateful that it didn't squeak when she pulled it open. Gina looked down the stairs, saw a soft glow at the end. Knew Tarika was somewhere beyond, out of sight.

Gina stood there, heard music, Tarika singing softly to a Jill Scott tune. She remembered how Tarika used to sing all the time and then one day just stopped. She remembered other things of their past, bits and pieces that made their history. Like the welts that used to line Tarika's legs and arms after her mother beat her.

Gina recalled Tarika lying up in the hospital after the miscarriage, her eyes fixed on the ward door for the sight of Sha-Keem. How every day her expectancy grew less and less until nothing could make her look that way.

But mostly what Gina remembered was how tight they had been, more like blood sisters than just friends. This was what propelled Gina down the steps, Tarika looking up from the folder full of torn magazine pages. "What you doing here?"

"Your uncle let me in."

"Why?"

"Because I have to tell you something, and he couldn't remember all that I had to say."

"Tell me what?"

"That you were right, and I was wrong. That wanting to do something with your life is a whole lot better than wanting to do nothing. That I miss the hell of out of you."

"I ain't down like that no more. I'm about something these days, you know?"

"I know you are. Shit—I mean, shoot, me too, that's what I came to tell you. I've gotten my shi—stuff together too."

"What you mean?"

"I got me a job, girl. A real one. At the library. Been seeing a counselor and everything."

"No lie?"

"No lie." Water filled Gina's eyes. "I've been through a lot of mess, but it's getting better for me." Gina sat down in a chair. "Got so much to tell you, Tarika. Could you do me a solid and listen?"

Dajah huddled under her blankets. Outside the wind was blowing a chilly thirty-seven, and just the idea of going out in it made her shiver. But it was just Thursday, the weekend still a day away, and she had a job to get to.

Wrapping her comforter around her, she made her way to the thermostat, saw it was set on sixty-eight and pushed it up to seventy-five. She stood over the floor vent in her living room, the comforter cocooned around her, and waited for the hot air to make it from the unit in the basement.

It did. She gave herself a few seconds of luscious heat, then headed back to the bedroom. Ditching her comforter, she went to her underwear drawer, then headed for the bathroom. Turning on the shower, she hand-tested the water until it was near scalding.

She added cold, getting the right temperature, stripped and stepped inside. She heard the phone ring but didn't even think about going to answer. It was still too chilly in her apartment for a naked and wet mad dash, Rick or not.

She knew it was him. That it couldn't be anyone else. The funky good-bye from the other night was still on her mind and no doubt on his. She'd hit him back when she got dry.

Feeling better, Dajah found herself singing as she soaped up and rinsed off. She was humming by the time she dried herself. Putting on her panties and bra, she hand-tossed her braids, added lip paint, waited sixty seconds and applied the gloss.

He had gotten over whatever it was that had claimed him, had climbed out of the black hole he had slipped into. They'd be okay.

She finished getting dressed, went to her phone and checked the last call received, certain Rick's number would appear. It didn't. Just a number she didn't recognize and the certainty, the joy, the confidence she'd just owned, vanished.

Rick hung up the pay phone, feeling ridiculous that he even had to use one, wanting to kick himself for forgetting his cell. Last night he had gone to bed tired and annoyed. This morning was a different matter.

This morning, last night with Dajah rose up like a dragon in need of slaying. The first thing he decided to do was to call Dajah as soon as he dropped Kanisha off at school. But she wasn't answering, and he knew why.

He had left a bad taste in her mouth, and letting her lug it around another day wouldn't help. Rick looked at his watch. It was five after eight. Dajah left for work at quarter after.

Ten minutes.

If he pressed on the gas, he could make it.

She did not recognize the Navigator until it passed her. Didn't know Rick was behind the wheel until their back tires crossed each other. Dajah turned her head and saw the plates. Eased up on the gas and applied the brake.

The SUV's rear lights popped on, began reversing back her way, the window easing down, his concerned face coming through. "I was trying to catch you before you left."

A car honked behind her. Dajah made a split decision. "Pull over." She eased her car to the curb. Got out. Waited for him to make a U-turn. He parked behind her, the passenger door opening wide.

She got in, eyes glancing at her watch, finding his quickly. "I have to leave in like two minutes."

He nodded. Took her hand. Kissed the back of it. "I was tired. That's all it was."

She felt the truth and let the anger fall away like dead leaves. "Why do I trip so?"

"Because you love me?" he asked.

"Do I?"

"Yeah."

"You ain't all that," the most she could offer. "I got to get going or I'm going to be late."

He squeezed her hand. "See you later then?"

"You sure you aren't going to be too tired?"

"I'm going home right now to catch some zee's. I'll be bright-eyed and bushy-tailed just for you."

"For me, huh?"

"Who else?"

Dajah had a list. Kept it to herself.

Chapter 25

Like the beat of a hummingbird's wings, the days went by swiftly, too fast to delineate, too immediate to dissect. Endless spans of twenty-four hours came and went, and in a blink of an eye the night before Rick's on-again overtime arrived.

They decided to spend the evening at Rick's. Ordered take-out and watched a movie on TV. The closing credits were still rolling when he flicked it off, the two of them getting into bed.

They made neither the best of love nor the worst, just somewhere in the temporal between. In the aftermath, Dajah's mind was where it had been since she'd found out that Gina would be taking care of Kanisha.

She knew her offer wouldn't be taken even as she spoke it. "Tell her she can call me if something happens."

"Who?"

"Gina. Just in case."

"She'll be fine. Besides, Jefferson'll be there."

Dajah wasn't convinced, but she forced the issue from her. "I'm going to miss you."

"Just a few nights of OT. Not like I'm going away."

"Feels like it."

He drew her close. Hugged her. "I'm right here."

But it wasn't the now she was worried about. It was the later. It was the past-midnight moment when he would ring Gina's door. How would she answer it? In one of those Victoria's Secret getups? Would she put on a robe with nothing else under it and loosely tie the belt? Would she seduce him? Would he let himself be seduced?

Dajah knew the power of the poonany. Knew because she had wielded it herself a few times. And yes, Rick might love her, but he had loved Gina first, and no matter what a person said or did, love was a permanent marker somewhere in your heart. It could not be willed away, lived away or loved away by someone new.

She rolled onto her back, nestled against the warmth of him. Dajah closed her eyes and tried to find some sleep, but everything inside of her was wired. Everything in her saying: *And so it begins.*

Nervous.

Rick didn't expect that. Kanisha *was* Gina's child. She had been raising her for years now. But it was all in Gina's smile. "She sleeping."

"Yeah, and I hate to wake her, but we have to get going."

"Well, you come in and try. She wasn't listening to me."

Rick entered the home of Jefferson Carter feeling as if he had stepped into a time warp. Heavy antique furniture was everywhere he looked, swallowing rooms and stealing light from the ceiling fixtures and table lamps. It gave the house a gloomy feel, as if cloudy days was all it knew.

"My room's up there," Gina said, pointing up the stairs.

He followed her to the bedroom, peered in and saw Kanisha dead to the world. Rick went over and shook her gently. "Kanisha, Kanisha. Come on. Wake up. We have to go." But Kanisha was in her seventh dream, and waking up was not on her agenda.

Rick looked around "Where's her bag?" Gina retrieved it from the corner. "Put her shoes inside. She did her homework?"

"As soon as we got in."

He scooped up his sleeping child and headed for the stairs. Took them slowly and continued toward the door. "Can you bring her bag to the car?"

Gina had no shoes on and her robe offered no warmth, but she nodded, following Rick out into the cold night. He hit the button on his alarm, and the doors unlocked. "Just toss it in the back," he asked, putting Kanisha into the seat.

Cold leather against her skin woke her. Kanisha came to, startled, doe-eyed. "I'm cold." She burrowed into the leather. Turned her back against the cold. Her feet curled up, trying to find warmth on the seat.

Rick snapped in the seat belt. Stepped back to close the door.

Gina stopped him. "Wait." She took Kanisha's coat and laid it across her. Leaned in and gave her a kiss. "Good night, Baby."

"Good night, Momma."

Gina closed the door. Hopped on chilled bare feet, hugged her arms over her chest. "Cold."

"Same thing tomorrow, okay?"

Gina nodded and hurried toward the house, the wind playing peekaboo with her robe, exposing brown thighs as she dashed up the steps.

It was a rotten schedule, and nobody liked it.

Not Kanisha, whose nightly sleep was interrupted a couple of times a week. Not Gina, who stayed awake past midnight so she could hear Rick ring the bell. And not Rick, who found the time it took to get Kanisha, wake her, drive home and get her back to sleep cut into his own sleeping time.

But life wasn't always about easy answers. Life was often about the hard. This was what Rick told himself, but as the weeks moved on, even he wasn't convinced.

It would be so much easier to have Gina bring Kanisha to his house. Kanisha would get her full night's rest, he would get the sleep he needed and Gina could stay in the third bedroom. She could bring a change of clothes, and he could drop her off at the library in the mornings.

It sounded so much better than what they had been doing. Sounded like an answer to it all. But Rick knew Dajah would neither appreciate it nor understand it. Knew he was heading for those same troubled waters they had recently got out of.

But lying wasn't a game he played. He told her straight, no chaser, as a rare night of dancing came to an end and he eased his SUV to the curb, cutting his engine. "I'm about to tell you something you're not going to want to hear."

"So don't tell me."

"You know that's not how I do."

"Let me guess. Gina's going to be watching Kanisha at your place, right? Because it's too much for everyone the way it's going now."

"Yeah."

She shifted in her seat, her gaze fixed on him hard. "How come I knew that? Because I'm psychic? No. But because I knew sooner or later it was coming to this." He reached for her, but she brushed his hands away. "Don't."

"It's only for—" He stopped himself. The song had played too many times already. "You want to do it? You want me to tell Gina never mind?"

Dajah didn't even have to think. "No."

"Then that leaves Gina. I know in your head you seeing all types of things that could and couldn't happen, but I'm telling you it ain't so. It's not like that. I'm not like that."

"Not yet."

"Excuse me?"

Dajah turned, on fire. She turned, unable to shut up another second about what she was seeing so clearly and Rick was refusing to even consider. "Bit by bit, you letting her back in."

"That's crazy."

"Is it?"

"Yes, it is."

"Why? Because you're done with her? But you're not. You never will be. You will go to your grave with Gina right there. Kanisha makes it so."

"She's her mother, yeah, but she's nothing to me."

"Yes, she is, Rick. She is the mother of your child, and once upon a time you loved her." Tears sprang into Dajah's eyes. "You loved that little woman-child so much you went through hell and high water to be with her." Dajah paused, her eyes filled with misery. "And love just doesn't go away. It stays even when you think it's gone."

He took her face into his hands, wiped at the tears that sprinkled her cheek. Dajah shifted her head from his touch. "Don't. You'll get makeup on them." But Rick ignored her. Continued to wipe away the wetness, foundation spreading along his fingertips.

"You're right. Love doesn't go away. But it's not just about who you love, it's about who loves you back. Gina hasn't loved me in a while. You do. I haven't felt anything for her since I met you, nothing. And I know it's just words, but damn, Dajah, I waited so long for someone like you, there's no way I'm going to do anything to risk it. I want you. I want to be with you. I love you."

"If you really mean it, then you won't let her back in your house, not even to watch Kanisha."

He pulled away. "I can't do that."

"Can't or won't."

"Can't . . . I'm getting letters from Kanisha's teachers about her falling asleep in class. Some nights I find myself falling asleep at the wheel. There's no choice here."

"So where is she supposed to sleep?"

"In the third bedroom."

"And you honestly think she's going to stay there?" Dajah didn't wait for an answer. "She wants you back, Rick. Did you know that?"

"She don't want me."

"Who left who?"

"I left her."

"I rest my case."

"Instead of trying to tell me who Gina wants, why don't you ask me who I want."

Dajah looked out the window.

"Come on, ask me. Because it's obvious you don't know."

Dajah said nothing.

"You won't ask? Fine, then I'm going to tell you. I want you. I wanted you from the first time I saw you and understood I couldn't have you then. I made hard-ass choices to be with you. And I know you think Gina got something over me, but truth of the matter is if anyone has anything on me, it's you. Because if Gina really had juice, I wouldn't be here now. So who got the real power, Dajah? Tell me, who got the real juice?"

She didn't want to respond. Did not want to leave her pedestal of authoritative opinion. She did not want to allow Rick's words to tear down what she knew in her heart to be true. But a blind man could see it—if Gina really did have Rick wrapped around her finger, Dajah could never have entered the picture.

"I do," she said softly.

He put his hand to his ear. "Sorry, what was that?"

She turned, an unwilling smile filling her face. "I said, I do. I got the juice."

"And it's all good, Dajah. Every single drop of you."

"Thanksgiving."

"What about it?"

"I want to spend it with you."

"Of course you will."

"But what about Gina and Kanisha?"

"Oh . . . yeah. Well, Kanisha will be sitting at whatever table I'm sitting at."

"And Gina?"

"You kidding? My folks won't even let her through the front door anymore."

But Kanisha couldn't see it or begin to understand it. Even at five she knew Thanksgiving was supposed to be with family. And her mother was family.

"How come Momma ain't coming?" was all she wanted to know the holiday morning as she and Rick sat at the table eating a hot breakfast.

"Because she's having dinner somewhere else."

"So how come we can't go there?"

"Because we're having dinner somewhere else."

"How come we can't have it together?"

"Because, Kanisha. Just because."

"She gonna be sad."

"Who?" But Rick knew.

"Momma. She said she was going to miss me for Thanksgibing. Her eyes got wet."

"That's just how it goes sometimes."

"Wasn't how it goes before."

"That was before. This is now."

Kanisha looked up at her father, her eyes soft, sad. "I liked before better, Daddy."

"Yeah, Baby, I know you did."

"Can it be like before? Can it? Granddaddy Jefferson said he'd help Momma if she wanted to move back. Said he pay her rent, if that's what she wanted."

"He said that?"

"Yeah."

Rick wondered why Gina hadn't told him. The Gina he knew would have been pulling up the moving truck by now.

But that was the thing. The Gina he knew was fading fast. The Gina who was brash, loud, foul with her language and selfish with her intent was becoming someone who was hospitable, considerate. Almost shy.

Every time Rick was around her, he felt her nervousness, as if she was afraid of saying the wrong thing, doing the wrong thing.

"Granddaddy Jefferson said he'd talk to you about if she wanted."

"Did she want him to?"

Kanisha looked away, her head shaking no. Rick spooned a forkful of grits and eggs into his mouth. Looked off. Chewed.

When Dajah had called her parents to tell them she wouldn't be coming to Thanksgiving dinner, she saw the disappointment on her mother's face, even though she was miles away. She had held the phone, hearing her mother sigh. "One Thanksgiving in thirty years. I'm just missing one."

"Well, why can't you and Rick come by after? You've been seeing him for a while, and we haven't seen him yet. It's like you're trying to keep him a secret or something."

Dajah had been. A big little secret. Its name—Kanisha. "That's not it at all. We're doing Thanksgiving over his folks' place. And for Christmas we'll come to yours."

"Seems like a long time to wait to meet him."

"Not that long. You'll blink and Christmas will be here."

"He is a good man, isn't he, Dajah?"

"Mom, you know me better than that. You know you and Daddy taught me better."

That sigh had come again. "Well, I'll tell your father."

"It's not like everyone else won't be there."

"Yeah, but our only child won't."

Which hadn't been Dajah's fault. Her parents having only one child was a decision God had made. "An only child who loves you both silly. An only child who's missing one Thanksgiving meal but promises she will never miss another."

"Well, come by the day after. Bring Rick. We'll save you some dessert."

"Okay."

But it had been a promise hinging upon whether or not Rick was working overtime the next day. As she waited for him to arrive Thanksgiving afternoon, she reminded herself to ask.

The SUV rolled to the curb. By the time Rick had gotten out to ring her bell, Dajah was already downstairs. "Happy Turkey Day." She kissed him. Felt Rick stiffen. Pulled back. Asked, "What?"

Rick pitched his head toward his vehicle. "Kanisha."

"What about her?"

"She's a little upset."

"About?"

"You being invited to dinner and Gina not."

"So I'm the bad guy, huh?"

"What can I tell you, Dajah."

Not a thing, she realized as she saw Kanisha staring, not a drop of happiness in those eyes.

As much as I did for that child? But that was all Kanisha was—just a child, as true, as open and honest with her emotions as anyone could be. She also realized that she couldn't blame Kanisha for what she felt.

Dajah fixed her face into something a little less hostile. "Let's go eat turkey," she declared. Opening the passenger door, her smile was bright. "Hi, Kanisha. You ready to do some serious eating?"

Kanisha looked away. Dajah waited for her to look back. Knew if she waited long enough, if nothing else, curiosity about what Dajah was waiting for would make her glance her way again. Kanisha did.

Dajah made her take a second look, all she wanted.

Gina had invited Tarika to the holiday table for a lot of reasons: to lessen the impact of meeting Jefferson's real children, having Kanisha gone from her side and being around her mother for the first time in months.

She had expected Jefferson's two daughters to be high mainte-nance and stuck-up. What they were were two overweight women in their forties with no husbands and kids her age. The two sets of fe-male cousins ended up in Gina's room before dinner. Gina hadn't in-vited them in, but they came in anyway.

"We thought you was a myth," one of them said. "Always heard about some little girl Granddaddy claimed but wasn't his."

"Yeah, you like the Candy Man or some shit," another offered.

Gina couldn't remember their names. Didn't try. All four of them seemed to be an effigy of who she used to be, from the too-tight clothes down to the endless tracks of weaves. One spotted her cleaned-out ashtray and pulled out a joint. Gina told her to put that back. "We don't do that here."

Gina looked at Tarika, and Tarika had given her a thumbs-up. Sitting there listening to them curse, be loud and trying to out-talk each other, Gina saw clearly for the first time the picture she had pre-sented. Was ashamed.

After dinner, when they all wanted to cram back up in her room again, Gina told them no. She told them that she had somewhere to go, and if they wanted to listen to music, they had to listen to the radio in the living room.

"Well 'sckews you,'" one them offered.

"Yeah, excuse me." She turned to Tarika then. "You ready?"

Tarika didn't know where they were going, only that she was down for the journey.

Thanksgiving dinner over, Kanisha fast asleep in the back and alu-minum foil-covered plates in her lap, Dajah looked over at Rick and smiled. "I had a great time."

He nodded. "Me too." His voice dropped to a whisper. "Glad you didn't take how Kanisha acted personally."

"How could I? I understand what's she feeling, and I'm not going to hold it against her. You're working overtime tomorrow?"

"Yeah."

"We were invited over to my folks'. They want to meet you and were kind of disappointed we couldn't come today."

"Another time."

"Sure, another time. Maybe Saturday."

"Maybe."

She leaned over and gave him a peck on the lips. "Get home safe."

"Will do."

The next day Dajah pulled up to the ranch, the grass in the yard brown with winter, spring flowers shriveled and gray. When she was a child, the house had seemed like a mansion. Now it felt like a cottage.

Time always changed perceptions; time the great transformer of all things. It stopped mattering where Gina laid her head or didn't. Dajah had Rick's words now. She was the one with the juice.

It made ringing her parents' doorbell, then using her key, all the much easier. Made Rick's absence bearable because she was assured that he would accompany her one day soon. It allowed for her parents' quizzing about "Where's Rick?" not to fester. "He's a corrections officer, and he's working now, but you're going to get the chance soon."

Rick's word had smoothed out all the lumps, the road ahead smooth and paved, not a ripple in sight.

Thanksgiving in the penal system always made the next day rough. While some families did make it their business to come visit with Tupperware full of turkey, dressing and cranberry sauce, too many never did. It was the unvisited population who made it bad for everyone else. Fights would break out, and the whole mood of the jail would be tense and foul the day after.

After nine years on the job, Rick was used to it and knew what to expect when he arrived at work that Friday. Still the hours of breaking up assaults and struggling to get unwilling inmates into solitary had taken a toll. Rick just wanted to leave it all behind, but getting off the island was in no way quick or easy.

He had to go through four different gates, five checkpoints and take a quick bus ride to his car before he could leave. At every step of the way, he had to be prepared to show both his badge and his ID if the guard on duty didn't recognize him.

His shift might have ended at midnight, but it was a while before he was in his car and driving over the bridge that connected Riker's Island to Queens. After midnight, the traffic along the Grand Central was light. As he drew nearer to his destination, he looked forward to getting home and into bed, wondering once again what he would find when he got there.

Gina in his bed. That's what Rick found.

Her body engulfed by the comforter, just her head tied in a black scarf showing. The sight was so disturbing, so unexpected, so irrational that he went to her, shaking her hard.

"What you doing?"

She came to, blinking. "Kanisha's bed too small for the both of us."

"You supposed to be in the third bedroom."

"Ain't no bed in there."

Rick had forgotten. Forgotten to bring Gina's old bed from upstairs down. His third bedroom was a rec room, filled with his giant-screen TV, audio and game systems and two chairs. He was supposed to have done it yesterday, but got caught up in Thanksgiving. He stepped back, face apologetic. "I'm sorry. I forgot."

Gina sat up, the comforter falling away, revealing a cotton topper with spaghetti straps. "I was gonna go upstairs, but then I didn't want to leave Kanisha down here. Then I thought maybe we'd both go upstairs, but you wouldn't know where I was."

She swung her legs out of bed. "Then I thought about the couch, but figured you wouldn't like that either." She stood. Scratched absently at a breast. "Where can I go?"

"You sleep here. I'll put Kanisha in here with you and take her bed."

Gina nodded, got back in. Was fast asleep by the time Kanisha joined her.

The next afternoon Rick made it his business to bring the bed from upstairs down. He waited until Dajah came over to help.

"So where did she sleep last night?"

"With Kanisha," Rick answered quickly as they lifted the full-sized mattress and made their way down the stairs. Plopping it on the floor in the third bedroom, they made the trek back up, four times in all, the most difficult piece being the box spring.

"Never knew they weighed so much," Dajah said, plopping down onto the mattress, spreadeagled, catching her breath.

"Don't tempt a wanting man."

"What?"

"You. Down there. Legs wide, chest heaving."

She looked at him sideways, sucked her teeth, laughed. Opened her arms and beckoned him. But Rick shook his head no, extended his hand for her to grab it. Pulled her up. It was Gina's bed, and there was no way he was going to do anything with Dajah on it.

Another tough shift finished, Rick pulled up to his house and saw the lights burning in the living room. Past midnight, the sight was unusual. Gina and Kanisha were usually fast sleep.

He hurried up the steps, unlocking his front door. He was about to call out to Gina when she appeared, a large cellophane envelope in her hand, his daughter's face peering out through the clear window. "Ain't she something?" Gina beamed, holding the school photo his way.

"When did this happen?"

"Took them a few weeks ago. I swear we got the prettiest little girl ever." Gina's eyes went back to the picture. "Look at the face. You ever seen such a sweet face? 'Course she look more like you than she'd ever look like me."

Rick moved in closer. "She has my eyes and my color, but the rest is all you."

"You think so?"

"Look," he said, moving a finger along the shiny plastic. "She has your eyebrows. She has your nose."

"But she ain't got my lips. Those are the most Rick-lookingest lips I ever saw. All nice and full, perfectly round." She looked up. Studied the original. Felt Rick's gaze, met it. Kissed him, a slow, partially opened mouth moving against his.

She felt him freeze. Eased back a little, searching his eyes for some sign of her soul in them.

Rick blinked. "Gina, I—" all he could manage, feeling an unexpected pulse.

She stepped back, head shaking, eyes away from him. "Damn, I'm sorry." Rick went to say something, to make the moment less impacting, but she turned away, put the picture of their child on the dining room table and hurried to the third bedroom, the door closing softly behind her.

* * *

It was just a photo, the type taken at most malls. It wasn't a great picture, but it was recent and inside the frame sat Rick, Kanisha and Gina, and it sat on Kanisha's dresser.

Dajah had gone in there to offer her perfunctory hello, her importance in Kanisha's life dwindled. There was little between them these days except polite words and quick hugs. Whatever ties had existed were gone.

She had been turning to leave when she saw the picture. Without thought she picked it up. In a flash, Kanisha was by her side, tiny hands reaching up and taking it back. She didn't snatch it away, but there was an urgency in her as she placed it back on her dresser, taking time to make sure the angle was right.

"I was just looking, Kanisha."

Kanisha didn't respond. Just sat on her bed and went back to her TV.

Dajah left. "When did you three go to the mall?" she asked Rick.

"What, last week? Why?"

"I saw the picture in Kanisha's room. The three of you."

"We'd gone to pick up some tights and a leotard. Kanisha's in the Christmas play, that's all."

"Christmas play?"

"Yeah. At school."

"Oh."

"I would have invited you, but you know . . . Gina."

"Going, right?" She forced a smile. "Maybe I could come anyway. Sit in the back."

"I was planning to go up to New Paltz next week, pick out the tree. Why don't you come along for the ride?"

"Next week?"

"Thursday. Think you can take half a day? They have this place where you can go pick a tree, and they cut it down fresh. It'll be a nice little ride for us, don't you think?"

Us. The magic word. Dajah said she'd love to.

The next week Rick, Kanisha and Dajah took the road trip. The excitement of a day off from school and going to get a Christmas tree making it okay that Dajah was joining them.

Leaving New Paltz, they headed to Harrow's in Long Island to buy Christmas decorations. The rest of the afternoon was spent listening to Christmas carols and decorating. Pulling out the ladder, Rick strung lights along the outside of the house, and at nightfall they stood in the front yard as Rick threw the switch.

"Looks good," Dajah told him.

"Yeah, I think it's going to be a very good Christmas." He turned to Kanisha. "Okay, young lady, bedtime."

"I had a good day," Dajah told him.

"Me too. I always wanted to do that. Drive upstate, get a tree. Spend the day listening to Christmas carols, putting up lights."

"Well, you've done it."

"Yeah, I did, didn't I?" Rick answered, amazement full in his voice.

Gina sat next to Rick in the auditorium of Kanisha's public school. On the other side of her was Jefferson, and next to him was her mother. Because of a filled-to-capacity crowd, some parents were forced to stand in the back.

They had checked the program and knew Kanisha's class would be the third. It was supposed to have started fifteen minutes ago, but they knew all about CP time.

"Just like black folks," Gina found herself muttering. "Can't do jack on time."

The lights dimmed. Shouts, whistles and applause went up. A middle-aged black woman came from behind the curtain, a cordless mike in her hand. "Good evening, mothers and fathers, family and friends. My name is Massie Smith, and I am the principal of this fine institution of learning." More applause broke out. "I want to thank each and every one of you who took the time to come and support our wonderful students and for being patient with us. Now I will ask you to sit back and get comfortable for one of the finest Christmas pageants you will ever encounter in your life.

"Our children have been working hard these last few weeks to make this show a success and I ask that you show your appreciation by saving your applause until the end of each number. Without further ado, I bring you the 2002 Christmas Extravaganza."

She disappeared behind the curtain. Three seconds later it began to rise. A hush fell over the crowd as rhinestones sparkled on the midnight-blue costumes of fifty kindergarteners, followed by a long, heartfelt *aaahhh.*

Gina blinked and blinked again, a fast hand to her eye. Rick knew just what she was feeling, a lump the size of Texas filling his throat.

"Ain't they sump'in," Jefferson whispered to nobody.

"Precious," Doreen Alexander found herself saying back.

The music came up. The little youngsters twirled and sang, some with much gusto, others petrified. But the effect was the same—the audience went wild, standing up on their feet, whistling hard and clapping harder.

By the time the curtains opened on Kanisha's class, Rick was so choked up, so overwhelmed, tears dotted his eyes.

"You see her, Rick? You see our baby girl?"

"I see her, Gina," Rick said softly, "I see her."

Kanisha stood dead center and at the front, the rest of her class behind her forming a pyramid. The cutest snowflake anybody ever saw. Even from where Rick and Gina sat, they could see how seriously she was taking her role.

She swayed her arms as though her life depended on it, her face beaming in a delight that could light the world. She spun on her ballet slipper-covered feet, keeping her circle tight and clean. She opened her mouth wide and belted out the song as if she was on Broadway.

Rick, Gina, Jefferson and Doreen were still standing and clapping long after the curtain had lowered. So much so that people began to turn and stare. "That's my baby," Rick said proudly.

"That's our little girl," Gina added.

"Yeah, but we want to see the rest of the show," someone offered, forcing them to their seats.

Doreen Alexander leaned past Jefferson. Tapped her daughter's leg. "She was the best one—that's why they put her in the front."

Gina nodded, prouder than two peacocks. "I know, Momma, I know."

Parents and children, some still in costume, milled around the front of the school. Despite the cold, no one seemed in a great rush to leave, the night still magical.

"Kanisha, you was just wonderful," Jefferson told her.

"Thank you."

"Was you scared?"

"Uh-unh, 'cause I knew everyone was out there watching me, and I wanted to do good."

"Better than good," Gina told her. "You was the best the whole night."

"You ain't never made Grandma prouder," Doreen Alexander said. "Never knew you was such a talented little thing."

"Momma helped me. She made me practice."

Eyes fell on Gina. She seemed unprepared for the scrutiny. "I just wanted her to be the best."

Jefferson looked around. "Well, folks, I don't know about you, but my bones don't like this cold too much. Y'all ready?"

Kanisha tugged at her father's hand. "Can Momma come over for a little while?"

"It's kinda late."

"Just for a little while, please?"

"One night of staying up a little late ain't gonna hurt nobody," Jefferson tossed in. "Besides, this here night is special."

Rick paused, thought about it. Agreed.

But whatever the little star had in mind for when they got home disappeared beneath exhaustion. The long day closed Kanisha's eyes two minutes after they got into the Navigator. She was snoring by the time they pulled up to Rick's house.

"Out like a light," Rick said, peering behind him.

"Like two lights. You hear them snores?"

"But she was fantastic tonight."

"Yeah, she was."

"Thank you."

"For?"

"For taking the time you take with her. You didn't even mention you made her practice."

"It's what I'm supposed to do. Help make her become the best at whatever she do."

Rick nodded. Reached for the car handle. Gina placed a hand on his arm. "Maybe you should just take me home. I mean, she is dead to the world."

"She might wake up and be disappointed. She did invite you."

"All right."

They got out, Rick scooping up his snowflake, Gina using her key and opening the door. She locked it behind her as Rick took Kanisha to her bedroom.

He had gotten off her ballet shoes and was about to take off her leotard when Gina got there. "Here, let me do it." With care, she slipped off one shoulder of the one-piece and then the other. She eased it down past Kanisha's waist and pulled it off her legs.

Next came the tights. "She don't need pajamas," Gina decided. "Her underwear's good enough." Rick gathered her up again as Gina pulled down her bedcovers. Stood back as Rick gently put Kanisha into bed, pulling the covers up to her neck.

"Good night, Baby," he whispered.

Gina said the same.

They stood there, parents of a wonderful child, arms touching, their gaze intent. "Sometimes I wonder how we did it. How we made such a beautiful child."

"Love." The word was out of Rick's mouth before he could check it, before he could weigh the implications, grateful for the chuckle Gina gave. Grateful that she turned and walked out.

She was sitting on the sofa when he got to the living room, one leg bent, a hand smoothing down her hair. Rick asked her if she was thirsty, and in truth she was both thirsty, and hungry.

"Got anything to eat?"

"You know where the kitchen is."

Gina got up, turning on the kitchen light. She opened the refrigerator, searched a while. Pulled out a loaf of bread, cheese slices, bologna. Butter. "When's the last time you had a fried bologna sandwich?"

"Fried bologna sandwiches . . . all you seemed to make for me back then."

"Yeah, but they were slamming." She got a frying pan. "You used to eat them up like they were going out of style."

"Because I was hungry."

"No, 'cause they was good." She turned the flame on beneath the pan, added pats of butter. "See, the trick is not to let the butter burn too soon. The bologna got to get that poky thing in the middle; then you slice it and press it flat."

"Oh, there's a science to it?"

"Not science, just the right way to do it." She added four slices of bologna. "Get some plates?" Asking, a new proclivity. Rick remembered when Gina didn't ask for anything.

He went to the cabinet and retrieved two blue ceramics. He laid them near the counter by the stove, stood back and watched her work. Like an assembly worker, she moved about with ease, flipping, frying, cutting and pressing. In no time flat, three fried bolognas with cheese were ready.

Rick took their plates to the table. Gina brought in two glasses of Kool-Aid. Sitting across from him, she took a bite, melting cheese burning her lips. "Hot."

Rick took a bite. "But good." Looked up at her. "Even got the Kool-Aid."

Gina smiled, took another bite. Her eyes dusted the ceiling. "That guy, he still want the apartment?"

"Last time I checked."

She nodded. Chewed. Picked up her Kool-Aid.

"You want it too, don't you?"

"I never stopped wanting it. That was the best place I ever lived. Just full of light and air and space. Living at Jefferson's is like living in a tomb. Everything all crowded in there."

"Yeah, I noticed." Rick finished off his first sandwich. Picked up his second. "How come you didn't tell me that Jefferson offered to help you pay the rent?"

Gina took her time answering, swallowing the food in her mouth. "Because it's not mine to have anymore. I know that. I messed up big-time. There was no way I could come and ask for it back."

"It was supposed to be for you. That's what this whole thing was about. Making a place for you and Kanisha."

"*Was* ain't is. There's a whole bunch of *was*es but none of them ain't." Gina got up, taking her plate with her. She went to the kitchen and put the stopper in the sink. Turning on the water, she slipped her plate inside.

She finished off her drink and put the glass in there too. Squirting dish detergent into the scrubber, she began cleaning up.

An old familiar sight, Rick found himself watching her wash and rinse. Found himself studying the back of her, the shape of her.

"You finished?"

He blinked, saw Gina staring at him over her shoulder. He nodded, went and handed her his plate and his glass. His arm brushed hers, and she jumped as if touched by fire. Turning, he left the kitchen, a part of him remaining behind.

Gina came out a little while later. "Can you call me a cab?"

"You can stay."

"Nah, tonight I want to go home. Can you?"

"I don't have that much cash on me." Which was the truth.

"So how was I supposed to get home?"

Rick had no answer.

She stood staring at him a long time. So long that Rick could not hold her gaze. "What you trying to do?" she asked as if her heart was broken all over again. She didn't wait for an answer, just went to the third bedroom and closed the door.

The phone rang.

Rick picked up, Dajah on the other end, wanting to know how the Christmas pageant went.

Chapter 26

Plan ahead; that was Dajah's new motto. No more surprises, no more assumptions. *Know.*

"What's the plan for Christmas?"

They were over at her apartment, a place that didn't see him often enough for her liking. It was less stressful on her own stomping ground, the gap between herself and Kanisha widening with every face-to-face.

"Christmas."

"Yeah, Christmas. Am I seeing you or spending it with you?"

"Seeing."

Dajah wasn't surprised. She *had* gotten Thanksgiving. "Dinner's at my folks'. They're having it around four. Can you make that?"

"Yeah, I'll be there."

"What does Kanisha want?"

"What doesn't she? She had a list two pages long."

"When are you shopping for her?"

"Tomorrow. I got it covered."

"Gina going with you?"

"Yeah.."

"They've gotten really close, haven't they?"

"They've always been. Gina *is* her mother."

"Unlike me, right?"

Rick refused the bait. Got up. "Getting some more wine. You want?"

"No, what I want is an answer."

"To what? Something you already know?"

Dajah stared, reading the signs that had not quite reached the surface. "When were you going to tell me?"

"Tell you what?"

"That you want her back?"

It took everything in him not to look away. Everything inside of him not to break contact with her eyes, angry eyes sprinkled heavy with hurt. More so, it took everything he owned to explore Dajah's question and find the truth.

There was no doubt that how he was seeing Gina these days, what he was feeling for her, was changing, shifting back into old emotions. But he had no plans to do anything about it. Wasn't sure if he wanted to. Rick told his truth. "I don't know if I do."

The knife blade stabbed her heart hard. Her head swam; her vision grew blurred. She was on her feet in a heartbeat. "Don't know or don't want to know?"

"Look, you asked, okay?"

"And that's supposed to make it right? I'm here with you, making plans for Christmas and you're considering walking and it's supposed to be okay?"

"Can I get some time to figure it out?"

"Figure out what, Rick? Who you want the most?" She took steps toward him. "I was supposed to be the one, remember? I was supposed to be the one with the juice, good to the last drop. That's what you told me. That's what I believed."

He looked at her, confused. "You were."

"Were? Were? But not now, right? Now that Gina has gotten it together, right?"

"She has changed."

"And that makes it okay? All the shit she did to you, almost sending you to got damn jail, and suddenly it's cool?" Tears spilled past her eyes. "To hell with me, right? To hell with the fact that I love you, that I've been here for you. To hell with all that, right?"

"It's not like that."

"No, then tell me. Tell me what the hell it's about?"

Rick sighed. "What are we doing?"

"I don't know what you're doing, but I sure damn know what I'm doing. I'm going to make this real easy for you, save you some thinking time. You want Gina, so you go on and get her. I hope you three have a fucking happy life." Her hand pointed toward her door. "I think it's time for you to go."

"I'm trying to figure it out, Dajah. Will you give me some time to do that?"

She opened her door wide, her answer.

Rick, the truth-speaker, telling lies.

No, not lies, just holding back truth. Holding back because he couldn't face it. Holding back because some part of him didn't want to know it. *Holding back because he does love you and wants to be sure.*

Dajah turned away from those thoughts the same way she turned into the corner of her bedroom. Swiftly.

She wished he had been a liar. Wished he had been a cheat and a fraud. Wished he could have lied right up to the end. That he'd gone on pretending until he got caught red-handed. Maybe then it wouldn't have hurt so much, stung so bad, torn at her soul.

She sat on her bed, hung her head until the moans ceased making her face ugly. Until a tiny bit of the feeling of being cheated, stolen from, left her.

But it would be months before it did, and life wasn't going to come to a halt. Dajah grabbed tissues off her nightstand, blew her nose and wiped her face. She sat there, sniffling up mucus until the flesh beneath her nostrils stayed dried.

She got up and went to her living room to turn out lights, her eyes dusting the space Baby used to occupy.

She had lost so much. She had lost time, energy, her life, things that mattered most. She wanted to kick herself, beat her own self down, because she had known from the very beginning, but had insisted it could work.

Who's the real liar?

Great big juicy fibs she had told herself in her dealings with Rick. Dajah had feasted on them for breakfast, lunch and dinner. But Rick never had. Not once, his words still ringing in her ears: *I was trying to figure it out.*

It took a minute to understand that his mind wasn't made up. That she was still in the running even if the most she could come in was second. Kanisha had first, always would. But Dajah wasn't a quitter. She'd come this far.

Picking up the phone, she called him on his cell. "You decide and quick." She hung up before he could speak a thing.

Rick and Gina moved through the aisles of Toys "R" Us as if they were on a mission. In truth they were. They were searching aisles, sorting through bins overspilling with merchandise in search of the toys on Kanisha's Christmas list.

With the holiday so near, the store was crowded for a Thursday afternoon, but Rick and Gina moved with speed and deftness, dodging other shoppers in search of the hottest toys and the newest games.

What they were doing took a while to find footing inside of them. Like a stone tossed onto a stilled lake, ripples disturbed the surface of parental sovereignty, a sovereignty with roots that had been buried beneath bitterness, unhappiness and personal visions.

"You gonna pay this much?" Gina asked, holding the Game Boy Advance in her hands.

"She wants it, right?"

"Shit, you can get a whole system for what they asking."

Rick looked at her. Gina immediately knew why. "I know, I know. But I'm trying, Rick, you got to give me credit for trying."

He did. It was all in his eyes. Eyes that were looking at her from new angles, different angles, Dajah's words a monkey on his back. Dajah's words making it easier, allowing him fuller disclosure.

Rick was taking this time to see who Gina was and wasn't these days. *So much better,* the thought no longer scaring him. The thought no longer causing him conflict, confusion.

"What you smiling about?"

He didn't even know he was. "I'm smiling?"

"Yeah. At me, like something funny."

"Not funny, Gina."

"Then what?"

Rick didn't answer. Gina didn't need him to. The other night she'd asked him what he was trying to do. But as they walked the aisles of Toys "R" Us, making a good Christmas for their child, she knew.

"I ain't trying to do no more wrong," Gina was telling Tarika later on that evening. "Ain't trying to mess nothing else up for nobody. But he acting like he wants to get back together."

"Is that a bad thing?"

"Yeah, 'cause somebody gonna lose."

"You mean Dajah."

"Ain't that a trip? Me caring about some other female? Some other female who got my man. But shit's changed so much for me, Tarika. How I used to be ain't how I am now. And she's good people. Did a lot of shit for Kanisha—I mean stuff. Things I'd never do. And like I said, I ain't trying to mess up nothing for nobody. 'Cause what you do comes back on you, did you know that?"

"You mean Karma."

"Yeah, that. I've done so much wrong, all that wrong just came crashing on my head, and I don't want that no more."

"So he say anything?"

Gina took a minute to think. "Nah."

"Done anything?"

"No, not really. Just this feeling I get when I be around him. How his eyes be looking at me."

"So what you gonna do, Gina?"

"Not a damn thing. He want me back, he gotta come out and ask."

Dajah had been one of the first people to really sit down and listen to her. She had taken good care of her child. Any hurt dished out this time, it would be on Rick.

Nine days.

Dajah could hardly believe it. Found it difficult to accept that she had been waiting so long for Rick's answer. That Christmas was less than nine days away, and she had not done any Christmas shopping. Hadn't even put up her tree.

All the Christmases past, Dajah had put a tree by her living room window and strung lights along the inside border. But this year not a drop of holiday cheer did her house possess. Scrooge had taken up residence, and she wanted the whole thing over and done with, so she could get on with her life.

Next month was January. Next month, the magic date. No more overtime, no more Gina in his house. Maybe, just maybe. But the strength of that maybe came and went like the tide. Some moments finding Dajah absolutely sure she and Rick would be together, other times saying she was beating a dead horse.

Yet she had never been a quitter. Rick would not make her one now.

Tarika and Gina stood inside the tiny apartment of the third floor of a house on 172nd Street. It seemed possible to stand at the entry door and spit all the way to the back, but it was filled with the soft light of a mute December sky, and the heat was moving about nicely.

"Ain't much," Tarika said, feeling Gina's thoughts, preparing her soul for the browbeating.

"But it's yours," Gina told her back, moving to the tiny kitchen window, peering outside. "And there's nothing more important than something being yours." Gina turned, pointed toward a doorway. "What's that?"

"Bedroom or living room, I haven't decided."

"Well, since it face the street, you should make it your living room. Make the one in the back your bedroom." Gina went inside. "You can put a couch in here, a TV. Stereo. Hang some curtains, girl, you'd be set."

Tarika smiled, drinking in the possibilities. The walls were painted a soft putty-gray, and in her mind she saw window treatments of soft shimmery white and rattan baskets holding wheat stalks of ochre.

This moment had not come easily for her. She had worked hard at McDonald's, going from cleaning up throw-up and washing windows to being on the register. Tarika had worked nine- and ten-hour shifts and saved every penny she could get her hands on.

She had returned again and again to that dark, dismal basement, reeking of cooking grease and wearied to the bone. She had feasted on loneliness, feeling as if no one was in her corner, but had fought against the nay sayers and persevered.

The signed lease was in her pocketbook. Tomorrow she would take a cab and bring over her few possessions. She had no bed. No dining room table. Not even a pot or pan. But she had her space, floor to ceiling all hers, the first milestone in her goal to get to where she wanted to be.

"So, how it feel?"

"Feels good, Gina. Feels real good. I did it, didn't I?"

"You sure did."

"What you doing for Christmas? I was thinking about making a dinner. You might have to sit on the floor. I ain't got no tables or chairs or nothing."

"Don't worry about that. They got them chairs on the Ave real cheap."

"I'm broke."

"Be my gift to you. Like a housewarming or something."

"You'd do that?"

"You my girl, 'course I would."

"So you'd come for dinner?"

"Yeah, me and Kanisha'll be here."

"What about Rick?"

"We gonna be over his place for the morning, but there ain't no plans for the afternoon."

Rick was still divided.

Some part of him thought that by the time he and Gina had finished Christmas shopping for Kanisha, after the two of them had hidden toys in the basement, he would know for sure.

He hadn't.

There were two Ricks: one who wanted to go back and nurture old dreams, and the other who wanted to go on with what he had.

He loved Dajah, and he still loved Gina. Standing on the sidelines, the best choice was clear. But he wasn't on the sidelines; he was in the middle.

He wanted to call Dajah but knew he couldn't without his answer. And all too soon he was back on his overtime routine. He became careful with the words he spoke to Gina, careful with how he set his eyes, his body language. He didn't want to give her the home-court advantage. Rick wanted his choice honest and fair when he made it.

When he made it.

Most of his life he had taken risks, but this was the riskiest of them all. Because if he chose wrong, it held life-long implications. If he chose right, the happily-ever-after could finally be his.

Saturday morning Dajah's phone rang bright and early, so early it woke her, so early, the sky outside was still dark. She struggled to wake, roll over, bring the phone to her ear. Dajah struggled to prepare her soul for words that would change her world.

"Hello?"

"Hey."

"Hey." She sat up. Stared at the shadows around her bedroom. Waited.

"Sorry it took so long."

"So you've decided." It was not a question.

"Yeah, I have."

"And?"

"You still want to do this?"

Everything in her wanted to say yes. Every fiber of her being wanted to give him an affirmative. "Yeah, I do . . . but I can't."

"What do you mean, you can't?"

Dajah wasn't sure when the bottom line had reached her, only that as the wait grew, things she had chosen to ignore began manifesting, hardening to the point that no excuse could reason them away, no alternative viewpoint would will them away.

"What I mean is, they got there first. They were in your heart first, and there's no room for me, that's what I mean."

"Of course there is."

"No, there isn't, and I can't be second. I thought I could, but I can't, and staying with you means that's all I'll ever be."

"You're not second, Dajah."

"But I am. Even you said so. You told me 'Kanisha will always come first.' I thought I could be okay with it, but I can't, because Kanisha means Gina too. You can't have one without the other, and you were thinking about going back to her, so how strong is your love for me if that even entered the equation?"

"But I didn't go back to her. I chose you."

It didn't matter because an old, long-ago lesson had come back to her, the one she had learned at the tender age of thirteen. She had forgotten, purposely and subconsciously, from the moment she met Rick. But it had returned to her in full force—she didn't do share. "But I'm not choosing you."

The silence on the other end told her she had hit a bull's eye. That he never suspected she had an option too. Dajah let the moment filter through him, allowed her proclamation to hit home, unsure of what he would say back.

She heard him swallow, felt his pain. Wished things were different, but the all of it was already set in stone. "You think I want to do this?" she went on to say. "You think I just want to walk away from you, that my heart's not hurting? I don't want to walk. I do hurt. It's three days before Christmas, and the last thing I want is to be without you, but what you can give me isn't enough. I can't be second fiddle, and it's taken me a while to understand that.

"I tried, you know how hard I tried, all we've been through because I loved you, Rick. I really did, but you were never really mine to love, and that's the sad awful truth."

"I do love you, Dajah."

"I know that. But you love Kanisha more. You still love Gina, and I can't share. I'm not going to share. I'm not going to spend the rest of my life wondering when you're going to backslide. That's not how things are supposed to go."

His voice was choked. "You mean this?"

"Yeah, Rick, I do."

"So this is it?"

"This is it. I'm sorry." She hung up the phone, wiped at her eyes. Looked around the darkness of the predawn morning, trying to find her way back to who she had been, the Dajah before Rick.

The beauty was gone.

The sky was gray, the ocean was gray, the world murky in shades of ash. The ocean roared, the wind howled and fought her every step of the way.

Dajah pressed on.

Head bent against the stinging wind, arms tight around her waist, she walked, the boardwalk her destination, the railing her final resting place.

She did not search the sky for the sun. Both its brightness and visibility were lost behind a wall of pewter. Instead she leaned her head down, closed her eyes, listening to the angry roar of waves beating the shore without mercy. It's blow, cleansing.

She needed to settle things within herself. Needed to go deep inside her soul and find the scattered pieces. Dajah needed to assemble the "why" with the "because", making a whole determination.

What was the point of being with a man who never could be hers? What had been the reason she had dived in, cautious and leery the whole time, but had given her all anyway? Why had she uttered those words to Rick when he had come to get his Mace?—*If you're ever free?"*—knowing in her heart he would never be?

Who were they now that they had come to the end of the line? Was anybody better for it? Had anybody reaped rewards from their lost battle? Dajah's gut tightened against the answer. She felt a true pain inside her heart. Yes, someone had reaped; someone's life had been made better.

Not mine, theirs.

Like an enlisted soldier, Dajah had signed up willingly and taken her marching orders. She had put herself on the front line and battled to near death. In the aftermath of surrender, two had remained standing; two had remained strong. In the aftermath Kanisha and Gina had become victors, their broken family now having the chance to heal.

She laughed, the sound lost in the harsh breeze. *That's what it was about, that's why I came into Rick's life, to give them a chance. But what about me? Where's my reward?*

Three days to Christmas, eleven to New Year's Eve, and she was standing out in the bitter cold day wounded and alone.

Dajah reached into her pocket, retrieved a tissue. She wiped her eyes and blew her nose. The vast, empty beach offered no comfort, the gray world around her no hope. With a heavy heart, she left the boardwalk. Made her way home.

Christmas morning arrived bright, sunny and cold. In the Trimmons household it was Kanisha who awoke bright and early, going first to Rick's bedroom to wake her father, and then to the other bedroom to wake her mother.

The three of them, two sleepy-eyed, gathered beside the Christmas tree, most of the brightly wrapped gifts bearing Kanisha's name. She went through them like a little tornado, ripping off the wrappings, eyes wide with delight for three seconds before she was off to the next.

By the time she was finished, she was surrounded by a mound of paper, bows and boxes stacked high.

"You like them?" Rick asked.

"Yeah."

He reached under the tree, pulled out two boxes, handed them to Gina. "Merry Christmas."

She put them aside, got up and retrieved four. She handed them to Rick. "Four?" he asked.

"You deserve more than that. But I don't make that much at the library. Go ahead, open them."

It had taken three weeks' salary just to pay for the shirt and pants and a loan from Jefferson to cover the cost of the jacket. She had gone to Hack's on 164th Street to make her selection, where nothing was cheap but the quality couldn't be beat.

Rick opened the first box and pulled out the shirt. He opened the second and pulled out the pants. He stood and laid them against him, checking the fit. It looked good. "I had my eyes on this—how did you know?"

"I asked Hack. Figured he would know."

He did not expect gifts. Did not expect Gina to go through the trouble of finding out what he wanted. Utter surprise filled him.

"Go ahead, open the third one," Gina said, anxious.

Rick did. What was inside— "*and* the jacket?"—overwhelming.

"What you wanted, right?"

Rick looked around his living room, the morning sun spilling in the windows, Kanisha surrounded by discarded Christmas paper and Gina looking at him with expectant eyes. "I guess I did."

What you trying to do? Gina had wanted to know weeks before, a question he had taken the time to answer, arriving at a different conclusion, bringing him a firm yes to wanting Dajah.

But Dajah had other plans, and Rick the Great Planner suddenly found himself without one. He found that great notions did not embrace the mysteries of the future, and in turn the unknown had led him.

But as Gina opened her present, the Enzio black leather boots he had bought her bringing tears to her eyes, Rick not only accepted what he had been trying to do, but embraced it.

Two seconds after midnight of the New Year, Dajah stood in Barry's too-crowded living room, draining the last of her champagne. Wall-to-wall with people, she felt out of the mix.

"Happy New Year, girl," Frieda whispered in her ear.

"Happy New Year to you too."

"You doing okay?"

"I'm doing all right."

"Ooh, ooh, six o'clock," Frieda said, excited. A dumb game, Frieda had been calling out possibilities for Dajah all evening. And though she didn't feel ready for any of them, it did make her smile.

Less than a minute after the New Year had begun, the hurt Dajah felt was still there. She still awoke from time to time at quarter to one in the morning thinking the doorbell would ring. But it never did.

Yet Dajah knew that every morning she woke up was a baby step. A baby step away from what she felt for Rick, a baby step toward the day it would be just a dull ache.

A man approached her, hand out. "Would you like to dance?"

The truth was, Dajah didn't. A lot of men had come up to her that evening, and she had obliged most of them. Now her feet were just danced out. She shook her head no.

"Can I get you a drink then?"

She shook her head no again.

"Well, is there anything I can get you?"

The fact that he was trying to be accommodating made her take a closer look. Not ugly, not super fine, he was somewhere in the middle. The sincerity that shone in his face, his need to be given the chance to do something for her, anything for her, was refreshing.

"You have any baby steps?" she found herself asking.

"Baby who?"

Dajah laughed then. A sound that came up from her soul and poured past her throat. "I was just joking, but no, I don't want to dance or a drink, but thank you for asking."

The man walked away, head shaking. Frieda came up to her. "What was that about?"

"Baby steps."

"Baby what?"

"Nothing." She reached over and gave Frieda a hug. "I made it past midnight. I'm going to head on home."

"So soon?"

"Yeah."

"Why?"

"Because it's where I need to be, for now." She saw that Frieda didn't understand. Explained it. "I came to the party because it was New Year's Eve and I had something to prove to myself. I had to show myself that I still have hope, even if most days telling myself I do feels like a lie. And right about now, that's all this is feeling like—a lie. I'm not having fun. I'm in a room full of people, including two people I know love me, yet I still feel all alone." She frowned. "I don't want to do that anymore—be in the middle of some lie. All those months I was with Rick, that's all I lived on—lies, lies, and more lies. It's not my style, Free. Never was. So I'm going home."

"You want me to walk you to your car?"

"It's right outside. I'll be okay."

Dajah went and said good night to Barry. "Don't tell me you're leaving?" he asked.

"Yeah, I'm heading home."

"You're sure?"

Dajah nodded. Accepted the disappointment in Barry's face and welcomed his good-bye hug. Then she was moving through the hot, crowded room, the front door her destination.

Dajah stepped outside, inhaled the cool, crisp January morning, and headed to her car, leaving baby steps in her wake.

TRUE LIES

Margaret Johnson-Hodge

ABOUT THIS GUIDE

The suggested questions are intended to
enhance your group's reading of
Margaret Johnson-Hodge's TRUE LIES.

Please feel free to visit Margaret at
her website *www.mjhodge.net*

DISCUSSION QUESTIONS

1. At the start of the book, it's been a year since Dajah broke things off with David and Dajah has come to regret it. Do you think she should have worked through her growing disinterest with him and stayed, or did she do the right thing when she called things off?

2. Despite warnings from friends and family, Rick got together with Gina even though he was eight years older and in a different mindset. Despite the problems that arose as a result, do you think being with Gina helped him or hurt him in the long run?

3. If Rick hadn't met Dajah, do you think he would have left Gina or would he have gone on being in that bad relationship? Why?

4. Gina gave Rick more grief than joy. Do you think she really loved him, or if she even knew what love really was?

5. Dajah became involved with Rick even though she 'didn't do share' (share a man with anyone). What do you think motivated her to do so, breaking a lifelong rule? Do you think she would ever do it again, if so, why?

6. Rick's plan to get a two-family house was faulty to anyone outside of his situation. Do you believe he really thought it could work, or was he just delusional? Why do you think he came up with that plan at all?

7. Gina's mother was extremely hard on her. Do you think her mother's actions were justified? If so, why?

8. Frieda was literally working herself into an early grave. Why do you think she refused to do something about it for as long as she did?

9. What do you think became a turning point for Tarika? What do you think motivated her to do something about her life? If

it were ten years from the end of the book, what would she be doing? Would she and Gina still be friends?

10. When the second floor apartment remains un-rented, Rick tells Dajah he has someone who wants to rent it in January. Do you think he really planned to rent out the apartment?

11. Whom do you think Rick loved more—Dajah or Gina? Why?

12. It is now two years since the end of the story. What do you think has become of Dajah, Rick and Gina?